promise me

Jill Mansell

promise me

REVIEW

First published in 2023 by
HEADLINE REVIEW
An imprint of HEADLINE PUBLISHING GROUP

1

Cataloguing in Publication Data is available from the British Library

ISBN 978 1 4722 8788 5 (Hardback)
ISBN 978 1 4722 8789 2 (Trade Paperback)

Map illustration by Laura Hall

Typeset in Bembo Std by Palimpsest Book Production Limited, Falkirk, Stirlingshire

Printed and bound in Great Britain by Clays Ltd, Elcograf S.p.A.

HEADLINE PUBLISHING GROUP
An Hachette UK Company
Carmelite House
50 Victoria Embankment
London EC4Y 0DZ

www.headline.co.uk
www.hachette.co.uk

This book is dedicated to some of my favourite people!

Marion Donaldson has for very many years been my wonderful, patient and endlessly encouraging editor.

Jane Judd has been my fantastic UK agent since day one of my writing career, which began back when I was – gasp – young.

My brilliant writer friends, both online and off-line, are the people who keep me going during good times and bad – I honestly don't know how I'd manage without all of you. I daren't list names, I'm far too terrified of missing out someone vital, but you all make this weird job so much more fun than it would otherwise be.

Thanks are also due to fellow authors Ruby Basu and Gillian McAllister, who answered my online cry for help and gave me excellent legal advice on the subject of wills for the purposes of this book. (The storyline subsequently changed, as storylines have a habit of doing, and most of it was no longer required, but I am still hugely grateful.)

And it goes without saying that I'm grateful to everyone at Headline, as well as to my other publishers, agents, editors, cover designers, publicists, marketeers, sales teams, booksellers and bloggers worldwide. I couldn't do this without each and every one of you, and your contributions are so appreciated.

Finally, if you've enjoyed any of my previous books and are planning on reading this one, huge thanks to you too – you have excellent taste!

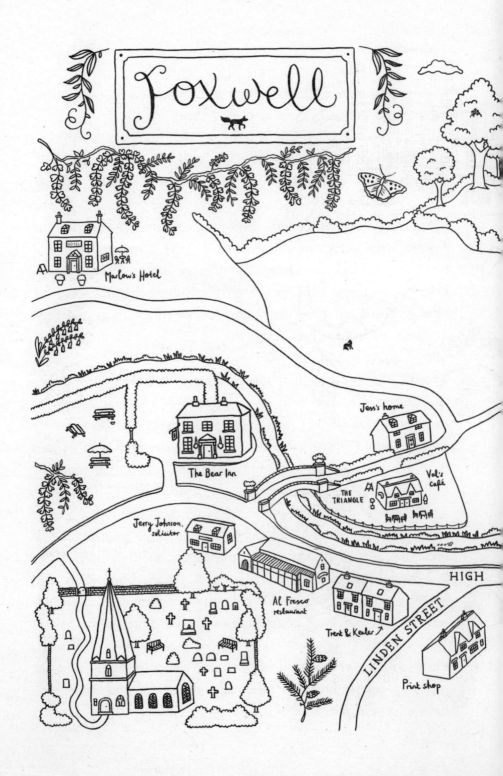

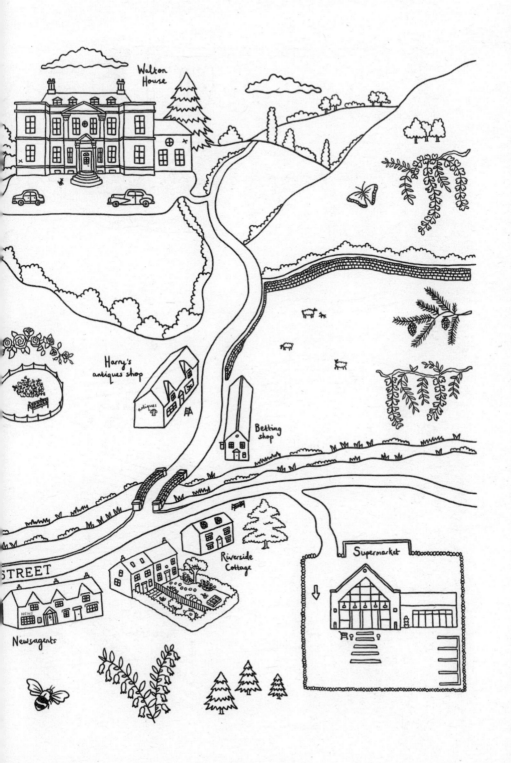

Chapter 1

'*How* much?' The old man ahead of Lou at the supermarket checkout was glaring in disbelief at the female cashier.

'Oh now, you always say that.' The cashier was evidently accustomed to his crabbiness. 'And the prices haven't changed since last week, my love.'

'They're too high anyway. Shouldn't be allowed. And don't call me love.' Paying with his credit card, the man took the plastic carrier she'd packed for him and limped over to the sliding doors, giving them a clunk with his walking stick when they opened too slowly for his liking.

'One day he might actually say thank you and I'll fall off my chair in shock,' the cashier observed with a good-natured smile as she rang up Lou's bottle of Merlot and box of apple dough-nuts.

'I'll say it for both of us,' said Lou. 'Thank you, thank you.'

Outside, it was a bright but blustery August afternoon and the old man was still making his way slowly across the car park. As Lou paused at the exit, wondering whether to break into the doughnuts now, she saw him brush past a dilapidated van with its crumpled bumper hanging off. The next moment, the

1

sharp side of the bumper caught the plastic carrier in his left hand. The man, taken by surprise by the sudden tug backwards, lost his balance and fell to the ground, the bag flinging its contents around him.

Racing over, Lou only had time to say, 'Are you—' before the walking stick swung round and clonked her on the head. Clutching her ear, she yelped, '*Ow.*'

'And there's plenty more where that came from, I can tell you.' The old man brandished his stick fiercely. 'Help, call the police, I've been mugged!'

'What? There wasn't any mugger.' Lou gestured around the empty car park.

'You tried to mug me. *HELP.*'

Honestly, what was he like? 'I'm not a mugger. You caught your bag on that broken bumper there. I came over to see if you're OK.'

'How can I be OK when I've just been attacked?'

'Nobody attacked you, you lost your balance and fell over. Look, are you hurt? Do you need me to call an ambulance?'

'Don't be ridiculous. I need you to pick up my shopping. Can you at least do that? Look at it all.' He gestured with irritation at the former contents of his bag, now strewn around them.

'Fine, let's get it done.' There was a gaping hole in the side of the carrier, so Lou stuffed the Merlot and doughnuts into her shoulder bag and used her own. In less than a minute she'd collected up the assorted tins, packets and ready meals for one. 'Now, how about you? Any pain?'

The old man shook his head. He'd crumpled rather than crashed to the ground.

'Want me to help you up, then?'

'No, I'd just like to sit here like a lemon for the next twenty-four hours. Of course I want you to help me up.'

Lou moved behind him, placing her arms under his and lifting him to his feet. 'There you go.' She passed him his walking stick. 'Right, where's your car?'

He pointed to an old grey Mini and she accompanied him over to it. When she'd put the bag of shopping in the boot, the old man shook his head and said, 'Oh for God's sake.'

'What's wrong?'

Producing a pair of spectacles and a single lens from his coat pocket, he held them up so she could see the broken frame. 'I must have landed on them when I fell.' He looked at Lou as if it were all her fault. 'How am I going to get home if I can't see where I'm going?'

He obviously couldn't walk any distance. 'Taxi?'

'No. Can you drive?'

'I can, but I don't have a car at the moment.'

'That's not a problem, is it? I do.' He held out the keys. 'You can take me home.'

He was saying it as if it were the only option. 'Where's home?'

'Top of the hill. Not too far.' Then, when she still hesitated, he added irritably, 'It's insured for any driver.'

'And how would I get back?'

'You've got legs, haven't you?'

Lou heaved a sigh. This was getting silly now; she'd got herself into a situation with a truculent pensioner who was a stranger to manners. And much as she wanted to say no to his demand, her conscience wasn't letting her. She knew why, too; it was those ready meals for one. He was grumpy because he was old, in his mid eighties at a guess. He was on a tight budget and presumably his wife had died. He was lonely and miserable, unable to walk without the aid of a stick and probably in constant pain from rheumatism or arthritis. She'd noticed the individual meals when he'd lined them up on the conveyor belt in the supermarket, but they'd looked even more heartbreaking strewn around him on the tarmac out here in the car park.

Plus, she'd always been a soft touch. Of course she couldn't walk away. Taking the keys from him, she said, 'Come on then, let's get you home.'

His eyes narrowed. 'And no speeding, either.'

He directed her out of the town and up a steep, winding lane overhung with trees and dappled with sunlight.

'Keep going,' he instructed. 'Mind the bend. Now slow down, it's up here on the left.'

Lou had been expecting a tiny cottage, maybe a bit dilapidated to match the dented grey Mini with its dusty tyres and scratched paintwork.

'Where now?' She paused on the gravelled driveway.

'You turn the engine off. We're here.'

'But where's *your* home?'

Irritated, he said, 'Are you blind? It's right there in front of you.'

He was gesturing at the majestic Georgian property constructed from custard-coloured Cotswold stone and overlooking the small town like a Roman emperor surveying his subjects. It was solid and square, with symmetrical rows of six-paned sash windows on three levels, a silver-grey slate roof, wisteria climbing up the walls and impressive stone pillars flanking the front door. Was it one of those grand country residences that had been carved up into many smaller apartments? Or could it be a retirement home? Either way, Lou was impressed. Switching off the ignition, she ran round to open the passenger door and helped him out before collecting his shopping from the boot. 'Here you are.'

He didn't take it. 'Bring it inside, will you?'

Oh well, it wasn't as if she was in a hurry to be anywhere else for a while. She waited as he unlocked a door at the side of the property, then followed him along a couple of corridors until they reached the kitchen.

It wasn't a retirement home then. Nor, from the look of the place, had it been divided into separate apartments.

'Will you put the food away for me?' He located a tube of Superglue in a drawer, then sat down at the scrubbed oak table to fix his broken spectacles.

Lou took a packet of two small frozen fishcakes out of the bag. 'Where's your freezer?'

'Through there, in the utility room.'

She grinned. 'So ten minutes ago you thought I was a mugger, yet now you're happy for me to poke around your house.'

He raised an eyebrow. 'It's the utility room. I don't keep sacks of diamonds in there.'

'Fair enough.'

'And I didn't say I was happy either. It's just a job that needs doing. And my leg hurts.'

The kitchen had a dusty, uncared-for feel about it, as did the utility room. Returning to get on with the unpacking, Lou said, 'Do you live here on your own?'

He nodded, opened a biscuit tin that was on the table and heaved a sigh upon seeing it was empty.

'But you have someone to help out?'

'No.'

Poor man, he sounded so weary, so resigned to being unhappy and alone. 'Did you lose your wife? I'm so sorry.'

'What? I don't have a wife. Never been married.' He regarded her with fresh suspicion. 'How can you not know that?'

Lou gave him a look. 'Maybe I haven't read your autobiography.'

Realisation dawned. 'Are you not from around here?'

'No. I live in Selly Oak.'

'Sellywhat?'

5

'It's in Birmingham.' She put the last few items away in the fridge, which was crammed with out-of-date food.

'You can put the kettle on now. Tea bags are in the blue tin. So what are you doing in Foxwell, then?' His tone was accusing.

'Visiting a friend. We were at school together in Cheltenham.' He was making conversation because he was lonely, she realised, though of course he'd rather die than admit it.

'What's her name?'

'It's a he. Sammy Keeler.'

'Keeler? One of the brothers, you mean? Which one's Sammy – the scruffy one with red hair? Always playing that damn guitar of his?'

As a succinct description, it was spot on. 'That's him.'

'Not your boyfriend, is he?'

'No.'

'What's the other one called?'

'Remy.'

'That's it. Two sugars. And don't take the tea bag out until it's done its job.'

Lou's phone rang as she was stirring his mug of tea.

'Hey,' said Sammy, 'are you there yet? I'm sorry, there's a problem with the train at Didcot and I'm not going to be home for another hour at least.'

'No worries, I'm fine. I'm in someone's kitchen,' Lou said cheerfully. 'We met in the supermarket car park, then he broke his glasses so I had to drive him home.'

'Who is it?' Having grown up in Foxwell, Sammy knew everyone.

'I don't know. He lives in a big house at the top of the hill. It's Sammy,' Lou explained to the man sitting at the table. 'He's asking who you are.'

'Allsopp.'

OK, bit of a funny name, but that wasn't his fault. Going back to Sammy, Lou said, 'His name's Allsopp.'

'Do you mean Edgar Allsopp?' Sammy started to laugh. 'Whoa! Are you telling me you're at Walton House?'

Walton, yes, that had been the name carved into one of the stone pillars guarding the entrance to the driveway. If she'd been on her own, she might have joked, 'Are you telling me he's a mad axe murderer?' But since Edgar was sitting less than six feet away, she said, 'That's right! I've just made him a mug of tea.'

'Good luck. He's a miserable bugger.'

She flashed Edgar a bright smile. 'I agree!'

'But if anyone can handle him, I guess it's you. Look, I'll call again in a bit, OK? I should definitely be home by six.'

When she'd put her phone away, Lou fished the tea bag out of her own mug and carried it over to the bin. As she reached it, her foot skidded and she almost went flying into the wall.

'Clumsy,' said Edgar.

'There's something on the floor. It's like an ice rink.' Crouching, she tested the surface with her hand. 'Did you spill oil on it?'

'No.' He bristled. 'It was butter.'

'Well, you can't leave a floor in this state. It needs cleaning up.'

Edgar looked horrified. 'What, with *my* knees?'

Shaking her head, Lou located an ancient scrubbing brush in the cupboard under the sink and filled the washing-up bowl with hot soapy water. As she scrubbed away at the black and white tiled floor, she said, 'You should get someone to come in and do this for you.'

'I did have someone. She left, same as all the rest of them.' He pointed at an area beneath a chair. 'You missed a bit.'

She sat back on her heels and looked at him. 'Any idea at all why they might not have wanted to stay?'

For a split second, Edgar looked as if he might be on the

7

verge of breaking into a smile. It didn't happen. He said, 'Too lazy, too afraid of an honest day's work,' and took a gulp of tea.

'Strong enough?'

'How would I know? I didn't ask them to lift the fridge over their heads.'

It was Lou's turn to smile. 'I meant the tea.'

'Oh. It's OK, I suppose. Could do with a bit less milk.'

When she'd finished scrubbing the floor, she said, 'Look, why don't you write out an advert and let me put it in the news-agent's window for you? I can do it when I leave here. Get yourself someone who can come and tidy the house up once or twice a week, how does that sound?'

He sighed as loudly as if she'd asked him to run a marathon. 'I'd need them here more often than that.'

'Fine, then say it!'

She found a pen on the dresser along with a battered tear-off pad. When she placed them in front of him, Edgar said, 'You can write it. Six mornings a week, general cleaning, cooking and helping out.' He paused, then added generously, 'They can have Sundays off.'

Lou wrote everything down as he dictated his phone number. When it came to the hourly rate, she said, 'Employers generally pay a bit more than that,' and with a sigh of annoyance, he upped it.

'I'll take this to the newsagent's and copy it out onto one of the postcards so it'll slot into the message board in the window.' She dropped the folded sheet of paper into her bag. 'What's the name of the woman who runs the shop?'

'How would I know?'

'How long have you lived here?'

'I was born here. Moved to London, then came back thirty years ago, after my parents died.'

'In that case, maybe you should find out her name. She's lovely, really friendly. We had a great chat while she was watering her hanging baskets outside the shop.'

'Hmph. Wait a minute.' He held out the pen as Lou hoisted her bag over her shoulder. 'Write down your number before you go.'

'Why?'

'Because I might want to call you. How long are you down here for anyway?'

'Just the weekend. Heading home on Sunday.' Scribbling the number on the notepad, Lou was briefly tempted to get it a bit wrong. But no, she couldn't bring herself to do that; it wasn't the kind of person she was.

'Do you have a job?' said Edgar.

'I do. I work as a carer. And I love it,' she added, because people sometimes liked to question her choice of career and she didn't need to get into that right now.

'Got kids?'

'No.'

'Husband?'

'Not any more.'

'Left you, did he?'

'Kind of. He died.'

At this point, anyone else would have exclaimed, 'Oh my goodness, how terrible. I'm *so* sorry.'

Not Edgar, though.

'When did that happen then?'

'A year ago.' Just over eleven months. Near enough.

'And how did he die?'

'Covered in trifle.' Lou winced; she hadn't meant to utter those words aloud. They'd spilled out in response to the mental image her brain had conjured up.

9

After a second's startled silence, Edgar gave a bark of laughter. It sounded rusty, as if he wasn't used to doing it, which didn't exactly come as a surprise. He put down his mug, sloshing tea over the rim onto the table. 'What does that mean?'

It was wrong of her to have said it. She shook her head and moved towards the door. 'Nothing. No need to get up, I'll see myself out.' Not that he'd shown any sign of rising from his chair. 'And don't worry, I'll put the ad in the newsagent's window.'

'Bye.' Edgar had already lost interest and was dragging a copy of last Sunday's *Telegraph* across the table towards him.

Lou left the house and pulled the heavy door shut behind her. Of course he hadn't said thanks. Just as well her choice of career meant she was used to dealing with all kinds of people. Even cranky, ill-mannered old men like Edgar.

Chapter 2

The woman behind the counter said chattily, 'Of course you can! For two weeks to begin with? Who's it for?'

Lou braced herself. 'His name's Edgar Allsopp.'

'Oh my word. Still on the hunt then, is he? Thought he'd given up. Sorry.' The woman flashed a bright smile. 'Relative of yours, is he?'

'Not at all. I just met him this afternoon, drove him home in his car after he had a fall. He's . . . quite a character,' said Lou.

'That's one way of putting it. Another way would be to say he's a complete nightmare.'

'Sounds like he's had a few home helps in his time.'

'Ha, more than a few. They don't last long, mind. My cousin worked up there for a week and he was impossible. She walked out after he complained about her singing as she was hanging out the washing in the garden.'

Lou grinned. 'Good luck to the next one then.'

'It's a pound a week to keep an ad in the window.'

She found two pounds in her purse and paid. As she did so, her phone burst into life, playing the opening chords of a song that told her it was a text from Sammy.

'Now why do I recognise that tune? Sorry, just me being nosy! It's familiar, but I can't place it.'

The text said: *Moving again, should be home by 5.30.*

'It's one of my friend's songs. Sammy Keeler?'

'Oh, of *course* it is. I heard him playing it outside the pub a few weeks ago. Such a lovely lad. Never gives up, does he? Just keeps plugging away, working his little socks off. Ah, it's a shame.'

'He's playing a gig at the Bear tonight,' Lou said. 'That's why I came down from Birmingham, to give him some support and cheer him on.'

'Ah, bless your heart, what a good friend you are.' As the woman slotted the postcard-sized advert into the row of polythene pockets in the window, she added sympathetically, 'Don't go expecting a big crowd, mind. You might be the only one.'

The wind had now dropped and the air was warm, which made sitting on one of the wooden benches beside the river no hardship at all. Having bought herself a takeaway coffee and a sausage roll from the café, Lou watched a family of quacking ducks chase after the pastry flakes she scattered on the grass, until between them the sausage roll was no more.

The shards of sunlight dancing on the surface of the water were dazzling, and she took out her dark glasses. It was nice to use them for their designated purpose, rather than for shielding her eyes from the curious gaze of others.

After Brett had died, memories of him had dominated pretty much her every waking thought. Now, almost a year on, it happened less often, but they were still there, like the reeds trailing from the riverbanks, undulating like hula skirts just below the surface of the water. Taking a sip of coffee, she found it happening again now, various significant scenes jump-cutting from one to the next, covering the two-year duration of their relationship.

It had all started so well – OK, of course it had, otherwise she would never have agreed to a second date, would she? And think of all the anguish that could have been avoided if *that* hadn't happened.

But the night she and Brett had first met had been so brilliant and had felt so right. It had seemed like a sign, a premonition of the future. Which just went to show how wrong you could be. Truly, you never could tell.

She'd been out with a group of friends from the nursing home where she was working at the time. After drinks in town, they'd all moved on to a nightclub. Not long after their arrival, on her way back from the loo, a tall, broad-shouldered man had approached her with a beaming smile and exclaimed, 'Lou! Hello, you're looking stunning tonight!'

He had nice eyes and an open, trustworthy face, and was clearly delighted to have bumped into her. Lou racked her brains, came up with nothing and admitted she couldn't place him.

'Oh dear, that's my ego battered.' But he was laughing, hadn't taken offence. 'Brett Miles. And it's great to see you again, even if you don't remember me.'

'I'm really sorry. I work at the Elms in Edgbaston, if that's where I know you from. Maybe you saw me there while you were visiting a relative.'

'No, that's not it. Look, I was just on my way to the bar. Can I get you a drink? Then I'll give you some clues. Honestly, though, I can't believe you've forgotten.'

Her friends were busy giving it their all on the dance floor. Intrigued, Lou accepted his offer of a drink, then spent the next twenty minutes sitting at a table with him, trying to work out when they'd previously met. Because just look at him, and he was *so* nice, how could she not remember someone like him?

Finally it was time to come clean. Brett admitted he had never seen her before tonight. Instead, he'd noticed her the moment she came into the club and had overheard one of her companions calling her name as they'd queued at the bar.

'Sorry.' He looked rueful. 'I'm no good at chatting up girls. I was desperate to speak to you but didn't trust myself not to mess it up. And you only get one chance to make a first impression, right? If I'd asked you to dance, you'd probably have said no. It's not easy trying to keep someone's attention when they're out with their friends. I thought if I pretended to know you, at least it'd give me a few minutes before you lost interest and walked off.' His shrug was self-deprecating. 'There, confession time over. I did it because I just had this feeling about you, that if I didn't give it a try, I'd never see you again, and then I'd regret it for the rest of my life.' He paused. 'And that was my best shot. Sorry again. If you've had enough of me, I'll understand. Feel free to go back to your friends.'

Charmed by the reason behind his fib, Lou said, 'What if I haven't had enough of you?'

His smile widened. 'Really? Well, that would make my day. Actually, it wouldn't, it'd make my week, my month . . . maybe even my year.'

'Steady on,' said Lou, and her stomach flipped as it crossed her mind that this could be the start of something significant.

'I know.' He was grinning now. 'I don't think I've ever felt like this before. Getting a bit carried away. Do you . . . No, forget it, nothing.'

There it was again, the swirl of mounting anticipation. 'What were you going to say?'

'Do you think you might feel the same way?'

It was like being in a movie, with the rest of the nightclub fading into the distance and the camera moving in for a close-up

14

of just the two of them while the cinema audience, entranced, held their breath.

Her own breathing shallow and her heart feeling as if it might burst, Lou heard herself say, 'I think I might.'

And that was when they'd shared their first kiss.

'So you managed to escape, then.' The voice behind her made Lou jump. And there was Sammy, as sweet and scruffy as ever, giving her a hug then throwing himself down onto the wooden bench next to her. 'Thought you might have been tied up and chucked in the cellar.'

'By Edgar?' she protested. 'He didn't even try. He doesn't do weird stuff like that, does he?'

'Just teasing. He's five hundred years old. Anyway, you're looking good.' He planted a kiss on her cheek.

'Thanks.'

'Now you have to tell me I'm looking good too.'

'You're looking exactly the same as you always look.' Lou regarded him with genuine affection; sartorial elegance was never going to be Sammy's thing. His rust-red hair was collar length and fluffily dishevelled, his freckles stood out against his pale skin and he was wearing comfortable old jeans and trainers with a blue and grey striped shirt and a black waistcoat that was missing two silver buttons. In all honesty, she'd seen more smartly dressed scarecrows, but Sammy's outfits were a part of his personality, and to dress him up like a Ken doll would be all kinds of wrong. People loved him for who he was, not what he wore. And no one who met him could fail to be won over by his friendly manner, kind eyes and impish grin.

Well, apart from Edgar Allsopp, obviously.

'I still remember the first time I came here,' Lou said as Sammy unlocked the front door and stood aside to let her into Riverside

Cottage. 'It still has that same gorgeous smell of stone and firewood and beeswax. And your mum was so brilliant.'

'She still is. And a lot more suntanned these days. I told her you were coming over, by the way. She sends her love.'

Lou's own mum had died when she was twelve. A year after that, not long after she and her dad had moved up from Exeter to Cheltenham, Sammy Keeler from her class at her new school had invited her along to his thirteenth birthday party and her dad had driven her over here to Foxwell. The party, held in the back garden of Riverside Cottage, had been raucous and chaotic, with a treasure hunt, karaoke and a tree-climbing contest. Lou had been at the stage of grieving where having a good time inevitably filled her with guilt, because what if people thought it meant she hadn't loved her mum as much as she should have?

But without even having met her before, Sammy's mother had sensed the turmoil she was going through. Thin and blonde, wearing a tie-dyed orange top, a pair of yellow shorts and loads of jangling bangles, she'd approached Lou while a couple of the other boys from her class were racing to climb the cedar tree and said easily, 'You know, your mum would be so happy to see you having fun and enjoying yourself.' She'd then given Lou's shoulder a quick reassuring squeeze before offering her a burger and moving on.

Lou remembered that day so clearly. It had felt like being given permission to be happy again, and the sense of relief had been incredible, because Sammy's mother was right. Her own mum had loved her to the moon and back; of course she wouldn't want her to be miserable for the rest of her life.

She hadn't planned on entering the tree-climbing contest, but ten minutes later, when Sammy had yelled across the garden, 'OK, who's next?' Lou had found herself calling out, 'Me!'

And with a highlighter pen tucked into the back pocket of

her jeans so she could mark the highest point reached, she'd clambered up like a monkey, beaten everyone else's best efforts and been rewarded with both a surprised cheer from the rest of the party and a reassuring wink from Teresa Keeler that had made her glow inside.

Now, Riverside Cottage was home to Sammy and Remy. Three years ago, much to her own surprise, Teresa had joined Tinder and fallen head over heels in love with a financial advisor called Maurice. Much to Maurice's surprise, within a matter of months he'd found himself casting off his tailored grey suits, resigning from his job in Slough and catching a flight with Teresa to Albufeira, where they now lived and worked ridiculously happily together running a beach bar on Praia de Vilamoura as if they'd been doing it all their lives.

'You don't have to sleep down here,' said Sammy when he saw Lou trying out the new sofa for length. 'Remy's away all week, so you can have his bed.' Proudly he added, 'I've even changed the sheets.'

'Did he say it was OK?'

'It'll be fine. He's on a plane right now, on his way to Texas to see a multimillionaire about a shopping mall.'

'He really won't mind?' Intimidated was the wrong word, but Lou had always been slightly in awe of Sammy's brother. Two years older, Remy was also several inches taller and significantly more attractive to look at. When they'd been at school, it had been generally acknowledged that Remy was the one with the stars aligned in his favour; with his striking good looks, spectacular sports skills and the ease with which he passed exams, he was regarded as the brother with all the talents. Sammy, by contrast, was unacademic, not great at sports, somewhat accident-prone and cheerfully unconcerned about his own less than prepossessing appearance. But if the differences between

17

them might have inspired resentment among some brothers, it had genuinely never been an issue for the Keeler boys. Remy was now a successful architect, while Sammy worked part-time as a delivery driver to pay the bills because all he really wanted to do was make music. Nevertheless, their love and support for each other remained unwavering and unconditional.

'He wants you to have his bed,' said Sammy. 'He was the one who offered it. Now, d'you want to give me a hand here? I'm going to make a lasagne.'

They chatted away as they worked together in the kitchen. Sammy was an enthusiastic cook rather than a skilled one, so it was always wise to keep an eye on what ingredients he might be impulsively adding to his creations along the way. The last time he'd made her dinner, there'd been an unexpected hit of aniseed in the coq au vin.

'So how did it go in London today?' said Lou as he energetically whisked the lumps out of a béchamel sauce.

'Three hours visiting pubs that aren't interested in having me play gigs for them. Two hours busking and getting told I'm a ginger twat by lads who think they're the first people to ever call me that. And the train ticket cost more than I earned, but what's new?' He shrugged, unperturbed. 'Hey, you never know, one day the right person could come along and be blown away by my music. If you don't get yourself out there, you'll never know.'

'Speculate to accumulate.' Lou tore open a packet of lasagne sheets.

'Exactly.'

'They could turn up this evening while you're playing in the Bear.'

'I know.' He was rummaging through the shelf of spice jars. 'It's just a shame it hasn't happened during one of the other seven hundred and forty times I've played there.'

18

'Well, I think you're brilliant.'

'And I think you're right.' He held up one of the jars. 'How about some of this in the white sauce? It could be the best discovery in the world.'

Lou shook her head, because it was fenugreek. 'It wouldn't be. It'd be gross.'

'Spoilsport. It's a good job I'm used to rejection.' The next moment, clearly struck by an idea, Sammy went on, 'Speaking of rejection, would you be my girlfriend tonight?'

There'd never been any kind of romantic connection between them; it had simply never materialised. But that didn't mean she couldn't do a favour for a friend.

'Who is it this time?'

'Her name's Tanisha. She moved here a few weeks ago to work on reception at Marlow's Hotel,' said Sammy. 'You should see her. Well, you will, because she's going to be at the pub tonight. I asked her out last week.'

'And?'

'She said no.' He shrugged. 'According to her friend, she goes for good-looking types.'

Like Remy, presumably.

'But if she sees you with me, she might have second thoughts?'

'Can't do any harm to give it a go.' He beamed, ever optimistic. 'I just need to win her over, make her realise that sometimes a fantastic personality is more important than boring old chiselled cheekbones and a six-pack.' Turning away, he sprinkled something into the pan of ragu sauce.

'What was that?'

'Nothing.'

Lou made a futile grab for the packet. 'It's ground cardamom. Sammy, you're a nightmare.'

'Don't knock it till you've tried it.' Unrepentant, he added

19

another shake of the powder to the saucepan. 'Anyway, how about you?'

'I'm not a nightmare.'

'I meant is there anyone out there you've got your eye on?'

'No.'

'Not even slightly interested?'

She held her thumb and forefinger a millimetre apart. 'Not even *this* much.'

'You never know, it could happen tonight. Someone might walk into the pub and it'll be like, *bam*. Love at first sight.'

It wouldn't happen, Lou knew that. After everything she'd been through, the thought of ever wanting to be with someone else felt about as impossible as winning a medal at the next Olympics. Emotionally, it was just beyond her. Sammy was sympathetic, but he couldn't truly understand the way she felt inside simply because he hadn't been through it himself.

But this was beyond boring for others to have to hear about. Far easier to stick on a brave face and pretend to be fine. She said cheerfully, 'It'd be just my luck for that to happen, then he'd see me pretending to be your girlfriend and his heart would be so broken he'd turn around and walk back out again.'

Chapter 3

The Bear Inn, overlooking the river, wasn't as empty that evening as Lou had worried it might be. Tanisha was indeed there with a couple of her friends from the hotel, which meant Sammy was happy. Having pointed her out earlier, he was now putting everything into his performance in the corner of the pub furthest from the bar, while grinning at Lou and even winking at her once or twice in a new-boyfriendy kind of way.

Would it do the trick and increase Tanisha's interest in him? It was a ploy that had worked for him once, many years ago, at the school Christmas disco, when a girl he'd had a major crush on had decided she fancied him after all and had gone out with him for a whole week as a result.

Not that it made any difference to Lou whether it worked or not; she was just happy to help out. Although from the way Tanisha was currently nudging her friends and eyeing up two burly guys in motorbike leathers over at the other side of the public bar, she wasn't holding out much hope for Sammy's wish to come true.

Poor Sammy. It couldn't have been easy for him growing up with a brother who'd had all the prettiest girls throwing themselves at him. Remy had never in his life needed to yearn for the attention of someone he liked the look of; it had been more a matter of how to reject them without hurting their feelings. He'd always been the one all the girls at school had secretly – or not so secretly – ogled.

Well, that had been then and Lou hadn't seen him for years, but presumably it was still happening. A couple of times Sammy had even been on dates with girls before belatedly discovering they'd only gone out with him as a way of getting to know his older brother. If only they knew what they were missing out on by not bothering to consider his merits. Because Sammy was good-hearted, genuine, thoughtful and funny, and whoever ended up with him would be the luckiest girl in the world.

The song he'd been singing came to an end and Lou clapped so hard it hurt her hands, earning herself a beaming smile from Sammy and yet another wink. OK, she was going to have to tell him to hold back on that; three was overkill and he wasn't even very good at it.

'Thank you, thank you. And now here's one of my favourite tracks, written by me about a girl who broke my heart back in school,' he announced, 'and cost me most of my GCSEs as a result. It's called: "I Failed It All For You".'

Lou applauded enthusiastically yet again, because this was one of her favourites too. Sammy's lyrics were deft and quirky, his compositions ingenious. If only the right person of influence could hear them, she knew they'd be blown away. Hopefully one day, one way or another, it would happen. But after all these years of remaining resolutely undiscovered, it had to get you down.

If only a diamond-encrusted Bentley could pull up outside now with Elton John in it. That would be perfect.

Over at the bar, the broad-shouldered bikers were now chatting to Tanisha and her friends. Several more people had wandered into the pub, which was good, then ordered drinks and carried them back outside to the garden, which was less good. Sammy was playing his guitar and singing, pouring his heart and soul into the performance, but half his meagre audience were chatting in low voices to each other and the rest were paying no attention at all. This was the problem with playing gigs in your local; all the customers had heard you a dozen times before, whether they wanted to or not.

'You were brilliant,' she told him when he'd finished his set.

'Ah, thanks.' He didn't bother to give her a boyfriendy kiss, because Tanisha and one of the leather-clad bikers had finished their drinks and left together ten minutes ago. 'I had fun, even if the audience wasn't so bothered.'

After a post-gig drink with Bob and Rico, who ran the pub, they headed back to Riverside Cottage and took the only slightly cremated lasagne out of the oven. Over a late dinner, they drank red wine and chatted non-stop, then played furiously competitive games of Bananagrams and Boggle while listening to music. The taste of cardamom in the lasagne lingered in the mouth, but opening a second bottle of Grenache helped to wash it away. Then Sammy picked up an acoustic guitar and started playing songs he was in the process of fine-tuning, scribbling down snatches of lyrics as they occurred to him.

Lou felt the tension leave her muscles as she rested her head against a faded velvet cushion. The living room was warm and his voice was so soothing it felt like being a child again, being sung to sleep by her mum . . .

'Ahem.' Sammy had stopped playing.

'Just resting my eyes.' She opened them and flashed him a smile, because it was what his own mum had always said after nodding off on the sofa.

23

'It's a good job this isn't a date. It wouldn't be flattering.'

'Sorry. I was up really early this morning.' She yawned, let him haul her to her feet and gave him a goodnight hug.

He ruffled her hair. 'No worries, you can sleep in for as long as you like. I won't wake you.'

At the top of the narrow stairs, he took a left turn and disappeared into his own bedroom, while Lou let herself into Remy's on the right. After several years away, initially at university and then in Edinburgh and London, where he'd worked for prestigious firms of architects, Remy had returned to Foxwell six months ago and joined a small company here in the town, partnering with an old friend of his mother's.

Appreciating the fact that he'd redesigned the upstairs layout of the cottage so that three bedrooms had become two, each with its own en suite, she brushed her teeth and changed into her jersey nightdress before sliding under a duvet that was far nicer than her own. It definitely felt weird knowing she was lying in Remy's king-sized bed with her head resting on Remy's pillows. This must be how it felt to spend the night in a bed belonging to a famous movie star. Oh, but these pillows were like clouds, and the sheets smelled amazing . . . Any sense of weirdness was offset by the knowledge that sleeping on the sofa would have been much less comfortable.

Revelling in the luxury of knowing she wasn't going to be rudely awoken by the alarm on her phone, Lou took in the sage-green walls, heavy bronze curtains and clever lighting, and the tiny home office set up against the opposite wall. She'd been good and not allowed herself to snoop in the wardrobe, but guessed that if she did, it would be hung with pressed suits and immaculately ironed shirts, probably with polished shoes lined up beneath them. By contrast, although she'd never inspected Sammy's bedroom, she imagined that if he were shown an iron and a coat hanger, it might take him a while to figure out what they could be used for.

Another yawn overtook her, almost dislocating her jaw. She switched off the overhead lamp before rolling over into the cloud-like luxurious centre of Remy's king-sized bed. Time to go to sleep . . .

Considering where she was, it perhaps wasn't surprising that Remy was making a guest appearance in her dream. He was throwing his baseball cap across the back garden like a frisbee, and every time she dropped it he said, 'I can't *believe* you're so bad at this. Come on, try again, I'm not stopping until you catch it.' But still she couldn't get it right, and the next minute he was throwing all sorts of different things at her: slices of cold pizza, fluorescent table-tennis balls, toy mice and handfuls of leaves that just disintegrated in mid-air and were impossible to catch.

'Oh my *God*,' he shouted, and in a daze Lou realised that something had happened, something wasn't right and someone who wasn't supposed to be in the room had woken her up.

'Waaah!' It came out as a strangled shriek. 'What's going on? What are you doing here?'

If she'd been more alert, she'd have been more embarrassed, because Remy Keeler was standing in front of her – *in real life* – with his blue and white striped shirt unbuttoned to reveal his tanned bare chest.

Recovering from the surprise of seeing her, he said, 'I live here. This is my . . . bedroom?' Pointing, he added, 'And that's my bed?'

'But you knew I'd be in it!' How could he have forgotten? Lou rubbed her eyes, then belatedly checked she was decent; sometimes her boobs managed to escape from her strappy jersey nightdress.

Not tonight, though. Thank God.

Remy raised an eyebrow. 'Does this look like the face of someone who knew you'd be in my bed?'

Her heart was thud-thudding against her ribs. 'Sammy said you were fine with it. He said it was your idea!'

But clearly it hadn't been. Too late, Lou remembered that Sammy had always been prone to harmless fibs. Not the mean or vicious kind, just innocuous ones that led to an easier life. Mortified, she pulled her nightdress down to her knees before flinging aside the duvet and throwing her legs over the side of the bed. 'I'm *so* sorry . . .'

'Wait, no.' He held up a hand to stop her. 'Me too. You can stay, it's OK, I'll sleep on the sofa.'

'No way. This is your room . . . *Oof*.' In her panic to get away, Lou reached down too fast to grab her bag and lost her balance, tipping forward and landing on her knees on the carpet.

'Here, let me help you up.'

'I'm fine, I'm fine.' A combination of too much red wine and less than two hours' sleep meant she was mortified *and* light-headed. 'Sammy said you were on your way to Texas . . .'

'My flight was delayed, then the meeting was cancelled anyway because my client's wife found out about his affair with the nanny and all hell broke loose. So it was a lucky escape really.'

'That's bad,' said Lou.

Remy shrugged. 'It can't have come as too much of a surprise for her. She was the family nanny when he was still married to wife number four. Look, I really don't mind sleeping on the sofa.'

'I couldn't let you do that. I'm going.' Hastily she collected her clothes and sponge bag, adding them to the pile in her arms.

'At least let me get you the spare duvet and pillows.'

'It's OK, they're in the airing cupboard, I know where that is. Sorry again.'

'See you in the morning, then. And no need to apologise. It was Sammy's fault for not mentioning you were here. He can cook breakfast for us tomorrow to make up for this.'

'He might sprinkle liquorice powder over it.'

Remy laughed. 'Or chuck in some oyster sauce and mustard. And now it's my turn to be sorry again – I've just realised who you are. It's Lou, right? Sammy's friend from school.'

Ouch. She could have described every inch of his face and most of his body in fine detail, right down to the freckle below his left ear, yet up until now he hadn't even recognised her. Then again, why would he? Since the time he'd gone to university, he'd never been here during her visits to Foxwell. Plus, Remy's life would have been far too full of excitement for him to bother remembering his little brother's gawky school friend, one of the many girls back then with a teenage crush on him.

Her face must have fallen a bit, because he went on, 'Hey, it's been a while. You look pretty different now. Didn't your hair used to be longer? And brown?'

OK, maybe he had a point. Her smile rueful, she said, 'That was before I discovered the magic of hairdressers and highlights. I'll let you get some sleep now.'

Clutching her belongings, Lou left the bedroom and made her way downstairs. In the hallway, she recoiled in fright from her reflection in the mirror – streaky blonde hair stuck up like a scarecrow's and splodgy mascara smeared beneath both eyes. Which meant there would be more on the pillows she'd left upstairs.

What a way to reintroduce herself to Remy Keeler.

Still, at over six feet tall, he would definitely have struggled to sleep on the sofa. At least she'd spared him that.

Chapter 4

It might have been a treat not to need to set the alarm, but her phone rang anyway. Blearily Lou winced at the time on the screen – *six forty-five, excuse me?* – then experienced that Pavlovian jolt of fear in the base of her throat, because a call at this hour surely signalled bad news.

'Hello?'

'It's gone.'

'What?'

'Can't find it anywhere. Did you take it?'

She sat up and said, 'Who's this?' even though it was painfully obvious.

'Edgar Allsopp. Have you got my walking stick?'

'No, I haven't. And do you have any idea what time it is?'

'Of course I do. This milk is sour. Can you get me some more?'

'*Me?*' Lou screwed up her eyes. 'It's not even seven o'clock.'

'If you know that, why did you ask me what time it was? I want a cup of tea and the milk's gone off.'

'You could drive down to the supermarket.'

'Except I can't, can I, because *someone's* stolen my walking stick.'

'Well, I promise it wasn't me.'

After a long silence, almost as if he'd looked up the next step in his Big Book of Basic Manners and Politeness, Edgar said gruffly, 'Please. A two-pint carton of milk. That's all.'

This was the drawback with being a member of one of the so-called caring professions. It meant your conscience was always on high alert and never gave you the day off, even when your less caring side kind of wished it would.

Ten minutes later, hastily washed and dressed, Lou let herself out of the silent cottage and made her way down the road to the just-opened supermarket. Sammy's battered blue van was on the driveway, but she didn't want to wake him to ask for the keys, which just went to prove how ridiculously nice she was. As for the black Mercedes parked alongside it . . . no way would she dare to get behind the wheel of that thing.

Cut to: another ten minutes later . . .

God, though, this hill was steeper than she remembered. The carrier bag containing a two-pint carton of milk swung from her fingers as she put one foot in front of the other, filling her lungs with crisp early-morning air. Far more air than they were used to being filled with at this time of the morning, but it was the thought of grumpy Edgar sitting all alone in his messy kitchen, longing for a morning cup of tea but unable to have one, that had propelled her off the living room sofa. How could she have rolled over and gone back to sleep? It must be awful to be eighty-something and infirm, no longer able to do what you wanted, even when it was a simple task most people took for granted.

Besides, he had said please.

Eventually she reached Walton House. Having paused to get her breath back, she made her way over to the front lawn to take in the view of Foxwell in the dip of the valley. Clusters of houses and other buildings glowed in the early-morning sunlight, their stonework the colour of custard creams. Rising up on the hill on the opposite side of the valley were more properties interspersed with a mixture of woodland and patchwork green fields, some containing cattle, others sheep. High above in an almost cloudless sky, birds swooped and danced.

She moved to the far end of the garden and studied the lanes and houses below in greater detail. From up here, it was like observing a model village. A red Royal Mail van was making its way along the main street, and a couple of people had just left their homes on bicycles. A woman in a yellow sundress disappeared through the sliding doors of the supermarket. And now that Lou had her bearings, she was able to pick out the newsagent's, the pub with its outdoor seating by the glinting river . . . and there was Sammy and Remy's place, with all the curtains still drawn, and the huge cedar tree at the far end of their back garden that she could probably still climb if the occasion arose, although would she want to?

A furious tapping on glass made her spin round. And there was Edgar, glaring at her through the window of what was most likely the living room. The next moment he'd shuffled across to the French doors and opened them. Now he was gesturing at her with what appeared to be – she couldn't help noticing – a walking stick.

'Are you going to stand out there all morning?'

Clearly not. For her own entertainment, Lou decided to see if she could win him over, maybe make him smile or even laugh out loud. Wouldn't that be a wonderful achievement?

'Hello! Isn't it the most gorgeous morning? I've forgiven you, by the way.'

'Forgiven me? For what?'

'Waking me up *so* early. And on one of my precious days off, too! But seeing your cheerful face makes up for everything.'

Edgar surveyed her for a couple of seconds as if she were a troublesome Sudoku he couldn't work out. Finally he said, 'I don't have a cheerful face. Did you get the milk?'

'I did. Ta-daaa!' She swung the plastic carrier bag containing the ice-cold carton. 'Here we are.'

'Is it full fat?'

'No, semi-skimmed.'

He snorted.

Lou said, 'It's good for you.'

Edgar gave her a pitying look. 'I'm eighty. I don't care.'

'OK, I'm sorry, but this is what I bought. If you don't want it, I can take it away with me.'

'Suppose it'll have to do.' Turning, he gestured for her to follow him into the house.

The living room was square and high-ceilinged, furnished with an assortment of mismatched antique furniture and decorated with sun-faded flock wallpaper the colour of porridge.

'You have a beautiful home,' said Lou.

'I know.'

'And you found your walking stick, I see.'

'This is the one I don't like. It's not comfortable to lean on.'

As they made their way slowly along the hallway, they passed another door, open to reveal a cluttered office with a window that this time looked over the garden at the other side of the house.

'Who lived here before you?' It was such a beautiful setting, with a paved Cotswold stone terrace surrounded by shrubs and flower beds, as well as that incredible view of the rolling hills beyond.

'My parents. Come on.' He shuffled through to the kitchen.

'Look, there's your other walking stick,' said Lou. It was propped up against the wooden dresser.

31

Edgar glared at her as if she'd left it there herself. 'Are you going to make me a cup of tea?'

She responded with a sunny smile. 'I might, if you ask nicely.'

'Fine. Will you make the tea, *please*? And have one yourself now you're here.'

It was so tempting to say no, but the strenuous hike up the hill had given her a ferocious thirst. Plus, he was an old man trapped in a spiral of misery and self-imposed loneliness. How could she refuse?

When she'd placed the two mugs on the kitchen table and pulled out a chair to join him, Edgar said abruptly, 'That comment you came out with yesterday, about your husband. What was that about?'

There, see? It served her right for being flippant.

But he'd evidently been thinking about it; his curiosity had been piqued.

'You want the full story? OK.' Lou stirred her tea. Sometimes she preferred to keep the details to herself; other times it felt freeing to let the words spill out. 'I married someone because I'd fallen in love with him and thought he was wonderful. But he turned out not to be wonderful at all. I fell for his charms, like an idiot, not realising the charm was part of the act. To begin with, I thought he needed to know where I was every minute of the day because he cared about me. I thought he came clothes-shopping with me because he wanted me to look my best. I didn't see what he was doing, gradually isolating me from my friends and controlling me.'

She hesitated; looking back now, it seemed crazy that she hadn't realised what was going on.

'When people read about relationships like that, they can't understand how it could possibly happen, but it does. And all the time he was doing it, he was sleeping with other women,

32

drinking too much, and taking cocaine, which I had no idea about. All I knew was that every time he lost his temper with me, it was my fault. I was the problem, because I was such a failure and a let-down.'

'You should have left him,' said Edgar.

Lou nodded; how many times had she heard those blithely spoken words from people who'd never experienced it? 'I know. And I was building up to it. You kind of need to reach rock bottom first, then get over the shame of finding yourself in that situation. You have to realise you aren't the one at fault.' It wasn't easy to explain how stupid and hopeless Brett had made her feel.

'Did he hit you?'

She shook her head. 'No, never. Maybe that was why I didn't leave sooner, because I didn't have any physical injuries to show for it. All he did was yell at me and break things in the house.'

'How long did this go on for?'

'A year, maybe? Like I said, it started off so gradually I had no idea what was happening. He was clever about it.' She paused again to take a gulp of too-hot tea; retelling the story was bringing back the panicky trapped-bird sensation in her chest.

'Go on,' Edgar prompted.

She exhaled slowly. 'It got worse. By then I knew something had to happen. I had a bag packed and hidden away, ready to leave if I needed to get out in a hurry. Because the yelling was so bad, I was pretty much expecting him to get violent sooner or later. But it was his birthday coming up, and he'd taken me to Paris to celebrate mine, so I thought I should at least make an effort. We were short of money by that stage, so I couldn't go over the top, but while he was at work, I made a special dinner with all his favourite things.'

Lou faltered, not bothering to mention that she was the one

who'd been short of money because Brett had somehow taken control of their finances. In her mind, she was back there now, picturing the dining table in their little flat, set with candles and flowers and gleaming cutlery on a red tablecloth.

'Smoked salmon roulade to start, then a rack of lamb with roast potatoes and broad beans, and raspberry trifle for pudding. I thought he'd love it.'

Edgar's eyes were fixed on hers; she had his full attention now. 'Did you kill him?'

Had she? Maybe inadvertently she had.

Another shake of her head. 'Brett had said he'd stop off at the pub after work for a quick drink with his friends and be home by seven. But he wasn't home by seven. Or eight, or nine, or ten. And his phone was switched off. I started to think he must have been in some kind of accident. I was actually worried about him.

'He arrived back just before midnight, and I told him I wouldn't be cooking for him again. That's when he completely lost it. I'd answered him back and he went ballistic. There was lipstick on the front of his shirt and he reeked of perfume . . . Yes, it was that much of a cliché.' The perfume had been Obsession by Calvin Klein, and now if she ever caught a waft of it on a stranger in the street it instantly made her feel sick. 'I accused him of having an affair and he said of course he was, because who wouldn't want to have an affair if they were stuck being married to me? Who could blame him? Which was nice to hear.'

Lou paused to take another swallow of tea, because her mouth was dry with remembered fear. 'That's when I told him I was leaving, and I absolutely meant it. And he knew I meant it. Which was when he stuck his finger into the trifle and tasted it, and told me it was fucking disgusting. So I said it wasn't as fucking disgusting as he was, and that was when he picked up the trifle and threw it at the wall. It was in a big cut-glass bowl that had belonged to my mum, and he knew how much it meant to me. And that was it, the bowl smashed against the wall, there was broken glass and trifle everywhere, and there was Brett screaming at me, yelling that I was going to regret this. The veins were bulging on his forehead, his face was purple and he was pouring with sweat . . . I was sure he was about to attack me.'

She paused for breath, marvelling at the way the words were spilling out so readily; of all the unlikely people to be telling her story to, who would have guessed a cantankerous virtual stranger would be the one to hear it?

'You can't stop there,' said Edgar.

Lou nodded. 'It was surreal. I thought I might be about to die, but I was also wondering if the cream from the trifle was going to leave grease marks on the walls and how much our landlord would charge us for it. Then Brett stopped shouting and started making awful gurgling noises in his throat. His eyes went glassy. He staggered a few steps forwards, then collapsed on the floor, just as someone started banging on the door. It was my neighbours, who'd heard what was going on. They helped me roll Brett over onto his back, and there was trifle all over him, mixed with splinters of glass. He wasn't breathing. One of the neighbours called 999 and I started doing chest compressions. I kept going, I didn't stop, and the paramedics arrived within minutes. They tried everything, but it was no good, they couldn't get his heart going again. He was dead.'

'Were you arrested?'

'No. I was questioned by the police, obviously, but my neighbours had heard everything. And the post-mortem was conclusive. He'd had a massive heart attack, helped along by a massive amount of coke, and he hadn't been out for a drink with his friends from work either. He'd spent the evening in a five-star hotel in Oxford with the girl he'd been seeing for the last six months. Who came along to the funeral and cried a lot more than I did. And that's it, there you have it.' She sat back and pushed her fringe out of her eyes. 'The story of the not-so-great love of my life.'

A fly buzzing around their heads was the only sound in the kitchen.

Finally Edgar said, 'And how did you feel after that?'

'I felt . . . everything. All the emotions. I'd married Brett because I loved him. So I was grieving for that person. It didn't feel like the answer to all my prayers, if that's what you're wondering. When they found out what he'd been like, plenty of people expected me to be glad he was dead.' She shook her head. 'But I didn't feel like that at all. It was really confusing. I'd had a big problem and now I didn't have it any more, but if I ever felt relieved, even for a second, there'd be this huge wave of guilt and shame.'

More silence. Then, 'And now? Got yourself a new boyfriend?'

'God, no. No *way*.' Lou brushed away the fly, which had now landed on the table. 'Look at what happened last time. I'd thought Brett was perfect to begin with, and I couldn't have been more wrong. I don't think choosing boyfriends is my forte. Anyway, that's enough about that.' She checked her watch. 'I should be heading off.'

Edgar looked at her, taking it all in. After a few more seconds he said, 'The light bulb on the landing's broken.'

What? Had she accidentally fallen asleep and woken up an hour later? But no, apparently not. Edgar was pointing to the dresser. 'The spare bulbs are in there. And the ladder's out in the garage.'

She finished her tea. 'OK, I can do that for you. But then I really do need to go.'

The ceilings in the house were high and cobwebby, and the stepladder was long. Once she'd finished fitting the new bulb, Lou returned to the kitchen and saw a packet of chocolate digestives on the table.

'Biscuit?' said Edgar.

'Thanks, but I'm fine. I have to get back now.' Slinging her bag over her shoulder, she said, 'And remember, when people apply for the job here, you must give them a real chance. You need someone to help out with things you can't manage yourself.'

'I've already told you, I tried that before.'

'Well, maybe make more of an effort not to get rid of them this time.'

'You don't know what they were like.' He grimaced. 'One of them chewed gum non-stop. Like a cow. It was disgusting.'

Just this once, maybe he had a point. 'OK, that *is* pretty gross,' Lou said cheerfully. 'Right, I'm off. Good luck with finding someone who doesn't chew like a cow. You have a lovely house and it deserves to be properly looked after. Oh,' she added, 'and remember what I told you about keeping a bit of emergency milk in the freezer.'

Edgar took a chocolate digestive out of the just-opened packet. 'Make sure you shut the door properly on the way out.'

'It's been nice to meet you.' Well, it was something to say. It was polite.

He nodded, using his sleeve to sweep a shower of biscuit crumbs off the table and onto the floor.

'You'll get mice if you do that,' Lou told him.

'Already got them, thanks.'

Chapter 5

Lou let herself into Riverside Cottage with the key she'd taken from the hook by the door.

Following the smell of frying bacon, she found Remy in the kitchen buttering thick slices of toast while wearing nothing but a pair of dark blue board shorts.

'You're back. I heard you leave earlier, thought you'd done a runner.'

What with the amount of butter he was using, he definitely didn't deserve that six-pack. 'Too early for running away. Sorry again about last night.'

'Not your fault. I wish you'd stayed in the bed.' After a beat, Remy said, 'OK, that didn't come out right. You know what I mean.' His eyes glinted with amusement. 'How did you sleep?'

'Really well.' Her stomach rumbled.

'Here.' He poured two coffees from the French press and passed them to her. 'Take these out into the garden. I'll be with you in a couple of minutes.'

The table was set up in a sheltered patch of sunlight and had his phone and laptop resting on it. When he joined her, he was carrying two plates of bacon sandwiches. 'Luckily I made extra.'

'Fantastic. Thank you.'

He waited until she'd finished wolfing down the first half of her sandwich. 'I didn't get the chance to say it last night, but how are you? I mean, how have you been?'

'Not so bad.' It was a question she was always being asked. At least this time it didn't come with the obligatory sideways head-tilt.

'Sammy told me all about it, obviously. Along with the back-story.' He paused, put down his plate. 'You've been through a hell of a time.'

'It wasn't great. At least I'm still here.' Lou licked a smear of ketchup from her finger and changed the subject. 'Are bacon sandwiches your speciality? These are outstanding.'

'When you have Sammy for a brother, you need to be able to cook.' Remy grinned. 'You know what I'm saying. How did his gig go last night?'

'Pretty good. Not too many people stayed till the end, though.'

'How about the new girl from the hotel . . . Tanisha? Any joy there?'

'She turned up. Then she . . . met someone. And they left.'

Remy pulled a sympathetic face. 'He gets his hopes up . . . Ah well, her loss.' His attention was caught by a blackbird singing noisily from the upper branches of the mature cedar tree at the far end of the garden. 'I remember you climbing that tree. It was Sammy's birthday.'

'I remember it too. I won.'

'Reckon you could still do it?'

'Of course I could. If I wanted to.' She picked up the second half of her bacon sandwich. 'Maybe not right now.'

'So what plans have you two made for today?'

'Nothing major, it's just nice to have the weekend off. We're meeting up with some of Sammy's friends this afternoon for a barbecue. Then this evening it's quiz night over at the Bear.'

Remy looked interested. 'That's always fun.'

He'd been expecting to spend this week in Texas. On impulse Lou said, 'If you fancy it, come along and join our team.'

He checked his phone. 'Thanks, maybe I will.'

Actually, having Remy on their team would be brilliant, what with him being super-clever and Sammy only knowing the answers to questions about music. Although to be fair, he did know almost everything there was to know about most types of music.

'Whoa.' Sammy himself appeared in the doorway minutes later, blinking sleepily and with his hair sticking up all over his head. He looked at his brother. 'What's going on, why aren't you in Texas?'

'Texas was cancelled. I drove back late last night. Found someone fast asleep in my bed.'

'You told me he knew.' Lou eyed Sammy. 'He definitely didn't know.'

'But I knew that if I'd asked him, he'd have said yes.' Sammy was unfazed, then his eyes widened. 'Oh wow, did he actually climb into bed with you?'

Imagine that. And now she *was* imagining it, which wasn't helping matters at all.

'Were you *naked*?' Sammy was laughing now.

'I wasn't naked. And no, he didn't try to get into bed with me.' If she'd had a paint chart to hand, what shade might her face be? Fuchsia Crush, possibly? Flaming Sunset? Rampant Raspberry?

Sammy joined them at the table. 'So where did you end up?' he asked Remy, while swiping the last sandwich from his plate.

Lou said, 'He slept in his room. I spent the night on the sofa. It was fine.'

40

Remy shrugged. 'I said she could have the bed, but she refused.'

'He did offer.' Lou leaned across and removed a stray feather from Sammy's tousled hair. 'And he might come along with us later to the quiz.'

'Cool,' said Sammy. 'If we have him on our team, we might even win.'

By eight o'clock, the pub was crowded and the quiz was in full swing. Thanks to Sammy knowing the name of the Smashing Pumpkins' first album, Lou's facility with mental maths and Remy being a whizz at everything else, they were doing well. 'How can you *know* those?' Sammy had shaken his head when she'd rattled off the answers to a series of questions about square roots of five-figure numbers, and she'd tried to explain that she didn't know them, it was simply a matter of working them out.

During a brief lull between the second and third rounds, her phone rang in her bag.

Around the room, the other teams called out good-naturedly, 'No cheating!'

'It might be work. Sorry, I have to answer it.' Pressing the phone to her ear, Lou said, 'Hello?'

'Can you come up to the house? There's something I need to talk to you about.'

OK, she was sympathetic, but this was getting too much. 'I'm afraid I can't.'

'What?'

'It's Saturday evening. I can't come now, I'm busy.'

'Busy doing what?' Edgar demanded.

'I'm out with friends.'

Rico, who was in charge of the quiz, said into the microphone, 'Right, we're on to Round Three now, and it's . . . biology!'

'Woo-*hooo*,' chorused the other teams.

41

Edgar said irritably, 'What's that racket? Who's making that noise? I can hardly hear you.'

'Question One, here we go . . .'

'Look, I'm really sorry, but I can't come and see you now—'

'Still can't hear you,' said Edgar, and the line went dead.

Which made her feel both guilty and relieved.

'Where on the body are the Islets of Langerhans?' said Rico.

An elderly woman sitting behind Remy gave him a nudge and cackled, 'No idea, but I'll show you mine if you'll show me yours.'

'In the pancreas,' said Lou.

Ten minutes later, the pub door flew open just as everyone was groaning in response to Rico's announcement that the next subject would be chemistry. Sammy leaned across and explained, 'He does this to taunt us because he knows it's our least favourite,' but Lou only half heard him, because she'd seen who was coming into the pub. As other heads turned, people began to nudge each other and surreptitiously point out the new arrival. Edgar Allsopp in turn surveyed the room without greeting anyone.

Clearing his throat and rustling his question sheet, Rico broke the silence by saying extra-jovially, 'I know you hate chemistry, but that's what makes it fun. Right, pay attention now, I want you to write down the atomic numbers of these three chemical elements . . . first, phosphorus.'

'Fifteen,' said Edgar.

'*Don't* call the answers out,' hissed a man at the bar.

'I don't mind if he gives us the answers.' A blonde woman snorted with laughter. 'I don't have a clue!'

'Shh,' said Rico. 'Second, gallium.'

'Thirty-one,' said Edgar.

The man at the bar said, 'Oh for God's *sake*.'

'If you want to join in with the quiz,' Rico addressed Edgar,

42

'there's paper and pencils on the bar and it costs two pounds to enter.'

'What's the prize?' said Edgar.

'A bottle of our very finest Spanish sparkling wine.'

'Good grief.' He grimaced and shook his head in disgust, his gaze sweeping the room until he found who he was looking for. He pointed his walking stick at Lou. 'There you are. Come outside, I need to speak to you.'

Had he spent his entire life not bothering to learn entry-level manners? It was time to make a stand. Lou replied calmly, 'I told you, I can't right now. I'm busy.'

'*Busy?* You're sitting down having a drink and answering ridiculously simple questions.'

They weren't ridiculously simple; some of them had been really hard. Lou said, 'If you wait until the quiz is over, we can have a chat then.'

'How long will that take?'

'It'll be finished by nine,' said Sammy. And because he was friendly and couldn't help himself, he patted the empty seat next to him. 'If you want to join in, come and sit with us. You can be on our team.'

Edgar gave him a stony look. 'I'll wait outside.'

Chapter 6

Lou went to find him forty minutes later, and there he was, sitting on one of the wooden benches without a drink.

She said, 'How did you know I was here anyway?'

'You sounded as if you were in a pub. I could hear there was a quiz starting. I drove around until I saw the sign outside this one.' He paused. 'Announcing that tonight was quiz night.'

'Good work, Sherlock. And do you never take no for an answer?'

'Not if I can help it, no.'

'Look, I'm sorry, but this is my night off and I'd really like to enjoy it. You have your car and your walking stick, so you can get hold of anything you need. If there are more jobs you want doing around the house, I'm sure they can wait until you've hired someone.'

'I agree. And I'm asking you to be that person.'

Had she suspected that this might be the idea he'd had in mind? Possibly.

Had it occurred to him that this might not be the world's most enticing offer? Clearly not.

Lou said, 'I already have a job.'

'I know. You told me. Hand in your notice.'

'I don't want to. I'm happy where I am.'

'I'll pay you more.'

'I don't want more.'

'Now you're being ridiculous. Everyone wants more.'

Not if it means having to work for a nightmare like you.

Lou exhaled slowly, because she couldn't say that. Choosing her words with care, she said, 'I look after a woman who's had multiple sclerosis for very many years. She's confined to a wheel-chair and most of the things she used to be able to do are no longer possible. Her coordination is poor and she needs a lot of care. And I love working for her because she's one of the most incredible people I've ever known.'

'Pass the sick bag,' said Edgar.

'It's the truth. She's kind and thoughtful, and endlessly patient. She never complains.'

'Did you ever see *The Sound of Music*? I bet you loved it.'

'OK, listen to yourself.' He was being deliberately obnoxious. 'Her name's Heather and it's a joy to spend time with her and her family. She has a wonderful husband and brilliant children who all adore her. So no, I'm happy where I am and offering me more money wouldn't persuade me to move.'

'Hmph.'

Since she wasn't nearly as rude as he was, Lou said, 'Sorry.' *Again.*

'What if I doubled the amount they pay you?'

This was getting silly now. She shook her head. 'Look, have you thought about moving into a residential home? There are some fantastic ones around, and you'd be able to make friends with the other residents—'

'You know what I'd rather do than make friends with other residents? Head over to the churchyard and dig my own grave.'

45

'Or you can keep yourself to yourself. You don't have to socialise if you don't want to.' Whipping out her phone, she googled 'retirement homes near me'. 'Look at this one; shall I get them to send you a brochure? Honestly, it's the perfect answer. You'll have staff there to take care of you, and fantastic meals cooked by a trained chef—'

'No.' He was shaking his head. 'If I can't put up with one irritating person in my own house, what makes you think having to deal with a whole gaggle of them would be an option? I'm not moving anywhere. It's my home, it's the only place I want to be, and I'm staying there until I die.'

'That's fine, too. It's allowed. But you're going to need to hire some help. Which means you have to stop being so picky.'

'I *know* that.' He spread his hands in despair. 'Which is why I'm asking you.'

Lou said, 'I don't know why you think I'd be any better than the ones you had before.'

'Because . . . I didn't mind you being in the house. Yesterday, or today. You didn't annoy me.'

High praise.

'Which just goes to show, you don't hate everyone.' She gave him an encouraging smile. 'So, start afresh and think positive this time. You've got the advert in the newsagent's window. When you interview the applicants, I bet you'll find someone else who doesn't annoy you. You never know, you might even end up enjoying their company.'

'I won't.'

Her phone buzzed and a text from Sammy flashed up on the screen: *Have you been kidnapped?*

'My friends are waiting for me. I'm going back inside now.' Lou stood up and fluffed her fingers through her hair. 'Good luck.'

'Did you win the quiz?'

46

'No, we came third. If we'd had you on our team, we might have won.'

'Hmph.'

'And you might have had fun.'

Edgar gathered up his walking stick and car keys. 'I doubt it.'

Did he realise he wasn't doing himself any favours? Lou watched him make his way slowly across the grass to the car park. Honestly, some people just didn't want to be helped.

Reaching the entrance to the pub, she almost collided with Remy coming out.

'Managed to get away from him at last?' His dark eyes glittered in the evening sunlight. 'He's a piece of work.'

'He offered me a job looking after him.'

'And?'

'I said no, of course.'

'Good decision. Look, I'm off now. And I won't be back tonight, so you're welcome to my bed.'

'Oh, OK, if you're sure.'

'I promise not to come home at two in the morning and wake you up.'

'In that case, thanks.' He really did have the most incredible smile; it was positively magnetic.

'It's been great to see you again. You're doing all right.'

He sounded as if he meant it. 'Thanks.' Lou managed to quell the colour in her cheeks. 'Good to see you too.'

Two weeks later, while being helped out of bed and into her wheelchair by husband Tony, Heather McLean fell heavily and fractured her pelvis. Six days after that, while Lou was visiting her on the orthopaedic ward, the couple broke the news to her that when Heather left the hospital, she would be moving into a care home fully equipped to handle her increasing needs.

'Tony's done his best, but it's too much for him now.' Heather's voice was slurred and indistinct, but Lou was able to understand her. 'It's better all round if I'm somewhere that can deal with me. Oh Lou, I'm sorry, we've loved having you here with us. I'm going to miss you so much.'

'You won't,' Lou told her, 'because I'll be coming to visit whenever I can. You're not getting rid of me that easily.'

Their friendship had deepened over the last two years. Coming to their house every day and spending time with Heather had made work a pleasure for Lou. Heather and Tony had both supported her during the dark period after Brett's death, and their uncomplicated love for each other – under the most difficult and stressful circumstances – had reassured her that some marriages were capable of being happy and enduring if only you were clever enough to pick the right partner in the first place.

'I do feel bad, though.' Heather's head wobbled from side to side as she dabbed at her eyes with a balled-up tissue. 'Like we're abandoning you. Now you're going to have to find another job.'

'Don't be daft. I'll get onto the agency, see what they have on their books. You don't need to worry about me,' Lou reassured her. 'Something will turn up.'

'And if it doesn't,' Heather's smile was wry, 'there's always Edgar Allsopp.'

'Ha, don't.' Following her weekend in Foxwell, she'd told Heather and Tony all about her initial encounter with Edgar as well as their subsequent meetings. Since then, Edgar had taken to sending her long, irritable texts about everything that wasn't meeting with his approval. These subjects ranged from the female newsreader on the radio who was clearly illiterate because she'd just mispronounced Clonakilty, to the fact that he'd been forced to wait eleven minutes – eleven! – in the newsagent's because the ridiculous woman in front of him had been spending her entire pension allowance on bloody scratch cards.

Lou pulled her phone out of her jeans pocket. 'He sent me another one last night . . . hang on, here it is: "A girl came for an interview this morning. She had a tongue piercing and a tattoo on her neck. She also told me she doesn't clean toilets because apparently they're – and I quote – 'like, totally gross'. Then, when I informed her she wasn't suitable for the position, she announced that she'd heard I was a miserable bastard and nobody wanted to work for me anyway."'

'Wow,' said Heather. 'He's a charmer. Is he still asking you to change your mind?'

'Every day. Sometimes twice a day.' Lou had been scouring the employment agencies online; he'd have to give up once she secured another position.

'And do you reply to every text?'

She shrugged. 'Only briefly. It just feels rude not to. I don't think he has anyone else to complain to.'

'You should block his number.'

'I know, but . . .'

'You can't bring yourself to do it, because you're too nice.' Reaching out to clasp Lou's hand in her own shaky one, Heather said, 'Lou, you've been so brilliant to have around. Wherever you end up, I hope the people at your next job appreciate you. They have no idea how lucky they're going to be to have you.'

'You see, it's kind of a cash-flow problem. I'm sorry, I wouldn't be doing this unless I really needed to. But I'm afraid I do need to.'

'Oh. Right.' Talk about a bolt from the blue. Lou looked at Dennis, her landlord, who was scratching his head with embarrassment and staring out of the window. The one-bed flat on the third floor of an old Victorian property might not be much, but it was hers. Except it wasn't, was it? It belonged to Dennis, who was evidently now in a financial pickle and desperate to turf her out so he could sell the flat to someone else and raise some capital, pronto.

Her mouth dry, she said, 'But I've got two months before I have to leave? That's what it says on the lease, two months' notice on either side—'

'I know,' he interrupted, grimacing. 'It does say that, and obviously I can't force you out before then, but if you could be gone sooner you'd be doing me a massive favour. See, a cash buyer's been in touch and I don't want to lose him. If you could be out in a fortnight, that'd be fantastic.'

'You want me to do you a massive favour?' This time Lou gave him the kind of puzzled look that implied she didn't understand. 'But I'm the one who's not going to have anywhere to go . . . and not even any money to pay for a B&B?'

Dennis sighed; he'd evidently hoped to get away with it, but she wasn't quite that much of a pushover. A wheeler-dealer to the end, he pulled a wad of notes out of his inside pocket and peeled off a number of fifties. 'OK, you're killing me, but fine. You can have this.' He waved them at her; it wasn't a huge amount, but better than nothing. 'So long as you're out by the end of next week. Deal?'

Lou took the money. 'Deal.'

Chapter 7

Sammy didn't particularly enjoy having his photo taken, but these things needed to be done every so often. His most recent gig, at a pub in Stroud, had attracted only a few punters and the landlady had suggested afterwards that maybe the poster they'd put up to advertise the event had looked a bit . . . well, *samey*.

'If you get a nice photo done of you wearing different clothes, people might think you're someone else and be more interested,' she'd explained helpfully. 'Just a thought, love.'

It had been a somewhat brutal thought, but she'd meant well, and you never knew, it might work. Which was why he was here now, sitting on the front step of Riverside Cottage wearing an actual shirt-shirt with a button-down collar rather than his favourite grey Ramones T-shirt with the holes in, and pretending to play his guitar while gazing into the distance, apparently unaware that he was being photographed for promotional purposes.

The plan had been for his brother to take the photos, but just as they were about to begin, a client called to tell Remy he needed to join a Zoom meeting as a matter of urgency.

'Shit,' said Remy, torn. 'I know what he's like. It's going to take ages.'

Now Sammy was all dressed up and looking quite unlike himself in black trousers teamed with a purple shirt he'd picked up in the charity shop and actually ironed with his own fair hand. The afternoon sun was at just the right angle, too. By the time Remy's meeting was over it would have disappeared from the doorway and the shirt would once more be full of creases.

'OK, here comes the cavalry,' said Remy, and Sammy half expected to see a horse galloping down the road towards them. Instead, swooshing into view came Jess Bailey on her bicycle.

'She'll make a better job of it than me anyway. Didn't she do a photography course not long ago?' Remy flagged her down and Sammy watched as Jess screeched to a halt, almost falling off her bike. Then again, Sammy thought with a rush of envy, she would do. He didn't doubt that if Remy asked her to jump out of a plane without a parachute, she'd leap through the hatch without a moment's hesitation.

'Yes?' Jess worked in her uncle's antiques shop halfway up the hill and, he guessed, had just finished for the day.

'Do you have ten minutes to spare? Ah, you're an angel,' said Remy when she nodded. 'I need to speak to a client and mustn't keep him waiting . . . Could you do the honours?' He thrust Sammy's phone into her hand. 'Just take loads of photos and you can't go wrong.'

'Look, it's OK,' said Sammy when his brother had disappeared down the road to the office he shared with his business partner, Briony Trent. 'You don't have to.'

'I don't mind. I'll do my best.' Taking in the outfit, Jess said, 'You look so different, I almost didn't recognise you!'

'It's for promo, to try and trick people into thinking I don't always look like an overflowing bin.' Self-consciously he reached up to touch his combed-back hair and the dark glasses perched on top of his head to make him seem laid-back and cool. 'Remy's worried that if he comes back in twenty minutes I'll have gone all crumpled and messy again. Plus the sun will have moved round.'

'He's probably right. OK, let's do this. What kind of mood are you aiming for?'

'Drop-dead handsome, obviously.' He grinned and crossed his eyes in case she thought he was being serious, then reorganised his pose so the shafts of sunlight through the branches of honeysuckle fell across his face. Previous smiley photos hadn't worked, so this time the plan was to look brooding and tortured. 'Like a serious musician,' he added.

Jess nodded again. 'OK, ignore me now, just let me get on with it. At my evening classes last year they taught us some tricks to use with a phone camera. This is going to be fun, like being a proper professional!'

It was less fun for Sammy, who'd spent a lifetime being unphotogenic, but needs must. He strummed a few chords on his favourite guitar, did his best to look suitably intense and resisted the urge to rake his fingers through his Sunday-best hair. Jess was taking her job seriously and moving from side to side, capturing him from all angles.

Like Sammy, Jess sometimes helped Bob and Rico out behind the bar of the Bear when they were busy. She was a hard worker, the owner of a mass of light brown ringlets and a gorgeous curvy figure, and he'd always assumed that, like most of the women in Foxwell, she had a bit of a crush on Remy. Over the years, Sammy had grown accustomed to being the younger brother hardly anyone fancied; he tended to get told he was a good laugh or, far worse, *sweet* instead.

'Oh my God, what are you doing to my brother?' Reappearing

twenty-five minutes later, Remy did a double-take at the sight that greeted him.

'OK, if I say so myself, I've been rather brilliant.' Jess, standing over Sammy, was flushed with success and artistic endeavour.

'We've got loads of moody shots.' From his position on the grass, flat on his back with the purple shirt unbuttoned and untucked and his no longer neatly combed hair fanned out around his head, Sammy said, 'It wasn't working.'

'He looked like he was going for a job interview in a bank. Here,' said Jess, stepping off him and scrolling back through the scores of shots taken to show Remy. 'I kept them all so you could see for yourself. They just weren't right.'

'So we thought we'd try a different angle.' Staying where he was, spread-eagled on the ground, Sammy said, 'My best song is "Angel in the Snow", agreed?' He swished his arms up and down to demonstrate. 'So this is me being an angel in the grass.'

He watched as his brother studied the photos. Finally Remy looked up and nodded. 'You're right. I like it. Especially these, where you're laughing into the camera. That's the real you.' He touched Jess's arm. 'Good job.'

She looked thrilled. 'Thanks. I just had the idea out of the blue and Sammy went along with it.'

'It's so much better than anything I could have done.' Remy had always had a way of praising people that caused them to melt with joy. The next moment Jess let out a yelp as a car blasted its horn behind her.

'Whoa, it's the lord of the manor,' said Remy. 'Looks like one of us has done something wrong.'

Jess said, 'Probably me. He came into the shop the other day and told me our prices were criminal. Then he got annoyed because a Georgian silver tray had a dent in it.'

Remy looked interested. 'Does he buy stuff from you?'

She pulled a face. 'Never buys anything. Just comes in, complains a lot, then strops out again.'

'Hey, you.' Having hauled himself out of the grey Mini, Edgar Allsopp was gesturing towards them from the other side of the front gate.

Remy said, 'Me?'

'No, of course not you. The other one.'

'Could be me, then,' Sammy said cheerfully. There was absolutely no point in getting het up; Edgar had always marched to the beat of his own drum. 'What can I do for you?' Although he could hazard a guess.

'That friend of yours. She came to stay with you not long ago.'

'I have lots of friends,' said Sammy. 'I'm incredibly popular.'

'Her name's Lou. Lives in Birmingham. She isn't answering her phone.'

'Oh, right. Maybe you took down the wrong number.'

'Of course I didn't. I've been texting her and she was texting back. Every time,' said Edgar. 'But now she's stopped doing it. And when I tried to call, there was no answer. So I want to know what's going on.' He narrowed his eyes at Sammy as if it were all his fault.

Sammy shrugged. 'I have no idea, sorry.'

'Can you at least tell her to reply to my messages?'

'Look,' Remy interjected, 'Lou's lost her job and her flat, so sorting out new ones is probably keeping her busy right now. Sometimes people just don't have time to answer non-urgent texts.'

'Well done,' Sammy murmured.

Remy looked at him. 'What? Why?'

Sammy shook his head and said, 'Nothing,' in the kind of voice that signalled it had definitely been something.

55

'Tell her I need to speak to her.' Leaning on his walking stick, Edgar made his way back to the dusty Mini. Over his shoulder, he added, 'And it *is* urgent.'

'Idiot,' said Sammy when the car had trundled on down the road.

'Me? What did I do wrong? It's true.' Remy was picking his expensive discarded sunglasses out of the grass. 'I was just trying to make him understand that she has more important things to deal with.'

'He's been pestering her to work for him. Practically every day, for weeks. It's been driving her nuts,' Sammy explained. 'And now you've just made it worse.'

'I honestly don't know what the problem is.' Remy shrugged. 'The man's a nightmare. If she doesn't want him pestering her, all she has to do is block him.'

'I already tried telling her that. The trouble with Lou is, she won't do it.'

Interested, Jess said, 'Was it Lou who was at the pub quiz with you the other week? We chatted for a bit in the loos. She was really nice.'

Sammy, busy shaking bits of cut grass out of his hair, said, 'That's Lou's problem. Sometimes she's too nice, and look where it gets you.'

'She's probably worried that if she blocks his number there'll be some kind of emergency and he'll try to call her but she won't know about it so then he'll die and it'll be all her fault.'

Sammy stared at her. '*What?*'

Jess shrugged. 'I saw a film once where that happened. It's why I don't block people. In case I accidentally kill them.'

'That's weird.' Remy shook his head.

She said defiantly, 'Anyway, he said Lou hasn't been answering her phone or replying to texts, so how do you know something hasn't happened to *her*? She could have been in a terrible accident and her phone was crushed by a bus.'

'*You're* weird,' said Sammy, starting to laugh.

'I'm not, I'm a catastrophist, I always expect the worst. Which is actually quite comforting,' Jess explained, 'because every time the worst doesn't happen, I feel as if I've won.'

Chapter 8

It wasn't as if Sammy believed for one moment that Lou had been in an accident, but the mental image of her in hospital did keep crossing his mind. After he'd finished putting together the new flyer for his shows and had used up all the coloured cartridges in Remy's printer making dozens of copies, he gave her a call to see how she was getting on with the search for a new apartment.

'I've been to see a few, but they were grim.' She sounded tired. 'There was one in Walsall that was OK, then just as the agent was showing me out, someone in the flat below started playing the trumpet. Turns out he practises for three hours every day.' She paused. 'Also turns out he can't play the trumpet.'

'Look, if you're ever stuck, you can always stay here. You know that. And yes, I did check with Remy this time.'

'Thanks, but I'll sort something out. A couple of friends up here have offered me a sofa if I'm desperate.'

'What are you up to now?'

'Just finished packing clothes and stuff into boxes. I'm lying on my bed eating custard out of a tin. Listening to the lovely sound of two angry drunk guys outside the pub opposite yelling insults at each other because they support different football teams.' She half laughed. 'Oh, it's a glamorous life.'

'Speaking of angry men, Edgar Allsopp dropped by to see me this afternoon.'

'He did? Aargh, *no* . . .'

Sammy could hear the guilt in her voice. 'He wanted to know why you've been ignoring him.'

'I've been busy! It's been non-stop here.'

'That's what we told him. Look, he asked you to call him, says it's urgent, even though we all know it isn't.' Sammy studied the printed-out flyers spread across the table in front of him, waiting for the gaps to be filled in in due course, giving dates and details of upcoming gigs. 'Anyway, he asked me to tell you, so now I have. Feel free to ignore. Remy says you should block his number.'

'I can't.'

'I know, I said that. So did Jess.'

'Jess with the curly hair, who was in the pub when we were there? I met her in the loos when she was scrubbing orange juice out of her top. She was lovely, and so funny too.'

'She helped me out this afternoon, taking photos for my new flyers.'

'Interesting,' Lou teased. 'I saw the way she was looking at you during the quiz. I reckon she likes you.'

As if. Sammy said flatly, 'She likes Remy. Any luck on the job front?'

'Nothing that jumps out, but I'll find something if I'm not too fussy. There's always work to be had in care homes, but the shifts can be such a pain. Or there's a mother of triplets desperate for a helper up in John O'Groats.'

'That's hundreds of miles away. I thought you were staying in Birmingham.'

'Nothing really to keep me here. I can go wherever I want, can't I? Have you printed the flyers yet?'

'Just finished.'

'Go on then, what are you waiting for?' said Lou. 'Send it to me so I can see what you've done.'

He pinged over a photo and waited. Seconds later, she laughed. 'Angel in the snow meets angel in the grass. Brilliant. That's my favourite out of all your songs.'

Sammy smiled; he'd known she'd get it straight away.

'And I love the spider. Stroke of genius.'

'What?'

'The spider.'

'*What spider?*'

'In your hair, just above your left ear.'

How many times had Remy told him he needed glasses? But he'd always shied away from the idea because it was just one more thing to lose or break or make him an object of fun. Although when Remy wore *his* reading glasses, it just earned him even more favourable attention. Bringing the flyer up to his face, Sammy peered more closely and made a strangled *urgh* noise in his throat, because there was the spider, a big one with hairy legs, practically waving at him from the top of his ear.

He shuddered. 'That is *so* gross.'

'It's a fantastic flyer anyway,' Lou told him. 'When people spot the spider, it'll be extra fantastic.'

'There's nothing good about knowing a huge spider's been that close to your ear.' Sammy grimaced; was he imagining that tickly feeling? 'What if it's still there, burrowing its way into my brain?'

'No worries, it'll probably just lay hundreds of eggs.'

'And to think I was about to wish you luck finding somewhere to live. Maybe you should go for that place above the guy with the trumpet.'

'You're all heart,' said Lou.

'And don't forget to call Edgar Allsopp.'

The next morning, Edgar beat her to it. Lou was waiting in the pelting rain for her bus to arrive when her phone rang and the now familiar number appeared on the screen. She took a deep breath, wiped the rain from the side of her face and held the phone to it. 'Edgar, hello!'

'Did he tell you to call me?'

'Sammy? Yes, he did but . . .' Oh thank goodness, here was the bus, at last.

'So why haven't you?'

'It was late last night and I thought you might be asleep, so—'

'And the times before that? I sent texts and you didn't answer them.'

She found a seat on the bus. 'I know, I'm sorry, there's been so much going on.'

'Were you trying to avoid me?'

'No! I've just been busy. I was about to call—'

'Not a very good liar, are you? And I'm not an idiot. Goodbye.'

Lou looked at her phone in astonishment. He'd hung up. To punish her, presumably. Which was a bit like being faced with a really unappetising plate of food then having it whisked away and being told you were no longer allowed to eat it.

The old woman sitting opposite had been behind her in the queue to get on. Shaking her head, she said sympathetically, 'Ooh dear, lover's tiff? Boyfriend in a strop? My Malcolm used to do that to me, slam the phone down when he wasn't getting his own way. Just leave 'em to stew, that's what I reckon. Teach 'em who's boss.'

'He isn't my boyfriend.' Lou hesitated, torn because now she

61

was picturing Edgar all alone in his dusty kitchen, feeling more rejected than ever.

She called his number. If he didn't pick up, at least she'd know she'd tried.

'Bet you any money he don't answer, love,' said the old woman opposite.

But he did. Unfortunately, at the exact moment an argument broke out between two teenage boys on the bus, so the first thing Edgar heard was one of them bellowing, 'You TOSSER.'

'Don't hang up,' Lou blurted out. 'That wasn't me.'

After a couple of seconds' silence, he said, 'You called me back.'

'Didn't you want me to?'

Another pause, then, 'I wanted to see if you would.'

And there it was. She'd been right. Her heart melted slightly.

'Well, I did.'

As she said it, the other teenage boy yelled, 'I'm going to rip your ears off!'

'Where in God's name are you?' The Hallmark Movie moment was over; Edgar was back to sounding irritable again.

'On a bus.'

'Get off it, then. I can hardly hear you.'

'If I get off now, I'll have a six-mile walk *and* miss my appointment. So if it's all the same to you, I'll stay on the bus.'

'What's the meeting about?'

Honestly, talk about blunt. 'It's . . . personal.'

'I hear you're looking for a job.'

'Sammy told you that?' He hadn't mentioned it.

'Not him. The other brother. And he reckons you need somewhere to live, too.'

Lou shook her head in disbelief; what was Remy playing at?

'So I think you should move down here and work for me.'

Here we go again. Behind her, the two boys were still arguing, although so far no actual ears appeared to have been ripped off. She said patiently to Edgar, 'You've asked me before. I'm afraid the answer's still no.'

'You can have your own section of the house . . . bedroom, living room and bathroom on the second floor.'

'Look, it's nice of you to offer.' Sometimes she was too polite for her own good. 'But it wouldn't work.'

'It would.'

'You only think that because it hasn't happened. Give it a couple of weeks and you'd end up hating me just as much as you hate everyone else. And no,' she added hastily before he could say it, 'I'm not moving in and giving it a go, because I know I'm right. It'd be a waste of my time and yours.'

'You're very stubborn,' said Edgar.

She smiled. '*You're* stubborn. I'm realistic.'

'But you're still looking for somewhere to rent, are you? Why aren't you buying a place of your own?'

'This is my stop,' said the old woman, standing up and showering raindrops from her plastic mac over Lou's knees as she squeezed past. 'And I don't know who it is you're talking to, love, but I'd tell him to get lost. You don't want to give men like that the time of day.'

'I heard that,' Edgar retorted. 'Who said it? Tell her to mind her own business.'

'OK, listen to me,' Lou began again when the old woman and her shopping trolley had left the bus. 'I don't have a car, I don't happen to have spare money in my bank account and I definitely don't earn enough to get a mortgage. It might be hard for someone like you to understand, but this is why I rent. Basically, I'm never going to be able to afford to buy somewhere to live, unless it's a one-man tent on a beach.'

'I was asking in order to make a point.' Edgar was unperturbed by her near-outburst. 'I have a suggestion to make. Come and work for me, and when I die, you can have my house.'

To Lou's right, a furious scuffle was followed by one of the teenage boys shoving a yellow baseball cap out through the narrow open window. The owner of the vanished cap let out a howl of rage and squealed, 'Are you fucking *kidding* me?'

'Not at all,' said Edgar. 'Never been more serious in my life.'

Chapter 9

There he was, as promised, waiting for her on the platform when the train drew into the station. Lou couldn't help it; her stomach did a little twirl of excitement at the sight of him. And he was a nice person too; not only was he amazing to look at, he'd volunteered to come and pick her up.

Well, Sammy had probably persuaded him.

'You didn't have to do this,' she told him. 'I could have caught the bus.'

'The bus takes ages. Besides, I had a meeting in Cheltenham earlier.' Remy flashed that irresistible, easy smile of his. 'So, this is a turn-up for the books.'

Talk about the understatement of the century. Lou said, 'Just a bit. I'm still half expecting it to be a joke. Actually, ninety-nine per cent expecting it. But he does seem to be serious.'

'I'm not sure Edgar knows what a joke is. Anyway, we'll find out more this afternoon.'

Lou had barely slept since Edgar had made his crazy offer, but strangely it had been the fact that he'd felt desperate enough to put it to her that had, in the end, made up her mind. He was lonely, clearly in need of company, and she felt sorry for

65

him. It just went to show, money didn't bring you happiness. Yes, of course it was nice – especially when you weren't used to having any – but it genuinely wasn't the reason she'd decided to take the job. She was a carer and a fixer by nature, and Edgar's slough of despond had finally got to her. Maybe it was fate, or destiny, but he'd essentially begged her to be the one to help him, and how could she resist a challenge like that?

Plus, Foxwell had Sammy and Remy in it, it was a beautiful little town and the residents – well, with one exception – seemed friendly. There were a lot worse places to live.

The interior of the car smelled of leather upholstery and Remy's citrussy aftershave, which beat both Sammy's battered van and the local bus hands down. When she'd called Sammy to tell him about Edgar's phone call, obviously they'd talked about it for some time, then he'd offered to accompany her when she came down to discuss it with Edgar and the solicitor. But when she'd contacted him again to let him know it would be happening late on Friday afternoon, Sammy hadn't been able to make it after all. A friend had recommended him to another friend, who'd booked him to appear at a music festival in Sussex. 'I know it's nothing major,' he had been apologetic, 'but it's a chance to be seen. Even if they've only booked me at the last minute because the guy who was meant to be doing my spot is in hospital with two smashed-up legs.' He added, 'I didn't smash them up, a car did.'

'Glad to hear that,' she'd told him. 'And of course you have to go. Don't worry, I'll be fine.' Although inwardly her heart had sunk a bit.

'Look, why don't I speak to Remy, see if he's free? He'd be better than me at that kind of thing anyway.'

And Remy had been free. He'd offered to come along with her to the meeting, be her wingman.

Glancing across at her as they sped along an empty stretch of road, he said, 'What's up, something on my arm?' and Lou realised with a jolt that she'd been admiring his beautiful hands and fingers. He had excellent wrists too.

'Just a tiny fly,' she lied. 'It's gone now.'

They drove in through the ancient lichened stone gateposts and parked at the head of the gravelled driveway next to Edgar's dirty grey Mini. If she was going to be working for him, the first thing she'd do was give his car a wash.

'Wow.' Climbing out of the car, Remy surveyed the house. 'I've never seen this place up close before. Only from a distance, looking up at it from the town.'

Edgar must have been listening out for them. The front door creaked open and he appeared framed in the doorway, leaning on his walking stick. Raising an eyebrow, he addressed Lou. 'I thought you were bringing the short, scruffy one.'

'Sammy's working in Brighton tonight.'

'So she brought the other one instead.' With a broad smile, Remy held out his hand. 'Remy Keeler. Good to see you again.'

Edgar shook the outstretched hand as if it were a carrier bag of cold casserole. 'You'd better come in, then. Johnson isn't here yet.'

Inside, Lou made cups of tea and carried them through to the cluttered living room.

'OK,' said Remy, once they were seated around the coffee table. 'I know you've talked this through with Lou, but can I ask you to explain it to me?'

'Sounds as if you don't trust me.' Edgar sniffed. 'It's perfectly simple. If I have to have someone helping me out and looking after this place, I want it to be this one here. When I offered

67

her the job, she turned it down. So I had to find a way to make her change her mind.'

'Isn't that a bit drastic?'

'Didn't have much choice, did I?'

'Do you know how much this property is worth?'

'Of course I do,' Edgar countered. 'I'm not stupid.'

Remy remained calm. 'And you want to leave it to Lou.'

'I don't know about *want*. It appears to be what needs to happen.'

'And you don't have any relatives expecting to inherit it?'

'None.' Edgar shook his head. 'No relatives full stop.'

'What about friends?'

He shrugged. 'None of those either. If this wasn't happening and I died intestate, it would all go to the government anyway.'

This was the main reason Lou was going along with the plan, which was otherwise too surreal to take seriously. She said, 'But why not leave everything to charity? Think of the good you'd be doing, the difference you could make . . .'

'Except I'd be dead, so it's not as if I'd be around to see it. So why would I care?' He raised an eyebrow at her. 'You said yourself I need someone here to help me out. And I've decided you're the one I want for the job. When I make up my mind,' he added unnecessarily, 'that's it.'

Remy said, 'Still, it's a huge amount of—'

'Money, yes, I'm aware of that, but once I'm gone, that becomes irrelevant to me. So it may as well go to . . . her.'

'You mean Lou? You could try calling her by her name,' Remy suggested. 'If you like her that much.'

'I didn't say I liked her. She just doesn't annoy me.'

'What if I start to annoy you?' said Lou. 'What if you change your mind and kick me out?'

'I won't.'

Hmm. 'But what if you *do*?'

'Fine.' He spread his hands. 'You'll still get the house. That's why we're having the will written by a professional. All options covered.'

Privately, Lou wondered how long she would be able to tolerate him. Maybe after a while she would be the one to give up and walk out, because it might turn out that life was too short to put up with people like Edgar if they were absolutely resistant to change. She said, 'But that's crazy, because how do you know I wouldn't be horrendous on purpose?'

'You wouldn't, though.'

'You don't know that. You hardly know me!'

Edgar turned to Remy. 'Would she?'

Remy shook his head. 'No. She just isn't the type.'

Lou didn't point out that Remy hardly knew her either. He was relying on her long-standing friendship with Sammy.

Plus, it was true. There was no way she could ever turn herself into a monster purely in order to get sacked. For the last few days she'd hardly been able to think about anything other than Edgar's bizarre offer. It still felt wrong to even contemplate accepting it, but in her current situation it was also the answer to a problem, and Edgar certainly seemed to have made his mind up. Even disregarding the whole house business, he was offering her a place to live and a decent salary to live on. And let's face it, both of those would come in handy right now. If he did prove to be completely insufferable, she would walk away, no harm done.

Edgar cleared his throat. 'There is one thing I haven't mentioned yet . . .'

Oh here we go. Lou exchanged a glance with Remy; if it was something weird, they were out of here.

'I'd like you to visit my grave regularly. Properly visit it,' he emphasised. 'I want fresh flowers. And don't just dump them and run, either. Keep it tidy, so when people are walking around the churchyard, they can see it looks cared for.' He paused, eyebrows furrowed, then went on gruffly, 'I don't want my grave to look neglected.'

Lou found this a touching request; he had no friends to do the job but didn't want it to appear as if that were the case. 'No problem,' she said, as the crunch of tyres on gravel outside the window heralded the arrival of Jerry Johnson, the local solicitor. 'I can take care of that.' If she were no longer around, she would arrange for someone else to do it; there were always people willing to help out in these situations.

'And I don't want anyone else knowing about this arrangement of ours. We keep it between ourselves, d'you understand?'

'Definitely.' Lou nodded. She didn't want other people knowing about it either, forming their own opinions and thinking she was nothing but a money-grabber, gossiping about her behind her back.

By the time they left the house, it was almost seven in the evening.

'Hungry?' said Remy when Lou climbed into the passenger seat and her stomach made a noise like a drain.

'I think so. I don't know. This whole thing just feels mad.' Before leaving, they'd followed Edgar on his stairlift up the imposing staircase so he could show them the section of the top floor that would be hers. It needed a good clean, obviously, but the rooms were large, the furniture was serviceable and the views from the windows were incredible. Taking in all the details, she'd been able to see that with a couple of coats of fresh paint, a few bright prints on the walls and her favourite colourful bedspread, it would be far nicer than any Birmingham bedsit.

Remy put the key in the ignition. 'Come on, I think we both need something to eat.'

'You don't have to cook for me,' Lou protested.

'I wasn't planning to. Al Fresco is open.'

'Oh, but . . .' She hesitated, mentally checking her bank balance, wondering just how expensive the restaurant was and if she could order the cheapest item on the menu. Or maybe pretend not to be hungry after all. The last couple of weeks of job-searching and flat-viewing had used up most of the money in her account.

'Hey, my treat.' Remy was evidently a mind-reader.

Lou exhaled with relief. 'Sorry. Are you sure?'

'I recognised that look. It's the one Sammy gets when he can't afford his share of the gas bill. And yes, of course I'm sure.' As he said it, his phone beeped with a message. 'Damn, I need to call into the office first and sort something out. It might take twenty minutes. Is that OK?'

Was he serious? Lou laughed. 'Hey, you gave up your whole afternoon for me. Take as long as you like.'

'Brace yourself,' Remy warned minutes later as he unlocked the door to the offices of Trent and Keeler, occupying the ground floor of a narrow building on the high street, just a few doors down from the restaurant.

'Why? It's fine.' The small room was painted pale green, the carpet was grey and there were framed certificates hanging on the walls. Apart from a plain desk and three chairs, there was only a single filing cabinet against the far wall. Lou had never ventured into an architect's office before, but somehow she'd expected more.

'This is where we see the clients.' He unlocked a second door, adjacent to the filing cabinet. 'OK, *now* brace yourself.'

He was holding the door open for her. Lou moved past him and caught her breath. Now she understood.

The second room was the Tardis, six times bigger and fifty times more crowded with cabinets, drafting tables, cardboard boxes and swivel chairs, mugs and crisp packets, lipsticks and cardigans and bottles of scent. There were also shelves and bookcases, scarves and sweet wrappers, and on every available surface teetering piles of papers, envelopes, more papers and assorted architectural magazines.

'Wow,' said Lou.

'I know.' Remy nodded.

'I thought you'd be . . . more organised.' He wasn't like this at home.

'It's not me, it's Briony. She's like a human hurricane.' He pointed to a framed photo on the wall of a fifty-something woman standing on a huge stage, being presented with an award. Her hair was long, straight and blue-grey, neatly pulled back from her face to accentuate her impressive cheekbones, and she was wearing an immaculate black suit with black patent court shoes. 'Looks good, doesn't she? And she is brilliant at her job. All this . . .' he gestured around the room, 'it's her guilty secret. Don't get me wrong, she's perfectly clean, just incredibly untidy. Her clients have no idea this is how she operates behind closed doors.'

'Does she know where everything is, though?'

'She says she does, but it's hardly ever true. We spend an awful lot of time looking for unfiled files.' Picking up an empty Coke can, he dropped it into a bin beneath one of the desks. 'And before you ask, we did have a cleaner, but she accidentally threw away some notes Briony had scribbled on the back of an envelope and it lost us a major account.'

'Yeesh.'

'Briony's a fantastic woman and a great business partner. I love her to bits and I'm so grateful for everything she's done for me.' Another text arrived on his phone. 'Anyway, grab a seat and I'll sort out what needs to be done.'

For the next twenty minutes, Remy searched for paperwork, located a set of architectural plans, made a couple of phone calls and answered the many questions of a client in Portland, Dorset. While she waited for him to finish, Lou did some gentle cleaning up, throwing away sweet and biscuit wrappers after checking there was nothing written on any of them. She collected eight coffee mugs and washed them in the tiny sink at the far end of the office. She found a dustpan and brush under the sink unit and swept up crumbs from the carpet. She steadied the more unstable towers of files so they wouldn't collapse on the floor, discovered a Cadbury's Advent calendar with only half the chocolates eaten, and shook many months' worth of crumbs out of the keyboard of the desktop computer on Briony's desk.

'Right, job done,' said Remy finally. 'Let's get out of here, shall we? Time for food.'

Chapter 10

Al Fresco, Lou was relieved to discover, turned out to be not too pricey after all. It was an old-fashioned family-run restaurant with checked tablecloths, framed photographs of Italy on the walls and exuberant opera playing in the background. Outside, it had just started to rain, but inside the lighting was golden and the atmosphere warm. Fat candles flickered in glass holders on every table, cutlery glinted and the cooking smells drifting from the noisy kitchen were out of this world.

When they were seated and a carafe of red wine had been brought to their corner table, Remy clinked his glass against hers and said, 'So, looks like it's happening. The beginning of a new life in the Cotswolds. Welcome to Foxwell.'

The wine was smooth and welcoming. Lou took a couple of swallows and felt the alcohol hit her empty stomach. 'It's going to be interesting.'

'Has the money thing sunk in yet?'

'Not at all. It's completely surreal.'

'Ten minutes ago you were wondering if you could afford a pizza. But you're set to inherit a house worth . . . well, a lot of money. Not to mention the rest of it.'

'I never thought anything like this could happen. In all honesty,' she said, 'I can't *see* it actually happening. He could live for another twenty years.'

'I couldn't cope with him for twenty hours,' Remy said bluntly.

'Exactly. And I might not be able to bear it for longer than a couple of months. To be frank, I can't see it lasting, which makes the money thing irrelevant anyway. But isn't *Edgar* interesting?' She lowered her voice and leaned across, although no one at any of the nearby tables was paying attention. 'I mean, he's lived here for all this time, never married, never made any friends . . . hasn't even tried to be nice, from what I can gather. It's like he doesn't care what anyone thinks of him.'

'It's sad. But it's always been his choice.'

'Exactly.' Lou took another swallow of wine, then raised an index finger to make her point. 'But then there's the whole business with the flowers and the graveyard, which makes me think he does care.' She frowned. 'And he could arrange to pay someone to do that without having to hand over his house. Oh God, my brain still can't get over it. But isn't it just the saddest thing, that he doesn't have anyone to leave it to? Not a single friend in the world?'

'Which is why he's leaving it to you.'

'It should go to some charity or other.' The amount of money was too daunting to consider keeping for herself, especially when she knew she hadn't done nearly enough to deserve it. Having given it much thought, Lou was pretty sure she'd feel compelled to hand it over if by some miracle she were still working for Edgar when he died. OK, she wasn't a complete saint; maybe she'd keep a small amount for herself.

'Of course he should do that, but he obviously doesn't want to.' Remy's dark eyes gleamed in the candlelight. 'For whatever reason, he's chosen you instead. He's lonely, he wants some company. And he might not be admitting it, but he likes you.'

'Hey.' She shrugged and broke into a grin. 'Who wouldn't?'

There was so much to talk about. When they ordered their food, Lou insisted she didn't need a starter, but Remy told her to choose one. 'And don't look for the cheapest thing on the menu, either. Have whatever you want.' He sat back, mouth twitching. 'It doesn't do me any harm to get into your good books. One day you could be the owner of the biggest house in Foxwell and everyone will have to bow and curtsey to you.'

He was joking. Lou said, 'I really can't see it happening. But knowing my luck, if by some miracle I do stick it out, he'll end up outliving me.'

She ordered prawns in a chilli, tomato and fennel sauce, and it was amazing. By the time their main courses arrived, she'd relaxed completely, possibly thanks to the wine. When her phone rang, it was Sammy FaceTiming from Brighton during the break between performances, wanting to know how the meeting had gone.

'It's all going ahead,' Lou told him. 'I'm moving down next week. We'll just have to see how long I last.'

'I was wondering if you'd be able to put up with him,' said Sammy. 'But I suppose if you know you'll be getting a bloody great house at the end of it, you can put up with anything. Even Edgar Allsopp.'

'That's just between us, though,' she reminded him. 'No one else needs to know about that bit. And the house isn't the reason I'm doing it.'

'You're mad,' Sammy said fondly. 'It'd be the only reason I'd do it. I wish Edgar liked me.'

Remy leaned across the table so Sammy could see him too. 'How's everything going down there?'

'Oh, you know. Same as ever.' The usual stoical grin filled Lou's phone screen. 'A small but discerning audience, most of them wishing I could've been the one who'd broken my legs.'

He worked so hard and never gave up. Lou said, 'Where are you staying tonight?'

'I'll be in the van. Hey, I'm used to it.' He laughed at the expression on her face. 'It's a luxurious establishment with quirky decor, fine dining facilities and first-class entertainment. Otherwise known as me and my guitar in a sleeping bag, with a can of Coke and something from the burger van to make my evening complete.'

'Tragic.' Remy angled his plate so it could be seen. 'We're having chicken parmigiana and salmon involtini.'

'And wine!' Some of it sloshed over the rim as Lou held her glass up to the camera.

'How are you getting home?'

'It's fine,' said Remy. 'I'm driving her back to the station. I've only had one glass.'

'If she wants to stay at ours, she can always have my bed,' Sammy said. 'OK, have to go, my hordes of fans are screaming for me to get back on stage. Anyway, great news about the job . . .'

When he'd ended the call, Lou said, 'Do you think the people around here will mind that I've taken the job?'

'Probably award you a medal for bravery. Everyone knows what Edgar's like.'

'But won't they think it should have gone to someone local?' As they'd passed the newsagent's, she'd seen that the advert had disappeared from the window.

'Plenty of them have had the chance to work for him. They didn't want to. You're the one he's chosen,' said Remy. 'Lucky you.'

77

'I didn't want to work for him either.' Lou put down her fork. 'It might be unbearable.'

'And if it is, you're always free to leave. No one would blame you.' He shrugged. 'If you can bring yourself to walk away.'

That was the dilemma. Could anyone really walk away from the life-changing deal she'd been offered? Edgar had handed her the responsibility of deciding whether to keep the house for herself or give the money to a worthy cause. Lou just hoped she wouldn't end up changing her mind and sacrificing months or years of her life for the worst reason of all.

'Hey, see how it goes,' Remy went on. 'Edgar's a nightmare, but you don't have to like him, do you? Just get on with the job and tolerate him, that's all you need to do. And hope he doesn't end up in the Guinness Book of Records as the world's oldest surviving man.'

Lou twirled the stem of her almost empty glass. Right now, she knew she wasn't going to change her mind. But she also knew she wasn't going to merely tolerate curmudgeonly Edgar Allsopp. Up until now, the idea had only existed inside her own head, but now she felt the urge to share it with Remy.

'I'm going to do better than that.' An adrenalin rush of determination accompanied her words. 'I'm going to find out why he is the way he is, and make his life better.' Feeling suddenly invincible and capable of anything, she went on, 'He might not like it, at least not at first, but I won't give up. I'm going to sort Edgar out and cheer him up.'

It was the obvious answer, wasn't it? She might be lacking in the money department, but she'd always been a naturally positive person, able to look on the bright side and make the best of any situation. Whereas despite all his wealth, Edgar had evidently been a stranger to joy, possibly for most of his life.

'Good luck with that then.' Remy was shaking his head, unconvinced.

'I mean it. I'm going to make it my mission.'

'If anyone can do it, it's you.'

He hardly knew her, but he was right. Lou acknowledged the compliment with a jokey sitting-down curtsey. The thing about Remy was, he had this amazing way of focusing his attention on you, making you feel special and interesting and kind of . . . glowy. OK, she'd had a fair amount of wine, quite a bit more than she was used to, but that didn't mean she was imagining it. And after the last tumultuous year, didn't she deserve to feel good about herself? She'd mourned the loss of Brett – not the horrendous mess their relationship had turned into, but what she'd hoped and expected it to be. It was a known fact, she'd learned, that bereaved partners whose relationships had been terrible grieved just as deeply as those who'd been idyllically happy together. It wasn't simply a matter of heaving a sigh of relief and moving on to the next one with a spring in your step.

It just didn't work that way.

Basically, after spending the last year in an emotional deep-freeze, tonight for the first time in what felt like for ever she was actually *feeling* something again. As in, back to normal. And now she was also feeling desirable, as if someone were finding her physically attractive. Because Remy might not be saying anything openly flirtatious, but – and she was almost certain she wasn't imagining it – he was looking as if he secretly wanted to.

It was a heady sensation, helped along by the golden glow from the candle on the table between them. If it was making Remy look this good, perhaps it was working its magic on her too. In response, Lou found herself smiling more widely, speaking more animatedly and listening more intently.

When she saw him pick up the bottle of San Pellegrino and refill his tumbler, she said, 'I feel bad, knocking back wine while you're stuck with boring old water.'

'It's fine.' He brushed aside her concern. 'Are you still OK to catch the train home?'

'I'm easy. I mean, whatever's easiest for you. If you'd rather have a few drinks, I'm happy to travel back tomorrow.'

'You choose.'

Ooh . . .

Were her eyes sparkling? They felt as if they might be. It wasn't as if she was throwing herself at him; they were just having such a lovely time, it seemed a shame for the evening to come to an end before it needed to. Glancing around the restaurant, Lou wondered if any of the other diners could possibly be enjoying themselves as much as she was, and if they were secretly wishing they could be the ones sharing a table with Remy Keeler. Leaning forward, she rested her chin on her clasped hands as if she were being photographed for an ad in a magazine. 'It's up to you. If you fancy a couple of glasses of wine, go for it. We can always order another bottle.'

And now everything seemed to be sliding into fuzzy-edged movie-style slow motion, the buzz and bustle of the restaurant fading away as she met Remy's steady gaze and awaited his decision. The corners of his mouth were curling and the index finger of his left hand was tapping lightly on the tumbler in his grasp. Silently willing him to make the right decision – *do it, do it, just say it* – Lou gave him a nod and an encouraging smile.

Chapter 11

'I think maybe . . .' Remy broke off, his gaze shifting to the door behind Lou, and the spell was abruptly broken. The next second, he was rising from his seat to greet the redhead who'd crossed the restaurant and flown into his arms.

'You're back!' He sounded delighted to see her, and Lou couldn't blame him. The woman might only be wearing a sleeveless khaki jumpsuit over a plain white T-shirt, but she was wearing it like Kate Moss, in such a way as to make everyone else in the vicinity look boringly overdressed. She was creamy-skinned and elegant, her hair shone like burnished conkers and she was wearing no make-up other than mascara.

'I wanted to surprise you, so I caught the earlier flight and drove down from Heathrow.' Holding his face in her hands, she planted a big kiss on his mouth before pulling back and turning to Lou. 'Sorry, how rude of me! Hi, I'm Talli, and you must be Sammy's friend. Waah, is that tiramisu? That stuff is heaven on a plate!'

'Lou. Nice to meet you.' Even while marvelling at the colour of Talli's eyes, as vivid as kiwi fruit, she was mentally kicking herself for having been so gullible. No, not even gullible; she'd

81

been fooling herself. Remy hadn't been remotely interested in her. Why would he be when he had someone like Talli in his life?

Another chair was brought to their table, another helping of tiramisu ordered.

'The trouble with surprises is, I arrived at your place and you weren't at home,' Talli explained, her hand on his forearm. 'So I went over to the pub, but you weren't there either. Luckily someone said they'd seen you coming in here.'

'You could have called me,' said Remy.

'But that would have spoiled the surprise! Now, shall we have some more wine?' Talli beamed at Lou. 'Where are you staying tonight?'

OK, this was starting to feel awkward now. Fumbling with her napkin, Lou said, 'We were just trying to decide. I was planning to catch the train home . . .'

'But you changed your mind?'

Remy said, 'We wondered if it'd be easier for Lou to travel back in the morning, then I could have a couple of drinks.'

'But it's fine,' Lou blurted out, because that sounded horribly wrong. 'It doesn't matter, whichever's easiest for you.' Except none of it was easy, was it? She'd had no idea Remy was currently involved with someone, because Sammy – like a typical male – evidently hadn't thought to mention it. And what had been a brilliant evening had now turned into a completely mortifying one.

'Hey, if you want a drink, you have one.' Talli gave Remy's arm a squeeze. 'You two order another bottle, I'll have an orange juice, and when we're finished here, I can drive Lou to the station.'

'Oh, but . . .'

'I *insist*,' said Talli as her pudding arrived. 'Now, Remy told

82

me you were thinking of taking a job down here. That's exciting! How did the interview go?'

'Well . . . good. I'm going to give it a go.'

'Fantastic! My God, this is the best thing I've ever tasted.' Talli was swooning over her bowl of tiramisu. 'Totally off the charts.'

Idiot . . . idiot . . . idiot . . .

The words tick-tocked through Lou's brain like a metronome in time with the chugging of the train as it made its way from Cheltenham Spa to Birmingham.

It was the last train of the evening, and a raucous group of girls at the other end of the carriage were screeching with laughter and swigging from cans of gin and tonic, having the best time. By contrast, the alcohol from earlier was seeping out of Lou's bloodstream and the realisation that she'd been close to making a spectacular fool of herself was slowly sinking in.

Basically, she'd fallen under Remy's spell. Spending time in his company had made her feel beautiful, his equal, as if they'd been forging a real connection. Until Talli had arrived and effortlessly demonstrated what a *genuine* connection looked like. Because now, looking back, it was blindingly obvious that Remy hadn't been flirting with her at all. He'd only agreed to help her out in the first place as yet another favour to his brother. And suggesting the restaurant had simply been a means to an end; they were both hungry and it was a place that served food.

Lou shuddered. It was a good job Talli had turned up when she did, because God knows how much more of a line she might have crossed – well, *tried* to cross, like a complete numpty – otherwise. Imagine if she'd invited herself back to Riverside Cottage, convinced that something incredibly romantic was meant to happen, and had made a move to kiss him . . . Aargh, what would he have *thought*? He already had a girlfriend who was stunning, stylish and supercool, and who had even hugged her goodbye after dropping her at the station. 'It's been so lovely to meet you.' Her green eyes had sparkled as she'd said it. 'We'll see you again soon. Now, mind you don't fall asleep on the train. Don't want to wake up in Edinburgh!'

See? She was nice, too. More than nice, truly lovely.

Well done me.

Her phone burst into life and Sammy's name flashed up on the screen. Hopefully Remy hadn't already called to tell him how embarrassing it had been, having to be polite over dinner while his old schoolfriend had come on to him like some over-excited and hopelessly incompetent groupie.

'Hey, where are you?' said Sammy.

'On the train.'

'Ask me how the second half of the gig went.' He was sounding cheerful, at least.

'Was it brilliant?'

'Not bad at all! People actually stayed to listen. And they clapped at the end. OK, they were pretty smashed, but it still counts . . . *and* this woman came over to see me afterwards; apparently her boyfriend's a famous music producer and she's going to tell him how amazing I am. I gave her one of my new flyers to pass on to him, so maybe coming down here was worth it after all.'

Lou smiled, happy for him. 'That's great. And where are you now?'

'Sitting on a bench next to the van, eating my burger and fries.'

'What's that noise?'

'There's a group of girls coming down the road. They're looking pretty lively.'

'They sound it.' Even from here, she could hear them singing 'Best Years of Our Lives' very badly indeed.

'Whoa,' said Sammy as she heard them scream with laughter. 'They just flashed their boobs at me. Thank you, ladies – hey, hang on, it's you!'

Lou heard a female voice say, 'Me? What's me, what did I do?'

'It's me, Sammy Keeler! From up on the stage, remember? Back at the festival, you told me I was brilliant. And I gave you a flyer to give to your boyfriend.'

'You did? Oh yeah!' The girl was laughing wildly. 'Some drunk guy threw up on my shoe, so I used it to wipe off the mess.'

'Oh. Well, never mind, my van's just across the road, I can get you another.'

'S'OK, I don't need one, my other shoe's fine. But you were brilliant! Bye!'

The girls resumed their terrible singing and clattered on down the road.

'Great.' Sammy sounded resigned.

'She might still remember your name and tell her boyfriend so he can google you,' said Lou.

'She's pretty drunk. She won't remember.' He heaved a sigh. 'She probably doesn't even have a boyfriend.'

Lou rested her forehead against the cool window and gazed out at the blackness whooshing by. She knew how that felt.

On the bright side, she hadn't flashed her boobs at Remy.

At least there was that.

Chapter 12

It took a while, but Lou eventually persuaded Edgar to come with her. Honestly, it was like dealing with a truculent teenager.

'Why do I have to go?' He eyed her beadily.

'Because I love it when everything's gone through the till and you look horrified and say *How much?*'

'Hmph.' But he put on his thick winter coat and stood by the front door, waiting impatiently for Lou to collect the shopping bags and car keys and take him with her to the supermarket.

'Hello there, my love, how's it all going?' Moira was in her usual position at the checkout. Never knowingly under-decorated, she was wearing flashing reindeer earrings and a huge Santa badge. As Cliff Richard trickled out of the shop's speakers, she sang 'Mistletoe and Wine' along with him. Beaming at them both, she pressed Santa's red nose on her badge, causing him to go *Ho ho ho!* 'I bought him in the pound store in Cirencester. Isn't he brilliant?'

'No,' said Edgar.

'I love it,' Lou told her. 'Do it again.'

Ho ho ho, Santa boomed tinnily once more, prompting Edgar to shake his head in disbelief. Moira said cheerily to Lou, 'What's he like, eh?'

Over the course of the last three months, following Lou's lead, the locals had begun to treat him with good-natured amusement.

There were boxes of mince pies piled high next to the checkout, and Lou added a packet of them to the items already on the conveyor belt.

'This is ridiculous.' Edgar scowled. 'It's only the first day of December.'

'Which means it's the start of Christmas,' she said patiently. 'Now, have you changed your mind about wanting a chocolate Advent calendar?'

'No. Come on, let's get out of here.'

For someone with nothing else going on in his life, he was always impatient to get home. When they were out together, he liked to accuse her of talking nonsense to other people. When she explained that it was just a matter of being sociable, he would respond with another of his stony looks and say, 'Why?'

Just as well she hadn't expected Operation Cheer Up Edgar to be easy.

Moira finished running the items through the checkout. 'That'll be forty-one pounds sixty pee, my love.'

'*How* much?' said Edgar.

'I call that a bargain,' Lou told him. 'Aren't you looking forward to having a lovely mince pie as soon as we get home?'

Edgar raised a critical eyebrow at Moira. 'And it's sixty *pence*, not *pee*.'

By way of retaliation, Moira pressed the nose on her badge, and when Santa had finished going *Ho ho ho* she said, 'Merry Christmas!'

Back at the house, Lou got on with unpacking the shopping and nudged the dial on the central heating up a couple of notches while Edgar wasn't looking, because what he considered fine was the kind of temperature that had people in Amsterdam skating on the city's canals.

She'd moved in three months ago, at the very end of August, on one of the hottest days of the year. Now it was December and frosty outside, the hills dusted with white and most of the trees bare. She'd survived an entire season of the year with the most taciturn man in Foxwell, and he was still taciturn, but she had no intention of giving up yet.

'Where are you going now?' he said as she placed a mug of tea and a mince pie in front of him.

Lou waved her iPad at him. 'Upstairs, to take some photos of the view while it's still frosty. With the sun out, it's looking fantastic out there.'

When she returned ten minutes later, the tea had been drunk and the foil case sitting on his plate was empty.

'How was it?' she asked.

'Dry.'

She smiled. 'Would it kill you to say you enjoyed your mince pie?'

'Yes, because it was dry.'

'Next time we'll add a drizzle of brandy and a splash of cream, then maybe you'll like it more. Now, have a look at these. What d'you think?' Pulling up a chair beside him, she ran through the photos she'd taken of the view from the top floor of the house. 'OK, I took loads, but I'd say this is the best one, because you've got the spectacular view and part of the house too, so people can see it was taken from an upstairs window.'

'What people?'

'I thought it would make an amazing Christmas card.'

'For who?'

'For you. To send.'

'Send to who?'

He was looking baffled. Lou belatedly realised this was an

88

alien concept. She said, 'I'm going to take it down to Dave and get some made up.'

'Who's *Dave*?'

'Dave Harding, at the print shop on Linden Street. He had a triple bypass in September but he's up and running again now. His wife's Sandy, she sells jams and cakes at the Saturday market and works as a teaching assistant at the school. Their son Ben's running a 10K for charity next weekend—'

'I only asked who Dave was. No need for a full biography. And I don't send Christmas cards.'

'Well I do, so why don't we give it a go this year? Humour me,' said Lou. 'It's nice! We can string ours up around the fire-place in the living room and have the tree in the alcove.'

'I don't have a tree either.'

'But this year we're going to get one.' She gave him her don't-argue-with-me look.

'What's the point? There's no one to see it.'

Last night, her dad had called to let her know he'd be spending the last week of December and the first week of January in Barbados with his partner, Kate. After breaking the news, he'd added, 'Will you be OK, Lou? If you can get away, you know you're welcome to join us.' Of course, she'd known she couldn't leave Edgar for that long, so she'd put on a cheerful voice and said, 'Thanks, Dad, but it's fine, I'll stay here. You and Kate have a great time.'

Now, she told Edgar, 'You're here. I'm here. Which means we'll see it. And this is me putting my foot down. Because I'm not spending Christmas in a house without a tree.'

After several seconds of mutinous silence, he said, 'Fine. But you're the one who has to do it all, because I'm not getting involved.'

'It's my job to do everything.' It was called making the best of a situation. Summoning up the spirit of Christmas by sheer force of will, Lou beamed at him. 'And guess what? I can't wait!'

Three days later, the enormous tree was delivered to the house. Lou drove into Cheltenham and bought tons of cheap and cheerful decorations, as well as pots of gold, silver and white paint. On her return, she raided the garden for armfuls of greenery and dried twigs, then clambered up the huge sycamore tree.

'What in God's name are you *doing* out there?' Edgar had flung open his bedroom window and was staring at her.

'We need mistletoe. I went to pick some up at the market, but they'd sold out. Then I thought, why buy it anyway when we've got some in the garden?'

'If you fall down from there, you'll break your neck.'

'I won't fall. Climbing trees is my superpower.' Lou was securely balanced on a hefty branch. She had a couple more to scale before reaching the oversized ball of mistletoe, but it would be a straightforward enough manoeuvre. Grinning at Edgar, she bent her knees and did a jokey pretend-wobble.

'Stop it!'

She clapped her free hand to her chest. 'Oh Edgar! Are you worried about me?'

'I'm worried about who's going to cook my dinner tonight.'

'OK, I promise not to fall.' Shifting onto her left leg and reaching up, Lou launched herself at the next branch, then the one above it. Finally she reached the football-sized bundle of mistletoe and sliced it off with the penknife she'd brought with her, tucked inside her bra.

'You're mad,' said Edgar when she'd completed her descent.

'Maybe. But I did it. And now we have mistletoe.' Triumphantly she held it above her head like the World Cup.

Evidently unimpressed, Edgar closed his bedroom window and disappeared from view.

Purely for her own amusement, Lou imagined she was acting in one of those festive TV movies where, little by little, she managed to win over the curmudgeonly old man who had no truck with Christmas. Maybe, just maybe, having seen her risk her life for a bunch of mistletoe, something inside Edgar's perma-frosted heart would start to soften. Then later he might shuffle grumpily into the living room while she was teetering on top of a ladder next to the tree . . . and when she accidentally dropped the silver star, he *might* pick it up and pass it to her . . .

After that, of course, Christmas music would begin to play, they'd start to sing along together, then the next couple of hours would be spent companionably decorating the tree while fat flakes of snow began to fall outside.

Plus, he would apologise for having spent the last three months being a caustic old git.

The scene conjured up by her ridiculously optimistic imagination didn't happen, of course, despite her playing all the right music and singing along while fixing strings of coloured fairy lights around the sash windows, then draping yet more lights over tree branches that smelled of Christmas. Coming into the room, Edgar had questioned what time dinner would be ready, before leaving to sit in his study and read his *Daily Telegraph* in peace.

Having finished clearing away dinner at seven Lou left the house to meet up with Sammy and Jess at the pub, and did briefly wonder if the fabulously decorated tree would still be standing when she got back.

Remy's car wasn't parked outside Riverside Cottage. He wasn't often around these days, instead spending most of his free time over in Cheltenham, where Talli worked as an orthodontist and lived in a spacious ground-floor flat in the upmarket district of

Montpellier. The two of them had been together for almost four months now, having first met at a party in Tetbury and hit it off from the word go – Talli had exclaimed laughingly that it had been love at first sight. And Lou had managed to get over her previous embarrassment by telling herself that she hadn't actually propositioned Remy that evening in Al Fresco and hopefully hadn't made as much of a fool of herself as she'd feared. Plus, if he *had* noticed her amateurish attempts at flirtation . . . well, he was Remy Keeler; by definition he was used to it.

Anyway, she had a spot of Cupid's-arrowing of her own to be getting on with, and if all went according to plan, tonight could be the night it finally happened.

Up until last week, Sammy had managed to remain oblivious to the fact that Jess was keen on him. It was as if his ongoing crush on Tanisha had taken over his brain. But a fortnight ago, two things had happened. First, he'd accidentally overheard Tanisha and her friends marking men out of ten for fanciability, and had discovered he was a two and a half. Snorting with laughter, Tanisha had gone on to say, 'I mean, bless his heart, he's a sweet guy, but can you imagine going out and getting trashed then waking up the next morning and discovering you'd slept with Sammy Keeler?'

The next moment, as if that hadn't been horrendous enough, another customer had pushed open the door behind which Sammy had been standing, revealing him and making the situation fifty times worse. Tanisha had blurted out defensively, 'Well I'm sorry, but I go for good-looking guys, don't I? It's not my fault you aren't my type.'

Sammy had pretended to find it funny, but Lou knew how much it had hurt him. On the upside, it soon became apparent that karma had also been eavesdropping that evening. Just five days later, Tanisha was sacked on the spot for having sex with a hotel guest when the man's wife caught them after returning early to their suite following a trip to the on-site beauty salon to get her legs waxed.

At least Tanisha was out of the picture now, having headed back to her mum's place in north Wales. Jess, having confessed her relief to Lou, had wondered if this meant she might now stand a fighting chance with Sammy. And Lou had spent the last week dropping crater-sized hints to Sammy that someone far nicer than Tanisha could have been right under his nose all along.

The first time she'd said it, he'd done a double-take then vigorously shaken his head. 'Jess? No.'

'Oh come on, she's brilliant, you two would be perfect together.'

'I'm not risking getting turned down again. I'd be the laughing stock of the town.'

'You wouldn't,' Lou told him. 'Because I'm pretty sure Jess wouldn't turn you down.'

This had taken Sammy by surprise. He'd genuinely had no idea. After that, Lou had dropped a few more casual comments, taking care to keep them subtle because otherwise Sammy might back-pedal and feel he was being pushed into it. He had his pride. She knew he needed to believe it was his decision, not hers.

Ah, but wouldn't it be great if she could make it happen? Maybe it wasn't set to be one of those thunderbolt-and-lightning *coups de foudre* – not on Sammy's side, at least – but some relationships got off to a slow start, didn't they? Then gradually grew into something wonderful. And Jess was exactly the kind of girlfriend he needed. Not flashy, not addicted to endless series of reality TV and not obsessed with online influencers peddling cosmetic surgery. She was low-maintenance, down to earth and good-hearted.

Well, seeing as cheering up a cantankerous octogenarian didn't appear to be working *at all*, Lou had decided to diversify; maybe the time had come to polish up her matchmaking skills and make other people happy instead.

Chapter 13

It was fun watching them notice – and pretend not to notice – each other. When she and Sammy walked into the pub that evening, Jess was waiting for them at their favourite table, scribbling away in a notebook. She gave them a quick nod and a wave, then went back to the notebook, a split second before Sammy did his own casual wave then hastily pretended to be smoothing his hair instead. Lou hid a smile.

While Sammy went up to the bar, Lou sat down next to Jess. 'What's all this, then?'

'My homework for the evening. Mum was telling me about this dog they're desperate to shift and I said why didn't they try posting an ad on Facebook? So now she's given me the job of writing it.'

Jess's mum, Babs, worked as a volunteer helper at an animal sanctuary midway between Foxwell and Cheltenham. Lou said, 'Why are they desperate?' and leaned across to see how she was getting on. 'Oh my God, you can't write that!'

Jess pulled a face. 'I know, it's risky, but the other way hasn't worked. The sanctuary said nice things about him on their website and had loads of interest from people wanting to adopt him. Until they met him for the first time and saw what he was really like, then they ran a mile.' Taking out her phone, she showed Lou a photo of a black and tan chihuahua with huge sticky-out ears and an intense, who-you-lookin'-at? expression on his face. 'This is him, this is Captain Oates. Doesn't look like the devil incarnate, does he? But he is.'

Lou read from the notebook:

Hi, my name's Captain Oates. (I'll explain later.) Nobody loves me because I'm just not lovable. I hate all sorts of people but mainly older women, possibly as a result of my first owner dressing me in a silver tutu. I also dislike small children (so loud, so *annoying*), men in bobble hats, and teenage girls who try to pick me up and call me cute.

They only try it once. Trust me, I'm not cute.

I need a home that contains none of the above. No other animals either, because I'll only fight them. And win. I don't like loud music. I don't like it when people dance and I really can't stand doors being slammed. When any of those things happen, I snarl and bark. Actually I do that a lot anyway; I just enjoy it. If you're the kind of person who thinks I might be won over and grow to love you, you're wrong.

So anyway, that's me. If anyone out there is up for the challenge, just give the sanctuary a call – they'll be *so* happy to hear from you. Oh yes, and my original owner called me Twinkle – you can imagine how much I enjoyed *that*. So this sanctuary place decided to change my name to Captain Oates. Because when I go out, I like to be gone for some time.

Sammy arrived at the table with their drinks.

95

'And remember, you'll need to be nice to me,' Lou read the last bit aloud, 'but don't for one minute expect me to be nice back.'

'Sounds like the messages I get sent on Tinder,' said Sammy.

'Read the whole thing.' Lou passed him the notebook.

When he'd finished, Sammy said, 'At least they'll know what they're getting themselves into. Can't complain they weren't warned. Is this him?' He picked up Jess's phone. 'You know, it's weird, but he kind of reminds me of someone.'

Lou laughed. 'Edgar.'

'Twin souls. A marriage made in heaven.'

'He hates dogs. Like, really can't stand them.'

Sammy shrugged. 'Captain Oates hates humans. So that makes them even.'

From his position at the top table, Rico clapped his hands and called out, 'Right, if everyone has their answer sheets, we're ready to start . . .'

★

They didn't win the quiz. Sammy was glad when it was over; his brain had been too full of other things, leaving him unable to concentrate. At 9.30, Lou headed back to Walton House to see if her Christmas tree was still in one piece. Well, that was ostensibly the reason; in reality, he knew she was leaving so he and Jess could be alone together.

Just the two of them.

God, he was hopeless at this. Always had been. Up until now, he and Jess had had an easy friendship. But discovering she *liked-him* liked him had come as a bolt from the blue. If Lou was even right, which wasn't a given; it could just be wishful thinking on her part. So now he was trapped here, struggling to work out what could be going on inside Jess's head.

Seriously, though, how did Remy find this kind of situation so easy to deal with, when it wasn't easy at all?

He took another swallow from his bottle of Stella and heard the audible gulp as it slid down his throat. And why did *that* have to happen every time he was on edge?

'Well, this isn't awkward at all,' Jess said finally.

Sammy rocked on the back legs of his chair. 'Sorry, it's that dog. I can't stop thinking about him.' *When in doubt, fib.*

She turned to look at him. 'That's not true, though, is it?'

'Sorry?'

'Lou told you, didn't she?' Except it wasn't a question.

'Told me what?' Another lurch. This time he nearly tipped over.

'Put the chair legs down before you end up flat on your back. OK, listen, we're both adults here. I can take it. Lou's told you I like you and you're not interested. Am I right?'

God, talk about direct. 'Well . . .'

'It's fine, it's *fine*.' Jess shrugged. 'Hey, you're not the first and you won't be the last. I'm used to it!'

'Me too!' Hastily he explained, 'But it's not that. It's just, I always thought you fancied Remy.'

'Why?'

'Because . . . everyone does.'

'I don't. I like you.'

'What about that time he asked you to take those photos of me? You were all flustered. When you saw him flagging you down, you almost fell off your bike.'

She frowned, then said, 'That was because *you* were there. Nothing to do with your brother.'

Whaaaaat?

The more Sammy thought about it, the more he found himself enjoying the idea of Jess preferring him to Remy. 'It's a bit of

97

a surprise, that's all.' He risked a cautious smile. 'Maybe it's a good surprise.'

'Oh Sammy, stop it. You don't have to be polite.'

'I'm not being polite.' His heart began to thud faster. 'This feels like one of those dreams where you open a door in your house and discover a whole new set of rooms you never knew existed.'

'I had that dream once! There was a swimming pool in the airing cupboard, and it was an outdoor pool with dolphins in it. Best dream I ever had.'

He laughed. 'I usually get the ones where I'm about to start singing on stage when I realise I'm naked. Or my teeth start falling out.'

Jess said, 'My worst one is when I'm on a high bridge that starts to collapse and I know I'm about to plummet into a ravine and die, and I start falling and falling . . . then I do a huge jerk and wake up. God, the relief when I realise I'm still alive.'

'Sometimes I dream I'm singing,' said Sammy, 'and there's only a tiny audience and most of them aren't even paying attention. Then I open my eyes and remember it happens all the time anyway.'

She gazed into his eyes. 'You know what, though? It shouldn't happen. I think you're an amazing singer and your music's brilliant.'

Adrenalin was swirling through his bloodstream, bursting out of nowhere and expanding like candy floss. He heard himself utter the words 'I want to kiss you' and couldn't quite believe he'd said them out loud.

'I want to kiss you, too,' said Jess.

In unison they finished their drinks, rose to their feet and oh-so-casually left the main bar via the side exit. Once out in the narrow corridor, they made it as far as the door that led through to the back garden before Jess stopped abruptly and turned to face him.

It was the best kiss he'd ever had in his life.

Even better, this was the door he'd been standing behind when he'd overheard Tanisha announce to her cackling friends that no way could she ever go for someone like him.

This, now, was a moment he knew he'd never forget. Jess's arms were wrapped around him, her body pressed against his, her warm mouth . . .

'Whoops, sorry to interrupt,' said Rico, appearing at the other end of the narrow corridor and grinning broadly as they sprang apart. 'Just wondered if you realised you've left your notebook on the table in the bar.'

He disappeared a split second later, leaving them staring at each other, breathless and in a haze of mutual lust and longing.

Finally Jess said, 'I can't leave it behind.'

'I'll go and get it,' said Sammy.

As he reappeared in the bar, a chorus of cheers and wolf whistles went up. It hadn't taken Rico long to spread the word.

Retrieving the notebook, Sammy said, 'If only you lot could be that enthusiastic during my gigs.'

'We've heard you singing enough times,' one of the old regulars chuckled. 'This has got more of the novelty factor. Not staying for another drink, lad?'

Sammy turned in the doorway to survey the laughing crowd. 'Funnily enough, I have better places to be.'

The good-natured joking followed him out of the bar.

'Ah,' said Jess when he reappeared in the corridor, 'the joys of living in a town where everyone likes to know your business.'

He kissed her again, then took her by the hand – God, even that felt fantastic – and led her out of the pub.

★

Two hours later, in Riverside Cottage, Sammy carried cold drinks upstairs to his bedroom and found Jess sitting up in bed, sending a message on her phone. Twenty seconds later, she received a reply.

'Who are you texting?' He climbed back in beside her and kissed her neck, which smelled delicious.

'Tanisha. Just letting her know she missed out on a treat.'

Sammy could still hardly take it all in. Earlier this evening, Jess had been a friend he'd found attractive but had held out no hopes for. Now, just a few hours later, his feelings for her had grown on an exponential curve. She was funny, passionate, endearingly honest and everything he'd ever dreamed of in a girlfriend. Not that she was his girlfriend yet, but this was surely no fleeting one-night stand. Now they'd slept together, he couldn't imagine them not being a couple.

He revelled in her naked warmth. 'I'm glad. Don't know what I ever saw in her. Come here.'

'Hang on, just need to finish this message.'

It wasn't to Tanisha. She'd been forwarding what she'd written about Captain Oates to her mother. Peering over at her phone screen, Sammy read the exchange:

Mum:
Thanks, love – that made me laugh! We'll see if the boss allows it. Anyway, where are you??

Jess:
I'm at Riverside Cottage. With Sammy.

Mum:
Oh dear. Is he playing his guitar and singing at you?

100

Jess:

Mum, no. And just to let you know, I won't be home tonight.

Mum:

Whoa! Well, this is a surprise.

Jess:

A wonderful surprise for me too.

Mum:

And?????

Jess:

He's amazing. It's been the best evening. Best

'Don't look,' said Jess as he reached across to swipe up. 'It's embarrassing.'

'Shh.' Scrolling until he could read the rest, Sammy saw that she'd messaged: *Best evening EVER. So so happy.* ♥♥♥

Pink-cheeked, she said, 'Told you not to look.'

'The thing is, I'm so so happy too, heart heart heart.' He felt as if he could burst with it; the relief was overwhelming. 'And I've never had an evening as brilliant as this, either.'

Ting went her phone as the next message arrived.

Mum:

Well I'm glad, love. Good for you, he's a lovely lad. Just one word of advice – whatever you do, don't have sex with him tonight. Always better to keep them waiting. Xxx

Jess texted back: *Night, Mum xxx*

Then, switching off her phone and turning to face him, she

kissed him again and pressed her beautiful voluptuous body against him. 'Stable door,' she murmured, sliding her leg over his. 'Horse.' Her tongue flickered against his upper lip. 'Well and truly bolted.'

Relieved, Sammy murmured, 'That was terrible advice anyway.'

Jess grinned. 'She's old. What does she know?'

Chapter 14

'Come on,' said Lou.

'Where are we going this time?'

'It's a surprise.'

'If it's a life-sized Father Christmas, you're not bringing it into the house.'

'Fine. I'll keep him in the garden.'

Twenty minutes later, she pulled up at the entrance to the Ivy Lodge Animal Sanctuary.

'Oh dear God.' Edgar, in the passenger seat, shook his head. 'No.'

'No what?'

'No to whatever it is you're thinking. No animals. Just . . . no.'

'Don't jump to conclusions. I'm not talking about adopting one. They need volunteer dog walkers and Jess told me last night about this dog nobody wants. He has issues, just isn't very lovable. And the thing is, I haven't been able to stop thinking about him.' This was true; unable to sleep last night, she'd lain awake fretting about the unloved dog who hated almost everyone. 'So I called them this morning and they said we could drop by for a visit, take him for a nice walk.'

'Well, don't expect me to have anything to do with it. One tug on the lead and I'd be on the ground with a broken hip.'

'Don't worry, you can stay at a safe distance. I'll do the hard work.'

The woman in the office greeted them with enthusiasm and took them through to the kennels.

'Here he is,' she said cheerfully. 'This is Captain Oates.'

'I thought you said it was a dog,' said Edgar. 'That's a rodent.'

Standing stiff-legged at the back of his wire-fronted kennel, Captain Oates eyed them with shuddery disdain.

'Come on, darling, these nice people have come to take you for a lovely walk.' The woman spoke in coaxing tones.

'Grrrr,' said Captain Oates, baring his teeth at them.

Edgar pointed at him. 'If you're not interested, that's fine. Because neither am I.'

Lou held her breath and watched them silently eyeball each other for several seconds. At last Edgar turned away and said, 'Forget it, he's not bothered. Let's go.'

'Oh my goodness, look at him,' the woman exclaimed, and by the time Edgar turned around once more, Captain Oates was on his hind legs at the front of the kennel with his front paws resting against the wire. 'He's never done that before.'

Opening the cage, she expertly fastened the narrow lead to the little dog's collar and offered the other end to Lou.

'I'll take it.' Edgar reached for it. 'Why's he called Captain Oates?'

The woman said, 'Because he likes to go for long walks outside.'

Edgar looked down at the dog, who was gazing up at him. Finally he said, 'So do I.'

The next day was cold and dank, with vicious flurries of rain. Lou was peeling potatoes for a cottage pie when Edgar came into the kitchen wearing his winter coat and scarf.

'Well? Are we going?'

'Going where?'

'To the animal place.'

She turned to look out of the window at the fat raindrops spattering the glass and the tree branches bending in the wind. 'It's not very nice out there.'

'Dogs need to be walked every day, don't they? Not just when the sun shines and it suits you to do it.'

Well, well. Talk about a turn-up for the books.

When they arrived at Ivy Lodge, the same woman came out of the office, delighted to see them again. 'Of course you can take him out, but only for twenty minutes. We'll need him back here by three o'clock sharp.'

'Why?' said Edgar.

'The thing is, it's the most wonderful news! Yesterday evening we put a funny post up on Facebook all about Captain Oates and what a tricky little chap he is. I'll be honest, I thought it would put people off, but they've been phoning up about him ever since; it's been mad here today. All of a sudden he's Mr Popular! And the first family's due at three; they're coming all the way from Cardiff. It's like a miracle, everyone's interested in him now!'

Twenty minutes later, Lou said, 'We should be taking him back.'

'I don't want to.' Edgar's chin jutted.

'It's nearly time. The other people will be waiting.'

He stopped walking. So did Captain Oates, who'd been trotting along at his side. Through the rain, Lou noted the identical expressions on their faces. She tapped her watch. 'We promised to have him back there by three.'

'Why don't I tell the sanctuary woman to name her price?'

Wow, he was serious. 'I don't think they're open to bribery.'

'Everyone's open to bribery.' Edgar eyed her meaningfully. 'If you offer enough.'

Touché.

It was seven minutes past by the time they arrived back at Ivy Lodge, and a middle-aged woman all in pink was waiting with her husband in reception.

'Here he is! Oh my Gaaad, look at him, isn't he just the cutest little thing you ever did see?'

She was wearing a pale pink sweatshirt with *I ♥ DOGGIES* emblazoned in magenta glitter across the chest. Bounding over to them, she dropped to her knees and squealed, 'Hello, baby, we are *so* excited to meet you!'

Captain Oates eyed her stonily and refused to wag his tail. When she held out a pink-taloned hand, he bared his teeth and began to snarl.

'Oh now, stop that, you silly billy, you're going to love us,' the woman exclaimed. Bouncing back to her feet, she reached over to Edgar for the lead. 'Hi, I'll take him, shall I? It's our turn now! Come along, baby boy, time to get to know your new mummy and daddy . . . Ooh, who's a little cutie-pie, hey? Yes, *you* are!'

'My God.' Edgar shuddered when the couple had left the reception area with Captain Oates reluctantly in tow. 'They can't let her have him. They can't.'

'Everything OK?' It was the cheerful woman from the office, clearly wondering why they were still here.

'Not at all. I want Captain Oates to come home with me. Tonight,' said Edgar. 'We want him. How much?'

Lou winced; he was clearly put out by the way the little dog had left with the other couple without so much as a backward glance.

'I'm afraid we don't sell our dogs,' the woman said brightly.

106

'You're welcome to register your interest, of course, but all applicants need to be thoroughly vetted and—'

'Five thousand pounds.' There was more than a note of don't-mess-with-me in Edgar's voice.

Sadly, the woman did mess with him. She said calmly, 'Donations are always extremely welcome, of course, but I'm afraid they in no way affect the decisions we make. The animals are our number one priority and they go to the best candidates, the ones most able to provide them with a safe and loving home.'

Other than distant barking from the other dogs over in the kennels, a tense silence reigned in reception. Lou sensed that Edgar was battling between being obnoxiously overbearing and standing a chance of being allowed to adopt Captain Oates.

At length he shook the rain out of his hair and said, 'In that case, I would like to register my interest.'

Lou raised her eyebrows and gave him an encouraging nod.

'I would like to register my interest,' Edgar said again, '*please*.'

Lou hid a smile and swallowed the temptation to say *Good boy!*

Edgar was awake and ready to leave the house before eight the next morning. By the time they reached the pet superstore in Cheltenham, he was driving Lou mad with his constant list-checking.

'We don't have to buy everything in advance. We could wait until we know for sure—'

'It looks better if we already have it when they come to check us out.'

'Look,' she attempted to manage his expectations, 'if we don't get him, there are plenty of other dogs to choose from.'

Edgar shook his head. 'I don't want any other dogs. Only Captain Oates.'

Lou was beginning to feel guilty. It had been her idea, but who could have imagined he'd fall this hard for the dog who'd been entirely unwanted until Jess had written that brutally honest plea for a new owner? Yesterday evening they'd heard that the Woman in Pink had also registered her interest, as had a third party. This afternoon, the manageress of Ivy Lodge was coming over to the house to assess it and themselves as potential adopters. If they failed the test, she didn't know how Edgar was going to react.

The teenage boy press-ganged into helping them inside the store was looking askance at him now. 'If it's a chihuahua, you only need the smallest-size bed. They're, like, pretty small, you know.'

'But sometimes he might want to sleep somewhere bigger. We'll have both,' Edgar ordered, indicating for the lad to add them to the already loaded-up trolley.

They had to buy one of every kind of dog food, because they didn't know yet which flavour or brand Captain Oates would like best.

Ditto shampoo, towels and worming powders.

And as for toys, oh yes, all the toys. Squeaky, chewy, furry, bouncy . . . whatever Captain Oates might like, he was to be provided with. Drily, Lou thought of yesterday's visit to the supermarket, when Edgar had complained about the price of the washing-up liquid she'd chosen. And now here he was splashing more cash than some people would spend on a holiday abroad.

There was barely any room left for the two of them by the time they'd loaded everything into the Mini.

Back home, all the items were carefully arranged around the house for maximum effect.

'We don't need to put out all six dog bowls,' Lou protested.

Edgar was sitting at the kitchen table like Laurence Llewelyn-Bowen, bossing her about and telling her what to do.

'Line them up neatly,' he ordered. 'I want them to know he can choose his favourite. No, put the silver one on the left.'

The manageress from Ivy Lodge duly arrived at lunchtime, armed with a clipboard and a long list of questions. Lou mentally braced herself, dreading an outburst, but Edgar was on his best behaviour. Which just went to show, he could be polite when he needed to be.

'I can walk him. I'm perfectly capable,' he told the woman, whose name was Mary. 'And Lou lives here too, so she'll be helping out whenever necessary.'

'That's good to know.' Mary ticked another of the boxes on her list. 'And I see you have a large garden.' Another tick. 'Now, you're eighty years old. If anything were to happen to you, who'd take over the care of Captain Oates?'

'Lou would. She'd take excellent care of him. What about that couple who came to see him yesterday?' Edgar blurted out the question he'd been bursting to ask. 'Do they still want him?'

'Yes, they do.' Mary regarded him frankly. 'I'm visiting them at their home tomorrow morning, then the other interested family tomorrow afternoon.'

'Is there any way I can persuade you to choose me?'

'No, Mr Allsopp, there isn't.'

'Not even if I offer—'

'*Don't*,' said Lou, before he started trying to bribe Mary. 'Just don't.' She wouldn't put it past him to whip a fat wodge of cash out of his pocket like a second-hand car dealer.

'We select the candidate most suited to the animal in question,' Mary continued firmly. 'Tell me, having never owned a pet before, why are you so interested in acquiring one now?'

'I don't want just any dog; I only want Captain Oates. He's

tricky and awkward and doesn't like most people. I feel as if I understand him.' Edgar stopped, pulling a clean white cotton handkerchief from the pocket of his grey corduroy trousers in order to blow his nose. When he'd finished putting the handkerchief away again, his eyes were damp. He gathered himself, then said gruffly, 'And sometimes when we look at each other, I think he understands me.'

Chapter 15

Having to wait was driving Edgar mad. Which in turn was driving Lou to distraction. The next day, out of sheer desperation, she drove down into Foxwell and collected the box of Christmas cards she'd ordered from Dave Harding in the print shop.

Anything to keep Edgar busy and his mind off the phone call that wouldn't be happening until much later this evening, if not tomorrow.

'Right.' She sat him down in the living room and handed him his favourite Parker fountain pen. 'Let's make a start on these, shall we? And you know who we'll be sending the first one to?'

'I have no idea. Surprise me.'

Lou began to dictate: 'To all the wonderful staff and volunteers at Ivy Lodge—'

'What? No way. Not unless we get Captain Oates.'

'But even if we don't, it'd be a nice gesture.'

'I'll give them a nice gesture,' Edgar snorted. 'No. Think of someone else.'

She made a quick list of all the people she'd got to know

since arriving in Foxwell, and kept her fingers crossed that at least some of them would understand what she was trying to do and reciprocate.

'How about the family who lived next door to you in London? You said they used to send you birthday cards. That was nice of them, wasn't it?'

'Can't remember their surname. Carter-something. Double-barrelled. No idea.'

Honestly, it was like trying to help a stroppy toddler. 'Maybe you have it written down somewhere.'

'It'll be in my address book,' Edgar said finally.

'And where's that?'

'Upstairs in my bedroom. On the second shelf of the bookcase. Blue leather. Over to the right, next to a book about moths.'

There was nothing wrong with his memory when it came to information he wanted to recall. Lou said, 'I'll go and get it.'

She found the address book with no trouble and idly flipped through it, because wouldn't it be great if it was filled with the names and addresses of dozens of old friends he'd forgotten to stay in touch with?

It wasn't, of course. There weren't that many entries at all, but she did come across a theatre programme, yellowed with age, slotted between the pages. And there were photos tucked inside the programme, she discovered when they started to slip out. Of Edgar in a smart, well-tailored dark suit and far darker hair than he had now, standing next to a woman who was younger than he was, rather beautiful and vaguely familiar. She was blonde and tanned, wearing an elegant primrose-yellow evening dress and a statement necklace like a silver waterfall trickling down almost to her navel.

Her gaze switching back to the programme, Lou saw that it was from a production that had run in one of the smaller West

End theatres thirty years ago. The name of the play didn't mean anything to her, but it had starred a couple of recognisable names and . . . Ah, of course, this was why the woman looked familiar. The blonde in the yellow dress was Della Lucas.

Ooh, and she was with Edgar. Interesting.

Back in the day, Della had become well known as the glamorous hostess who'd assisted a comedian through several series of *Make My Day*, a popular game show on ITV. He'd supplied the jokes and she'd gone along with being the butt of them in the way that had been acceptable back then. Once the show had run its course, she had moved into acting and discovered it was harder than it looked. In the ensuing years she'd appeared in a variety of those random TV quiz shows requiring guest stars. She'd also continued to pop up at parties, movie premieres and in women's magazines.

Flipping through the rest of the photos, five of them in total, Lou saw that they all featured the two of them together, at different events.

OK, she couldn't stay up here any longer. Time to get back to the living room and hear the story behind this unexpected discovery.

'Done one,' Edgar announced upon her return.

He was concealing something under the table.

'Well done.' Checking to see he hadn't written anything that could get him arrested, Lou saw that he'd scrawled *Best, E. Allsopp* inside the first card. 'Who's it for?'

'No idea. You can choose.'

Honestly. Hopeless.

From beneath the table came the sound of a high-pitched bark, which meant he'd been secretly watching the video he'd recorded of Captain Oates during yesterday's walk in the woods behind Ivy Lodge.

'You don't have to hide it,' Lou told him. 'I know what you're doing.'

'Woof-woof,' said Captain Oates, eyeballing her in a confrontational manner as Edgar replaced his phone on the table.

Glad to be able to distract him, she sat back down and waved the address book. 'Anyway, I found something interesting!'

'It's an address book.'

'I'm talking about what's inside it.'

'Been snooping, have you?'

'I didn't plan to. They just fell out when I took it off the bookshelf.' She showed him the programme and the photos. 'Look at you, all handsome and debonair with a celebrity on your arm!'

Edgar sighed and switched off the video as Captain Oates broke into a fresh volley of barks. 'She wasn't a celebrity, she was an actress.'

'But I recognised her. She's still a bit famous now. And these were all taken on different occasions, so that means you properly knew her. Look at this one!' Holding up the photo that had been taken in a garden, Lou said, 'You're actually laughing. You look so *different*.'

'It was a long time ago.'

'You can see how happy you were.'

Edgar took the photo from her and examined it. 'I was. Didn't last, though, did it?'

'Were you actually a couple? I had no idea.'

'Of course you didn't, because I didn't tell you.'

'This is wild. How long were you together?'

'Almost a year, I suppose.' He swallowed. 'On and off.'

Lou hesitated; she'd been on the brink of asking him if he'd been in love with Della Lucas but didn't want him to clam up. Besides, it was pretty likely he had been. Instead she said, 'It must have been wonderful. She looks so much fun.'

'She was.'

'What happened?'

'She married someone else.' Edgar's tone was flat.

'Oh no.' Della had broken his heart. 'That's sad.'

He put the photograph down. 'Why am I even telling you this?'

'Because I asked.' Lou gave a tiny shrug. 'And I told you all about my terrible marriage. Sometimes it helps, you know. To share the bad stuff.'

The hint of an eye-roll told her what he thought about sharing. 'Anyway, it's all in the past.'

'You didn't stay in touch?'

'No point. She had her husband and then she had her kids. Are we going to get on and do these stupid cards or not?'

'They're not stupid. And yes, we are.' Indicating for him to pick up the fountain pen, she said, 'Write: "To Babs and Bob—"'

'Who are *they*?'

'You can reel off every element of the periodic table, but you don't bother to learn the names of people in your own town. It's polite to know these things. Put: "Wishing you a merry Christmas and a very happy new year".'

She watched as he wrote: *Happy Christmas, E. Allsopp.*

'No,' she said. 'You have to sign it "Edgar".'

He looked mutinous. 'They wouldn't know who it was from.'

'Oh, they will. Trust me, they'll know.' Struck by a brilliant idea, Lou exclaimed, 'You could send one to Della Lucas!'

'What? Why would I do that?'

'Because it's nice getting cards out of the blue from people you knew years ago. You can write a short message, say you hope she's well . . . Wouldn't you like it if she sent you one? Of course you would. It's just . . . friendly. The spirit of Christmas!'

115

'She wouldn't send me one,' said Edgar.

'Fine. It was just an idea.'

'She's married.'

'OK, no worries.'

'There's no point.'

'Right, let's forget it. Why don't you look up those old neighbours of yours and send one to them instead?'

While he was doing this, Lou took out her own phone. By the time Edgar had found the surname of his old neighbours in Kensington, she'd discovered far more.

When he'd successfully completed his first card, she said, 'Do you ever google Della?'

'No.'

She'd guessed that surfing the internet wasn't something that interested him. 'Well, I just did. There's loads of stuff about her online. She married Barry Lloyd thirty years ago. They had two children, a son called Tom and a daughter, Fiona. They—'

'I know that,' he interrupted. 'I saw her being interviewed once on TV.'

'They lived in Brentwood, Essex, where Barry ran a nightclub. Four years ago, he suffered a heart attack and died.'

'He's *dead*?' That made Edgar sit up and take notice. 'Good grief. And he was twenty years younger than me.'

This was enthralling. Had he and Barry been love rivals?

'Did you know him?'

He shook his head. 'No.'

'How did you meet Della?'

'At a party.'

'Edgar!' Lou teased. 'I didn't know you liked parties!'

'I didn't want to go.'

'But you did. And you met Della Lucas. That's the thing, isn't it, about parties? You never know if they're going to be boring and a complete waste of make-up, or if this could be the one where you meet someone amazing who changes your whole life.'

'She didn't change my life.'

'You were together for almost a year. It must have changed you in some way.' Lou couldn't stop gazing at the photos lying face up on the table, imagining the two of them as a couple all those years ago. She'd seen Della on TV often enough to know that she was glamorous, elegant and vivacious. 'Look at her. I bet you had so much fun together.'

'Are we going to write these cards or not?' Edgar changed the subject.

'Of course we are. Now, are you going to send one to Della?'

'No.'

It had been like forcing a reluctant child to do their maths homework, but finally the job was done. Stamps were fixed to the cards that would be posted. The local ones were going to be slipped through letter boxes around Foxwell. Lou had added her name to these. Next, she persuaded Edgar to drive down into the town and wait while she hopped in and out of the passenger seat, delivering them to pretty much everyone she'd met during the last three months. As darkness fell, Christmas lights came on in the shops and houses. One of the homes had been decorated with a plastic Santa on the roof and a whole family of inflatable reindeer in the front garden. A ten-foot snowman was singing Christmas songs by the front gates, and there were giant plastic robins chirping away on the lawn.

'Why do they *do* that?' said Edgar.

'Because it's fun and cheers people up.'

'Doesn't cheer me up.'

'No, well, grumpy old men aren't the target market.'

'Where next?'

'The newsagent's.' She'd made him do a card for Belinda.

It was as he was parking between a blue van and a red Volvo that Edgar's mobile phone began to ring.

'That could be her.' Braking abruptly, he fumbled in his coat pocket and pulled the phone out, hand trembling. 'Hello? Yes?'

Lou tried her hardest to eavesdrop, but he had the phone pressed so tightly to his ear that all she could make out was a blurry female voice. The multicoloured Christmas lights outside were reflecting off Edgar's face as he listened in silence. She braced herself for fury, then saw the silhouette of his Adam's apple jumping in his throat as he swallowed. Finally he said, 'Yes, first thing tomorrow. Thank you. Thank you so much.'

When he turned to look at her, overcome with emotion, she saw the sheen in his eyes.

'Is he yours?'

Edgar cleared his throat and nodded. 'He's mine.'

Chapter 16

The next morning, Jess's mum, Babs, was waiting to greet them in reception.

'I probably shouldn't be telling you this,' she whispered to Lou across the desk, 'but that other woman was a nightmare. She'd posted on Facebook that she couldn't wait to get her new doggy home so she could paint his claws pink to match her favourite handbag.'

'Edgar won't be doing that,' Lou promised her.

'I don't have any nail polish that matches my favourite handbag,' said Edgar, and his tone was so dry that it took them a few seconds to realise he'd made a joke.

'And the other party turned out to have a pet parrot, which would have been carnage waiting to happen. So anyway,' Babs went on, 'we thought that all in all, you and Captain Oates would be a good match for each other.'

'We will be.' Edgar nodded firmly.

When the necessary paperwork had been completed, Captain Oates was brought out to them. He bared his teeth and snarled at Babs, ignored Lou entirely and stood stiff-legged on the floor in front of Edgar, visibly waiting.

119

'You're coming home with me,' Edgar told him, carefully bending to pick him up.

Babs blurted out, 'Mind he doesn't—'

'Bite me? He's not going to bite me. Are you, lad?'

Captain Oates hesitated, looking for a moment as if he might be tempted. Then he tilted his head forward and sniffed cautiously at Edgar's neck. Watching them, Lou held her breath and prayed he wouldn't go feral.

Captain Oates, not Edgar.

The next moment, the little dog rested his front paws against Edgar's shoulder, then reached up and licked the side of his new owner's face. In response, Edgar broke into a genuine smile.

'Oh my goodness, I never thought I'd see the day,' Babs cried. 'It's like a Christmas miracle!'

Captain Oates twisted round and bared his pointy teeth at her.

'OK,' Babs amended, 'maybe not.'

'That's my boy.' Stroking the top of the dog's head, Edgar said with pride, 'Come on, lad, nothing to worry about. Let's get you into the car, shall we? We're taking you home.'

They were twin souls, Lou realised almost instantly. Sometimes when they looked at her, the expressions on their faces were identical. But it was the love and pride emanating in waves from Edgar that was the biggest revelation of all. Captain Oates had been settled into his chosen dog bed in the kitchen before they'd retired last night, but an hour later, she'd heard the familiar clunk-and-whir of the stairlift descending to the ground floor, followed by its slow return upstairs accompanied by a few muffled barks.

'He was lonely on his own.' Edgar's tone was defiant when she questioned him over breakfast the next morning.

120

'And did he sleep on the floor? Or the bed?'

'On the floor.'

Lou shook her head. 'You're such a rubbish liar.'

His gaze softened as he looked at the new arrival. 'It was the best night's sleep I've had in years. Can we take him out for a walk now?'

Still in her pyjamas and dressing gown, she said, 'Am I allowed to get dressed first?'

'Hurry up, then.'

It wasn't just a gentle stroll around the garden Edgar wanted either. They drove down the hill into Foxwell and found a parking space outside Jess's uncle's antiques shop. Spotting them with Captain Oates on his lead, Jess came rushing out to make a wary fuss of him. And she was right to be wary; the dog bristled and growled, then resolutely turned away and refused to look her in the eye.

'He doesn't like many people,' Edgar said with relish.

'I can tell. He's definitely his own dog.' Jess backed away.

'He's the best dog.'

Twenty minutes later, Lou said, 'You look so happy.' It was as if a dark cloud had lifted. It might have been her imagination, but even his walking seemed to have improved. And the people they encountered along the way were delighted to admire the most recent addition to the town.

Edgar had been casting sidelong glances in shop windows as they passed, admiring the sight of himself with Captain Oates trotting along at his heels. He said, 'I feel like Clark Gable.'

'Now you've lost me.'

'In *Gone with the Wind*. When Rhett Butler and Scarlett O'Hara had a baby called Bonnie Blue, he used to take her for walks in her pram. Everyone in the town used to admire her. That's how I'm feeling now.' He stopped as they reached one

121

of the empty benches overlooking the river, then sat down and lifted Captain Oates onto his lap. 'Let's have another photo, shall we?'

It was touching to see the two of them posing for her. Lou snapped away, catching them from all angles, before finally capturing the moment they stopped gazing directly into the lens and looked into each other's eyes instead.

'Here we are, this is the one.' She showed him the shot; there on the wooden bench was Edgar in his charcoal wool coat with the crimson scarf she'd bought him for his eighty-first birthday wrapped around his neck. Perched on his lap was Captain Oates, bright-eyed, with his ears sticking up and out, Gremlin style. And behind them was pale blue sky, the row of shops with their Christmas decorations up ... and a figure over to the left emerging from a black Mercedes.

'That spoils it.' Edgar pointed to the figure on the screen. 'You'll have to crop him out of the picture.'

'Crop who out of the picture?' Unbeknown to Edgar, Remy had crossed the frosted grass and come up behind him. 'I hope you're not talking about me. Oh my word, this must be the famous Captain Oates. Hey, little chap, I've heard all about you.'

'He doesn't like you,' Edgar announced with satisfaction as the dog, unimpressed by Remy's spectacular good looks, bristled and regarded him with disdain.

'He's a character. You two are so well matched.' Cheerfully Remy turned to Lou. 'Can I see?'

She passed him her phone.

'It *is* me getting cropped out. And you'd be right to do it. Then it'll be a great photo. You should get copies printed off and sent to everyone you know.'

'We should.' Edgar nodded in agreement, then addressed Lou. 'We could do it now.'

She nodded. 'The print shop's closed today, but we'll get it done tomorrow.'

'That's no good. Isn't there anywhere else around here?' Edgar was characteristically impatient.

After a couple of seconds, Remy said, 'Tell me to mind my own business if you want,' and in unison Edgar and Captain Oates turned to give him a basilisk stare.

'About what?' said Edgar.

'I was just going to say, we have a printer in the office and you're very welcome to use it. But if you'd rather not, that's fine. I understand.'

Silence. Lou was careful to keep a straight face, because Edgar wasn't accustomed to finding himself on the receiving end of good deeds from anyone, let alone one of the Keeler brothers, of whom he'd disapproved for so long.

On the other hand, she knew he really *really* wanted copies of the photo.

'Right,' he said at last, with some difficulty. 'Let's do that.'

'Are you sure?' Lou looked at Remy and clasped her hands in deliberately over-the-top delight. 'Oh, that would be fantastic! Thank you *so* much.'

Forcing Edgar to nod and mutter, 'Thanks.'

'You are most welcome,' Remy told him with a broad smile. 'Always happy to help.'

Edgar and Captain Oates stayed outside on their bench by the river. In the back office of Trent and Keeler, still as cluttered as before, Lou duly cropped Remy out of the photo, then emailed it to him so he could print off twenty copies.

'You're a star for offering to do this.'

'Oh, it was worth it to hear him have to thank me.' Remy grinned. 'And I have to say, the dog is a master stroke. You're in danger of turning Edgar into an actual human being.'

As the printer hummed and efficiently clicked its way through the process, Lou breathed in the smell of Remy's aftershave without looking as if this was what she was doing. He was wearing black jeans and a black cashmere sweater, and it might have been a while ago, but her skin still prickled with embarrassment at the memory of their candlelit dinner together in Al Fresco.

Hopefully it had slipped his mind; after all, it had been over three months now. And he and Talli were still going strong.

'This is great.' She picked up the first of the glossy printed-off photos. 'We should have chosen it for the Christmas card.'

'Thanks for ours, by the way. I'm guessing it's all part of the rehabilitation process.'

She'd sent one to the three of them, at Riverside Cottage. 'Trying my best.'

'You're doing a good job.' Turning to smile at her, he caught her surveying the office. Briony was currently out with a client, but there were three different scarves and two coats hanging on the back of her chair, and five mugs littering her desk. There were also two lipsticks, three single gloves, several torn-open sugar sachets and a plastic bottle of mayonnaise with its lid flipped up.

'Sorry.' Lou raised her hands. 'I won't touch them, I promise.' Oh, but her fingers were itching to restore order to chaos.

'Speaking of jobs, Sammy said you were thinking of taking on a couple of shifts at the supermarket.'

She hesitated, tempted for a moment to confide in him. Maths had always been her favourite subject at school; it had come easily to her, and she'd loved the satisfaction of fitting numbers

124

together, knowing that the answers were predetermined and definitive. If you did it correctly, it was always right. The plan back then had been to do her GCSEs, then take A levels including pure and applied maths, with a view to moving into accountancy.

But a bout of glandular fever had fogged her brain, confining her to bed and resulting in her missing the GCSEs, and that summer she'd found herself falling into a part-time job at a nearby hospice. By September, having discovered how much she enjoyed working with the patients, she'd decided to leave school and stay on. After that, it had been many more years before the lure of accountancy had returned, but by that time she was newly married to Brett, and . . . well, he'd made his feelings on the subject only too clear.

With an inward shiver, Lou dismissed both the hideous memory of that time and the thought of sharing it with Remy. It made her sound weak, and he wouldn't understand how skilfully Brett had indoctrinated her, making her feel incapable of managing the amount of studying the course would entail. Even now, all this time later, she still worried that he might have been right.

Anyway, why would Remy want to hear about it? It wasn't as if her failed hopes and dreams would be of interest to him.

'It was just an idea.' She shook her head. 'I'm only doing thirty hours a week up at Edgar's, which leaves me with some free time. And I like to keep busy, so I thought it might be fun. But I need something more flexible, to fit in with Edgar . . . If he needs me at home for any reason, I can't just disappear . . .'

Remy was collecting the photographs as they emerged from the printer. He said slowly, 'Look, feel free to say no, but if we needed help getting this place in order, might you be interested? Because I've managed to persuade Briony that we can't carry on like this; something has to be done about it. I'm thinking maybe two or three stints a week, six hours in total, probably in the evenings? Nothing too complicated, just cleaning and tidying up, then sorting out the filing system and keeping everything organised from one week to the next . . . Would something like that suit you?'

It might not be a course in accountancy, but it was a job she knew she would enjoy. 'Are you kidding? That would be perfect.' Lou could have kissed him . . . except of course she couldn't. 'Are you sure?'

He grinned at the look on her face. 'Wouldn't ask if I wasn't. And we'd pay a bit more than the supermarket.'

'I'd love to sort this place out. Once it's properly organised, you'll both be able to find everything.'

'You'll have to be patient with Briony. She's a lost cause. And everything'll need tidying up every time you come in.'

'I can't wait to start,' said Lou. 'Thank you so much.'

'Thank Sammy, he's the one who mentioned you were looking for something else to do. And thank you, too.' Remy shook his head. 'You're going to make my life a hundred times easier. If you can stand to work for us, that is.'

The last photos slid out of the printer and he gathered them up. Taking them from him, she said, 'I've had plenty of practice with tricky employers. Somehow I'll cope.'

When they returned to the bench at the river's edge, this time Edgar said thank you without prompting – another Christmas miracle.

'No problem. Any time you need a hand with anything, just ask.' Remy glanced at Captain Oates, then added genially, 'I don't bite.'

After dinner that evening, Edgar tackled the final batch of Christmas cards, adding one of the photos into each envelope after scribbling: *Season's greetings from me and Captain Oates* on the back of each one.

'I thought about what you said,' he told Lou. 'Sending a card to Della. But I don't know where she's living now, so I can't.'

Lou looked up, delighted by his change of heart. 'Is there anyone you can ask?'

'No. That's why I'm telling you.'

She took out her phone. 'This is the kind of challenge I like.'

It took a while, but she got there in the end. Directory enquiries drew a blank because, predictably, Della was ex-directory. Raymond Carrera Associates, her talent agency, stated on their website that fan mail and autograph requests could take three months to receive a reply. A small but keen fan group on Facebook, however, had put up numerous photographs of Della and her family, gleaned from various magazines over the years. Someone a while back had won a competition to have afternoon tea with her, and had uploaded over thirty photos of the occasion, as well as a blurry one of the exterior of an imposing Victorian residence that had evidently been turned into flats. *X marks the spot*, he'd written triumphantly beneath it. *This is where she lives, on Frobisher Square.*

The numbers on the doors were too small to read, but a couple of the flats had identifying features that made the rest of it easy. Thanks to one on the first floor that had a massive chandelier visible through the front window, and another one two doors away with lime-green curtains, Lou was able to make her way around the square on Google Street View until she found the third-floor flat that on Facebook had been marked with an X.

This time the number of the house in question was clearly visible. Thanks, Google.

'Well?' said Edgar when she looked up from her sleuthing.

'One two seven Frobisher Square, north London.'

'How do you *do* that?' For an intelligent man, he was stubbornly reluctant to engage with the internet.

'I started by—'

'Never mind, that's what you're here for.' Captain Oates was nestled, eyes half closed, on his lap. Reaching past him for another Christmas card and one of the photos, Edgar hesitated. 'Is this stupid? Should I be doing it? Or not?'

Touched by the unexpected display of vulnerability, Lou said, 'Of course you should. There's nothing not to like. All you're doing is making contact with an old friend – where's the harm in that? I'd love to be sent a card by an old friend out of the blue!'

Edgar frowned. 'Well, don't get your hopes up, because I'm not sending you one.'

'Can you manage OK with him on your lap, or shall I take him off you?' She reached over to lift Captain Oates out of the way.

'Grrrrr,' snarled the little dog, determined to stay where he was.

'Watch out,' Edgar said happily. 'He'll have your fingers off. If you get blood everywhere, you're the one who's going to have to clean it up.'

'Oh!' Briony Trent lived in the flat upstairs. Returning home from dinner with friends, she clapped her hands to her chest and froze in the doorway, staring in disbelief at the transformed office.

Well, semi-transformed.

'We haven't finished yet,' said Lou as the older woman noticed her desk and gasped. 'This is just the start.'

'But it's . . . oh my goodness . . . it's so *different*.' Tears had sprung into Briony's eyes, and Lou turned to Remy, pride turning to dismay. They'd been working together for the last three hours, and she'd been excited to be restoring order to months of accumulated mess. If this was the moment he admitted Briony hadn't known it was going to happen, she might have to kill him.

Remy put down the sky-high pile of files he'd been carrying and said, 'Oh Bri, please don't cry . . .'

'It's OK, I'm not upset.' She pulled a tissue from her pocket and wiped her face, then dropped the tissue onto the floor before breaking into a huge watery smile. 'I just can't believe how . . . how . . . *empty* it all looks. There's so much space everywhere!' She gestured to her chair, no longer buckling from the weight of half the contents of her wardrobe piled on the back of it, then to the desk, cleared of everything that didn't need to be there. 'And it all looks so *clean* . . .'

'I haven't thrown anything away. Well, nothing to do with work,' Lou said hastily, because old food wrappers obviously didn't count. She pointed to the black boxes lined up against the far wall. 'Each box is labelled, see? And your make-up, snacks and jewellery are all in these separate drawers. We haven't started on the filing system yet, but I promise it'll help to keep everything—'

'Tidy. Organised. I know.' Nodding, Briony unwound the iris-blue silk scarf from around her neck and flung it onto one of the tilted drawing tables behind her. 'What happened to my bag of chips?'

Lou braced herself for an outcry. 'Bin.'

'Oh phew, thank goodness you didn't eat them. They were mouldy!'

Lou managed to keep a straight face. 'I know.'

'Really, thank you so much for this.' As Briony addressed

129

them, she rummaged in her coat pocket until she found a lip balm, applied it, and dropped it onto her desk, whereupon it promptly rolled off and landed under her leather swivel chair. 'It's time, I know it is. It's going to make life easier.'

'For both of us.' Remy's smile demonstrated his genuine fondness for her.

'Oh, I'm a nightmare, I know that too. I honestly don't mean to make a mess.' Oblivious to the fact that she had just taken a crumpled Mars bar wrapper out of her other pocket and tossed it onto her desk, Briony shrugged and said helplessly, 'Somehow it just happens.'

Once she'd whirled out of the office in her smart purple coat and left them to it, Remy said, 'Can't imagine how.'

'She has no idea.' Lou picked up all the bits and pieces Briony had abandoned in the space of five minutes. 'And it's so funny, because to look at her, you'd think she was a complete neat-freak. She's immaculate.'

'Just goes to show, you never know what people might be like beneath the surface. This is Bri's guilty secret.'

'Mine's eating slices of cold butter sandwiched between prawn cocktail crisps,' said Lou.

Remy's face was a picture. 'That's terrible.'

She laughed. 'If it wasn't, it wouldn't have to be a guilty secret, would it? You can't say: Ooh, my guilty secret is that I have perfect teeth and look amazing in a bikini.'

'Fine, I won't say it. Even though it's true.' He gestured at his body. 'I think I look pretty great in a bikini.'

They carried on working together, sorting through the catastrophe that was the largest filing cabinet. When Remy picked up one of the buff folders, a fossilised cheese sandwich fell out. They spread all the folders out on the carpet, rearranged them in alphabetical order, then began refilling the cabinet.

130

Occasionally their hands and elbows bumped together, the contact sending zings of excitement up Lou's arm and down her spine, but it was fine because he had no idea he still had that effect on her and she was determined to get it out of her system. She worked on this by chattering away happily about Talli, and about Sammy and Jess, and about the joys of trying to give an outraged Captain Oates a bath after he'd wriggled and rolled in fox poo.

'Right, that's enough for tonight,' said Remy as the church clock chimed ten.

'Thanks for helping out and showing me where everything needs to go.' Lou straightened up and stretched her aching arms. From here on, he or Briony might sometimes be working in the office when she turned up, but now that she knew what needed to be done, she would be in sole charge of maintaining order.

Leaving together, they were greeted by the sight of Foxwell in all its night-time festive splendour. The sky was alive with stars and almost every building was lit up with multicoloured Christmas decorations. A sparkling frost had fallen, coating roofs, cars and tarmac, and a recent bonfire had left the smell of woodsmoke hanging in the still, wintry air.

Lou shivered and dug the keys to the Mini out of her coat pocket. In the distance, music was playing; she could hear Mariah Carey singing like an angel about all she wanted for Christmas.

Remy finished locking up and turned to look at her. 'Thanks again,' he said, and a cloud of condensation hovered in the air in front of his mouth.

'I enjoyed it.' She'd loved every minute, but it wouldn't do to sound too overexcited.

As she crossed the street, heading to where she'd parked the Mini in a pool of golden light beneath one of the ornate street lamps, Remy called after her, 'You forgot to ask me what my guilty secret is.'

Lou stopped and turned back to face him, silhouetted in the office doorway. God, he was beautiful. Those shoulders, those long legs . . . and that *voice* . . . She breathed in a lungful of icy air and woodsmoke and felt her heart rate quicken as she called back, 'Go on then, tell me. What's your guilty secret?'

He could be about to say anything. If this were a movie, this could be the moment when he blurted out that he hadn't been able to stop thinking about her . . .

His hands were stuffed into the pockets of his brown leather jacket. He hesitated, half smiling as if deciding what to say, because of course people as cool as Remi Keeler didn't have the kind of secrets they needed to feel guilty about.

Then, as her teeth began to chatter, he took one hand out of his pocket and pointed in the direction of the distant music. 'Don't tell anyone. This is my favourite song. In the world.'

Just as well she hadn't expected her fleeting movie fantasy to come true. 'Wow.' She shook her head sorrowfully. 'For your sake, I hope Sammy never gets to find out that your favourite song in the world isn't one of his.'

Chapter 17

Life had been so much lovelier years ago. Della still made as much effort as she always had, but the rewards were far fewer nowadays. The fizz had faded and the excitement of having once been a celebrity was on the decline. People sometimes still stopped her in the street and exclaimed with surprise at having recognised her, but sometimes they couldn't quite remember her name or where they knew her from. They thought she might have been a weather girl or someone who'd appeared on *EastEnders*. On one occasion, she'd even been told she was the spitting image of someone called Marlene who ran a fish stall at the local market, yet when she'd gone to check this out, Marlene had looked like an older, rougher, *far* less attractive version of her.

Talk about mortifying.

Which meant, of course, that even when she was only popping out to the bank, like now, she felt compelled to do her hair, dress nicely and put on enough make-up not to frighten the horses, so that members of the public couldn't gleefully declare to all their friends how old and past it Della Lucas was looking these days.

An hour later, returning from her trip to the bank – when of course *no one* had bothered to stop her in the street to tell her how wonderful she was looking – Della let herself back into number 127 Frobisher Square. The post had arrived and her back gave a twinge as she retrieved the envelopes from the black and white tiled floor behind the communal front door. God, sixty-one years old and she was turning into the kind of person who said *oof* when they bent down.

At least she could still run up three flights of stairs without getting out of breath.

Tom was in the kitchen making toast and coffee, blonde hair uncombed, chin sporting golden stubble and lilac shirt untucked from his holey jeans. But because he was thirty and ridiculously handsome, he could get away with it.

'You're home,' said Della, shrugging off her coat.

He grinned. 'Well spotted. Toast?'

'No thanks.' She leaned against the fridge and began sorting through the post. Electricity, ugh. Bank statement, ugh again. A glossy invitation to view an over-sixties holiday village in Surrey, no thanks. A Christmas card from her friend Michelle who lived in Puerto Pollensa. And another card whose handwriting on the envelope she didn't recognise.

'You haven't asked me why I'm here,' said Tom.

'Sorry, darling. Why are you here?'

'We broke up.'

'Oh no! Oh, that's sad!' For a split second the latest girlfriend's name escaped her, then she remembered it was Emily. Or maybe Emma. But to be fair, there'd been so many, was it any wonder she struggled to remember all their names? 'What happened?'

'She got hold of my phone while I was asleep, used my fingerprint to get into it and found some texts from another girl.' He grimaced. 'Not too happy. So that's over.'

134

'It's only been a few weeks. At least now you won't need to buy her a Christmas present.'

He slathered butter and Marmite onto his toast. 'Every cloud. What's up?'

As she'd been opening the card inside the envelope, the past had rushed up to greet her. Della scanned the handwritten message, written in proper ink, then studied the photo that had been tucked inside the card. Eddie Allsopp. Yes, it really was him. Sending his condolences for the loss of her husband in his careful slanting handwriting. Showing her his newly acquired chihuahua. Wishing her a good Christmas.

'Who's it from?' said Tom. 'You look as if you've seen a ghost.' He paused. '*That* would be a good opening scene for a film, getting a card from someone who's dead.'

'This one isn't dead.' How long had it been? Thirty-one years. Eddie had been fifty and she'd been thirty. She wasn't proud of her behaviour back then, but hadn't everyone done things they'd later regretted? At the time it had seemed . . . well, fine. All you did was compare your own relatively minor transgressions with other people's more eye-popping ones, and yours no longer seemed so terrible after all.

Then again, it hadn't been entirely one-sided, had it? Each of them had taken what they'd wanted from the relationship, had both benefited from it in their different ways. Quid pro quo.

Della studied the photo. He looked old. He *was* old. But it was actually quite sweet. The expression on the little dog's face was cute, in a pugnacious kind of way. You could see the connection between them.

Turning over the Christmas card and studying the front of it for the first time, she saw a frosty, hilly scene of a small town surrounded by countryside, viewed from high up and including, on the left, a part of the Cotswold stone building from where the photograph had been taken.

On the back of the card was the name of the company that had printed it, as well as that company's address: 5 Linden Street, Foxwell.

'Let's see?' Tom swallowed his mouthful of toast and took the card from her, while something else stirred in her memory. Eddie's elderly parents had lived in Foxwell, hadn't that been the name of the place? She'd never visited it nor met them, but vaguely recalled him once showing her a photo of the family home and being impressed by its grandeur. Was this where Eddie lived? Of course his parents would be long gone, but had he moved in after their passing? Was he married, with children and possibly grandchildren of his own? Was he happy, and what was his life like now?

'Let me guess. Some old actor you worked with?'

'No. He was a . . . friend.'

Tom did a jokey double-take. 'Not *that* kind of friend.' Then he saw the look in her eyes and said, 'Oh God, really? He's *ancient*.'

'He was a suitor. He was very keen on me. I was . . . young and single.'

'Wow. How long ago was this?'

'Before your father.'

He spluttered with laughter. 'I should hope so!'

'It was never serious.' Not on her side, at least.

'Going to give him a call?' He pointed to the phone number written at the bottom of the card.

'I don't know.' Now that the original shock was wearing off, her curiosity was growing. 'Maybe.'

'Is he rich?'

'No idea. He used to be.'

136

Tom shrugged and reached for another bit of toast. 'Well then. What have you got to lose?'

★

Edgar's phone rarely rang. Other than irritating sales folk in faraway call centres, people tended not to bother him. The last two days had been agonising, wondering if the card had reached its destination yet and if Della would make contact. He deliberately hadn't included his address; the thought of receiving a polite card in return was no longer enough. He wanted to hear her voice, speak to her, find out how she was.

It had been like walking around clutching a grenade, waiting for it to go off.

In the event, when it happened, he was sitting down on the wooden bench in the garden, watching as Captain Oates trotted around exploring the flower beds and the various patches of grass where wild animals had left their marks. His phone rang and he felt a rush of adrenalin because it was a number he didn't recognise, which meant it could be a stranger in a call centre on the other side of the world . . .

Or it could be Della.

He took a breath. 'Hello?'

'Eddie? Hello! How *are* you, darling?'

And there it was, the voice he'd longed to hear, instantly recognisable and remarkably unchanged. She was the only person who'd ever called him Eddie. And no one else had called him darling since their break-up, that was for sure. For a moment his throat closed and he couldn't speak.

Except that would never do. He swallowed and ordered himself to get a grip. 'Della. It's so good to hear from you. You sound just the same. I'm well. How about you?'

137

'Oh, not so bad, considering. Can I ask how you found out my address?'

Edgar braced himself; he didn't want her to think he was a stalker. 'My helper found some old photographs of the two of us together the other day, inside an old address book, and it brought back memories. I thought, why not send you a Christmas card? Then when we looked you up online, I saw that you'd lost your husband. I was so sorry to hear that. I don't have much to do with the internet, but my helper found out where you lived.' He paused; it was so good to hear from her. 'I hope you don't mind that I used the address.'

'Oh darling, of course I don't mind – it was wonderful to open the card and discover it was from you! And such a beautiful card too. Is Foxwell where your parents lived?'

'It is.' Flattered that she remembered, Edgar said, 'They died not long after I last saw you, just a few months apart, and I took over the house. Been here ever since.'

'I've forgotten what it's called . . .'

'Walton House.'

'That's it, of course. And you must live there with your family?'

He paused; she'd automatically assumed he had married and raised children as she had. 'It's just me.'

'Eddie! Have you been widowed too? I'm so sorry!'

'I didn't marry.' His voice sounded stiff to his own ears. 'Or have children.'

'Oh, but . . . why ever not?'

She'd always been blunt too. The honest answer was that he'd never found anyone to match up to her. Nor even tried, really. He'd loved her far more than she'd ever cared for him and he'd known that right from the start. His feelings had never been properly reciprocated. He'd tried his best to win her over, but it hadn't happened.

And he had turned into a bitter, unhappy curmudgeon as a result.

'I just didn't.' He held out his free hand as Captain Oates trotted across the damp grass towards him with a stick clamped between his teeth.

'So you're all on your own?'

'I have my live-in helper. And my dog.'

'Oh Eddie, your little dog looks wonderful. And you do, too. Are you happy?'

Happy? Hardly ever. What might his life have been like if he *had* managed to win her heart?

'I'm happy talking to you,' he said truthfully as Captain Oates dropped the stick, spotted something that bothered him in the direction of the house and began to bark with irritation. Turning to look behind him, Edgar saw that Lou was watching them from the landing window on the top floor.

'We should meet up,' Della went on gaily. 'Have lunch next time you're in London. Would you fancy that?'

What a question.

'That'd be . . . yes, yes, I would. Any time that suits you.'

'OK, let me think, I'm free on Friday . . .'

'This Friday it is.' He couldn't get the words out fast enough. 'I'll book a table somewhere nice.' He remembered how much she'd always loved being taken to the Savoy.

'You mustn't be shocked when you see me, Eddie. I'm all wrinkly and raddled now, an old crone!'

'I know that's not true.' He wouldn't even care if she was. 'I'm glad I sent the card now.' It was the weirdest feeling; something that might even be joy was bubbling up inside him.

'Oh Eddie, I'm glad, too. Will you pick me up here? At around midday?'

'Of course I will.'

He ended the call and sat thinking about what had just happened. Finally he heard a scuffle of dry leaves behind him.

'I saw you talking on the phone,' said Lou. 'Was that her?'

'It was.'

'And?'

'I'm meeting her for lunch in London. On Friday.'

'Oh wow, quick work.' Seeming genuinely delighted, she clapped her hands. 'That's brilliant!'

'I know.'

'Look at you, you're freezing. Come on inside now and get warm.'

Edgar bent to pick up Captain Oates, who snuggled into the crook of his arm.

'Phone the barber and book me in for Thursday,' he announced. 'I need to get my hair cut and have a proper shave.'

★

Two could play at googling.

'Walton House, Foxwell,' said Della, and Tom keyed the words into the search engine.

It came up in Images. The dozen or so photos told them everything they needed to know.

'It's beautiful,' Della gasped. 'Georgian. Like something out of *Bridgerton*.'

'Call him back,' said Tom. 'Tell him you'll go down there. Then you can take a proper look around.'

It made sense. She *wanted* to see it. She reached for her phone.

'Eddie, darling, me again. Listen, why should you have to schlep up to London when it's so much easier if I come to Foxwell? That would be nicer, wouldn't it? I'd love to see where you live. Yes? Great, we'll do that then. Can you arrange a car for me? Thank you so much. Can't wait!'

140

Chapter 18

'It's like I'm the fairy godmother,' said Lou. 'And you're Cinderella.'

And to prove that Edgar was turning into a whole new person, he'd actually laughed. OK, maybe not properly laughed, but it was close, along the lines of getting a fishbone caught in his throat. It had definitely been noisier than a smile.

Which was pretty miraculous, you had to admit.

He'd had his steel-grey hair cut and the barber had given him a wet shave. Then Lou had driven him into Cheltenham and helped him choose a new outfit for the occasion, smart dark grey wool trousers, a cream shirt, a brass-buttoned blazer and a striped tie. A tad formal, but it was what he wanted to wear. He had even bought a new bottle of Givenchy Gentleman because the seldom-used bottle on his chest of drawers was, she'd discovered, over thirty years old.

That had been yesterday. Now, today, Della was due to arrive at midday and Lou had been up since five cooking the elaborate buffet-style menu Edgar had written out for her, presumably made up of Della's favourite things to eat.

By 11.30, she was done, everything was laid out prettily in

the drawing room and the chauffeur from the car company had called to let them know he was twenty minutes away.

'Right, that's it,' Edgar told her. 'You can go.'

'What? Can't I stay?' Lou had been looking forward to meeting Della Lucas; he hadn't warned her that she was to be banished from the house.

'No.'

'How about if I promise not to come out of my room?'

'It'll put me off if you're here.' He was on edge, elegantly dressed and wearing a generous helping of the Givenchy Gentleman. Having expected to be introduced, Lou had smartened herself up a bit, too.

'How long before I'm allowed back?'

'I'll send a text, let you know.'

'Why did you need to hire a driver to bring her down here? Why couldn't she catch the train?'

'Why is it anything to do with you?' Edgar countered snippily. 'If you must know, it's not easy for her, being well known. It's a nuisance being bothered by fans.'

Because of course people would want to mob a faintly recognisable ex-game-show-hostess-turned-minor-actress.

Lou kept a straight face and said, 'Why, is she bringing Beyoncé?'

He flapped a dismissive hand. 'I have no idea what she's bringing, and I don't know what a beeonsay is. Come on now, out you go.'

As she was about to leave, the letter box went *plunk* and more post than usual thudded onto the mat.

'Bill. Bill. Junk mail, junk mail, junk mail.' Sorting them onto the kitchen table, Lou put down the final five envelopes. 'And these are Christmas cards.'

'You can open them,' said Edgar.

142

'They're from kind people who are sending you cards in return for the ones you sent them.' Efficiently slicing open the envelopes, she said, 'Isn't that nice? Doesn't it make you feel all warm and fuzzy and Christmassy? Look, this one's got glitter on it. Ah, it was drawn by Moira's granddaughter!'

'It looks ridiculous.'

'She's six years old!'

'Are you still here?' Edgar shook his head at her.

'I'm just saying, put them up with the others in the drawing room so Della can see them. It makes you look popular.'

'Go,' he said impatiently. 'I'll let you know when you can come back.'

There was champagne chilling in the fridge. He was as jumpy as a cat. Lou really hoped the visit would go well. She said, 'Do you want me to take Captain Oates with me?'

'Of course not. He's staying here with me.' Edgar looked at her as if she was out of her mind. 'Della will want to meet him.'

★

Having dropped her on the gravelled driveway, the car headed off and Della paused to admire the house, every bit as impressive in real life as it had appeared online. So this was the ancestral home, lived in by generations of Allsopps and majestically overseeing the town below. And Edgar had been here for the last thirty years. What had his life been like all this time?

Well, she was about to find out. The heavy oak front door opened and there he was, framed between the stone pillars flanking the doorway, smartly dressed and leaning on a walking stick.

'Eddie, so wonderful to see you! My goodness, you don't look a day older . . . and just as handsome as ever!' She flung her

143

arms wide and hastened over to greet him with a hug and a fond kiss on each cheek. Once an actress, forever an actress. She'd always been capable of putting on a good show.

'You look incredible.' He let her go, then studied her at arm's length. 'I can't believe you're here.'

From inside the house came the sound of barking. 'Well I am! And that must be your gorgeous doggy, I can't wait to meet him . . . Oh, your home is wonderful . . .' Following him across the imposing but gloomy wood-panelled hallway hung with scenic paintings in ugly frames, Della said, 'I can't believe you never married or had a family.'

Edgar opened another door and there was the dog, yapping at her in an aggressive fashion. 'He doesn't like many people.'

'He's very high-pitched, isn't he? I do like dogs, though. Now, I'm so *hungry*. Where are you taking me to lunch – somewhere gorgeous, I hope?'

'I thought we'd eat here.' Picking up the furious chihuahua, Edgar said, 'The food's all ready and waiting, so—'

'Oh no! Darling, this is supposed to be a joyful reunion. I've been looking forward to going out and celebrating in style!' As someone who hated any form of cooking, eating delicious meals in restaurants had become, now more than ever, a welcome respite from frozen ready meals, bowls of cereal and mountains of toast. Clutching his sleeve, then hastily letting go before the snarling dog could sink his teeth into her hand, Della said, 'The driver's waiting down in Foxwell, so we can call him back to come and take us wherever we want to go. There must be some lovely places nearby.'

He'd always agreed to everything she wanted. Wasn't that why she'd carried on seeing him? She gave him her most winning sparkly-eyed smile.

'Fine, we'll do that,' said Edgar.

'Grrrr,' Captain Oates snarled at her from the crook of his arm.

'Oh stop it,' Della told him. 'Naughty boy!'

★

It was sunny and cold outside, but comfortingly warm inside Val's, the café on The Triangle, where you could gaze out of the window at the river on one side and the shops along the high street on the other. The air was steamy with the mingled scents of freshly ground coffee and home-made cakes and snacks. Christmas songs were playing on the radio in the kitchen and there were fairy lights galore strung up around the café and zigzagging across every window.

Luckily it wasn't too busy, which meant Lou didn't need to feel guilty about having settled in for the duration. She'd bagged one of the cushioned window seats on the high street side of the café, ordered a blackberry doughnut and a coffee, and was now chatting to Heather on Messenger, keeping her updated with the latest goings-on in Foxwell.

Lou:
Ooh, and did I tell you about my thrilling love life? No? Well, that's probably because I don't have one. Not any kind of love life.

Heather's condition had continued to deteriorate since she'd moved into the nursing home, but she was still able to send messages on her iPad. Now she typed:

Heather:
Does this mean you're starting to feel ready to meet someone at last?? Because that's progress. I'd also say it's about time.

Lou replied: *Not really, I'm OK as I am. Don't want to make a fool of myself again like I did that time with Remy.*

She hadn't mentioned it to anyone else; Heather was the only person she'd confided in. The cringeworthiness might be fading but it was still there, three months on.

It'll happen, Heather typed back. *When you least expect it. One day you'll bump into Ryan Reynolds in the queue at the post office and he'll say, Where have you been all my life? and sweep you off your feet like a superhero . . .* 😂😂😂😂😂

Chapter 19

Moments later, Lou heard the bell ring above the door as a new customer entered the café. A good-looking customer at that. Belatedly she realised she still had a grin on her face from reading Heather's last message and the reason the newcomer was smiling at her was because he thought it had been directed at him. Which meant she now needed to casually glance back at her phone and break into a fresh grin, so he understood that this was what had been amusing her in the first place.

Honestly, was life this complicated for everyone or just her?

Oh, but customer-wise he was a bit out of the ordinary. Maybe a couple of years older than her, he was tanned and handsome with swept-back blonde hair, bright blue eyes and a lovely broad mouth. Surreptitiously observing him as he unwound a navy wool scarf from around his neck and selected a table in the opposite corner of the café, she took in his battered jeans and the faded blue sweatshirt worn over a red polo shirt. Having hung his puffa jacket over the back of his chair, he sat down and began to study the menu on the table. When he glanced up, he caught her watching him and said in a friendly way, 'Warmer in here than out there.'

His voice was nice, drawly and quite *Made in Chelsea*. Lou nodded and said, 'It is' – *oh great, riveting stuff!* – before returning her attention to her phone. She heard the new arrival order a cup of Earl Grey from Val and swiftly typed:

Lou:
You aren't going to believe this, but a good-looking guy just came into the café. Nice face . . . nice body . . . nice smile!

Heather's reply was: *WOW.*

Lou:
And he's ordered Earl Grey tea. Posh!

Take a sneaky photo, Heather prompted.

Lou:
I can't, he'll see me. He's settled down to do some work now.

Heather:
What kind of work?

Lou:
No idea. He's sitting across from me using one of those stylus pens on his tablet.

But minutes later, still furtively observing the newcomer from beneath her lashes, Lou began to suspect he wasn't writing at all. She typed: *OK, sounds weird, but I think he might be drawing me.*

Heather:
What?????

Lou:

He keeps stopping, glancing over, then looking back down and carrying on. Like people do when they're sketching someone.

Heather:

Ooh, maybe he's a famous artist – this is so exciting! Ask him if that's what he's doing.

Lou:

No way. What if he isn't? I'd sound like a right berk.

Heather:

Wait till he glances up again, then give him a smouldering look and strike an exotic pose. See what happens.

Lou:

OK, I'll definitely give that a try.

Heather typed: *It's what Madonna would do.*

At this, Lou gave an involuntary snort of laughter, which she tried to disguise as a cough. The man sitting across the room looked up and said, 'You OK?'

And there it was again, that crooked, complicit smile. She ended her pretend coughing and nodded. 'I'm OK.'

'Sure you don't need a pat on the back? Because if you do, just say the word.'

'I'll be fine. But thanks.' She paused, watching as he scribbled some more then looked up at her once again. 'What are you doing?'

A flicker of . . . was it guilty amusement? 'Nothing. Well, maybe something. Why?'

'I just wondered. It felt as if you might be drawing me.'

149

He put down his screen pen and took a sip of tea. 'And if I have been drawing you? Would that be allowed?'

On her phone, the next message from Heather had popped up on the screen:

Heather:

You've gone quiet! What's happening? Are you two doing a sexy tango in the middle of the café???

OK, it was a good job he wasn't able to see her messages. Lou said, 'Are you an artist?'

'I . . . dabble. In my spare time. If you really don't want me to sketch you, I'll stop.'

'You don't have to stop. Can I see it, though?'

'I'll show you when I've finished. I'm shy.'

'I can tell,' said Lou.

Heather:

OMG, you are! You're too busy doing the sexy tango with your sexy stranger to talk to me. This is SO unfair.

Looking serious and important, Lou wrote back: *He IS sketching me!! We're chatting. No tango happening . . . yet . . .*

'So are you incredibly busy, or am I allowed to talk to you?' He was still working away, strands of his straight blonde hair falling over his forehead as he tilted his head in order to study her more closely. 'Or am I being too forward? If I am, just say.'

The faint fluttering sensation in her chest was back. The last time she'd experienced it, Remy had been the cause. Now, three months later, it was happening again, this time in response to a complete stranger. Who undoubtedly had a wife or girlfriend every bit as gorgeous as Remy's Talli.

No wedding ring. Not that this proved anything either way. Someone really should invent some foolproof method of signalling to interested parties that you were single and available.

'We can talk,' said Lou.

His mouth stretched into an even broader smile. 'Hooray. Can I ask you questions?'

'If I can too.' She finished her coffee and he signalled to Val to bring a refill.

'Of course. Name?'

'Lou. You?'

He gave a nod of approval. 'Tom. Monosyllabic names are the best. And are you local?'

'I am now. Moved down from Birmingham a few months ago. Your turn.'

'Oh, I move around. Spent last year in Austria. Amsterdam before that. Now I'm giving the UK another go. OK, next question. Are you going to finish that doughnut?'

'Not while you're drawing me. It's never a good look.' She was starting to relax and enjoy herself now.

Helloooo? I'm still here, Heather reminded her impatiently.

Lou wrote back: *His name is Tom. He's charming and fun. THIS HAS NEVER HAPPENED TO ME BEFORE.*

Heather:
Yay! Oh bum, physio's here. Back in twenty minutes. Don't do anything I wouldn't do.

Helpfully, Heather added: *Try to keep your clothes on.*

'And what's it like living here?' said Tom. 'Are the natives friendly?'

Val, carrying the fresh drinks over to their respective tables, winked at Lou as she put her cappuccino down in front of her. 'Most of us are, aren't we, love? One or two exceptions, mind

151

you.' Resting a hand on Lou's shoulder, she turned to address Tom. 'But thanks to this one here, we're making some progress, I reckon. Little marvel, Lou is.'

'We're getting there, slowly.' Lou added sugar to her coffee, then jumped as someone double-knocked on the window to her left.

Remy came in through the door and Val said, 'Speaking of friendly natives. Hello, my love. Oh, now look what you made her do!'

Having spilled sugar over the table, Lou was surreptitiously sliding the scattered crystals off the edge into her cupped palm.

'Sorry, all my fault. Hi, Val.' Not sorry at all, Remy gave her a warm hug. 'How've you been?'

'Missing you terribly.' Val and Remy's mother had attended school together, Lou had learned, and Val had known him all his life. 'Every time you go away, my profits drop like a stone. What can I get you, love?'

'Three sausage rolls, please, and a black coffee to go. And I'll have a couple of those custard doughnuts to keep me going. Sorry, can't stop, I'm heading over to meet clients in Bath. Just dropped by to call into the cottage and pick up my post.'

'All going well with the new girlfriend then?'

'Seems to be.' He looked amused.

'Practically a world record, isn't it? Could this be The One?'

Remy said, 'You never know, Val. Have to wait and see.'

'Ah, there'll be some broken hearts around here when you get married. Won't there, love?' Back behind the counter now, Val was bagging up Remy's order while cheerily addressing Lou.

Oh great. Floundering for a second, Lou said, 'Um . . . I guess so?'

From the other side of the café, Tom was looking as if he was trying hard not to laugh.

152

'Sorry,' he said when Remy had left. 'It was the look on your face. It was quite funny.'

'Thanks so much.'

'So does that mean you'll be one of the broken-hearted admirers?'

Lou shook her head and prayed her neck wasn't going red. 'No. We're just friends. Known each other for years.'

'He's a good-looking guy.'

'Charming, too,' Val chimed in, as helpful as ever. 'If he and this latest one break up, maybe you'd get your turn, love. I mean, couldn't say no to an opportunity like that, could you?'

OK, this really wasn't helping. Lou said, 'Maybe I already have someone.'

Tom raised an eyebrow. 'Ah, that was going to be my next question, before we were interrupted. So are you single or not single?'

'Single,' Val called across the café.

'There could be someone you don't know about,' Lou protested.

'There could, but Sammy and Jess would know, wouldn't they? And they told me there isn't anyone at all.' She directed a beaming smile back at Tom. 'How about you then, my love? I'm enjoying this twenty questions. Your turn.'

'I'm single, too,' said Tom.

'How about that? I feel like Cilla! Anyway, don't mind me, you two carry on, I've got sandwiches to be getting on with in the kitchen.'

When Val had left them to it, Tom said, 'I'm starting to like it here.'

'It's fine so long as you don't mind everyone wanting to know everything about you.'

He frowned. 'Could be an issue if you're an undercover cop. Or a secret agent, or a drugs smuggler.'

'Or a bigamist with another family nearby.'

'Damn, that's ruined it for me.'

More customers piled into the café and Val returned to serve them. After another five minutes, Lou said, 'How long does it take you to sketch someone?'

'As long as possible. I'm enjoying myself.' Tom paused to take a swallow of his tea, which had to be cold by now. 'No, don't worry, nearly finished.'

It was a weird feeling, posing for someone without looking as if you were aware of them, while tinglingly conscious of their gaze on you and knowing they were taking in every last detail of your face. She was still sending messages so that Heather could read them all as soon as the physio was finished with her.

What an unexpected turn this day had taken. But while it was a fun situation to be in, she really didn't know a thing about him, not even what he was doing here. Given her luck, she'd never see him again anyway.

'There, done.' He threw the e-pen down onto the table with a flourish.

'Show me.'

'I'll text it to you. But if you don't like it, please don't laugh.'

'I won't.'

All of a sudden, he was no longer confident. 'Promise?'

The lack of self-assurance came as a surprise, and actually made her like him more. Lou said, 'One hundred per cent.'

'OK, what's your number?'

She reeled off the string of figures. He keyed them in, then crossed his fingers and said, 'Right, sending it now.'

Her phone pinged. She opened the text, which said *#BeKind*, and downloaded the image. Which revealed itself to be a page full of badly drawn cartoons of cats, stick people, lollipop trees, random swirls and spirals, and a space rocket. Beneath it, Tom had written: *I didn't say I could draw. But it got us chatting, didn't it? And now we have each other's numbers. I call that a win. Xxx*

Looking up, Lou met his gaze and felt a frisson of excitement, because there was a definite attraction and it might even be mutual. 'Well done.'

'I told you, I'm very shy. You're not cross?'

'I'm not cross.'

'I've never done that before, by the way. But sometimes it's hard to strike up a conversation out of the blue. The idea just came to me and I thought I'd give it a try.'

'It worked.' She was glad he hadn't attempted to sketch her and not been successful – that would have been far worse.

'Can I come and sit with you? Or is that too forward? It's all right, you can say no.'

Lou smiled; there was that frisson again. If they sat together, she'd be able to get an even better look at those incredible blue eyes. 'Why not? Saves having to shout at each other across the room.'

But as he was gathering up his things, her phone rang.

'It's me,' said Edgar, because it didn't matter that his name came up on her phone, he still had to say it every time.

'Hello, you. How's everything going?'

'Good, good. Except you need to get home.'

Her heart contracted. 'Why, what's happened?'

'We came out for lunch. We're at Grey's Hotel over in Turville, but I'm worried about Captain Oates. Della said it would be OK to leave him at the house, but now I'm worried he's lonely and feeling abandoned. So you have to go and make sure he's all right.'

'Is he in the kitchen?'

'Yes.'

'But that's why we've been putting him in there, to get him used to the idea.' Tom had pulled out the chair opposite her and was sitting down. He had really nice hands. Lou said into the phone, 'Honestly, he'll be fine.'

'You don't know that, do you? He might be traumatised. Just go back and make a fuss of him. We'll be a couple of hours yet. Bye.'

And as always when he'd said his piece, Edgar ended the call abruptly.

Chapter 20

Damn.

Damn. And how typical that this should happen now, just when she was enjoying herself.

Tom said, 'Something wrong?'

Lou hesitated. Edgar was being over-cautious, and the thing was, Captain Oates was a dog. If she stayed here for another hour, it wasn't as if he could tell on her, bark out his complaint that she *hadn't* rushed straight back and catered to his every doggy need.

More to the point, unless Edgar was the one doing it, Captain Oates didn't even *like* having a fuss made of him. Whenever she'd tried it, he'd given her one of his disdainful what-do-you-think-you're-doing? looks and turned away.

But . . . Oh God, having a conscience was such a pain. She heaved a sigh.

'What's the problem?' said Tom.

'I'm sorry. I can't stay.' The fleeting idea that she could go and collect Captain Oates then bring him back with her to the café flickered and died, because dogs weren't allowed in here. And with the temperature outside hovering at zero degrees, inviting Tom to join her for a walk with them was hardly an enticing offer.

'Oh no.' He looked genuinely disappointed. 'Why not?'

'My boss needs me to get back to the house.'

'Is he the one locked in the kitchen?'

Despite her disappointment, Lou smiled. 'I wish. No, Captain Oates is my boss's new dog and he's worried about leaving him at home while he's out for lunch . . . so it looks like I have to—'

'Hang on.' Tom did a minuscule double-take as she dropped her phone into her bag and began to pull on her coat. 'His name's Captain Oates?'

'I know. It's one of those joke names, because he likes to be out for a long time.'

'Is he a black and tan chihuahua?'

Lou stared at him in disbelief. 'Yes! Do you *know* him?'

'Is your boss . . . Eddie somebody?'

Wide-eyed, she nodded. 'Edgar Allsopp. You know him too?'

'I don't. But right now he's having lunch with my mother.'

The penny dropped.

'Your mum's Della Lucas? Are you serious? Oh my God, this is mad . . .' She started to laugh. 'We didn't know you were coming down too.' A thought occurred. 'Hang on, does your mum *know* you're here?'

'Well, seeing as I was sitting next to her in the back of the limo, she probably noticed.' His ultra–blue eyes sparked with amusement. 'This is crazy. I wasn't doing anything else today, so I thought I'd come along for the ride, seeing as the car was booked anyway. Then after the first couple of hours, once they'd had their lunch, I was going to join them so Mum could introduce me to Eddie.'

'It sounds so weird to hear you call him that. He's always been Edgar to me.'

'She hadn't heard from him in over thirty years. Then he sent her a Christmas card out of the blue,' said Tom.

Lou said proudly, 'I was the one who took that photo.'

'And there was another one inside, of him with the dog.'

'I took that one too.'

'Whose idea was it to send them to Mum?'

'Mine. Well, after he'd told me how they used to be friends,' she added.

Val, still happily eavesdropping as she served mince pies to a table of new arrivals, said, 'Made him send loads out, didn't you, love? We all got them. Nearly passed out with the shock when I opened ours and saw who it was from! I said to my hubby, whatever next? At this rate, she'll have old Edgar dressing up as Santa for the Christmas Fayre. Hahaha, your face . . . Don't worry, only joking. Don't mind me!'

Tom was shaking his head at Lou, still marvelling at the connection. 'This is like discovering we're related.' The corners of his mouth twitched. 'Except better, because we aren't related.'

'I do need to get back.' Flustered, Lou dug out her keys.

'So, can I come with you? No, sorry, I'm being too forward. I should probably stay here.'

But he didn't want to stay here, she could tell. And he wasn't really a stranger, was he? Not any more. Lou considered the options, the likelihood of him being a murderer, and weighed them up against the fact that he was Della Lucas's son and she instinctively liked him. Quite a lot, in fact. Plus . . .

'Look, I made tons of food for them to have for lunch. If they've gone out to eat instead, it's only going to go to waste. So if you want to come and meet Captain Oates, let's go.'

She drove them up the hill in Edgar's grey Mini.

'Nice place you have here,' Tom said as they crunched their way across the frosted gravel driveway.

Lou shrugged. 'It's not so bad. You should see my mega-yacht.'

'I could come and visit you on it. Does it have a helipad?'

'It has three, so my friends don't have to queue up to land.' She unlocked the front door and braced herself for a volley of outraged barks. 'OK, he's not the cheeriest, so don't expect an ecstatic welcome. He doesn't bite, but he looks as if he will.'

When she opened the door to the kitchen, however, Captain Oates was peacefully asleep in his dog bed. Opening one eye and evidently finding them too uninteresting to merit a reaction, he closed it again and began to snore once more.

'Panic over, I guess,' said Lou. 'Shall we have some of that food I spent ages making this morning?'

'We can do whatever we like. If Eddie says they won't be back for another couple of hours, that means we have some time to kill.' As he followed her through to the drawing room, Tom's eyes lit up at the sight of the ice bucket containing the Veuve Clicquot. 'This'll do nicely, for a start.'

Oh well, he was a guest, and she knew there were two other bottles chilling in the fridge.

'I have to fight with myself every time I do this.' Easing out the cork and giving the bottle a little shake, Tom said, 'I know I should be doing it gently, but I just love it when it—'

Pow went the cork as it shot out and ricocheted off the ceiling.

'Whoops.' Lou stuck two glasses under the cascading eruption of foam, most of which had already landed on the rug.

'He'll never know.' Once the glasses were filled, Tom clinked his against hers. 'Here's to us. This is turning into a far nicer day than I was expecting. Cheers.'

'Cheers.' He had perfect teeth, white but not Hollywood-white, and a winning smile. 'Here, have a plate. Help yourself to anything you want.' She indicated the food, far too much of it. 'And there's salmon mousse and chicken salad in the fridge . . .'

He put down the plate and eyed her solemnly. 'You're beautiful.'

'Me? No I'm not.'

'Don't say that. You are. I'm so glad I came down here today.'

'It's not the kind of afternoon I was expecting.' Lou was experiencing that fizzy sensation in her chest again, but the last time it had happened was when she'd been having dinner with Remy and had stupidly imagined he'd felt the same way.

Whereas today, she knew she wasn't imagining anything.

'In a good way, I hope?' His eyes were blue and sparkling, his tone playful. Placing the champagne glass on the table next to the wild mushroom vol-au-vents Edgar had instructed her to make because they'd always been Della's hors d'oeuvre of choice, Tom reached out and drew her closer. 'You did say I could help myself to anything I want . . .'

He kissed her once, twice, three times, lightly on the lips. The third time, he lingered there. Then, pulling back in order to gauge the look on her face, he said, 'More? Or would you prefer me to stop?'

Lou's breathing had quickened. How long was it since anyone had kissed her properly, as if they meant it? Now she remembered what she'd been missing out on. Kissing the right person was better than just nice; it was fantastic, out of this world. She murmured, 'Don't stop,' and lifted her face up to his for more.

Minutes later, Tom stroked her hair back from her temple, twirled a strand of it around his index finger and said playfully, 'You could always give me a guided tour of the house, if you want. Show me your bedroom . . . I'd love to see it.'

And for a long, heart-stopping moment, she was tempted. Tempted to nod and say yes, then take him by the hand and lead him upstairs to her room . . .

She imagined the scene, a no-holds-barred sexathon to make up for all the sex she hadn't had during the course of the past fifteen months. Plenty of people would go ahead and do it without even pausing to wonder whether it was a good idea . . .

What was it like to be one of them?

Because she couldn't go through with it; she just wasn't that impulsive. Amazing though the last hour and a half had been, it was only an hour and a half. She might be attracted to Tom Lloyd, and he definitely seemed nice, but she didn't really know him, did she?

And there were other reasons, too. Her bedroom was in a right state. She'd thrown her sheets and duvet cover into the washing machine earlier, which meant the mattress and pillows were bare. Plus, she had no condoms in her room and—

'Yip yip yip-yip-yip,' barked Captain Oates, having chosen this moment to wake up, scratch furiously at the closed kitchen door and demand attention.

Tom said with good humour, 'I'll take that as a no, then, shall I?'

Was she crazy to have passed up the kind of offer that could end up being life-changing? Then again, if he was that keen, there'd be another opportunity, surely? Lou nodded and took a glug of icy champagne. 'I think it's best.'

'Fair enough. But you were tempted.' He slid an arm around her waist and dropped a final kiss on her mouth. 'Definitely tempted.'

'Maybe, a little bit.' She smiled, because he wasn't stupid. He knew.

'That's good enough for me.' He gave her a quick squeeze. 'Makes me like you more.'

And the fact that this was his reaction was what made her

like *him* more. They appeared, Lou realised, to be caught up in a delicious mutual-attraction spiral.

By the time they heard the limo pulling up outside, they'd made decent inroads into the buffet, finished the bottle of Veuve Clicquot and taken Captain Oates outside for twenty minutes of exploration in the garden. She'd given Tom a tour of the ground floor of the house and responded diplomatically to his questions about Edgar. And despite being eyed by Captain Oates with utter disdain, they had continued to flirt with each other in quite a thrilling and adrenalin-surging way.

'How about that then?' Della exclaimed when they went out to greet the two of them at the front door. 'You're already here! How did this happen, darling?'

Tom briefly updated her. Then he shook Edgar's hand and went on, 'Hi, I'm Tom. I've heard so much about you. Fantastic to meet you at last.'

'Della told you about me? Excellent. Good to meet you too.' Edgar actually sounded as if he meant it. He was even smiling, in his creaky, out-of-practice way. He turned his attention to Lou. 'Is he OK?'

'Of course he's OK! We've had a great time . . . *Oh.*' Belatedly realising he meant Captain Oates, and aware of Tom trying hard not to laugh next to her, Lou said, 'Yes, he's absolutely fine.'

As Edgar ushered Della inside out of the cold, she stood back to admire the oak-panelled hallway and the imposing Georgian staircase with fronds of ivy, pine cones and red ribbons entwined around the newel posts. 'Eddie, you're so lucky; this really is the most stunning house. Perfect for entertaining. And just look at it, all decorated and ready for Christmas.' She gestured expansively, encompassing the grandeur. 'If you're planning to hold a gorgeous party here any time soon, I do hope we'll be invited?'

Chapter 21

The text arrived at 5.30:

Edgar:
You can come downstairs now.

Lou, banished to her room shortly after Edgar and Della's return, had never felt more like a lowly under-housemaid in a Victorian TV drama. Having heard footsteps and voices at the front door minutes earlier, she had hovered at her second-floor window, gazing down as Della and Tom climbed into the waiting limousine. Neither of them had looked up to see if they were being watched. With a swoosh of tyres on gravel, the driver had borne them away and Edgar had returned to the house, closing the front door behind him.

Now he presumably wanted her to make him a mug of tea and clear away all the plates of uneaten food in the drawing room.

Lou looked at her own phone, which remained silent, even though Tom Lloyd had her number. She waited a couple of minutes more, giving him time to send her an apologetic text for having left without saying goodbye, but when her phone went *ting*, it was only Edgar again.

Edgar:
Hurry up, I'm waiting.

So much for her fateful and oh-so-promising meeting with Tom in Val's Café.

Just as well she hadn't slept with him.

'There you are,' said Edgar when she found him in the drawing room. Captain Oates, his tiny tail wagging, was sitting on Edgar's knee licking a Twiglet.

'How did it go? All good?' Lou forced herself to smile at him; yes, she was disappointed, but it wasn't his fault she'd yet again made the mistake of thinking someone nice might actually be attracted to her.

'All very good. Didn't you think it went well?'

'It wasn't that easy to tell, what with me being upstairs.' *Hidden away like the madwoman in the attic.*

'It couldn't have gone better.' Edgar sat and watched as she began stacking up the serving dishes, ready to carry them back through to the kitchen. 'And we're having a party.'

The plate of Emmental goujères tipped sideways and most of them ended up rolling across the carpet. 'Who's having a party?'

'Us. Me. You'll be organising it.'

'Where?'

'Here, of course. Like Della said, this is the perfect place for one.'

Lou collected up the fallen goujères and offered one to Captain Oates, who gave her a look that indicated she had a nerve offering him food that had been on the floor.

She frowned. 'Hang on, I might be hallucinating. You? *You* want to throw a party?'

Edgar's stony expression was eerily similar to Captain Oates's. Then he gave up and said, 'Della thinks I should. She wants to come back and meet all my friends. So . . . we have to make it happen.'

She wanted to meet all his friends? Lou said, 'Who are you going to invite?'

'I'll leave that to you.' He stroked the underside of Captain Oates's chin. 'You can decide. Anyone you think will come along.'

Her eyes widened. 'When?'

'How am I supposed to know? Boxing Day . . . New Year's Eve? Whichever's best.'

Lou thought fast. 'Neither of those, because most families will have made plans for those dates by now. We need to go for the boring bit in between. How about the twenty-ninth?'

'OK.' It wasn't as if he had anything else filling up his jam-packed schedule.

'How many guests?'

'As many as you can find.' He thought again. 'No idiots, though.'

She was going to have to beg people to turn up. 'You'll need to use private caterers. I can't organise that much food by myself.'

'Fine.'

Phew, that was easier than expected.

'But I want you to get a couple of guest bedrooms sorted out,' Edgar went on. 'They need redecorating.'

'Why?'

'So that Della and her son can stay.'

Did that mean Tom had already announced he'd be here? Lou's pulse quickened, but she'd made decorating plans of her own. 'I was going to do my room, remember?'

'And you can, so long as you do the others first.'

There was no point in arguing. 'Fine, I'll make a start tomorrow.'

'After we've been into Cheltenham.'

'Why are we going into Cheltenham?'

Edgar stroked Captain Oates's velvety sticking-out ears. 'I want to buy a new car.'

★

'Well?'

Della opened her eyes; the wine with lunch followed by half a bottle of champagne back at the house had caused her to doze off in a pleasantly fuzzy fashion within minutes of the car leaving Foxwell. Now they were on the motorway heading back to London and she'd woken up with a dry mouth.

'Pass me that bottle of water, darling. And well what?'

Tom gave her a look. 'How did it go?'

'Lunch was great.'

'I meant Eddie. Have you fallen madly in love with him all over again?'

'I was never madly in love with Eddie. He took me to wonderful places and treated me like a queen. He was my biggest fan and he put me on a sky-high pedestal.' Della unscrewed the lid of the water and took a long swallow to quench her thirst.

'You told him you couldn't wait to meet all his friends.'

'I was just being polite!'

'Well, if he does invite you to a party, I think you should go.'

She closed her eyes; Tom was about to start nagging her about the future again, she could tell. He was always telling her off about her terrible relationship with money. As if it was her fault she no longer earned enough to support the kind of lifestyle she deserved to lead. When Barry had been alive, he had taken care of the boring financial side of things, and he'd been successful

167

enough that she'd been able to buy more or less anything that took her fancy.

But now that Barry was no longer here, the practicalities of life had become more of an issue. He hadn't gone in for putting money aside for a rainy day, which meant there hadn't been much in the way of savings, but at least they'd had their house in Essex. By selling it for a good price and moving into rented accommodation in north London, she'd assumed it would be a simple matter of living off the capital. But what with actually having to pay off the random bills that kept coming in – some of them every *month*, for heaven's sake – the amount remaining had dwindled at an alarming rate. What she'd imagined would keep her going for at least the next fifteen years was about to run out, and when she'd enquired at the bank about getting a loan to tide her over, the man asking the questions had practically laughed in her face. It had been all she could do to bite her lip and refrain from replying icily that unlike some people, at least she didn't have sweat patches on her shirt and a shocking case of dandruff.

She took another swig of water and tilted her head sideways to look at her son. 'I don't think there'll be a party. He looked pretty startled when I said it.'

Tom shrugged. 'But if there is one, you should go.'

'Fine.' She smothered a yawn. 'What was the girl like? I've forgotten her name.'

'Lou.' He smiled briefly. 'She was great. I liked her.'

Not that this meant much. Show Tom a pretty girl and the chances were that he'd make a play for her. Della said, 'Well, if I have to go, so do you.'

'And I will. Don't write him off, that's all I'm saying. He's a wealthy man and you definitely need a helping hand in the money department.'

168

She grimaced. 'He's eighty-one years old.'

'Exactly. Look at that as a good thing.'

'Easy for you to say. You're not the one who'd have to spend time with him. Anyway, shush.' She put a finger to her lips and indicated the back of the chauffeur's head. It didn't do to be indiscreet.

'Hey, no worries.' The chauffeur met her gaze in the rear-view mirror and said cheerfully, 'You can say anything you want in front of me. I'm like a priest in a confessional.'

A text arrived on Della's phone and she squinted at the screen. 'It's Eddie. He's decided to have the party. Does the twenty-ninth of December suit us?'

'Suit you, you mean.'

'You're coming too. You've promised.'

Tom shrugged. 'OK, the twenty-ninth is good for me.'

Della texted back: *Perfect, we'd love that. Can't wait to see you again and meet everyone.* She paused, then said, 'You never know, maybe I'll meet someone wonderful at the party. Just as much money as Eddie and ten times the charm. Ooh . . .' Quickly she added to the text: *Darling, don't forget to book another car, will you? So much easier than all the faff of having to catch trains. Xxxx*

Tom said, 'If you put kisses, he'll think his luck's in.'

'Good point.' She deleted them.

'But you don't want it to look unfriendly. Maybe one kiss.'

'Thanks, darling.' Tom was so good at text etiquette; he always knew what was what. Della added one small kiss, then replaced it with a larger one. Then she pressed send.

Chapter 22

Lou had never ventured inside an upmarket car showroom before. It smelled *expensive*. There was free coffee, who knew? And bowls of sweets to make you feel special. There were salesmen in suits who acted as if you were their long-lost best friend and pretended not to mind that you had a mutinous-looking small dog with you who might wee or worse on the glossy tiled floor at any moment. And there were also cars bearing mind-boggling price tags, all polished and gleaming to within an inch of their lives.

It was crazy, but it was what Edgar wanted to do, and within twenty minutes he'd done it, choosing a berry-red Bentley with a six-litre engine and the kind of throaty roar that made your feet vibrate. After a short test drive, during which he'd driven at a stately twenty miles an hour down the nearby dual carriageway, he'd returned to the showroom and given a nod of satisfaction, job done. 'I'll take this one.'

'Are you sure?' Lou was startled; she'd lived in houses that cost less.

'Why, do you want to give it a trial run?'

'No way.' She shook her head vehemently. 'What if I crashed it?'

The smooth salesman attempted to conceal his alarm. 'I think it's probably better if you leave the driving to your grandfather.'

'She isn't my granddaughter.' Edgar turned to Lou. 'You can stick with the Mini.'

'Thank you.'

'When can I take this one home?' He returned his attention to the salesman.

'It won't be until the beginning of January, I'm afraid, what with everything that needs to be—'

'If I can't have it by December the twenty-ninth,' said Edgar, 'I'm not interested.'

'I understand, sir, but—'

'No? Fine, we'll go elsewhere.'

Suddenly pale, the salesman audibly swallowed. 'Sir, that won't be necessary. We'll make it happen, you have my word.'

Lou took Captain Oates outside while Edgar sat down with the grovelling salesman to deal with the necessary paperwork. It was the first time she'd ever witnessed first-hand the truth of the phrase *money talks*.

As Della had been leaving the house yesterday, she'd apparently made some jokey, disparaging remark about the modest grey Mini parked on the drive. When she arrived at the party, Edgar was clearly determined to impress her with a car she couldn't laugh at.

Unable to help herself, Lou pulled out her phone and read – for maybe the seventh time – the text that had woken her when it had pinged up on her phone at two o'clock this morning:

Tom:

Missing you already. Have a great Christmas. See you on the 29th. Xxx

She'd spent the whole evening convinced he wouldn't be in touch – triggered by Brett's habit once they were married of not making contact when he'd said he would. She needed to keep reminding herself that not all men were untrustworthy. Tom Lloyd was a good person, far nicer than Brett. She needed to learn to relax and believe that.

And he was looking forward to seeing her at the party.

Lou hugged this information to herself like a secret. She couldn't wait.

'Done,' Edgar announced, rapping his walking stick on the ground to attract her attention. 'Let's go.'

'Home?'

'No. We need to buy the paint for the spare bedrooms so you can get started on them straight away.'

Two hours later, Lou lugged the heavy cans upstairs and said, 'I'm not going to be able to finish both bedrooms in time, not on my own.' She'd already explained that a professional would do a better job, and Edgar had agreed that this was true, but ringing around the local decorators the week before Christmas had met with a distinct lack of enthusiasm.

He looked at her now as if she were being difficult on purpose. 'But it has to be done.'

'Well, it's only going to happen if I have a friend to help me. But he'll need paying.'

Edgar shook his head. 'What d'you think I am, made of money?'

Was he joking? Lou couldn't quite tell. But she called Sammy, who was still in bed at midday, busy honing the lyrics of his latest song.

'Would you like to come and hone them up here, and do something useful at the same time?'

'When?'

'Now. Wear something that it doesn't matter if it gets wrecked.'

'That's everything in my wardrobe,' he said.

The doorbell went twenty minutes later while Lou was perched on a stepladder taking down the curtains in the yellow bedroom. By the time she'd reached the top of the staircase, Edgar had opened the front door. Leaning over the balustrade, she heard him say, 'Oh, it's you. I hope you know what you're doing. I don't want any accidents.'

Sammy grinned, undeterred. 'Don't you worry, I'm a decorator extraordinaire. Thanks for the invitation, by the way.'

'What invitation? Oh, right. Yes.' From her vantage point, Lou saw Edgar remember the email they'd constructed and sent out last night, letting everyone know about the party. Evidently also recalling her stern instruction to him to be nice to all those invited, he went on, 'Thought it would be good to have a get-together for . . . you know, the people around here.'

'I think it's a fantastic idea. If you want, I could bring my guitar and—'

'No need for that.' Edgar shook his head firmly. 'Anyway, Lou's upstairs, she'll show you what needs doing.'

What needed doing was a *lot*. The furniture was piled in the centre of the room, covered in old sheets. At a guess, the last attempt at redecorating had taken place decades ago. Lou scrubbed the walls with sugar soap while Sammy got started on the ceiling. The sash windows needed sanding back, then priming and re-glossing, as did the skirting boards and dado rails. As he worked, Sammy sang his most recent songs with gusto, which was fine when he knew the words, but the latest one wasn't finished yet, and hearing the same melody repeated over and over on a loop with different lyrics each time was wildly frustrating. It was a love song about Jess, and every time Lou tried to make a helpful suggestion, Sammy said, 'Stop it, the words have to come from *me*.'

By six o'clock they'd put a first coat of mango yellow on the walls and only spilled a couple of drops on an exposed patch of carpet. Sammy and his purple sweatshirt and jeans were splattered all over with yellow and white emulsion, but the lyrics for the song were finally completed and that was all he cared about.

'D'you think she'll like it?'

The title was 'Christmas Day with You' and with the addition of sleigh bells would be wonderfully festive. Lou said, 'How can she not? It's fantastic. And who wouldn't want a song written about them? Well, apart from Edgar.'

'I'm saving it for Christmas morning. Then I'll sing it to her.' Catching the look on her face, Sammy added, 'Don't worry, I've got her some proper presents too.'

'Phew. Not that the song isn't great on its own . . . *Waah*.' She ducked as he brandished a roller.

'It's going to be the best Christmas. I've never felt this way about anyone before. Next year's going to be amazing.' He ran his free hand through his red hair and discovered how much paint was in it. 'Is it too soon to tell her I love her?'

'Do you?'

'I think so. Pretty sure. I mean, yes, I know I do. But it still seems crazy that we've known each other for years and been kind-of friends . . . then *pow*, this just happens out of nowhere. It feels like the last piece of a really tricky jigsaw fitting into place.'

'It didn't happen before because you were so convinced she was besotted with Remy,' Lou reminded him. 'That's why you wouldn't even think about making a move yourself.'

Sammy's smile was rueful. 'I guess.'

'If you like someone, never assume they wouldn't be interested in you.' Oh, it was easy to dole out advice when you weren't the one on the receiving end. As if she was some kind of expert.

He nodded. 'Lesson learned. And look at me now, I've found what I always wanted. My missing puzzle piece. It feels like we've been together for months, but it's only been three weeks. Are you sure that's not too soon to say it?'

Lou pointed out of the bedroom window with her paintbrush. 'Look at Edgar and Captain Oates. That was love at first sight. Like, the moment they looked into each other's eyes it happened. I saw it for myself. And they've been inseparable ever since. They'll be together for ever. Compared with them, you're being slow.'

'I don't want to scare her off by coming on too strong, that's the thing.'

She smiled; it was so lovely to see him like this. No one deserved to be happily in love more than Sammy. 'Hey, relax. I'm pretty sure you won't scare her off.'

At seven o'clock they heard the clunk-and-whir of the stair-lift transporting Edgar up to survey their progress.

Sammy murmured, 'He's probably bringing us a couple of beers each. Going to tell us what a fantastic job we're doing.'

When Edgar appeared in the doorway and surveyed the scene, he frowned and said, 'You're going to have to work faster than this.'

Sammy left at ten that evening. 'Don't worry,' he told Lou as he headed out to his van. 'I'll be here by eight tomorrow. We'll get it done.'

The next morning, at just gone seven, her phone rang.

'Hi,' said Jess. 'Look, Sammy's really sorry, but he won't be able to help out today. He's been puking all night.'

'Oh no, poor thing. What's wrong?' Dismay mingled with sympathy and frustration; there was still so much to do.

'Don't feel too sorry for him. I made a macaroni cheese last night but he wanted to use up some chicken that was past its sell-by date. Except it smelled weird, so he covered it in curry sauce to hide the taste, because he thought that was the sensible thing to do.' Jess heaved an affectionate sigh. 'Basically he's thrown up about fifteen times so far and his face is the colour of pistachio ice cream.'

'Eurgh.' Lou wondered how she'd manage on her own. Oh well, if the job didn't get done, it didn't get done. Simple as that.

'But no need to panic. He managed to call in a favour between puking sessions. His stand-in's heading over to you as we speak.'

'Oh God, who?' Please not Bez Shackleton, who was one of the Bear's most enthusiastic customers and widely regarded as the worst decorator for miles around. Once tasked with painting a client's drawing room, he'd painted the children's playroom instead, because that was where the walls had been covered in drawings. Bracing herself, Lou said, 'Is it Bez?'

'That name did crop up.' Jess laughed. 'Don't worry, I persuaded him not to go there.'

'Thank you.'

'So you've got Remy instead.'

Ohhhhhhh . . .

And there it was, that oh-so-familiar lightning charge of adrenalin that occurred every time she heard his name. Lou exhaled silently and willed it to disperse; was it *ever* going to stop happening?

Into the phone, as if it made no difference whatsoever, she said breezily, 'Great.'

'Sorry I'm late,' Remy announced forty minutes later.

He was giving up his Sunday morning.

'Honestly, you don't have to do this. I'm the one who works for you, not the other way round.' Lou tried not to notice the way his mouth curved up at the corners; somehow his did it better than other people's. 'Anyway, it's Edgar's fault for wanting it finished at such short notice. If it doesn't happen, there's nothing he can do about it, is there?'

'Hey, no problem. Sammy asked me to step in as a favour to him. If I was working, I'd have had to say no, but I didn't have anything else on, so . . . Hi,' he went on as Edgar appeared in the hallway.

'What's he doing here?' Edgar frowned at Lou. 'What happened to the other one?'

'My brother has food poisoning,' Remy explained. 'So I'm helping out today instead.'

'Take your hat off,' Lou yelped, and Remy removed his black beanie just in time as Captain Oates trotted out into the hall. Having eyed the new arrival with suspicion for several seconds, the little dog then disappeared back into the kitchen.

'He doesn't like men in hats,' said Edgar.

'Me neither.' Remy stuffed the beanie into his jacket pocket. 'By the way, thanks for inviting us to your party.'

'*Us?* How many more of you are coming?' Catching Lou's stern look, Edgar said hastily, 'Doesn't matter. Everyone's invited. I'm going into my study now.'

Chapter 23

Lou led the way up the staircase and Remy followed. When they reached the yellow bedroom, she said, 'Thanks again for this. I'm learning not to apologise when he comes out with something rude. This party means a lot to him.'

'I know, Sammy told me.' He surveyed the room, assessing what needed to be done next, and took off his jacket.

'You don't have to turn up. Hopefully enough people will come along.' She'd panicked and messaged everyone whose name she recognised on Foxwell's Facebook page.

'Wouldn't miss it for the world. Shouldn't think anyone else will either.' Remy pushed up the sleeves of his pale grey sweatshirt and got busy with a large screwdriver, expertly levering the lids off the tins of paint lined up against the wall. 'All these years we've seen this house from a distance but hardly anyone's been inside it. I bet people can't wait to have a good look around. Right, ready to start? Shall we have some music?'

Lou exhaled with relief. 'Yes please.'

Just as before, in his and Briony's office, they worked well together and the hours flew by. Much as she loved Sammy, not

178

having to listen to him endlessly tweaking his lyrics was a treat. Instead, she and Remy took it in turns to play their favourite tracks. Sometimes they sang along, other times they chatted as they worked, and the conversation flowed as effortlessly as it had last week. They talked about the teachers they'd both known at school. Lou related anecdotes from work and Remy told her about his years at university, then they broke off to turn up the volume and join in with the chorus when it was the turn of 'Sweet Caroline' to blast out of the speakers. At lunchtime she went down to the kitchen and put together some food for the two of them, then they video-called Sammy, who was lying on the couch still feeling wrung out, but happy at least that the throwing-up had stopped.

'Is Remy singing?' he asked Lou.

'We both are.'

'I sing better than he does.'

'But I get less paint over me,' Remy pointed out, because streaks of yellow and white emulsion were still visible in Sammy's uncombed hair.

When the call had ended, Remy said, 'So how do you feel about him and Jess?'

'Me? I think it's great. She's brilliant. They're a dream team.'

He took a swig of Coke, then tilted his head. 'It doesn't bother you?'

'Why would it? We're just friends. We've always been friends.'

'Right. OK, well, that's good. I didn't know if you'd maybe . . . been hoping for something to happen.'

A tidal wave of relief flooded through her, because if this was what he'd been thinking, it meant he hadn't realised who she'd actually had the crush on.

'I *was* hoping,' she told him, giddy with freedom, 'but not for it to happen with me. I couldn't be more delighted for him and

179

Jess. They're both so lovely, they deserve to be happy together. And from the sound of things, it's already pretty serious.'

'It is.' He nodded, finishing the last bite of his toasted cheese sandwich. 'I like her too. You're right, they're a great match.'

'Same as you and Talli.' There, see? She could sound convincing, as if she truly meant it. It just meant putting on a good front and successfully concealing her own feelings, because nothing could ever come of them anyway. When it came to perfect couples, Remy and Talli were so well suited it was ridiculous.

'That reminds me. Has Sammy said anything yet about Christmas Day? He didn't know if you were seeing your dad?'

Lou shook her head. 'No, he and Kate are going to be in Barbados. It's fine,' she went on hastily. 'In my job I'm used to working over the holidays.' And last year, still reeling from Brett's death, she hadn't celebrated at all.

'Talli wondered if you'd like to join us at the cottage. Nothing spectacular, just us and Sammy and Jess.' His dark eyes softened. 'You don't want to be stuck here on your own, do you?'

Oh, that gaze, those incredible eyes . . . No, stop it, don't get carried away.

But she was deeply touched by the offer. 'Oh, thanks. I mean, technically I wouldn't be on my own, I'd be here with Edgar, although he did say I could take the day off. I wouldn't do that to him, but maybe I could pop down for a couple of hours.'

'That's settled, then.' Remy broke into a smile. 'Come for the afternoon. Otherwise he'll just have you working non-stop to get this place ready for the party.'

Lou felt her shoulders relax; he was right. And it would be nice to spend at least some of the day with friends, even if she would be the only singleton thrown in with two loved-up couples. 'I'd like that. Thanks so much.'

'Brilliant. And don't worry about dinner, it's all sorted. We're not letting Sammy anywhere near the food.'

'I love him to bits,' said Lou, 'but I'm so happy to hear that. It's a relief to know we won't be having turkey with coffee gravy.'

'You should have been there last Christmas.' Remy pulled a face. 'He put mint and raspberries in the bread sauce.'

What happened two hours later was Beyoncé's fault. 'Single Ladies' was playing at top volume and Lou was dancing on the stepladder while cutting away a strand of old wallpaper that had previously been hidden by the curtain pole.

'All the single ladies,' she sang, digging into the annoying bit of paper with her knife.

'All the single ladies,' Remy joined in, busy glossing the skirting board on the other side of the room.

'All the single ladies.'

'All the single ladies!'

BAM, something huge smacked into the window inches from Lou's face and she let out a shriek, losing her balance and falling backwards off the ladder. She crash-landed on the floor, knocking over a paint pot and throwing herself sideways to catch it before Mango Magic matt emulsion could spill everywhere and sink through the dust sheets into the carpet beneath.

'Oof . . . *ow*.' She'd saved the carpet from disaster, thank goodness. Lying on her back now, she assessed herself for damage. Feet . . . legs . . . head, all OK. By some miracle the window hadn't broken, but there was the dusty white imprint on the glass of a large bird with its wings outstretched.

'Oh God.' Remy appeared, standing over her and looking aghast.

'It's OK, I'm fine. Not hurt at all.' Eager to reassure him, Lou reached for his outstretched hand in order to be hauled back to her feet. 'Is the bird all right, do you know? It's my own fault for cleaning the windows – if I'd left them dusty, he'd have known the glass was there.'

But Remy wasn't looking at the window; he was gazing in horror at something on the ground next to her, and when Lou moved her left arm, she touched liquid and thought the paint must have spilled out after all.

Except it was warm, which was weird.

'Don't look,' Remy ordered. 'It's a bit grim. Close your eyes, hold your arm in the air and tell me where I can find a clean towel.'

'Airing cupboard, along the landing, third door on the left.' Touched that he'd remembered her telling him how she was fine dealing with other people's blood but less keen on seeing her own, she obediently raised her arm and heard the drip-drip-drip of it landing on the dust sheet. The Stanley knife had fallen out of her hand upon impact, and when she'd rolled over in order to grab the paint pot, she'd landed on the blade and sliced open her left forearm.

Remy was back in no time, wrapping a white towel around the injury and helping her to her feet.

'Make sure you close the door so Captain Oates can't get in,' Lou told him as they left the bedroom.

Remy said, 'God knows what he might turn into if he drinks your blood.'

'What's going on now?' Edgar was at the foot of the staircase when they reached it. Frowning, he said, 'I hope you haven't got paint on that towel.'

'She's cut her arm,' said Remy. 'I'm taking her to A&E to get it sorted.'

'So who's going to paint the bedroom?'

'If you want to drive her to the hospital, that's fine. I can stay here and get on with the job.'

'And leave you in the house on your own? Poking through my private things?' Edgar shook his head. 'No, you can take her. Just don't be long.'

'Um . . . I'm feeling a bit . . .' A wave of light-headedness and nausea caused Lou to sway. Mortified, she found herself needing to lean against Remy as he helped her out to his car.

'That man's a piece of work,' he murmured once she was in the passenger seat. Leaning across, he fastened her seat belt. 'Try and keep your arm up.'

His hand had accidentally brushed the sensitive skin of her neck, and now she was feeling light-headed for a different reason. Forcing herself not to replay the sensation in her mind, she said, 'Shall I stick it out of the window?'

He laughed. 'If you do that, I'll just have to keep turning left.'

'And then we'd never get there.'

The good news was she was no longer feeling sick and faint. The less good news was the realisation that her crush on Remy, the one she'd worked so hard to keep in check for the last few weeks, had come bursting back with all the force of a charging rhino.

It was the physical contact that had been the trigger. The warmth and strength of his arm supporting her had brought back all those electrifying feelings she'd worked so hard to suppress. Breathing slowly, she concentrated on the pain instead, which was coming in stinging jabs superimposed on a steady dull ache.

'Thanks so much,' she said when they reached the hospital. 'You can just drop me here. No need to stay when it could take hours.'

'Why don't we find out first?' Spotting a parking space, Remy

183

expertly reversed into it. 'If you're going to feel faint again, you'll need someone around to catch you.'

Which was the very reason it would be better if he left, but she couldn't tell him that.

When he accompanied her into A&E, the receptionist behind the desk exclaimed, 'How about that? You couldn't have picked a better time. Looks like everyone's too busy getting ready for Christmas to want to come and see us this afternoon! Sit your-selves down and the triage nurse will call you through very soon.'

'I may as well stay,' said Remy as they took their seats. 'The last time I was here I had to wait six hours.'

'When was that?'

'I was fourteen, Sammy was twelve. He dared me to ride my bike along the top edge of the bridge in Foxwell. So of course I fell off, landed in the river and broke my ankle.' He grinned. 'He thought it was hilarious until Mum told him he had to be my servant until I could get around without crutches again. Which was great, because from then on I had him waiting on me every five minutes.'

In no time, the triage nurse called Lou through and unravelled the bloodied towel, examining the injury and telling her how lucky she was not to have damaged a nerve. Once the wound was cleaned, the curtain was pulled back and a cheerful doctor with Christmas ribbons in her hair said, 'Hello there! Let's get you stitched up now, shall we?'

The queasiness returned with a vengeance and Lou felt the colour drain from her face. How embarrassing. She swallowed and exhaled, and the doctor laughed. 'Oh dear, my husband's squeamish too! Are you a fainter? Is that your husband out in the waiting room – do you want us to call him in to hold your hand?'

Your husband. Imagine if that were true. Just for the secret thrill of it, Lou didn't correct her. 'It's OK, I'll cope.'

And she did, by gritting her teeth and looking the other way, and digging the nails of her right hand into her palm. To further distract her, the doctor chattered on about marriage and husbands in general and Lou managed to nod and smile and not faint. Once she was thoroughly bandaged up, she was led back out to the waiting room and the doctor said to Remy, 'Here we are, all done! Your wife was very brave!'

Which was slightly awkward, but it had to be the kind of thing that happened all the time in hospitals. Luckily Remy didn't recoil in horror and exclaim, 'Oh my God, are you joking? Do you seriously think I'd marry *her*?'

Instead he said, 'Thanks so much,' and gave the doctor one of those irresistible smiles that had been melting the hearts of females everywhere since his time at school.

'Where's the towel?' said Edgar when he opened the front door and saw her neatly bandaged arm.

'It was too far gone. Couldn't be saved. And I'm fine,' said Lou. 'Thanks so much for asking.'

'That was my favourite towel.'

'I'm sorry. I'll buy you another.'

'Where's he going?' Edgar watched as Remy drove off.

'Home to see his girlfriend. Sammy's feeling better, so he'll be back tomorrow to help me finish the room.'

'Just as well it was only your left arm. At least you can still work.'

Honestly, what was he like? 'I know,' said Lou. 'Thank goodness for that.'

Chapter 24

Christmas had been and gone. For Della, it had been pretty quiet but still somehow unaccountably expensive. It was now 29 December, and here she was, back at Walton House, inwardly hoping that tonight might be the night she met the man of her dreams but at the same time somehow sensing it wasn't going to happen. Already Eddie's eagerness to please was making her want to escape.

'Look, it's lovely,' she said now, as he proudly showed her the bedroom, 'and you've done a wonderful job, but the smell of paint is quite strong . . . It would give me a terrible headache. I think it's best if the driver just takes us home tonight once the party's over.'

'We could open the windows.' Edgar sounded desperate, and her heart sank; he'd evidently been counting down the hours to seeing her again. From his texts she'd guessed he'd been hoping she'd still be here tomorrow, once the ordeal of the party was behind him. 'Or you could have my room instead, if that—'

'Eddie, it's kind of you to offer, but Tom and Fia are keen to head back tonight . . . You know how it is, things to do, people to see.' This was a fib; then again, it was all very well for Tom to be encouraging her friendship with Eddie, but he wasn't the one being forced to spent time with an eighty-one-year-old for whom conversation had never been a strong point. In all honesty, she'd rather take her chances on Tinder again and hope to meet someone both wealthy and closer to her own age, even if the sixty-something men these days only seemed interested in women in their forties.

Oh well, they were here now, and hopefully this party would be entertaining in its own way. And at least they could all fall asleep in the back of the limo on the way home.

Not that the flat on Frobisher Square would be their home for much longer, the way things were going. Honestly, why did life have to be so difficult? Not to mention cost so much.

★

The house had filled up quickly while Lou had been busy supervising the staff in the kitchen, hired for the evening to pass around trays of hors d'oeuvres and drinks. The food looked and smelled good, the house was festively decorated and the guests were in high spirits, enjoying the novelty of being inside Walton House at long last and being offered free drinks to boot.

Then a voice behind her said, 'There you are, I've been looking everywhere for you,' and Lou's heart lifted, because she hadn't known he'd arrived.

'Come here.' Tom wrapped his arms around her and gave her a kiss. 'You look fantastic.'

Compared with their first meeting, she certainly did. Tonight she was wearing a red velvet dress with a deep V neck and assorted silver necklaces decorating her best attempt at a cleavage. Her hair was just washed and falling to her shoulders in a blonde curtain, and her make-up included silver eyeshadow, black liner

187

and mascara, and a beigey kind of lipstick because a red one always ended up Joker-style around her mouth.

'Not so bad yourself.' She stepped back to admire his electric-blue shirt, black jacket and narrow black trousers.

He indicated her bandaged forearm. 'What have you been doing to yourself?'

'Fell off a stepladder onto a Stanley knife, like an idiot. While I was redecorating one of the bedrooms for your mum. But it was worth all the hard work,' she told him. 'It's all done now and looking amazing.'

'Except we're not staying,' said Tom. 'We're heading back tonight.'

'Oh!' All that hard work for nothing. Not to mention the stitches.

'Hey, don't look so disappointed.' He leaned closer and murmured in her ear, 'We can always sneak up later and christen it.'

'In the middle of a party?' Lou laughed as he ran an index finger down her spine. 'Probably not ideal.'

'You see, I disagree. I can't think of a nicer way to make the evening go with a swing.'

Was he joking, or did he actually mean it? She was aware of other women casting admiring glances in his direction. Taking a drink from a passing waiter's tray and hastily changing the subject, she said, 'How was your Christmas?'

'Oh, you know, the usual chaos and madness. How about you?'

'Quiet. But nice.' She'd spent the afternoon down at Riverside Cottage, which had been wonderful, of course it had, but the guilt of leaving Edgar on his own had kicked in and she'd left early to come back and spend time with him instead. Not that he'd seemed to appreciate the gesture, but she'd felt better about herself, just being here. She had actually sent a quick text to Tom that evening wishing him a happy Christmas, but hadn't received a reply. Well, if his day had been mad and chaotic, he wouldn't have had time.

'It would've been nicer if you'd been with me.' He dropped a kiss on the side of her neck. 'I've missed you. Are you sure you don't want to take me upstairs and show me your room?'

'It's my job to keep an eye on the caterers.' Her attention distracted by movement on the first floor, she glanced up as Edgar's stairlift came into view, making its usual whirring and clunking noise as it trundled around the curve of the staircase – with someone other than Edgar on it.

'Woo-hooooo!' squealed the vision in pink, waving her arms and kicking her legs in the air as the lift slowly descended to the ground floor.

'Who is *that*?' said Lou.

When she looked at Tom, he was rolling his eyes. 'That's my sister.'

★

At the other end of the crowded hall, Sammy and Jess were chatting with friends from the pub when Sammy heard a high-pitched *Woo-hooooo!* and turned to see who was creating all the noise.

For a moment he struggled to make the connection. The girl had long streaky pink and white hair and her body was encased in a pink-sequinned catsuit. She was extremely pretty and certainly not suffering from lack of confidence, swinging a bottle of wine by the neck and kicking so vigorously that one of her high heels flew up into the air.

Sammy frowned, because she definitely wasn't from around here but he knew he'd seen her somewhere before. Could it have been on TV or online, maybe?

The next moment the stairlift reached the bottom step and

ground to a halt in the hall. The girl in pink jumped off it, retrieved her kicked-off stiletto and did a happy shimmy that made her boobs jiggle inside the low-cut outfit.

At his side, Jess commented, 'She's shy,' and in that moment it came back to him. It was the jiggling that had served as the reminder.

'The last time I saw her,' he said, 'was back in September. She flashed her boobs at me in the street.'

Jess did a double-take. 'What, here in Foxwell?'

Sammy shook his head, feeling suddenly hot. God only knew how she came to be here tonight, but what if this was fate's way of offering him a second chance?

'It was in Brighton.'

'I've been there.' Jess nodded sagely. 'In Brighton, stuff like that happens all the time.'

'Hi,' said Sammy. 'Hey there. Remember me?'

The girl in pink was busy plucking king prawns out of a vol-au-vent and discarding the puff pastry case on someone else's plate. She raised her eyebrows, looked perplexed. 'No, but don't get a complex about it. I forget people all the time.' After studying his face for a couple of seconds, she said doubtfully, 'Did we . . . ah . . . have sex?'

'No. No!' Sammy felt his cheeks redden.

'Phew. Well that's a relief.' She shot him a dazzling smile. 'I mean, no offence, but I usually go for guys who are a bit more . . . you know . . .'

He nodded. 'I do know. And who could blame you?' She was stunning and he was nothing if not realistic; how could he take offence? 'You saw me playing at a festival in Brighton three months ago. You thought I was amazing.'

'Did I? Are you sure it was me?'

'Definitely. I couldn't forget a face like yours. You told me

190

your boyfriend was a music producer,' Sammy reminded her. 'I gave you one of my publicity flyers to give to him. Then some guy threw up on your shoe and you had to use the flyer to wipe it off.'

'Actually, that does ring a bell, now you mention it.'

'Then you and your friends all flashed your boobs at me,' Sammy prompted.

'OK, that definitely sounds like us.'

'I can't believe you're here. Who *are* you?' More importantly, was her boyfriend who she'd said he was?

'I am . . . ready for another drink.' Abandoning her empty wine bottle, she grabbed a glass from the tray of a passing wait-ress and tapped it against Sammy's. 'Cheers. And my name's Fia. My mum used to know the old guy who lives in this place and she dragged us down here with her. That's my brother over there, talking to the flat-chested girl in the red dress.'

Sammy made the second connection. The brother was Tom, who had captured Lou's attention in Val's Café a couple of weeks ago. Their mother was Della Lucas, the glamorous woman who'd been on the telly years ago; he'd already glimpsed her earlier, in the crowded drawing room, standing next to Edgar but directing her attention at Steve Crane, owner of a local haulage company and flashy watch-wearer extraordinaire.

'She really should get a boob job,' Fia went on. 'I could give her the name of my surgeon if she doesn't know anyone. He's great.'

Which meant Sammy was now forced to avert his gaze from anywhere in the vicinity of Fia's frontage. 'I don't think Lou wants them bigger. Anyway, it'd cost more than she could afford.'

'Oh, come on, it's only a few grand, and who wouldn't want gorgeous ones like mine?'

Still not looking *there*, he changed the subject. 'Can you really not remember me from Brighton? You thought my music was brilliant.'

'I'm sure it was. It's just my memory that's crap.'

He cleared his throat and began to sing in an undertone, 'You're an angel, my angel, my long-lost angel in the snow . . .'

Fia continued to look blank. Sensing that he was on the verge of losing her, he blurted out, 'Wait here, don't move, I'll be back in one minute.'

Because sometimes the universe gave you another chance and only a complete nincompoop would risk losing out again.

He raced out of the house and down the driveway to where his van was parked on the verge further along the lane. Edgar hadn't seemed enthusiastic about him playing his guitar at tonight's party, but he'd brought it along just in case. The lock on the back of the van had iced up and he had to huff hot breath on it before the key would go in. Then he almost slipped and went flying on the gravel as he ran back to the house. He hadn't dared yet ask Fia who her boyfriend was, but as she and her friends had been clattering off after the event in Brighton, he'd been almost certain he'd overheard her mention the name Shiv.

And let's face it, there was only one well-known music producer with that name. If it was Shiv Baines, who in their right mind wouldn't do whatever it took to get noticed?

Letting himself back into the house, he searched the crowded hallway – no sign of her – then made his way through to the drawing room. There she was, knocking back shots with several boisterous members of the local rugby team. Squeezing past other guests, he strummed the opening chords and began to sing 'Angel in the Snow', prompting a few howls of protest from the rugby players. But he carried on regardless and gave the song his all. And this time Fia paid attention. She nodded and waved her arms, and even sang along with the last line of the chorus. Then she clapped and exclaimed, 'I *do* remember it. You're good!'

Good was OK, but incredible or a genius would have been better. Mentally crossing his fingers, Sammy blurted out, 'If I give you another of my flyers, could you pass it on to your boyfriend? Or even better, maybe you could arrange for me to meet him.'

Nothing ventured, nothing gained.

Fia looked bemused. 'If you want. But he probably wouldn't want to hear you sing. He hates music.'

'He's a music producer.' Sammy blinked. 'He can't hate music.'

'Oh, I'm with you now. My boyfriend's a sculptor. I *used* to go out with Shiv Baines,' she explained. 'But we broke up.'

And there it was, the story of his life. So near yet so far. 'Right,' said Sammy.

'He's not the settling-down kind,' Fia went on.

He'd heard as much. Every time he saw a photo of Shiv Baines in the paper, he seemed to have a different girl on his arm. 'Oh well. Never mind.'

'Throws great parties, mind you. I can't wait for his New Year's Eve bash at the Duquesa Club.'

'Are you going? Even though you aren't together any more?'

'Of course I am. It's going to be a blast. Shiv knows everyone.' Fia stopped and eyed him with curiosity. 'You know, you have a really interesting face. You aren't good-looking, but you do look kind of cute. And I really do like that song of yours, it's still in my head now.' She paused again, then said, 'I've just thought of something. If you do want to meet him, you should come to the party.'

'Yeah, right.' Sammy gave a snort of laughter, because this was completely ridiculous.

'No worries, it's OK if you don't want to.' Fia shrugged. 'You're probably busy doing something else anyway. I just thought if you did fancy it, you could come along as my guest.'

Chapter 25

Lou was dancing with Tom and feeling happy and desirable when his sister came up and tapped him on the shoulder.

'I've made a terrible mistake,' Fia declared. 'Someone has to help me.'

Lou winced, because an hour ago Sammy had been beside himself with joy, telling her all about Fia's invitation. Surely she wasn't regretting it and looking for an excuse to backtrack and get out of taking him along with her to Shiv Baines's party on New Year's Eve.

'What's new?' Tom turned back to Lou. 'This is the girl who could win Olympic gold in making terrible mistakes.'

'It's this outfit, it's killing me. I know the sequins are on the outside, but they're attached to netting that's scratching me all over, and every time I move it's like being attacked by a million wasps. I can't bear the feel of it a minute longer . . . Look what it's *doing* to me!' Fia grimaced and unzipped the front a few inches to reveal the reddened skin beneath.

'Come upstairs with me,' Lou told her. 'I'll find you something to change into.'

Tom grinned. 'You mean that was all I had to do to get

invited up to your bedroom? Complain about my sequins hurting me? Because I'm telling you now, my sequins are giving me gyp.'

Upstairs, Lou opened her wardrobe while Fia peeled herself out of the problematic catsuit. 'Phew, that's better. Oh dear, where are the rest of your clothes?'

'This is all of them. I don't have that many.'

'You have hardly *any*. I'd take more than this lot on a week's holiday. Except I probably wouldn't, because they're not the kind of thing you'd want to wear on holiday, are they? Sorry! Am I being rude? I don't mean to be, it just comes out. Let's have a look . . .'

After rummaging through the limited contents of Lou's wardrobe, Fia clambered into a pair of black leggings and a tight black T-shirt, then studied her reflection in the mirror. 'Hmm, not great, but I can't exactly go downstairs naked. Do you have scissors?'

Three minutes later, the T-shirt was sliced to the bone, the sleeves removed, the neck slashed to an asymmetric V and the body reduced from hip length to just below the bottom of Fia's emerald-green bra.

'That's better.' She did a twirl. 'You don't mind that I cut it, do you? How much did it cost?'

It had been Lou's favourite T-shirt, but this was Tom's sister. And it had only cost a couple of pounds in the charity shop.

Plus, Fia was doing Sammy a favour that was priceless.

'No worries, you don't have to pay me. It looks great on you.'

'Thanks. And I wasn't actually offering to pay you. I don't have any cash on me,' said Fia. 'I thought you could have my catsuit instead, as a swap.'

Lou spluttered with laughter. 'Thanks, I've always wanted to know how it feels to be stung by a million wasps.'

Out on the landing, they paused to look down and survey the party in the crowded hall below. Leaning on the balustrade, Lou spotted Sammy and Jess, then Moira from the supermarket, and over there were Remy and Talli chatting to . . .

'What's that noise? Sounds like scratching.' Next to her, Fia straightened. She followed the sound along the landing and began opening the door to Edgar's bedroom.

Lou yelped, 'Don't go in there. He hates people and noise . . .'

Predictably, Fia ignored her. Less predictably, she emerged from the room seconds later with Captain Oates in her arms.

Most startling of all, she was nuzzling Captain Oates's nose – and he was nuzzling hers, apparently delighted to join in.

'My God, who *are* you?' Lou addressed the dog in amazement. 'And what have you done with the real Captain Oates?'

'He's a sweetheart,' Fia exclaimed, still happily nuzzling away.

Lou held out a warning hand. 'Careful, he can get snappy.'

To prove it, Captain Oates turned and bared his teeth at Lou.

'Oh, I *love* him. He won't snap at me.'

Was it weird to feel a spasm of jealousy because the dog clearly preferred Fia? Lou tried not to mind, but it felt so unfair, especially as she was the one who had to go around picking up Captain Oates's many tiny poos.

'He likes you too,' she said, as the dog wagged his tail and – *oh, this is unbelievable* – licked Fia's cheek. 'But he really doesn't like crowds and noise. Edgar said he has to stay up here.'

'I suppose. Isn't he just so gorgeous, though? Let's put you back, baby . . . Ooh, wouldn't you look cute in a fairy costume?'

Snuggling happily against her front, Captain Oates licked her face again and Fia dropped a last kiss on his nose.

Once he'd been returned to his basket in Edgar's room, they headed back downstairs. Fia's change of outfit attracted almost as much attention as the pink sequinned catsuit had done. Eyeing the jagged edges of her micro-top, Sammy asked, 'Did Captain Oates do that to you?'

Wide-eyed, Fia said, 'Why's everyone making out that dog is such a crosspatch? He's an *angel*.'

★

Meeting new men was always fun. Well, it was fun if they were the interesting kind. But it wasn't so easy, Della was finding, when you had Edgar clinging to you like a barnacle the whole time.

OK, not physically clinging, but he'd remained at her side all evening and wasn't giving her any chance to escape. She'd also realised he didn't actually know the names of most of his guests, although they all seemed to know him. Or *of* him, at least. Each time they moved on to a new group of people, he would proudly introduce her as Della, then wait for each of them in turn to tell her their own names. It was the strangest scenario; Eddie had always been an introvert, but social interaction had clearly become even more difficult for him over the years.

She was gracious, though. Friendly towards everyone, especially a couple of men in their sixties who seemed well off and whose eyes had lit up at the sight of her. But it was a relief to know she could leave soon. By eleven she would feign exhaustion and signal to Tom and Fia that it was time they made their escape in the car that was waiting for them outside. Tom was keen to get back tonight because his latest girlfriend was flying in from Italy first thing tomorrow.

Della heaved an inward sigh. Christmas was over and January threatened to be the most depressing month yet. She'd run out of money and didn't know what to do about it. Tom was still urging her to hit Eddie up for a loan, but that was easier said than done, because how could she ever repay it? As far as her son was concerned, why would she even want to worry about repaying it, but she wasn't that much of a bad person.

Well, not yet. It was a slippery slope. As time went by, who was to say her scruples wouldn't trickle away?

'Hi, my name's Belinda,' said a cheerful woman, and Della realised that while she'd been daydreaming, Eddie had found someone else to show her off to. 'I run the newsagent's on the high street.' Enthusiastically the woman shook her hand. 'I'm a big fan of yours, I used to love watching you on TV in that game show when I was a child. I always thought you were so beautiful back then . . . Oh God, sorry, you're still beautiful now!'

Della forced a smile; it was the kind of comment she was used to. If she had a fiver for every time she'd heard something along these lines, well, she wouldn't be having to worry about paying the bills now. But she nodded and said charmingly, 'Thank you so much. It's wonderful to meet you.'

Belinda, visibly delighted, pulled out her phone. 'Wait till I tell my mum I've met you. Is it OK if we have a selfie so I can show her?'

At her side, Della could sense that Eddie was positively bursting with pride. She *wasn't* a bad person, was she? She'd come here this evening out of the goodness of her heart, practically as a favour to him. If only he would offer to lend her enough money to help her out. That would be so much easier than having to ask for it.

But she widened her famous smile, held out her arm so that Belinda-from-the-newsagent's could stand beside her and said brightly, 'Oh my darling, of course you can!'

★

It was almost eleven o'clock and a few of the older locals were starting to drift away. All in all, the evening had been a success.

Moving among the groups of people, collecting up discarded glasses, Lou saw Talli ahead of her, wondering where to put down her empty plate. Hastening over, she said, 'Let me take that for you,' and a second later felt a hand on her elbow.

For a moment she couldn't place the attractive brunette in a grey silk trouser suit. Then the woman laughed and said, 'People never recognise me when I'm out of my scrubs! Hi, how's the arm now, all healing nicely? I hope that husband of yours is doing his share around the house!'

Oh great. Lou felt herself grow hot. Talli was now regarding her with a playful, questioning smile. And how typical that Remy should choose this moment to end his conversation and cross the room towards them.

'My arm's fine,' Lou blurted out, 'thanks so much! So, fancy bumping into you here . . . Do you know Edgar?'

'Not at all! My husband's one of those rowdy rugby players over there. Hi,' she turned to Remy, 'I stitched up your wife's arm last week. I was just telling her to make sure you do your share of the housework while she's recovering from her injury.'

'Wow.' Talli looked amused. 'Did you two secretly get married? I had no idea.'

Lou said to the doctor, 'We're not married,' and wished she couldn't feel herself blushing. It didn't help that Remy was smiling too.

'No? Oh, I'm sorry, I thought you said you were. My mistake. Anyway, I'm glad you're on the mend.' The doctor melted away into the crush.

'Well,' Talli said lightly, 'how could she even think you were a couple? If she makes mistakes like that, I'm not sure I'd trust her in a hospital. She might amputate the wrong limb by mistake.'

★

Slow music was playing and Lou was swaying in Tom's arms ten minutes later when Della waved from across the room to attract her attention. Typical, just as she was enjoying herself.

'There's not many girls who could get to me like you have,' Tom was murmuring into her ear, 'but you've managed it. I haven't been able to stop thinking about you.'

Now he was kissing the side of her neck and it felt incredible. Across the room, Talli and Remy were dancing too. For a moment, while Talli was saying something to him, Lou saw Remy glance over, and their eyes met. Had Talli said something about her? Or was he watching her while not listening to Talli? In the next split second, she imagined that the lips on her neck belonged to Remy and not Tom. For goodness' sake, what was wrong with her? She needed to put a stop to these fantasies, and everyone knew the best way to do that.

'You don't have to go back tonight,' she said in a low voice. 'You could always stay.'

Tom stroked her cheek with an index finger. 'You're killing me. I'd love to, but I can't. I have a breakfast meeting at the Wolseley first thing, and it could be a life-changer.' Releasing his hold on her, he turned as Della reached them. 'Mum. Everything OK?'

'I'm shattered, darling. Completely exhausted. It's been lovely, but now we need to leave.' Della glanced once more around the room. 'Except I can't find Fia anywhere. She's done one of her disappearing acts. Have you seen her?'

'Not for a while. She might be outside,' said Tom.

'But it's icy out there.'

'I have an idea where she might be,' said Lou. 'Let me go and look.'

Fia wasn't in Edgar's room. Then again, neither was Captain Oates. Making her way along the landing, Lou opened each

200

door in turn before finally reaching the yellow bedroom, the one that had been so painstakingly prepared for Della.

Fia was fast asleep in the centre of the bed, curled up on her side with Captain Oates clutched to her chest. As Lou leaned over to give her shoulder a gentle shake, Captain Oates opened one eye and bared his pointy teeth at her in a half-hearted fashion.

Fia mumbled, 'Go away.'

'Your mum's waiting for you. They're about to leave.'

'Fine, let them.'

'But you can't stay.' Lou gave her another shake. 'You need to get home.'

'Grrrrrrr,' said Captain Oates, wriggling closer into the crook of Fia's arm.

'Leave me alone.' Fia's eyes remained closed. 'Or I'll call the police.'

Back downstairs, Lou said, 'She's asleep. I couldn't get her to move.'

'Oh, that girl.' Della sighed. 'Once she's like that, a herd of elephants couldn't drag her out of bed. Right, we'll leave her here. She'll just have to find her own way home tomorrow. Come along, darling, let's make a move . . . Oh, here comes Eddie. I suppose we'd better say goodbye.'

Outside, Lou and Tom loitered in the doorway while the driver warmed up the limo and Edgar took the opportunity to show Della his new car.

'It's a Bentley,' he said with pride.

'That friend of yours I was chatting to earlier, Steve Crane, he was telling me he has one of those, too. A silver one.'

Lou watched as Edgar, who evidently had no idea who Steve Crane was, said, 'Mine's better. Look at it, immaculate paintwork. And it's only done six thousand miles.'

'Well, it's an improvement on the Mini.' With a dramatic shiver, Della hugged the collar of her coat around her neck. 'I'm cold. And tired. Tom, are you ready? We need to go.'

'I wish I didn't have to leave.' Tom kissed Lou, then shook his head regretfully and stroked her cheek. 'But I must. See you again soon, I hope.'

He was lovely. And a good kisser. They both watched as Della gave Edgar a quick hug and a fleeting air-kiss a couple of inches from each cheek. Lou said, 'I hope so too.'

Chapter 26

The morning after Edgar's party, Sammy had been up early to collect a consignment of parcels from the depot and deliver them all before midday. Now, arriving back in Foxwell, he stopped off at Val's café to pick up a couple of hot chicken pies, one for himself and one for Jess, who was working too.

When he reached the antiques shop, he heard Fia Lloyd's voice before he saw her.

'I'm in love. That's it, completely in love! I *have* to have it.'

The door swung shut behind him and Sammy saw she was sitting on a incredibly ornate throne chair upholstered in peacock-green velvet, its wooden frame finished in fuchsia-pink matte paint that was in turn decorated with splashes of gold leaf.

It wasn't an antique, nor was it subtle in any way whatsoever, but Sammy knew that Jess's uncle had picked it up as part of a job lot a month ago and had been desperate to sell it ever since. Everyone who walked into the shop immediately sat in the chair for a joke, but so far no one had wanted to buy it.

'Hi.' Fia waved when she spotted Sammy. 'Fancy seeing you here. Don't you think I need to buy this amazing chair? It's so me it's not true!'

'It really is. And I definitely think you should buy it.' This would earn him brownie points with Harry.

She was sniffing the air. 'And what have you got there? It smells like heaven. Can I have some?'

'Chicken pies. I bought one for Jess and one for me.' Torn, Sammy glanced across at Jess, who was applying beeswax polish to an armoire; he'd been up for six hours and his stomach was rumbling. On the other hand, this was Fia Lloyd. On the *other* other hand, did she even remember what she'd said to him last night?

'Here you go.' He handed over one of the bags containing a wrapped-up chicken pie. 'How are you feeling today? Lou said you crashed out in one of the bedrooms last night.'

'I had tons to drink. Luckily,' Fia went on gaily, 'I don't get hangovers. You know, I reckon I could pimp this up and sell it for a profit.' Lovingly she stroked the ornate carved arms of the chair.

'I'd say it's been pretty pimped up already,' said Sammy.

'Eurgh, I can't pay that much.' Fia examined the price tag and frowned.

'I'll knock off two hundred,' Jess said promptly. 'Seeing as it's you.'

'Deal.' Fia clapped her hands, then said, 'So long as you deliver it to our place in London.'

Jess shook her head. 'Sorry, I can't do that.'

Thinking fast, Sammy said, 'How are you getting home?'

'Oh, who knows? I suppose I'll have to catch the train.' Fia was wearing borrowed wellies and last night's jagged black top and leggings with one of Edgar's many grey cashmere cardigans slung over the top.

'It'll cost a fair amount to get the chair sent up. If you want, I could drive you back and take the chair. In my van.'

'Deal,' Fia said triumphantly as, behind her, Jess raised her eyebrows at Sammy.

Sammy said, 'Hey, what are friends for? Seeing as you promised to take me along with you to Shiv Baines's New Year's Eve party, I'd say it's the least I can do.'

He held his breath and watched as Fia did a slow blink, belatedly recalling their conversation last night. He saw the words sink in as she weighed up the deal they'd just struck. Finally she looked at the brown paper bag in her hand, then back at Sammy and said, 'Sure. No problem.'

Jess said, 'So you're buying the chair? That's great. And how would you like to pay, cash or card?'

'Um, card.' Fia opened her purse and took out three credit cards. Everyone then held their breath as Jess brought over the card machine. The first two were declined. Luckily the third one worked.

Once the chair had been loaded into the back of Sammy's van, Fia swallowed the last mouthful of chicken pie and wiped her hands on the sides of her black leggings. She looked at Sammy. 'There, all sorted. Can we go now?'

Once she was installed in the passenger seat, Sammy said a quick goodbye to Jess. 'At least you've got rid of the chair. Harry'll be pleased.'

'I just hope she keeps her promise.' Her tone was dubious.

'I'll stay up there, sleep in the van, then drive back on New Year's Day. Is that OK with you?' He willed her to understand; this was something he had to do, it felt like a chance he couldn't pass up.

Jess wrapped her arms around him. 'I just hope it works out. I'm going to miss you.'

'I'll miss you too. But it'll be worth it. Happy new year.'

Winding down the passenger window, Fia called out, 'Sammy?

I'm still starving. If your girlfriend doesn't want the other pie, can I have it?'

'Sorry.' Jess half smiled. 'I'm hungry, too. You can take my boyfriend, but there's no way you're taking my chicken pie.'

★

Walton House felt empty. Edgar felt empty. He didn't miss the inhabitants of Foxwell, who had turned up in their droves to take a look around his home, eat free food and drink free drink, but he was missing Della more than ever. It was like a hunger, an almost primal need to see her again.

And he did, briefly, when a video call came through for Lou from Sammy and Fia, in the flat in Frobisher Square.

'Hiya, just to let you know we're here,' trilled Della's excitable daughter. 'And we managed to get the chair upstairs. Is Captain Oates there? Can I say hello?'

Video-calling was out of Edgar's comfort zone, but Lou turned the phone in front of him and he held up the dog so Fia could see him on the screen.

'There you are! Hello, boo-boo, I miss you!' Fia waved and blew kisses, and Captain Oates, with a whimper of adoring recognition, wagged his tail. 'Oh look, he's so happy to see me . . . Eddie, if you ever decide you don't want him any more, I'll have him.'

The cheek of the girl. Edgar peered more closely at the screen. 'What are you wearing? Is that my cardigan?'

Fia beamed, evidently without shame. 'Yes, well spotted! I was so cold I had to grab something to wear.'

'You could have borrowed something from Lou.'

'I know, but she didn't have anything nice. This is cashmere, it's so cosy. And Mum said you wouldn't mind, didn't you, Mum?'

Edgar held his breath, then there she was, appearing in the

background wearing a peach satin kimono and nodding in agreement as she sipped a cup of tea. 'I did! I knew you wouldn't want her to be cold. You aren't cross, are you, Eddie?'

'Of course I'm not cross. It's fine.' Well, what else could he say?

Lou, peering at the screen, said hopefully, 'Is Tom there too?'

Fia shook her head. 'No, he had to meet a friend. Anyway, just wanted to check in and say hi to Captain Oates, make sure he hadn't forgotten me. We're off out now. Sammy wants to buy a new shirt for tomorrow night.'

From the look on Lou's face, Edgar gathered that Sammy buying anything new was a rare occurrence.

Lou said, 'That's great. So he's definitely invited to your ex's party tomorrow night?'

'Of course he is. I said I'd take him, didn't I?' Fia gave Sammy, at her side, a friendly punch on the arm. 'I wouldn't let him down!'

Three hours later, Lou served Edgar a bowl of home-made soup then headed upstairs for a shower. Sitting at the kitchen table, he tasted the chicken and vegetable soup and gave a brief nod of approval, because it was very good indeed. Not that he'd admit as much to Lou, but persuading her to come and live here had worked out better than he'd ever imagined. She was a cheerful person and a great cook. She was also a hard worker and barely annoyed him at all.

A *ting* caused him to put down his spoon and glance over at the phone she'd left on the table while she took a shower. The screen lit up with the name Heather, whom Edgar knew was the woman with MS who had been her previous employer.

What was she saying to her? He didn't make a habit of reading other people's messages. It was only the thought that this Heather person could be trying to lure Lou back to her that prompted him to lean sideways, give the phone an accidental tap with his forefinger and take a look at the screen. If she noticed, he would tell her Captain Oates was the one to blame.

There was a long chain of messages. Edgar didn't scroll through them in case Lou would be able to tell he'd done so – he definitely couldn't blame the dog for that – but he studied those that were visible.

Lou had written: *No, I'll go down to the Bear tomorrow evening. It'll be packed, but good fun.*

Heather had responded: *Will Edgar be OK on his own?*

Lou:
He'll be fine. He wouldn't enjoy the pub.

Heather:
Well, let's hope he has a nice evening.

Lou:
I hope he dies.

Edgar froze. That was what Lou had sent to the dear friend and ex-employer with whom she'd always got along so well. And the reason the screen had lit up just now was because Heather had replied:

Hahaha, you might want to delete that! Followed by a string of those yellow laughing faces.

Edgar felt as if he'd turned to stone; the shock was sudden, unexpected and so brutal it felt like a punch in the chest. Then logic asserted itself. He'd been taken in by the girl's sunny demeanour, but all this time it had been nothing more than an act. She was polite to his face because she was employed by him. But it didn't mean she liked him, and why would she?

He'd needed to resort to bribery to get her to agree to come here in the first place. Beneath the smiley, cheerful surface and all those comments about money not being important, of course she despised him and couldn't wait for him to die.

It made sense, but it was still chilling to discover the kind of things she was saying about him behind his back.

Not until Captain Oates jumped up onto his lap and licked his face did Edgar realise his cheek was already wet. He couldn't remember the last time he'd shed a tear.

The joy of seeing Della again last night had disappeared along with Della herself. The sensation of being the perpetual outsider was back. And it hurt – it physically *hurt* – to know how Lou felt about him.

Should he say something to her? Let her know he knew?

No, he wouldn't. That would just be even more humiliating.

'You and me, boy.' His voice cracked with emotion as he stroked the little dog's ears, because the one thing he could be sure of was that Captain Oates's love for him was unfaltering.

He pushed back his chair and rose to his feet. The screen of Lou's phone had turned black once more, her cruel words no longer visible.

'Come on, lad, let's go out for a walk,' said Edgar. 'Before it gets dark.'

At least Captain Oates would never let him down.

★

The following afternoon, as the rest of the world was preparing to celebrate the end of the current year and the start of a new one, Edgar's name appeared on Della's phone for the second time.

Oh God, not again.

But a truly terrible festive film had just finished on TV and she was lying stretched out across the sofa with nothing better to do, so this time she answered it.

'Hello, it's me. Eddie. I just wanted to wish you a happy new year.'

Della sighed and said, 'Thank you.' Since losing her husband, the celebrations had lost their allure. 'And to you, too.'

'So. Off somewhere glamorous tonight, are you?'

'No, I was invited to go out with a group of girlfriends, but I'm not going.'

'Why not?'

Della tilted her head and looked over at the pile of post on the coffee table; of all the days, how cruel was it that three different bills should have arrived this morning? If she went out with her wealthy divorcee friends, they would be buying bottles of champagne all night long and she'd be forced to take her turn.

'Hello?' said Edgar. 'Are you still there?'

She remembered Tom's words to her about tapping Eddie for a loan to help her through the next few months.

'I'm still here. Oh Eddie, you want the honest truth? I can't afford to go out. I can't afford to go anywhere or do anything, and I certainly can't pay my rent. My life is just . . . You couldn't begin to understand what a mess I'm in . . .' Tears burned her eyes and she took a shuddery breath. 'I didn't want you to know. I'm so ashamed. But since Barry died, things haven't been easy.'

'I'm so sorry to hear that.' He sounded taken aback.

'And the bills keep c-coming in,' Della hiccuped. 'It ought to be against the law to send them on New Year's Eve. I haven't stopped crying all day. I feel like such a failure.'

'Look, let me have a think . . .'

Della crossed the fingers of her free hand and silently willed him to do the right thing. It hadn't even been a lie; she'd shed tears of despair when she'd opened the bills, and it had happened again during the sad part of the ridiculously schmaltzy film. Her voice wobbled as she said, 'I just don't know what I can *do* . . .'

'I don't like to think of you on your own,' said Edgar. 'Why don't I see if I can hire a car to bring you down here tonight? We could see in the new year together.'

Della closed her eyes in frustration. No, she couldn't face it. Why couldn't he just take the hint, ask for her bank details and dump a huge amount of money into her account? Was that really too much to ask?

'It's so kind of you to offer.' She did the tragic-but-brave wobbly thing with her voice again. 'But I wouldn't be good company. I'm just going to stay here on my own tonight, while I still have a home to stay in. Anyway, happy new year to you, Eddie. And give Captain Oates a kiss from me.'

Chapter 27

It was a while since he'd last driven such a distance, but there was no reason why it couldn't be done. He had his new car, which was far more comfortable than the old Mini. He'd learned how to programme the sat nav. And he also had a plan.

Not to mention a grudge to settle and spur him on.

Edgar left Foxwell at 4.30. According to the navigation system he had eighty-five miles to drive and would reach Frobisher Square at 7.22. He was wearing his smart white shirt and charcoal-grey suit, and the aftershave Della had always liked. In addition, his spirits were high because the new year now promised to be better than expected.

It was almost eight o'clock by the time he'd found a parking space on the square and parked the Bentley. Having made his way to number 127, he pressed the intercom and was greeted by a female voice yelling, 'OK, wait there, on my way!'

Then he heard a clatter of high heels and the door was yanked open. Della's daughter, Fia, did a double-take.

'Oh, I thought you were Sammy.'

'Well, I'm not,' said Edgar.

'I can see that now.'

Then a male voice behind him said, 'I'm here,' and Edgar turned to see the scruffy red-headed Keeler brother emerging from his even scruffier blue van.

'Mum,' Fia bellowed up the stairs, 'you've got a visitor! Sending him up now!'

Fia and the Keeler boy disappeared down the road. Thankfully there was a small lift installed in the hallway opposite the staircase, otherwise it might have taken Edgar until midnight to reach the third floor.

Then the door to the flat opened and there stood Della, her mouth falling open in shock at the sight of him. 'Eddie, what are you *doing* here?'

She was wearing the same peach-coloured dressing gown as yesterday and no make-up. Her streaky brown and blonde hair hung loose around her shoulders and she looked pale but still beautiful.

She would always be beautiful to him.

He said, 'I had to come and see you. I want to help.'

'Oh Eddie . . .'

'I love you.'

'You don't.'

'I do. I always have.'

Della paused, her hands thrust into the pockets of her dressing gown. Finally she said, 'Eddie. You're a good man. But I don't love you.'

'I know.' He nodded. 'I know that.'

'I'm sorry.'

'I still want to help you, though.'

'Do you? Do you really? Oh Eddie!' Della promptly burst into tears. 'You have no idea how grateful I am. Just knowing we won't be kicked out of here would mean the world to me

. . . well, to all of us! Thank you, thank you so much . . . Oh, come here, you're a *lifesaver*.'

She wrapped her arms around him and, still sobbing, gave him a huge hug. Eddie hugged her in return, but he knew he mustn't kiss her. 'You don't have to worry about being kicked out of this place. I want you to come and live with me in Foxwell.'

Della's arms dropped and she took a step back. 'What?'

'You can stay as long as you want. I won't charge any rent. It won't cost you a penny.'

The tears of relief had stopped, he noticed, as abruptly as a tap being turned off. The outburst of emotion had been down to her assumption that he would be giving her enough money to sort out her life.

'Eddie, it's so kind of you to offer, but I don't know that living out of London would suit me terribly well.'

He looked at her. It wasn't the answer he'd wanted to hear, but he'd half expected he might.

Luckily, he still had his Plan B.

'To be clear,' he continued, 'I wouldn't expect anything in return. Nothing . . . romantic, if that's what's bothering you. Just friendship.'

'I still don't think I could do it.' Della tightened the belt of her dressing gown. 'I mean, there's my career to consider. I need to be . . . available.'

There was no career to speak of and they both knew that. It was just an excuse.

Outside, a firework exploded into the night sky, followed by a stream of crackerjack-style explosions like gunfire.

The words on Lou's phone screen yesterday flashed through Edgar's mind.

I hope he dies.

Followed by her friend's laughter and the reply:

214

You might want to delete that!

Oh yes, he was used to feeling alone and unwanted. God knows, over the years he'd had enough practice.

'Come and live with me on a friends-only basis,' he said evenly. 'And when I die, you'll inherit everything. Walton House will be all yours.'

★

The Duquesa Club in Mayfair was somewhere Sammy had heard of, of course he had, but he'd never imagined one day being invited here. Well, kind of invited. By proxy.

It was huge inside, designed by the duquesa who'd bought the building and transformed it into a nightclub a decade ago. Trying to look cool and not gawp like an overawed tourist, Sammy took in the crimson lacquered walls, the turquoise pillars and gold ceiling, and the emerald pool in the centre of the club. The mood lighting beneath the surface of the water shimmered and danced, and the background music was all from Shiv Baines's stable of stars.

He still couldn't believe he was here. When he and Fia had driven up to London yesterday, he'd hoped she'd offer to put him up for the night. But as soon as the throne chair had been installed in the hallway of the flat, she had said carelessly, 'That's great, thanks. So I'll see you tomorrow, yeah? When you get to the Duquesa, just tell the guys on the door that I said you could come in.'

Whoa, no chance. Sammy had replied firmly, 'But they might not believe me. Tell you what, I'll pick you up from here tomorrow and we'll go to the club together.'

'You mean you don't trust me?'

'Of course I do. It's other people I don't trust. Especially night-club bouncers. You have no idea how important this is to me.'

215

She had laughed and thankfully not taken offence. 'Fair enough. Pick me up at eight. I promise I'll be ready.'

He'd managed to contact a mate in Enfield and spent the night on his sofa. Then, just to be on the safe side, he'd driven back to Frobisher Square in the afternoon and waited in the van until eight o'clock.

And now here they were, inside the club. So far everything was going according to the plan he'd been thinking about non-stop since yesterday morning. In his shirt pocket was the USB stick containing his ten best songs. Terrified of inadvertently saying the wrong thing, he wasn't even taking advantage of the free drinks and was determined to stick to water all evening. Well, unless his ultimate fantasy came true, in which Shiv Baines took the USB stick, plugged it into the club's sound system and after listening to the first couple of tracks pronounced him a magnificent genius and announced to everyone in the club that he was going to sign him on the spot.

In the fantasy, everyone then leapt to their feet, whooping and applauding, and Shiv Baines ordered magnums of champagne to be opened so they could all raise a toast to the greatest new discovery since Adele.

If that happened, Sammy told himself, he'd have a drink.

He hung back for now, watching from the sidelines as Fia greeted people she knew. The guests were glamorous and there were plenty of recognisable faces: several models and actresses, a TV chef, a Formula 1 racing driver and more footballers than you could shake a stick at, as well as loads of people in the music business. There was a lot of posing going on and photos being taken. The only person missing was the host himself.

Which was slightly panic-inducing, but apparently Shiv invariably turned up late to his own parties. With any luck he'd be here soon.

In the meantime, as Fia shimmied around the dance floor with her friends, Sammy was content to sip his water while leaning against a wall, half taking in the scene and half conjuring up more imaginary scenarios. There was that girl from the latest MTV series over there, Amy Klein . . . maybe once she'd heard his music and seen him being lauded by Shiv Baines, she'd introduce herself and start flirting shamelessly. But despite the fact that she was gorgeous and *very* keen, Sammy fantasised, he would let her down gently and explain that he was sorry, he already had a girlfriend . . .

'Oh my God, it's *freezing*,' shrieked one of the glamorous women, dipping a toe into the pool and hastily snatching it out again.

'Drink?' offered a pretty waitress, carrying a tray over to Sammy.

'No thanks, I'm fine.' The nerves were kicking in now; a double whisky would help him no end, but he wasn't going to risk anything going wrong. Nodding over at the pool, where the woman was still hopping around in over-acted shock, he said, 'Is the water really that cold?'

The waitress nodded. 'They keep it at two degrees to stop people jumping in for a laugh.'

'It would stop me.' He grinned at her.

'Every so often they chuck another bucket of ice cubes in there, because they look pretty bobbing around on the surface,' she explained. 'It's so cold in there, they take for ever to melt. Are you signed to Shiv Baines?'

'No.' *Not yet.*

'Are you famous?'

'Sadly not. But I am a musician.' His tone rueful, he added, 'Not a successful one, though.'

'Ditto. Which is why I'm waitressing in this place. Hey, we have to look on the bright side, don't we?' As she prepared to move away with her tray of drinks, the girl said, 'We need to tell ourselves we have the talent, we're just still waiting for our big break.'

217

Chapter 28

The Bear was bursting at the seams, people were drinking and singing uproariously along with the band hired for the night to play crowd-pleasers, and Remy was discovering just how easy it was for one person to ruin what would otherwise have been a great night.

'I can't get over it, bumping into you like this – oh my God, how *are* you?'

That was how, an hour earlier, Holly Merton had greeted him. The last time he'd seen her had been fifteen years ago, when they'd been in the same year at school. Tonight, turning up out of the blue along with her older sister, she'd hailed him with amazement and delight, then caught him up with a blow-by-blow account of everything – husband, divorce, another husband who'd done a bunk – that had been going on in her life since they'd last met.

She had also drunk several rum and Cokes, becoming more garrulous as each new drink arrived. Now it was 10.30 and Remy still hadn't been able to get away from her.

'OK, shall I let you into a secret? I'm going to tell you the truth.' Nodding to emphasise just how secretive she was being,

Holly stage-whispered, 'When my sister was waitressing up at the big house here the other night, she heard someone ask what you'd be doing on New Year's Eve. And you said you'd be coming here.' Her gaze was adoring. 'And I've always fancied you, so I thought, why don't I turn up and see how things go, know what I mean?'

Remy could hazard a guess. He frowned slightly. 'But didn't your sister mention that I was at that party with my girlfriend?'

'Yes, she did, but your girlfriend said she wouldn't be here, she was driving up to see relatives in Yorkshire. So I thought this could be my chance and I'd be mad not to take it. So I did, and here I am, and here *you* are . . .'

'Sorry,' Remy interrupted when she paused for breath, 'there's someone over there I need to speak to.' The door to the pub had just swung open and he'd never been so glad to see anyone in his life. There in the doorway stood Lou, bright-eyed and wrapped up against the cold, casting her gaze around the bar.

'Who is it? Oh, is that thingummy whose mum died? I remember her! Wasn't she friends with your brother?'

'She still is, and I need to speak to her urgently . . . Excuse me.' Disentangling his arm from Holly's grasp, Remy made his way through the crush to Lou. 'Hi, good to see you. At the risk of sounding fifteen years old, could we look as if we're having a private discussion that mustn't be interrupted?'

'It'll cost you a drink.' She hung up her coat. 'Who are you trying to avoid?'

'Over by the fireplace, blue top, white skirt.'

Lou peered across the room. 'Wasn't she in your year at school?'

He nodded. 'I haven't been able to escape. She's a bit . . . over-keen.'

'I'd have thought you'd be great at fending off eager women.'

'Not this one, apparently. OK, she's still watching us. We have to keep talking.' Gazing intently at Lou, he said, 'So, it's almost eleven. Why so late?'

'I'd planned to be here earlier, but Edgar did a bunk this afternoon. He drove off in his new car and I had no idea where he was. He finally answered his phone, and it turns out he's in London with Della.' She shrugged. 'Goodness knows what's going on. But he'd left Captain Oates behind, and I couldn't go out and abandon the poor creature. So I'm just here for a quick drink, and he's waiting for me out in the car.'

'Oh God, she's coming over.' Remy exhaled in disbelief.

Holly appeared in front of them. The look she gave Lou was suspicious. 'You know he's got a girlfriend, don't you?'

'I do know that.' Lou nodded politely. 'Her name's Talli.'

'OK, but you can't keep him to yourself all evening. I've come a long way to see him again, so it's only fair to share him. Come on,' Holly urged, gazing up at Remy adoringly, 'let's have a dance, shall we? I've been looking forward to this all day!'

In her jeans pocket, Lou's phone went *trrrrinnggg* and she reached for it.

'Text from Sammy,' she told Remy. 'Apparently the party's amazing, Shiv Baines has just turned up and Fia's going to introduce him any minute now. He says this is the best night of his life.'

'Play your cards right and this could be the best night of *your* life!' Reaching for Remy's arm, Holly cried, 'Ooh, I love this song. Come on, dance with me . . . woo-hoo, let's have some fun . . .!'

Remy removed her hand from his sleeve and pointed behind her. 'Actually, let's not. I'm busy and I think your sister wants to see you.' Swiftly he steered Lou through the pub and out into the garden, where a marquee was set up alongside the barbecue. Once armed with food and drinks, they settled down with friends at a table, but before long, Holly came teetering out and spotted them.

'There you are,' she said, her eyes shiny with tears. 'Are you trying to hide from me? My sister says I'm making a show of myself, but I didn't mean to. I haven't had a proper night out for months and this one isn't going the way I wanted it to go.' Sitting down on a bench, she proceeded to gaze forlornly at Remy from a distance, intermittently wiping her eyes like a teary chaperone.

Talk about awkward. And uncomfortable. From the corner of his eye he could see she was still watching him. Remy wondered what he'd done to deserve this. He was glad Sammy was having the best night of his life up in London, because thanks to Holly, this was in danger of turning into one of his worst.

'OK, I'm calling it a night.' He rose to his feet, shaking his head in resignation. 'I think it's best. Enjoy the rest of your evening, everyone. Happy new year.'

Minutes later, when Lou emerged out of the darkness, he said, 'You don't have to leave too.' But somehow he'd known – or hoped – she would appear. It was why he'd waited out here in the car park, next to her car.

'She's still out there. Dancing on her own now. Her sister came out and told us she gets like this, kind of fixated on men, and tonight was your unlucky night. Hello, you!' Lou tapped the car window and wiggled her fingers at Captain Oates, who glared back at her like a furious Gremlin. 'It's OK, we're going home now. We'll sit outside and wait for the fireworks, shall we?'

The dog eyed her balefully.

Remy took a deep breath. 'You don't have to head home right away. I'm going back to the cottage. If you like, the two of you could stay for a bit and watch the fireworks with me.'

He saw Lou hesitate, then she nodded. 'That'd be good. It's always better seeing them with other people.'

This was true. But also, what was he doing?

Except he knew, didn't he?

Of course he did. Not that the plan was to actually *do* anything. But the thoughts were all there, clamouring for attention in his head.

Remy knew his feelings for Talli were on the slide; they had been for weeks now. She hadn't done anything wrong – it would be so much easier if she had – but the sensation was familiar enough by now. It was like carrying around a bag full of sand with the tiniest hole in the bottom. Every day, so stealthily as to be almost unnoticeable, a fine trickle of grains was escaping from the bag.

He'd hoped this time would be different, because who in their right mind wouldn't want to be with someone like Talli? But that explosion of initial attraction hadn't lasted. It never did.

Instead, something was happening to him that had never happened before. For the first time in his life he was experiencing a slow-burn connection instead. As a teenager, he had only vaguely been aware of Lou. She'd been a friend of Sammy's, two years younger than himself, and back then he simply hadn't considered any kind of relationship with that much of an age gap. Then he'd moved away, gone to university and begun the next stage of his life, and that had been that.

But then Lou had come back to Foxwell for the first time in years and had caught the attention of Edgar Allsopp. That weekend she'd caught Remy's attention too, when he'd come home and found her – like Goldilocks – fast asleep in his bed.

That had been the start, and it had continued from there. Edgar had been intrigued and interested in her, and he hadn't been the only one. Remy had since given the situation a lot of thought, and he was pretty sure the only connection he'd made with her on that first occasion had been one of platonic friend-ship. He'd liked her, had liked everything about her, but purely in a just-good-friends way. Plus, of course, she was a long-term friend of his brother, and it had occurred to him back then that maybe that friendship might develop and grow into more, which meant he couldn't even think of her as a potential romantic interest for himself. Which was fine; he'd just enjoyed getting to know Lou and learning more about her. Being in her company had been so effortlessly easy from the word go. It had just felt . . . right.

The next stage, the rapidly increasing attraction, had come out of nowhere, a real bolt from the blue, catching him completely by surprise. And it had carried on growing, despite nothing physical happening between them. Nor would it happen so long as he and Talli were still together. But over the course of the last week, Remy had sensed he was reaching a tipping point. His relationship with Talli wasn't destined to last, he knew that now. Which meant he needed to end it.

Then again, who knew if Lou even felt the same way about him? He could be getting it completely wrong, imagining the chemistry between them simply because he so desperately wanted it to be there. Just because he was experiencing this incredible back-to-front attraction didn't mean it was reciprocated, after all. He could be risking making a fool of himself . . . just like poor Holly Merton, back at the pub.

Plus – and this was an even more important reason – Lou's abusive husband had died in front of her sixteen months ago and the degree of trauma involved had clearly been immense. Up until last week, as she'd explained to him while they were painting and talking together, she had steered clear of any involvement with the opposite sex. Emotionally she had been shut down, and even the thought of it had been too hideous to contemplate.

Well, this was all entirely understandable, Remy knew that. The grieving process needed to be gone through at its own pace. Hopefully the brief flirtation with that guy who'd come down from London with his mother meant she was getting over the grief and starting out on the road to recovery. When he had seen the two of them together at the party, he'd taken an instant dislike to Della Lucas's son, who looked pleased with himself and too smooth by half. Clearly they weren't suited and nothing would come of their fledgling relationship.

He sincerely hoped.

Having left the Mini in the pub car park, the three of them made their way down the frosted road to Riverside Cottage. Captain Oates trotted along at Lou's heels in his funny, high-stepping doggy way. The Christmas lights were still up along the high street, the night sky was clear and spangled with stars, and the sounds of music and excited voices were drifting over from the Bear. It was now twenty minutes to midnight, which meant they had plenty of time to open a bottle of wine and bring the garden chairs round to the front of the house, where they'd get a far better view of the fireworks than at the back.

'Isn't it a gorgeous night? Except it's killing me not knowing what's going on with Sammy. Oh!' Stopping dead in her tracks, Lou pulled out her phone once more and fired off a rapid text. 'If it hasn't happened yet, he can get someone to video it for us! Why didn't I think of that before?'

★

In London, Sammy read the text and said, 'It's Lou.'

'Who?'

He'd already worked out that names weren't Fia's forte. 'My

friend, remember? The one who works for Edgar. She says can we record the big moment when I meet Shiv, so she can see it happen?'

'OK, I can do that. Put that antique away.' Fia grimaced at his battered four-year-old phone with the drastically cracked screen. 'We'll use mine.'

'Shall we do it now?' Sammy could feel his heart speeding up. Since Shiv Baines's arrival in the club, the great man had been surrounded by acolytes and there'd been no opportunity to get close. But a few seconds ago, the crowd around him had largely dispersed in order to get a better view of an inebriated reality star who was staggering around the dance floor with an ice bucket on his head. Shiv was now conversing with a middle-aged man in a grey suit; this could be the best chance Sammy was going to get. If all went well, he fantasised, he might still be chatting to Shiv when the clock struck midnight and the new year was rung in . . . they could even end up linking arms and singing 'Auld Lang Syne' together, if such a thing happened among people as cool as this.

'Right,' he said to Fia, awash with adrenalin because it was going to happen at last. 'Get your phone ready. Let's do this.'

His heart pounded as Fia pressed video-record and said with a giggle, 'OK, here we are in the Duquesa, I'm about to introduce Sammy to Shiv, and let me tell you, he's convinced this is going to change his life. Ah, bless him, look at his little face. Come here and let me just try and do something with your hair . . .' She reached out like a fond mum with a five-year-old and brushed his messy fringe off his forehead.

Sammy said nervously, 'Do I look OK?'

'No, but it's too late now. Off we go.' As they moved forward, Fia waved madly with her free hand and called out, 'Hey, Shiv, hi, how *are* you? I've got someone here I want you to meet!'

They were only a couple of metres away when everything seemed to go into slow motion. There was Shiv Baines, deep in conversation in front of the emerald-green pool . . . and there was the drunk reality star losing control of the ice bucket on his head . . . and now ice cubes were skittering in all directions across the shiny dance floor, but that wasn't going to stop Sammy, except, *whoa*, shit, help, aaargh, *noooooo* . . .

His left foot had shot out sideways, knocking him off balance and propelling him forward so he crashed into the back of the man in the suit, who let out a shout of surprise and crashed like a skittle into Shiv Baines. Sammy landed flat on his face on the floor, his nose making brutal contact with the edge of the pool and sending a starburst of pain through his head.

The fact that his eyes were squeezed shut meant he didn't see the crowd's reaction but heard the gasps and cries of alarm, followed by the sound of two hefty splashes as Shiv Baines and Grey Suit both hit the icy water.

Amid the horror of knowing he was responsible for their yells of outrage, Sammy felt himself being roughly lifted up off the floor and into the air by the burly bald security guy who'd spent the evening keeping an eye on Shiv Baines from a discreet distance. His bodyguard, he belatedly realised.

'If you've lost me my job,' the man hissed into his ear, 'you're fucking dead, mate.'

The next moment, still in slow motion and with the sound of the Pogues' 'Fairytale of New York' competing with the shrieks ricocheting around the club, Sammy found himself being hurled into the pool and discovering at first hand just how close to sub-zero the water was.

By this time, the security team had hauled out Shiv Baines and Grey Suit. Mortified, Sammy gazed up from the pool as Shiv – looking confusingly different – glared down at him.

Through violently chattering teeth he said, 'I'm s-s-so s-sorry, it was the ice, I just s-s-slipped and—'

'Get out,' Shiv seethed. 'Get out of here now. I don't know who the hell you are, but I never want to see you again, you . . .' Evidently unable to conjure up an epithet terrible enough, he gestured in disbelief and turned to his minders. 'Just get rid of him.' The next moment, glaring at a group of girls who were giggling at the sight of him, he added, 'And get rid of them too.'

'L-look, it was an accident. I wanted you to listen to my m-m-music.' Searching frantically in his sodden pocket, Sammy pulled out the USB stick and offered it up like Oliver Twist. But it was too late. Shiv Baines had turned on his stacked heels and marched off, disappearing through a door marked *Private*.

'You heard, sunshine. Out you get.' Half a dozen security guards gathered at the edge of the pool indicated that it was time to go. Shivering dramatically, Sammy hauled himself out of the water and in desperation looked over at Fia as he was frogmarched past her in front of everyone in the club.

'Not my fault,' she called out. 'I tried to help you. I didn't know you were going to do *that*.'

As he was hustled to the exit, Sammy saw the drunk reality star who'd dropped the bucket of ice cubes and caused his plan to go so drastically wrong. Shaking his head, the drunk guy said slurrily, 'There he is. What a twat.'

★

The clock on the mantelpiece clicked forward; it was now five minutes to midnight. Della switched on the TV so they could watch the massed crowds gathered in Trafalgar Square and along the banks of the Thames. Two cheerful young commentators were gushing with excitement. Some of the residents of Frobisher

227

Square were outside; she could hear them through the slightly opened windows.

But it was hard to concentrate on anything other than the thoughts still swirling around her head. Since Edgar had made his extraordinary offer, she'd tried calling both Tom and Fia, but neither of them was answering their phone. Eddie had played his hand and was waiting for an answer. And of course it wasn't what she *wanted* to do, but how could she possibly say no? It was a curveball that had come swooping out of nowhere. It would mean a complete change of lifestyle. And it would mean never having to worry about money again.

She'd even furtively googled the average age a man with Eddie's year of birth was likely to reach. Although knowing him, he'd live until he was a hundred and twenty just to spite her.

'Two minutes to midnight,' squealed the female commentator on the TV. 'And the atmosphere out here is electric!'

'Well?' Eddie turned to look at Della. 'Yes or no?'

He'd already explained his plan in great detail. They would visit a solicitor here in London and the will would be drawn up. There was no need for everyone else to know about it; as far as they were concerned, she was coming to stay with him as a friend.

She double-checked. 'And Tom and Fia can come and live there too, if they want?'

'Fine.' He paused. 'So long as they behave themselves.'

Well, that was highly unlikely. But he didn't need to know that. Just imagine, though – it would mean that at some stage she would become the outright owner of a multimillion-pound property in a sought-after corner of the Cotswolds. OK, maybe it sounded a bit mercenary when she thought of it like that . . . but on the other hand, talk about a dream come true.

'We have a deal,' she said, as the countdown to midnight

228

began on the TV, and outside the window the first fireworks jumped the gun, prematurely exploding into the sky.

'Thank you.' Eddie's face registered relief as he clinked his glass against hers.

She smiled at him; thank goodness he'd made it plain that he wasn't expecting anything more than friendship. All he was asking for was the pleasure of her company. She could cope with that.

. . . Bong. Bong. *Bonggg* . . .

'Here's to new beginnings,' said Della. 'Happy new year.'

★

'I think that's her,' said Lou as they heard a voice that sounded like Holly's in the distance screeching along to a Tina Turner track.

'So long as she's over there and not here, I'm happy.' Remy tilted his head to look sideways at her. 'Sure you're warm enough?'

'Completely. This is great.' And it was true; the temperature might be hovering around zero, but she was well wrapped up in her coat and gloves, and after carrying the table and chairs round to the front garden, he'd brought extra blankets as well as a bottle of Veuve Clicquot and two glasses out of the house. There were candles burning in glass tumblers on the table, and the delicious smell of woodsmoke from a nearby fire hung in the cold night air.

Lou gave a secret shiver of delight. Was this what true happiness felt like? She couldn't imagine being anywhere nicer than this right now.

And now it was almost midnight. Remy loosened the wire cage around the neck of the bottle and popped the cork, sending it sailing across the road and landing with a tiny plop in the river on the other side. Bubbles foamed up and Lou held the

229

glasses as he filled them. Then they clinked them together, listening to the noise level increase as everyone over at the Bear spilled into the pub's back garden. The boisterous countdown started at twenty, and Captain Oates growled gently in Lou's lap, clearly offended by such frivolity but not offended enough to poke his face out from beneath the warm blanket covering his head.

'Well, this year's been better than the one before,' said Lou. 'So all I can hope is that next year will be better again.'

'I'm sure it will. Cheers,' said Remy.

She touched her glass to his for a second time. 'And for you and Talli, too.'

He nodded and looked at her, and for a moment she sensed there was something he wanted to say. But it didn't happen. He tilted his head back instead and gazed up at the sky. It must have been something to do with his and Talli's plans for the future. At a guess, this would be the year they got engaged or bought a place together, or even planned to get married . . .

'I can't *believe* he left like that.' Holly's voice rose momentarily above the rest of them in the pub garden. 'We came all this way and I didn't even get a kiss off him.'

Remy laughed briefly, then said, 'Thank God,' with feeling.

Lou was glad of the darkness hiding the colour in her cheeks. If he could read her mind now, he'd discover Holly hadn't been the only one thinking about kissing him. Not that Lou would do it, because he already had Talli. And not that Remy would do it either, obviously. Oh, but there were some things you couldn't help imagining, just wondering how it would feel if it *did* happen.

'Nine,' bellowed the raucous pub crowd, having reached single figures. 'Eight . . . seven . . .'

This was the moment when it struck her that if they'd still been in the pub, the moment the countdown was over everyone

230

would be kissing everyone else and no one would think twice about it. But being here, just the two of them alone together, was going to feel – and look – completely different.

'Six . . . five . . . four . . .'

They were sitting side by side. It would be weird if they exchanged a kiss and weird if they didn't. How had this not crossed her mind before now? Oh God, it was going to be *so* awkward . . .

'Three . . . two . . . one . . . YAAAAAYYY!' The pub crowd broke into ecstatic cheers and the church bells rang out in celebration. They could hear 'Auld Lang Syne' being played and sung with gusto.

'Happy new year,' said Remy, touching his glass to hers once more, and it suddenly occurred to her that he could be thinking the same thing, wondering if she was going to lean over and kiss him, and most probably praying it wouldn't happen, what with her being someone he'd hired to clean and tidy his office.

'Here's to a happy new year. For both of us.' She'd taken off her woollen glove in order to hold her glass without dropping it, and as they re-clinked, the side of her hand brushed against his. The brief moment of contact with his warm skin sent a jolt of adrenalin up her arm, and in that exact moment the first huge chrysanthemum firework detonated overhead, lighting up the sky.

Also in that exact moment, she saw the colours from the firework reflected in Remy's dark eyes and realised he was leaning towards her, his face moving closer as if he'd realised it would be wrong not to exchange the traditional new year's kiss and it was something he was required to do after all. And now Lou's stomach felt like a nest of snakes because it was going to happen – not a proper kiss, of course, just a brief polite peck on the cheek, but it was still the most giddily alive she'd felt in years. And *BOOM-BOOM-BOOM* went the next huge fireworks, emerald and gold, followed by a sky full of squirly silver ones zooming in all directions while emitting high-pitched squeals, followed by another kind of sound far closer, which caused an audible intake of breath from Remy and a sensation of icy wetness on Lou's thigh because her glass of Veuve had tilted sideways and the contents were now soaking into the leg of her jeans.

'Grrrrrr.' An unimpressed Captain Oates made his feelings known as he shifted beneath the blanket.

Remy took out his ringing phone. 'It's Talli. Wanting to FaceTime.'

Of course it was. And of course she'd be wanting to speak to her boyfriend face to face. Flustered, Lou blurted out, 'Should I go?'

'No.' He pressed answer and greeted Talli with a grin. 'Hi, happy new year.'

'Happy new year to you, my darling! Oh wow, I can see fireworks! Are you at the pub? Where's everyone else?'

Pow, POW-POW-POW went the next burst of explosions in the sky. 'No, I'm in the front garden. Had to escape from someone really annoying at the pub.'

'Haha, let me guess, was it—'

'Lou's here, too,' Remy cut in quickly, and Lou felt her cheeks burn. Was *she* the person they had agreed was really annoying? Did that mean they'd been laughing about her behind her back?

But Remy had now angled the phone so Talli could see her and wave. 'Lou, hey there! Have you had a fab evening?'

Oh, the agony of having to look and sound as if you'd done absolutely nothing wrong . . . when you hadn't done anything wrong. Lou beamed and said, 'It's been great. No word yet from Sammy, though.'

'Oh, he'll be having a wild time. *Whoa* . . .' The final triumphant volley of fireworks set the whole sky alight, followed by cheers and applause filtering over from the pub garden. As soon as the noise had subsided, Lou said, 'That's it then, all done. Right, time I was heading home.' She stood up, holding onto Captain Oates, who had treated the firework display with the contempt it deserved by ignoring it completely. 'Bye!'

'Bye,' said Remy, and she suspected he was relieved to see her leave.

On the phone screen, Talli waved cheerfully and called out, 'Happy new year, Lou. See you soon!'

Reaching her car in the car park a couple of minutes later, she saw Jess carrying a crate of clanking empties out of the pub and adding it to the pile in the outhouse.

'Whew, that was a busy night.' Straightening up, Jess rolled her shoulders, then took out her phone. 'Have you heard from Sammy at all? I haven't.'

Lou shook her head. 'Me neither. We were dying to find out how it's going. Maybe he hasn't had a chance to meet Shiv Baines yet.'

'He said he'd definitely call me,' said Jess. She pressed call on her phone, then listened and shook her head. 'Still dead.'

'He'll be fine. He's just run out of battery.' Lou paused. 'You're not worried about him, are you?'

'Oh, it's just me being silly. I'm not the jealous type.' Jess pulled a face. 'Never have been. It's just that he's up there with Fia, and she seems a bit . . . I don't know. I mean, what do you think? If she made a play for Sammy, would he say no?'

'Are you serious? Of course he'd say no! He isn't interested in Fia!'

'But she's stunning.' Jess sounded unconvinced. 'Far more stunning than me.'

'Hey, what did he tell you on Christmas Day? That he loves

233

you. *So much,*' Lou exclaimed. 'And this is Sammy we're talking about. He wouldn't dream of doing that to you. Guaranteed.'

Jess smiled sadly. 'I guess. It's just me being silly. Anyway, better get on with the cleaning up. Where did you and Remy go, back to the cottage?'

'We sat out in the front garden. Watched the fireworks from there.' To make it sound as unromantic as possible, Lou said, 'Talli FaceTimed from Yorkshire.'

'Ah. She's lovely, isn't she?'

'Yes.' The lingering worry that she'd been the annoying person they talked about behind her back was still niggling away.

'And did Tom call to wish you a happy new year?'

He hadn't. Lou shook her head. She'd hoped for a message, even if only a text, but nothing. 'Must be busy, out with his friends.'

'Him and Sammy both. Typical men, eh?'

They exchanged rueful smiles as Rico appeared at the back door. 'There you are,' he exclaimed. 'Still plenty of clearing up to do in here if you're interested.'

'On my way.' Jess rolled her eyes and grinned at Lou. 'Typical men.'

Chapter 29

Sammy had waited outside the club as the new year was rung in, on the off chance that once the singing and celebrating was over, Fia might come out in search of him.

But this hadn't happened. As fireworks continued to explode overhead, the cold intensified and she failed to appear. His phone hadn't survived being immersed in the pool, and passing revellers seemed to find it hilarious that he was so completely soaked to the skin. No taxis would stop for him either; they slowed down, then took one look at the state of him and speeded up again.

He'd never been so chilled to the bone in his life. Nor as miserable. This wasn't how his momentous encounter with Shiv Baines was supposed to have turned out.

To add insult to injury, he was also fairly sure his nose was broken. It really hurt.

It took an hour to walk back from Mayfair to Frobisher Square. The only way not to succumb to hypothermia had been to adopt a brisk marching pace, swing his arms a lot and pick up a hot coffee along the way. There were lights on in Della Lucas's third-floor flat, but was she actually awake, and would she even answer the door at this time of night? He wasn't going to risk it. Jess, he knew, would have been calling him over and over, wanting to wish him a happy new year and wondering why he wasn't answering his phone. Same with Lou, and probably other friends too.

All he wanted to do now was go home.

There were dry clothes in the back of the van, at least. And the temperamental heater took pity on him and chose to behave itself for once, so by the time Sammy reached the motorway, he'd stopped shivering at last. The roads were eerily quiet now, at almost two in the morning, but random fireworks still intermittently lit up sections of the sky. He concentrated on telling himself that he hadn't *lost* anything – he might have pinned all his hopes on Shiv Baines loving his music, but it was really no different from spending your last tenner on a Lotto ticket and not winning the jackpot.

Well, except he'd lost his phone and was probably now condemned to be blackballed from the music industry for life.

Bump-bump-BUMP went the van, and the sensation was too familiar for Sammy not to recognise what had happened. Pulling over onto the hard shoulder, he climbed out and took a look at the wheels on the passenger side. Yes, tonight of all nights, *of course* he had a flat tyre.

Because nothing good could ever happen to him, could it? The universe was well and truly on his case, determined to teach him a lesson he'd never forget.

Wearily he opened the back doors and took out the spare wheel.

The windows of a passing Citroën were buzzed down and a bunch of lairy late-night revellers bellowed, 'Haha, *loser*,' at him as they roared past.

Sammy resisted the urge to hurl the car jack after them. Talk about kicking a man when he was down.

Happy new year to me.

★

Sammy heard himself yelp, 'I'm sorry, don't kill me.' This was because he'd been grabbed by Shiv Baines's minder, who was backing him into a corner of Val's Café while shaking him by the shoulders. 'No, no,' he went on as the shaking intensified. 'I didn't mean to do it, it was an *accident* . . .'

Then he realised it simply wasn't practical for this to be happening in Val's Café, and the minder was wearing a teddy-bear onesie, which also seemed unlikely under the circumstances. Relieved that this meant it had to be a dream and he was at home in his own bed, he opened his eyes and saw that his brother was the one doing the shaking. Oh, and not just Remy; Jess was here too. Looking . . . well, like he'd never seen her looking before. As if she could be on the brink of spontaneous combustion.

'What is it? What's going on?' As he struggled to sit up, the weirdness of the dream subsided and the real-life horrors of last night came whooshing back. He felt instantly sick with fear. Had Shiv Baines accused him of assault? Was he going to be sued for millions? Were the police waiting downstairs to arrest him? Would he go to prison?

Also, ouch, he'd forgotten about his broken nose.

'Honestly.' Remy shook his head. 'We can't leave you alone for five minutes, can we? Happy new year, by the way.'

'Oh come here and give me a hug,' Jess cried, launching herself onto the bed and squeezing him so hard she emptied all the air from his lungs. 'Why didn't you call me? We were so worried!'

'My phone's dead.'

'You need to put it in a bowl of rice,' said Remy. 'That might do the trick.'

Sammy frowned. 'How do you know it got wet?'

'Call it an educated guess. Jess just showed me the video.'

237

'What video?'

'Are you serious?' Remy started to laugh.

'The one that has a million views on Instagram and TikTok,' said Jess. She glanced down at the phone in her left hand. 'Actually, make that one and a half million.'

'Fuck. What? Oh *fuck*.' Sammy felt sick.

'Looks like you managed to make . . . quite an impression,' said Remy.

His brother might find it funny, but Sammy didn't. Taking Jess's phone, he saw that Fia had uploaded the video in the early hours. He braced himself, then pressed play and watched himself, with hope and reverence on his face, approach the God-like entity that was Shiv Baines.

In the seconds that followed, in what felt like a long, horrifying episode of déjà vu, he saw the ice cubes hit the floor, then his own foot land on one of them and shoot sideways, knocking him off balance so he careered forward into the two men. Over the side of the pool and into the water they went, one after the other, like dominos. But it wasn't until they broke the surface that Sammy noticed for the first time what else had happened. For years, people had suspected Shiv Baines of wearing a toupee. Like a younger and extraordinarily vain version of Simon Cowell, with shark eyes and zero sense of humour, he had always vehemently and furiously denied it.

Until now. Because somehow the fall had knocked the hairpiece sideways in a way that was both unflattering and highly comical, so that in a flash the years of speculation were over. Hastily straightening it had been a fruitless exercise; by then the truth was out and it was too late.

Above the gasps of horror and delight from the assembled onlookers came Fia's voice as she exclaimed, 'Oh Sammy, you're *so* dead,' then burst out laughing. 'Good luck, babe, you're going

238

to need it – oof!' At this point the huge minder picked Sammy up and hurled him into the icy water. Seconds later, one of the other security guys approached Fia and ordered, 'Switch that thing off,' while putting his hand up to make a grab for her phone. After a swoosh of blurry movement followed by a close-up flash of cleavage, the screen then went dark as, at a guess, Fia thrust the phone for safe keeping into her bra. That was the moment the video abruptly ended.

'God,' Sammy groaned now, 'it's even worse than I thought. The *wig.*' This was why, in his highly traumatised state, he hadn't been able to work out why Shiv had, just for a few seconds, looked so different.

'Nearly two million views now,' Jess marvelled. 'Look at the comments! Everyone thinks it's hilarious, the best thing ever.'

'That's because it isn't their life that's just been ruined.'

'So you didn't get a chance to give him the USB stick,' said Remy.

Wearily Sammy shook his head. 'No.'

'How did you manage to get dry?' Jess was looking puzzled. 'Although I suppose they had warm towels and changing rooms somewhere out the back.'

'Warm towels and changing rooms? For the likes of me, who'd just done *that* to the man whose party it was? No, they didn't offer me that courtesy, funnily enough.'

'But . . . you must have been freezing!'

'I was. And,' said Sammy, 'I had a flat tyre on the way home.'

'Oh baby.'

'This is the worst thing that's ever happened to me.' He let out another groan and squeezed his eyes shut, which made his nose hurt more. 'I'm never going to live it down. I'll probably be banned for life from singing in public.'

'But you've still got me.' Jess gave him a huge, comforting

hug. 'I love you. When you didn't call me last night, I was scared you'd gone off with Fia instead.'

'What? *Never.*'

'So this is actually a good day for me.' She kissed him on the mouth and Sammy managed a glimmer of a smile, because she was right. They still had each other and that was all that really mattered.

Remy, looking at Instagram on his own phone, said, 'Tash Janssen has just posted a comment.'

Tash Janssen was a rock star with a massive worldwide following. Sammy winced and said, 'It's probably just someone pretending to be him.'

'He's got twenty million followers and it's a verified account.'

'Oh God, what's he said?'

Remy grinned. 'According to him, it couldn't have happened to a better person than Shiv Baines.'

And that was what swung it for Sammy. If his phone had been functioning, it would have exploded. As it was, he logged into his social media accounts on Remy's spare tablet and almost exploded himself when he saw the thousands of comments online.

Shiv Baines might be world class at what he did, but a sympathetic character he was not. Years ago, he had appeared as a judge on a popular TV show that whittled down singers until a winner was finally found. Shiv's bluntness, his acid put-downs and the fact that he couldn't care less how many hearts he broke had made him famous, along with the annoying but undeniable fact that he had a nose for talent and was exceptionally good at his job. His departure from the show after just two series had left it without its chief critic – and minus all the best insults – but by then he had become both a tabloid regular and a popular villain. People loved to hate him.

The same people, it turned out, who loved to see him getting what he deserved in the form of a good old dunking in an ice-cold pool.

Quite without meaning to, and because it so clearly *hadn't* been a publicity stunt, the unknown and unsigned musician Sammy Keeler had achieved a level of fame he'd never imagined. With nothing more pressing to do on the first day of January, people logged on to their social media accounts and laughed out loud at the sight of a thirty-second video in which Shiv Baines received his long-overdue comeuppance.

It was the viral sensation of the new year.

*

'Has he missed me?' said Edgar, arriving home from London in the afternoon.

'Of course he has.' Well, it was what he wanted to hear. Lou carved a slice of the bara brith she'd just made because it was his favourite. 'He was fine last night, by the way, just the same as on Bonfire Night. The fireworks didn't bother him at all.' She began buttering the tea bread. 'Did you have a nice time with Della?' All she really wanted to do was find out if he'd heard from Fia about Sammy's disastrous experience, but it was only polite to ask how his night had gone first.

Edgar nodded. 'I did. I wasn't bothered by the fireworks either.'

A joke! He was in a good mood. Lou smiled at the sight of Captain Oates scrambling up onto his knee and placed the plate in front of him on the kitchen table. 'Glad to hear it. Did you see Tom while you were there?' She floated his name into the conversation casually; she knew Tom had seen her friendly happy new year text, but he still hadn't replied.

'No, he was out with friends. The girl didn't come back either.'

'So you haven't heard what happened with Sammy?' She

grinned and reached for her phone. 'You won't believe it. Wait till you see this, it's just the most—'

'Della's coming to live here,' Edgar interrupted.

Lou put down the butter knife. 'What?'

'She's moving in.'

'Wow. That's . . . a surprise.'

'Not until the end of the month.'

He was looking happy and proud and the tiniest bit defensive, as if worried that she might not approve. Lou's heart went out to him; what kind of person did he think she was? Breaking into a broad smile, she said, 'This is wonderful news! Does it mean the two of you . . .?'

'Just friends. She's been struggling financially. The rent on her apartment is more than she can afford. So she's letting it go and moving in with us instead.'

'And if the flat's going, what about . . . um, Tom and Fia?' Lou felt her pulse speed up. 'Where will they be living?'

'Della hasn't had a chance to discuss it with them yet. It's their decision,' Edgar said flatly. 'If they want to move in with friends in London, they can. But if they decide to come down here with her, that's fine too.'

Tom could be living right here? In this house?

Her heart was really starting to gallop now.

'If all three of them move in,' said Edgar, 'you'll have to redecorate another bedroom.'

Please please please make it happen.

'No problem,' said Lou.

Happy new year to me.

Chapter 30

Shiv Baines arrived on the doorstep of Riverside Cottage three days later.

'Who's that?' said Jess as the doorbell rang downstairs.

Next to her in bed, Sammy was eating toast made to his latest experimental recipe: blackcurrant jam sprinkled with grated cheese and Aleppo pepper. 'Could be Lou?'

Jess shook her head. 'Lou doesn't press the bell for as long as that.'

He watched as she wrapped herself in his dressing gown – God, he loved her body so much – and crossed to the window. Peering down, she said, 'There's a big fancy car outside, and three men who look like . . . Oh my *God*.' Scuttling backwards, she stared at Sammy in horror.

'What?' He put down his toast. 'Is it journalists?'

'Worse than that. Much worse.' The colour had drained from her face. 'I think it's Shiv Baines.'

'Are you joking?' The blackcurrant and cheese instantly began to churn in his stomach.

'It looks like him. Except he's bald, so it's hard to be sure.'

They both jumped as the doorbell was pressed again in a peremptory, don't-waste-my-time kind of way.

'I'm not answering it,' said Sammy.

'I'll tell him they've made a mistake and you don't live here.' Tightening the belt of the dressing gown around her waist, Jess fluffed up her curls and took a lungful of air, then headed downstairs.

Sammy held his own breath and crept out onto the tiny landing, eavesdropping for all he was worth.

His chest tightened as he heard the front door open and Shiv Baines announce, 'Looking for Sam Keeler.'

Fuck *fuck*.

'Who? He doesn't live here.' Jess sounded like the world's worst liar.

'Yes he does.'

'Well, OK then. But he's not at home.'

'Quite sure about that?'

'Of course I'm sure!'

'Fine. We'll just wait until he comes back.'

'That'll take a while. He's going to be gone for the next week.'

'Is he? Or is he maybe hiding upstairs?'

Sammy flinched; did the man have a drone hovering overhead with a thermal-imaging camera attached?

'Look,' he heard Jess say slightly desperately, 'it was an *accident*. He didn't do it on purpose.'

Shiv Baines replied, 'Tell you what, why don't you let him know I'm here?'

Silence.

'Or,' he went on, 'why don't *I* do it?'

The next moment, Sammy's cheap new phone began to ring in his hand.

Of course it did. He wished with all his heart that Remy could have been here now to back him up.

'Honestly,' Shiv Baines drawled, 'some people. Away from home for a whole week and they don't even bother to take their phone with them.'

The silence that ensued was now excruciating. Sammy pulled on a crumpled T-shirt and ripped jeans and made his way downstairs.

'And like a miracle,' Shiv's voice dripped with his trademark sarcasm, 'he appears.'

He was wearing an expensive-looking black Crombie-style coat over an orange and black checked shirt and black trousers. His hands were thrust into the deep pockets of the coat and for a split second Sammy wondered if there could be a pistol in one of the pockets. But it was the loss of the oh-so-familiar toupee that made it impossible to tear his gaze away; without his hair and with his head closely shaved, Shiv Baines looked completely different.

Jess blurted out, 'Can I just say, you look so much better like that?' She pointed to his head. 'It really suits you.'

'Not that I had much choice in the matter,' Shiv said evenly. 'You can make me a cup of tea if you like. Strong, two sugars.'

Sammy sent up a silent prayer that she wouldn't accidentally give him the mug with *I'M A TWAT* printed on the bottom.

Jess raised her eyebrows. 'What are you doing here anyway?'

'I've come to see this one, *obviously*.' Shiv nodded in Sammy's direction.

'Why?'

'Does it make a difference as to whether or not I get the tea?'

She shrugged. 'Might do.'

'OK, I want to sign him to my record company.'

What? Sammy's ears began to buzz, drowning out the tension in the living room. Had Shiv Baines really just said that?

More to the point, did he mean it?

'I'll make the teas.' Jess's eyes widened. 'But if you're lying . . .'

'Let me guess, you'll spit in it.' Shiv waved her off.

Jess had disappeared into the kitchen but left the door open so she could still hear what was going on. Sammy looked at Shiv and said, 'Are you serious?'

'You think I came all the way down here just for fun?'

Shiv Baines was famed for never doing anything for fun. Sammy shook his head, belatedly remembering his manners. 'Sorry. No, of course not. Please, sit down.'

'I'll stand. You sit.'

He did as he was told, mainly because his knees had begun to tremble.

'I've been finding out about you. Listening to your music. Watching the videos on YouTube. You've made me a laughing stock.'

'It wasn't deliberate.'

'I want to sign you to my label.'

Sammy swallowed. There, he'd said it again. As if he *did* mean it. 'Why?'

'Because I like what you've written. You have talent. And it's the last thing anyone would expect to happen.'

This was certainly true. Sammy nodded, aware that his mouth had fallen open and he probably looked completely gormless.

'But it means we have to move fast,' Shiv Baines continued. 'Make the most of what's happened before the story goes stale. How many decent songs d'you have?'

'Me?'

'No, that pot plant over there.'

246

'OK, dozens. I've been writing them for years. I had the best ones on a USB to give you at the party, but—'

'Yeah, well, don't play me them now. You can email them to me. But the ones I've already heard, I'm happy to go with.' He clicked his fingers at one of his minions, who passed over an A4-sized envelope. 'And you need to sign a contract. Unless you don't want to work with me.'

It was an actual proper contract. Full of complicated sentences and words Sammy didn't understand. As his gaze ricocheted randomly from page to page, he saw the amounts of money mentioned and felt faint. He licked his lips and said, 'Can I get someone else to look at this before—'

'Fine, you've got twenty-four hours to get a lawyer on to it, then as soon as it's signed, we can put out a press release and make plans to get you over to LA.'

Sammy gaped at him. 'LA? You mean . . . Los Angeles?'

'What d'you think I mean, Librarians Anonymous? C'mon, I can't hang around all day; all you have to do is let me know you're on board. Or I might change my mind about wanting to work with you.' Shiv shrugged. 'Your choice. I may be called a lot of names, but I'm the best at what I do. And you already know that.'

This was true. Still in a daze, Sammy nodded and said, 'I'm on board.'

'Welcome to my world, kid.' Shiv shook his hand, then passed him a business card.

'Thanks.'

'I'm guessing Morton Kendrick hasn't been in touch.'

Morton Kendrick was the American equivalent of Shiv Baines; they'd been rivals for years. Sammy said, 'No.'

'Too slow, see.' Shiv gave a nod of satisfaction. 'I got word last night that he was about to make a play for you. So I made sure I beat him to it. Right, passport up to date?'

'Uh . . . um . . . I think so.'

'Make sure you know so. We'll get you onto a flight before the end of the week. Email me the rest of that music asap.' He picked up the mug of tea Jess had placed on the table, took a swig from it and pulled a face. 'My PA will be in touch with the details. Right, we're off.' He turned to address Jess. 'You the girlfriend?'

A proud nod. 'I am.'

'Don't hold him back.'

She bristled. 'I wouldn't.'

'Good.' He pointed to the mug. 'You put too much sugar in that tea.'

When Shiv Baines and his mini entourage had left, Sammy grabbed hold of Jess and held her tight. 'Did that really just happen?'

'It really did.' She gazed into his eyes. 'Your life is going to change.'

He ran his hands over her forearms. 'You've got goosebumps.'

'I can't help it. I feel . . . oh, I don't know how I feel.' She pulled him close and whispered in his ear, 'Excited. And so *so* happy for you. And . . . a bit scared.'

Don't hold him back. Sammy instinctively sensed what she wasn't saying. He kissed her on the mouth. 'No need to worry. And don't even think it, because nothing like that's going to happen. I *love* you.'

Her eyes filled with tears. 'I know.'

'Hey, I mean it. This is me, remember? I'm hardly a sex god. It's not as if the girls over there are going to start suddenly throwing themselves at me.'

She nodded, wiped her eyes. 'I know, I'm just being stupid. It's all been so sudden . . . I still can't believe it's happening.'

'Me neither. I'm about to be signed by Shiv Baines. He's

flying me to LA. He's watched my videos on YouTube and he really likes my music.' An unstoppable smile spread across Sammy's face as he reached for his phone. 'I have to call Remy and tell him. He'll think I'm having him on.'

'Do it. Put him on speaker so I can hear everything.'

His smile broadened as he raked his free hand through his slept-on, sticking-up hair. Next, he would call his mum in Portugal, then his dad in Swansea, and Lou, of course. But Remy was the one he really couldn't wait to tell.

'This is so mad. I never thought it would happen. For the first time in my life, my big brother's going to be proud of me.'

Chapter 31

'Look, I wish I could be there to help you out,' said Sammy, 'you know that. But I'm stuck here in this hell hole . . .' As Lou watched, he moved the phone away from his face and slowly revolved it to show her the sparkling azure water of the swimming pool, the even more vivid turquoise sky, the palm trees and the serried ranks of bright flowers bordering the pool.

'You poor thing, how terrible.' She retaliated with her own view of the rain lashing down from a pewter sky, the bare trees bending as a howling gale whipped through them, and the stripped walls of the bedroom she was less than halfway through redecorating.

'I was going to say don't knock Shiv into the water, but who wouldn't want to swim in a pool like that?'

'He never goes near it. He works all night and sleeps all day, like a mole. But he's better than I thought he'd be to work with,' Sammy added. 'Sometimes when he drops the big-man attitude he can actually be quite funny and nice.'

Lou found that hard to imagine; maybe Shiv had brainwashed him into believing it, Svengali-style. 'So how's everything going?' She propped her phone up on the undercoated windowsill and levered the lid off a tin of Farrow & Ball Vert De Terre with a chisel.

'Just being in the recording studio is like a dream come true. And the session musicians are fantastic. Basically the whole team is amazing.'

'So I see.' Lou grinned as a group of elaborately styled girls in micro-bikinis approached, giving him a wave and calling out, 'Hey, Sammy, hiya, babe!'

'That's Shiv's new girl band. They're called Tempt You.' He raised a hand in greeting as they wiggled past him on multi-coloured high heels.

'They look incredible.'

'They're just finishing the video for their debut single.' Sammy paused, then said, 'I heard this morning from Shiv's PA. They want me to stay out here a bit longer. Another couple of weeks. Maybe three. Do you think Jess'll be OK with that?'

Oh. They were midway through January. Lou knew Jess had been counting down the days until his return. Now he might not be back until the first week of February. But how could she complain when Sammy was finally on his way to becoming a success, famous for something other than a viral video involving ice cubes and a wig? She said, 'Hey, it's not your fault. She'll understand.'

'I know she will. I just don't want her to feel . . . you know, abandoned.' He was wiping his forehead with the back of his hand, huffing damp strands of hair out of his eyes. 'I know she trusts me, but she might still worry about stuff. The publicity people are hell-bent on building up stories, you know? Even if they aren't true.'

'What kind of stories?'

Sammy pulled a face. 'One of the girls in Tempt You broke up with a footballer just before Christmas. They think it'd be

251

cool if we got together. I mean, I said no, but they won't drop the idea.'

'Get together?'

'Not *really* get together. Just hint at a bit of, you know, flirting and stuff. To create more interest in both of us. It's their job to come up with these fantasies. The company's investing a ton of money in us, the publicity woman said. They have to do everything possible to make sure they don't lose it. I know, it's crazy. But what can I do? I don't want them to change their minds about me and decide I'm not worth the effort.' He gave Lou a pleading look. 'Let's face it, this is my one and only chance.'

Everything he was saying made a twisted kind of sense. In the world he was now entering, his audience demanded entertainment in whatever form possible, and an endless supply of it. Lou said, 'I'm sure Jess'll understand. So long as you warn her about it before it happens. Just explain everything exactly like you've told me.'

'OK.' Sammy nodded, as another gaggle of near-naked glamour girls appeared, one of them blowing a kiss at him as they sashayed past.

'Just an idea, but when you call Jess, it might be better to do it from your hotel room,' said Lou.

★

What with it being cold and drizzly outside, and with half the regulars doing Dry January, the Bear Inn was going through a quiet phase. Bob and his family had taken the week off to go skiing in the Swiss Alps, leaving Rico in charge. Jess was working with him this evening, but the customers were few and far between, leaving her with plenty of time to chat.

Lou, perched on a high stool at the bar, peered at the phone screen to see the photo Jess was showing her.

'I mean, I *do* understand,' said Jess. 'But it still feels a bit weird. Kind of . . . humiliating. Like I'm being airbrushed out of the picture because I'm not a good fit for the story.' She shrugged. 'Which I suppose I'm not.'

They were three weeks into January now. The PR department of Shiv Baines's record label had wasted no time in going ahead with their plan to concoct a story that would benefit both Sammy Keeler and Frini Papadopoulos. Frini, the lead singer of Tempt You, was a stunning brunette from Manchester with a model figure and an adorable smile. According to Sammy, she was actually really shy, although it had to be said she didn't appear shy when she was dancing in their just-released music video, gyrating in eye-boggling fashion against a succession of oiled-up male backing dancers.

The official line, currently, was that Sammy and Frini were most definitely *not* a couple, while the many photos released suggested that of course a wildly romantic mutual attraction was blossoming but *shh*, it was a secret because Shiv himself had decreed that his signings needed to concentrate entirely on their music and no shenanigans were allowed.

'He'll be home soon,' Lou said now, her tone reassuring.

'I know. Can't wait to see him again.' Jess glanced down at her body in a clinging cream sweater and too-tight post-Christmas jeans. 'Maybe I should go on a diet before he gets back.'

'Oh don't say that, you don't need to. He loves you the way you are.' Lou clicked off the photos of Sammy and Frini exchanging smouldering looks on the beach (smouldering looks *really* weren't Sammy's forte), then glanced up as the door was pushed open and three girls from the Marlow Hotel came in.

Well, two girls from the Marlow, along with Tanisha, the hotel's disgraced ex-receptionist.

'Hi, it's me!' Never shy, Tanisha greeted Lou and Jess with enthusiasm. 'God, this place is dead tonight! Just think, last time I was here, remember how Sammy had that massive crush on me and I broke his heart? He was so gutted when I wouldn't go out with him . . . I bet I could sell that story to the papers! And look at him now, living his best life in LA, hobnobbing with the stars and sleeping with more stunning girls than you can shake a stick at!'

'He isn't sleeping with anyone out there.' Jess stared at her.

Tanisha clapped a hand over her mouth. 'Whoops, I'd forgotten you two had got together. Sorry! But isn't he seeing that Frini girl now?'

Jess's cheeks reddened. 'They're making it look like he's involved with her, but there's nothing happening. It's just for publicity.'

'If that's what Sammy says, then I'm sure you're right. Anyway, this place is too quiet for our liking.' Tanisha turned to her friends. 'Let's head over to the Dog and Duck instead. Bye, Jess. Give my love to Sammy, tell him I said hi.'

When the three girls had left, Lou said, 'Don't let it bother you.'

'She's only saying what everyone else is thinking. I'm going to have to get used to it, aren't I?' Jess bit her lip. 'I don't have much choice.'

'Large Scotch, please, no ice.' Steve Crane had walked in just as the girls were leaving. While Jess found his favourite tumbler and poured out two measures of Laphroaig, he beamed at Lou. 'So you've been busy, I hear, getting the house shipshape and ready for the new guests.'

'I have,' Lou agreed; the bedrooms were now finished and she couldn't wait. On the outside she might be playing it cool, but knowing that Tom would be moving in next weekend was something to look forward to. Hopefully he would distract her from thinking about Remy.

'Only six days to go,' Steve continued with relish. 'I like what you've done to Della's room, by the way. The furniture looks great.'

Lou frowned slightly. Della had complained that the dark wood furniture in the yellow room was not to her taste, so she had sanded down the old French-style armoire and the chest of drawers before painting them chalk-white and slubbing the surfaces with silver gilding wax for a fetching shabby-chic effect. She'd then taken photos of the end result and Della had been delighted.

'Have you been up to the house?' If he had, Edgar hadn't mentioned it.

'No, no.' Steve shook his head. 'Della sent me a couple of pics. She can't wait to move in. I can't wait for her to move in either,' he went on cheerfully. 'We're having dinner together. I managed to bag a table at Colworth Manor.' He gave an exaggerated wink, because he was Steve Crane, who drove around in a silver Bentley and was the winky type. 'Reckon things are going to liven up around here once the divine Della's settled in.' Another wink, just in case Lou and Jess had managed to miss the first one. 'Someone like that's right up my street. And the way things are going, I reckon the feeling could be mutual.'

Chapter 32

Snow was falling, dusting the fields and the surrounding hills, as Remy headed back from a meeting with a client in Bath. Sammy had left a voicemail on his phone earlier to let him know he was going to be on the Mara Stillman show, his first ever TV appearance, and it was going out live, which was both exciting and terrifying, and was Remy going to watch it?

The show aired at midday in California and was viewable online here in the UK at 7 p.m. It was now 6.50; he would be home in time after all. Driving through Foxwell, he slowed to let an elderly woman cross the street pulling her wheelie shopping basket behind her. Glancing to the right, he saw the lights on in the office window of Trent and Keeler, which meant Lou was in there doing one of her twice-weekly cleaning stints.

He hadn't seen her for almost a week; she'd been busy getting the house ready for the new arrivals. Which was obviously nothing at all to do with him, but that didn't mean he was happy about it. On impulse, he parked behind Lou's grey Mini. He wouldn't admit to anyone how much he'd missed her. Plus, she might not know about Sammy's imminent TV appearance, which gave him a good excuse to drop by.

And there she was. He paused in the doorway and watched her with her back to him, vacuuming energetically while she sang along to the music playing into her ears through earbuds.

Well, sang was being generous. Since she evidently knew the tune but not the words, there was a lot of la-la-laing and dee-dah-deeing going on as she wiggled her bottom from side to side and bent to push the vacuum cleaner under the desk, where Briony had dropped a biscuit and trodden crumbs into the carpet.

'. . . you and me, da da da, meant to be . . . only when the hills have eyes and the la-la-la never gonna exercise . . .'

Remy smiled, because his mother had always done the same, substituting her own words when she didn't know the real ones.

And Lou still had no idea he was here. Her hair was tied back in a high ponytail that revealed the nape of her neck. Remy wondered how it would feel to kiss the sensitive skin there. He wasn't going to do it, but he was allowed to imagine it, wasn't he? There were silver hoops in her ears – lucky silver hoops, bouncing against the sides of her neck as she bobbed her head in time with the music. And she might not be wearing anything special – just a faded purple sweatshirt and navy leggings – but to him, everything about her was special.

There was no getting away from it, the feelings he had for Lou weren't going away.

Quite the opposite, in fact.

'Oh woo hoo hoo, you're my pea-green kangaroo, and I'll never ever . . . oh!' Mid wiggle, she spun round and yanked out her earbuds. 'Hi, sorry, didn't hear the door with these things in. Edgar hates me singing along, so it's a treat to be able to do it when I'm on my own.'

Remy's heart flipped, and that was when he knew for sure.

257

Lou was grinning, entirely unembarrassed at having been caught out.

'Sing away. I don't hate it. I especially like the pea-green kangaroo.' He checked his watch. 'Did Sammy tell you about his TV thing?'

'He did! I was going to watch it on my phone . . . Ooh, it starts soon. Don't worry, I won't stop working.'

'Why don't we watch it on the desktop?' He switched on the computer. 'And you're allowed to stop working when it's something as special as this.'

Remy found the website, expanded the screen to full size and pulled over another chair so they were sitting side by side. Being so close to her – but not touching – was thrilling in a way he hadn't experienced for years.

Who was he kidding? More like decades.

Then Sammy's segment began, and it was time to concentrate on him instead. Mara Stillman was in her thirties, massively popular in the US, with a warm and enthusiastic manner. Introducing him, she announced, 'And now it's a complete thrill for me to meet my new hero, the wannabe singer-songwriter all set to become the next big thing in music . . . the young Brit who sent Shiv Baines flying into the water on New Year's Eve – yes, you've *all* seen the video many times over. Please welcome . . . Sammy Keeler!'

Lou pressed her hand to her chest. 'My heart is racing.'

'Mine too,' said Remy, although his was doing it for a different reason.

'He's so scared he's going to swear in front of millions.'

On the screen, Sammy said, 'Hi, Mara. I can't believe I'm here. My friends are watching at home, waiting to see if I accidentally swear.'

Mara Stillman laughed. 'Please don't! Oh, but you are getting so much *attention* paid to you. It must feel so strange, after years of playing to tiny audiences, that all of a sudden everyone's falling in love with your music. Over seven million people have watched the old videos you put out on YouTube. They're comparing you with Ed Sheeran. And I have to tell you, pretty much all the girls in our office here have a bit of a crush on you!'

Sammy said, 'Well, that's definitely something that's never happened to me before. I mean, I'm not exactly good-looking—'

'Oh, now stop that – you're adorable! You have the cheekiest smile, and those blue eyes are to die for . . . and a little bird tells us we're not the only ones to fall for your charms. First you bag yourself an incredible contract with the big, bad music man himself, then you catch the eye of a rather stunning girl out here . . . and there she is!'

A photo flashed up on the screen of Sammy and Frini Papadopoulos laughing together at a table beside an infinity pool.

'We're just friends,' said Sammy.

'And it's always nice to have friends,' Mara exclaimed teasingly. 'Especially when they're as beautiful as this one!'

'Oh God, poor Jess,' said Lou. 'Even though we know it isn't true.'

'We wish you so much success, Sammy. You won us all over on New Year's Eve, and you did Shiv Baines a huge favour when you made him realise he didn't need to wear that hairpiece any more. In fact, our studio crew are grateful, too, because when they popped into the thrift store this morning, guess what Shiv had just dropped off there?' One of the cameras panned around to show half a dozen beaming crew with joke-store black nylon wigs perched on top of their heads.

'We really are just friends, though,' Sammy repeated quickly

259

as everyone else in the studio laughed at the wigs. 'There's nothing going on, I promise.'

'I'll believe you, millions wouldn't,' Mara joked. 'Thanks for coming in to see us today. Everyone, this is Sammy Keeler. He's already a total hero, and we predict he's going to be a megastar!'

As the segment ended, Lou's phone pinged with a text. Next to her, Remy saw her eyes widen as she saw who'd sent it. A smile spread across her face and he could practically feel her excitement as she read the message.

'It's Tom. He says they're all ready to move in on Saturday.' Her eyes were shining. 'And he's really looking forward to seeing me again.'

Maybe he was being unfair, seeing as he didn't really know the man at all, but Remy instinctively didn't like him. He wouldn't trust Tom Lloyd further than he could throw him. Then he realised Lou was looking at him as if wondering what was going on in his mind. And much as he wanted to, he knew he had no right to tell her how he felt about the first man who'd captured her interest in years. Switching off the computer, he said, 'Sounds like he can't wait.'

Lou pushed back her chair and reached for the vacuum cleaner, ready to get back to work. 'Neither can I!' she said cheerfully.

★

Moving-in day arrived. The hired van came trundling up the driveway, driven by its owner, and minutes later, Edgar's Bentley appeared behind it. He'd driven to London yesterday, and was returning today with Della, Tom and Fia in the car, while their belongings made the journey in the grubby white van Tom had been forced to hire when Edgar had evidently baulked at the idea of footing the bill for a removals company himself.

260

Lou and Captain Oates ran out to greet them.

Edgar did a double-take. 'What have you done to your face?'

'It's called make-up, Eddie,' Della chided good-naturedly. 'For when we want to look our best.'

Lou gave her cheeks a surreptitious rub; maybe she'd got a bit carried away with the blusher.

'Ignore him.' Tom wrapped his arms around her. 'You look fine. Also, hello. I've missed you so much.'

'He says that to all the girls.' Fia, crouching down to greet Captain Oates, exclaimed, 'Hello, baby, I missed you too! Brrr, it's so cold out here, let's get inside and find something to drink. I'm in the mood for cocktails.'

'Ooh, me too.' Della clapped her hands. 'An espresso martini – perfect!'

'Red wine for me,' said Tom.

The van driver, watching as they headed into the house, called out, 'Oi, who's gonna help me with this lot?' He indicated the vehicle.

Edgar gestured dismissively. 'Lou, you can give him a hand.'

'Seriously?' The driver watched as the rest of them disappeared.

'Don't panic,' Lou told him. 'I'm stronger than I look.'

As they began to unload the various cases and items of furniture, she said, 'Did the blonde guy help you get everything out of the flat?'

'What, you mean the one who's gone into the house? Mr Red Wine?' The driver laughed. 'He only rocked up as we were finishing. I had to get the old bloke in the ground floor flat to give me a hand. Thought he was going to have a coronary lifting this bloody thing into the van.'

'This bloody thing' was the spectacularly over-the-top throne chair bought by Fia and driven up to London by Sammy. Now it was back in Foxwell. Maybe if Fia hadn't fallen in love with it, Sammy's fateful meeting with Shiv Baines would never have happened.

It just went to show, you never knew when one seemingly insignificant action might cause another that was capable of changing your life.

Although deep down, Lou couldn't help wishing Tom had come back outside and said, 'What was I thinking? Of course I'll help get everything into the house. Here, let me take that.' As much as she didn't want to compare them, she knew that Remy and Sammy would both have been there like a shot.

At six o'clock, Della changed into a sapphire-blue wool dress, redid her make-up and announced that her friend Steve would shortly be picking her up and taking her out to dinner at Colworth Manor.

'Remember how crazy you used to be about Dennis the Dashing Dachshund?' Laughing at Fia, she sang a line from the song made famous by the suave cartoon character who'd originally featured in a series of bestselling children's books. 'The old guy who invented Dennis bought Colworth Manor and turned it into an amazing country house hotel. He's retired now but still lives there, and his daughter Daisy runs the hotel. Steve says Hector's a fantastic guy, the best fun, and after dinner we'll probably end up having a singalong with him in the bar. I can't wait!'

'And is he single?' said Tom.

'Sadly not.' Della fastened sparkling studs into her ear lobes. 'Apparently he's madly in love with his wife.' She laughed. 'But Steve is divorced, so fingers crossed!'

Edgar was looking put out. 'I didn't know you'd made arrangements for tonight.'

'Oh Eddie!' Gaily Della flung a violet scarf around her neck.

'I didn't arrange it, Steve did! You don't mind, do you? When you move to a new area it's only natural to want to get to know the locals. Now, don't worry about waiting up, I'll probably be late back. And don't worry, I've got my key. Bye!'

Lou felt sorry for Edgar, who tucked Captain Oates under his arm and headed upstairs shortly afterwards.

An hour or so later, she felt sorry for herself when Fia announced, 'Right, time we checked out the nightlife in this place. Are you coming with me or letting me go out on my own?'

She was addressing Tom, who looked amused. 'OK then, you've twisted my arm.'

'Lou, which is your favourite pub around here?'

'The Bear's the best one,' said Lou, 'and the people who run it are great.'

'Cool, will you drop us down there?'

She hesitated, waiting for one of them to invite her to go with them. When it didn't happen, she said, 'I suppose so.'

Ten minutes later, as she pulled into the pub car park, Fia said, 'Thanks so much. We'll give you a call when we want picking up.'

OK, this was getting ridiculous. Lou revved the Mini's engine and breathed on her hands to warm them up. 'Sorry, I won't be able to do that.'

'Oh! Why not?'

'I'll be asleep. I've had a long day.' She saw the look of surprise; Fia was clearly used to getting whatever she wanted, whenever she wanted it. 'Don't worry, it's not far to walk back. Only a mile.'

A very-much-uphill mile . . .

At last Fia shrugged. 'Fine. I'm sure we'll find someone to give us a lift.'

'Knowing some of the regulars,' Lou couldn't resist adding, 'it'd probably be safer to walk.'

But much later, she was woken by a tap-tap-tap on her bedroom door.

Her eyes snapped open. In her dream, she'd been trying to clean the Trent and Keeler offices, but Talli was there, flinging handfuls of rice, grass cuttings and liquorice allsorts all over the floor. Laughing at the mess, she'd said to Lou, 'God, you're useless, I'm going to tell Remy to sack you.'

That was the moment Lou had jerked awake, and frankly it had come as a relief; being mocked by Talli was *horrible*.

The tapping came again. She checked her phone, saw that it was ten past midnight and said blearily, 'Yes?'

The door creaked open and a figure appeared silhouetted against the dim light of the landing.

'Hey, it's me.' Still dressed, Tom closed the door behind him and crossed the bedroom. 'Are you OK?'

The upsetting dream slithered from her mind. 'I was asleep.'

'Never mind. You're awake now.' Sitting on the bed next to her, he reached for her hand and gave it a squeeze. 'I wanted to apologise for earlier. I would have invited you to come along, but Fia was dead set on it being just the two of us. She hates feeling like the new girl in school, being introduced to everyone by the form teacher. So I'm really sorry about that. I hope you didn't mind.'

He was stroking her arm now, his body close to hers, his warm breath on her cheek.

'I didn't mind,' Lou fibbed.

'I've missed you so much. Will you show me around the town tomorrow?'

'If I have time. How did you get back here in the end?'

'Fia charmed some guy into giving us a lift. Can't remember his name, but he runs a printing shop.'

'Dave Harding.'

'Anyway, did I mention how much I've missed you?'

'Once or twice.' Lou smiled into the darkness, because he was nuzzling her neck now. He was here, he was single and he'd succeeded in chasing away the terrible dream featuring Talli and herself in Remy's office.

'And have I told you lately how beautiful you are?' He dropped a trail of tiny kisses along her collarbone.

'Not that I can remember.'

'Well, I'm saying it now. Can I sleep in your bed tonight?'

Could he? Now wide awake, Lou wondered if the sensible thing would be to tell him no and send him back to his own room. Then again, why should she be sensible? Practically everyone else she knew was paired up, one half of a couple, enjoying that feeling of being both wanted and desired. As her own friends had predicted, getting over the shocking and abrupt end to her marriage had taken time, but it had happened. Brett was gone, and now her body was healing, craving normality.

Of course, having a wayward mind of its own, her body had chosen to crave normality – love, sex and everlasting happiness – with someone who was both out of her league *and* unavailable. Like marching up to the counter in a kebab shop and requesting lobster thermidor . . .

OK, so the dregs of the dream hadn't entirely evaporated. It still hurt to remember being made fun of by Talli, who'd never been anything but kind to her.

Dammit, though, here she was, lying in bed next to Tom Lloyd. He might be the second-best option, but he was still attractive, single and keen.

He'd missed her. He thought she was beautiful. And she really

265

had to do her best to get over her massive – not to mention completely pointless – crush on Remy.

She heard Tom's intake of breath as she began to unfasten buttons, first those on his shirt, then the ones at the front of his jeans.

His teeth gleaming in the darkness, he whispered, 'And there was me thinking you might say no.'

Outside, an owl hooted. She ran her hand over his warm chest and felt the *bump-bump-bump* of his heart. Tom *wanted* her. Taking a deep breath, she murmured, 'I decided it's time to say yes.'

Chapter 33

In a life overflowing with disappointments, Edgar supposed he shouldn't have expected the last ten days to have been any different.

Yet somehow he had still hoped they might be.

Della's companionship was what he'd yearned for, more than anything, but it wasn't proving to be anywhere near as much fun as he'd imagined. She was missing London, she'd explained with characteristic bluntness. And her friends, and the glittering shops of the West End. Consequently she'd taken to spending more and more time cocooned in her bedroom making phone calls, watching TV and giving herself beauty treatments. When she was downstairs she painted her nails, ate endless packets of crisps and watched yet more TV. Sometimes she would play a card game with him, and he'd been trying to teach her the rules of backgammon, but it was never very long before she would apologetically declare herself exhausted and head back up to her room for an afternoon nap.

Plus, on four separate occasions so far, she'd spent hours doing herself up to the nines before heading out for the evening with Steve Crane.

As for her son and daughter . . . well. At least Tom was spending most of his time up in London, allegedly working on a screen-play with a friend who also called himself a writer. There was something about Tom that Edgar didn't care for one bit, but he couldn't tell anyone about that.

Then there was the daughter, Fia, who was at least fond of Captain Oates but was in all other respects a living nightmare. She played terrible music all day long, screeched with laughter whenever she was on the phone to her friends – which was most of the time – and was also forever riding up and down the stairs on his chair lift, *just for fun*.

Edgar waited until the clouds had dispersed and the sun had come out, then went in search of Della. She was in the drawing room, flicking through a copy of one of Fia's glossy magazines.

'I thought we could go for a walk,' he announced.

She glanced up. 'A walk? With your hip?'

'I don't mean a five-mile hike. Just once around the church-yard.'

Della wrinkled her nose. 'Oh darling, I don't think so.'

But Edgar fixed her with a look. 'Please.'

There was clearly enough of an edge to his voice to change her mind. She put down the magazine and said, 'OK, if we must.'

As he drove through the entrance to the churchyard, she said, 'Why are you bringing me here, anyway?'

'You haven't seen it yet. The plot I've reserved for myself.' He pulled up at the end of the driveway.

'Darling! Are you not feeling well?' Della turned, placing a concerned hand on his forearm.

She might never have been a great actress, but it had been her job once. Was she secretly filled with hope?

Edgar said, 'I feel marvellous. Never better.'

'Well, I'm very glad to hear it!'

Did she even mean that? Edgar wondered if she had any idea that she'd comprehensively broken his heart all those years ago and was still managing to break it now.

They left the car behind them and took the path to the right of the ancient church. He was slow, but it mattered less here. There were gravestones to be read, people to imagine, stories to uncover.

'Here's where I'll be,' he said finally. He pointed with his walking stick to a grassy space beneath a mulberry tree, currently bare of leaves.

Della frowned. 'Where are your parents? Aren't they here?'

He shook his head. 'They're in London. Highgate Cemetery.'

'And you don't want to be buried with them?'

Edgar's chest tightened. They'd chosen to join his sister; there had never been any question that they wouldn't. And he'd always known they wouldn't want him there with the three of them. But he'd never confided in Della about Elizabeth; some memories were just too painful to share. Gruffly he said, 'No, I'd rather be here.'

On my own. Always on my own . . .

'Why did you buy it in advance?'

'So I didn't get landed somewhere I didn't want to be.' He indicated the neighbouring plots, well cared for and belonging to people who'd died of old age. 'No beer cans, no balloons. No wind chimes to drive you mad. And no artificial flowers,' he added pointedly.

'Oh, but artificial flowers can look incredible! And they last for *ever*,' Della exclaimed.

'I prefer fresh.' He paused, then looked at her and broached the subject for the first time. 'When I'm gone, will you visit my grave? And bring flowers?'

269

Della looked surprised, then said, 'Oh Eddie, of course I will!'

'Not carnations. I don't like them.'

'Darling, I wouldn't dream of doing that to you. It'll be lilies and roses all the way.'

'No lilies either. The pollen can kill cats.'

'Fine. I shall buy beautiful flowers that are non-harmful to animals. No expense spared!' She rolled her eyes in amusement, as if his request was slightly ridiculous.

'You won't need to worry about money. You know that.'

She nodded and moved closer, shivering and tucking her arm through his. 'Brrrr, it's cold. I do know that. And obviously it's lovely to know you're leaving everything to me, but that could be – will *hopefully* be – many years in the future. The thing is, though, darling, I'm in a bit of a pickle with the bank *now*, so I was wondering if you could spare me a tiny amount in advance . . .'

She was gazing up at him, her blue eyes wide with hope, and Edgar knew he'd have to agree, because only last night he'd passed comment on the endless deliveries of items she'd ordered online and she'd exclaimed that out here in the middle of nowhere, what else was there to do? He'd almost been waiting for this request to be made. And maybe, just maybe, she would be grateful enough to spend more time in his company once the cash was transferred to her account.

'OK, I'll sort something out.' He nodded and was rewarded with an enthusiastic arm-squeeze.

'Oh thank you so much. That's a huge weight off my mind.' Her coral-lipsticked smile was dazzling. 'And it's not as if you can take all that money with you, is it, darling? Let's use it while we can!'

★

Remy and Talli were on their way to Al Fresco at lunchtime on Saturday afternoon when Talli pointed and said, 'There's Lou and thingummy.'

Turning, Remy saw Tom Lloyd and Lou further along the high street. As always, his heart did a flip at the unexpected sight of her. Today she was wearing a bright turquoise jacket over a short black skirt and opaque black tights. For a moment she glanced sideways and he thought she'd spotted him, but no, she said something to Tom and they headed across the grass to the stone bridge over the river.

As Remy watched, Lou wrapped her arms around Tom and reached up to kiss him on the mouth. Then she produced her phone and shifted position in order to take a photo.

'Ah, don't they make a lovely couple? Let's go and say hello.' Veering across the road, Talli waved to attract their attention and called out, 'Hi, Lou, love the jacket! I was just saying to Remy how perfect you look together. No need to ask how things are going between you two!'

'Oh, hi, everything's going great.' Lou's free arm was still curled around Tom's waist. Turning to look up at him, she said, 'Isn't it?'

'I'd say so.' Tom seemed pleased with himself. *As well he might.*

Talli clapped her hands. 'Fantastic! Hey, why don't I take a few photos of you? It's always better if it isn't a selfie . . . Here, give me your phone.'

Remy waited while the photos were taken, capturing Lou and Tom together on the bridge with the best view of the river and the trees behind them. He wondered if Tom was slightly less enthralled to be doing this in public. Was it his imagination or was his smile not quite so enthusiastic as Lou's?

'There you go, all done. What a beautiful couple you make. Ooh, I've just had a thought,' Talli went on as she returned the

271

phone. 'We're heading over to Al Fresco for lunch. Why don't you join us?'

Remy's heart sank; he didn't want to have lunch with Tom Lloyd.

Luckily Tom swooped to the rescue. 'Thanks, but we can't. I have to get back to London. Lou's dropping me at the station.'

'That's a shame,' Remy lied.

Talli said, 'We've just been watching Sammy's new music video on YouTube – it's brilliant. Have you seen it?'

'Only about fifty times since it came online this morning.' Lou grinned, looking as proud as a new mum. 'It's great.'

'And who would have thought it'd be so . . . you know, sexy?' Talli mimed fanning herself. 'Have you seen the things people are saying in the comments section? Phew!'

'But it's not real, it's just a video. I called Jess,' said Lou, 'and she's fine. Not bothered at all.'

'I'm sure you're right, and good for her.' Talli pulled a face then gave Remy's arm a squeeze. 'But I wouldn't be fine with it if it was me!'

Tom pushed back his sleeve and took an exaggerated look at his watch. 'I think we need to make a move. Don't want to miss my train.'

'OK.' Lou nodded, checking out the photos on her phone. 'I can't decide which one I prefer. Which one do you think I should put up on—'

'Please don't,' Tom interrupted. 'There's no need to post stuff online. Come on, let's go.'

'What do you make of him?' said Remy as they reached the restaurant.

'Good-looking. Pleased with himself. Thinks he can get away with anything.' Talli paused. 'Bit of a dick.'

272

It wasn't just him then.

Torn between wanting Lou to be happy and not wanting her to be with someone who didn't deserve her, Remy nodded. 'Same.'

'But we mustn't say anything.' Talli unwrapped the tartan scarf from around her neck as they pushed open the doors and were greeted by garlic-and-wine cooking smells. 'Nobody likes a killjoy, do they? Poor Lou, she's been through so much. And now for the first time in ages she's properly happy.'

'But—'

'I mean it, don't even think of telling her he's a dick. She's having fun again, having amazing sex again . . .'

Remy's chest tightened; this wasn't welcome news. 'Did she tell you that?'

'No, but it's pretty obvious. Look at her! And him! Of course they're having sex, and good for her. I hope it's mind-blowingly *fantastic*—'

'*Buongiorno*,' exclaimed Beppe Romano, materialising in the nick of time to lead them to their table.

Relieved, because the very last thing he needed to hear was speculation about just how amazing Lou's sex life was, Remy said hastily, 'Beppe, how *are* you? Good to see you again!'

Beppe beamed and pulled his phone out of his jacket pocket. 'We were all in the kitchen watching your brother's video. Have you seen it? *Mamma mia*, he's like a movie star now! You must be so proud!'

Beppe's wife Gina came bustling over, arms outstretched to greet them. 'To think he used to work as our washer-upper, and now he's famous – our cheeky little Sammy! Next time we see him I'm going to ask for his autograph!'

Just then they heard screams in the kitchen. Remy thought someone must have had a horrible accident. But when the

273

chef came rushing out of the kitchen, he was waving his own phone.

'Someone on TikTok just asked one of those Kilnishian sisters what she wanted for her birthday, and she said a steamy night in a seven-star hotel with Sammy Keeler!'

Once they were seated at their favourite table by the window, Remy caught a flash of grey as Edgar's old Mini sped up the road with Tom in the passenger seat and Lou behind the wheel, driving him to the station at Cheltenham Spa. He really wished he could delete the thought of them in bed together from his brain.

Talli said teasingly, 'You know, when we first got together, I thought I'd bagged the best brother.' Her green eyes sparkled. 'But now I'm not so sure.'

★

'Connie Kilnishian has sixty million followers on Instagram,' said Jess. 'I have eighty-three.'

'Stop it.' Lou topped up Jess's glass with red wine. 'Your followers are lovely and you know them all.'

Jess twanged the waistband of her leggings. 'She's a size six. I'm a size sixteen.'

'And I know who I'd rather hug. I know who Sammy would rather hug too.'

'She's a teetotal clean eater who treats her body like a temple and runs ten miles every day.'

'Shush, have another piece of cheese. She doesn't know what she's missing.' They were in Jess's house, watching favourite episodes of *Schitt's Creek* on Netflix and intermittently keeping up with Sammy's own rocketing social media numbers. Jess might have been joking about the explosion of interest in him, but it had to feel weird. Lou said, 'You're OK about it really, aren't you?'

Sitting cross-legged on the rug in front of the fire, Jess broke into the wedge of creamy Cambozola with the side of her fork. 'Oh, I can cope. It's surreal, but it's everything he's ever wanted. He called me earlier and said they've moved his flight home again. Which means he's not going to be able to come with me to Dan's wedding.'

'Oh no.' Dan was an old friend of Jess's who'd moved to Southampton.

'But I can go on my own, and it can't be helped. It's not his fault. They've booked him to appear on *Saturday Night Live*, and apparently that's a big deal.'

'He loves you,' Lou reminded her. 'He'd much rather be here with you.'

Jess licked her fingers and nodded. 'I know.'

Two hours later, her phone began to chirp.

'What is it?' Lou saw Jess's smile fade as she looked at the screen.

Jess handed it over. Her follower count on Instagram had shot up, and gleeful strangers were now posting comments about her appearance, making fun of her clothes and telling her she needed to sort herself out.

'Apparently my hair's a mess, I need a nose job and new teeth, and Connie Kilnishian is, like, a billion times prettier than me.' Jess paused and took a deep breath. 'How kind of them to let me know.'

'Don't look. Just block them.' The jibes and insults weren't being directed at her, but Lou still felt sick on Jess's behalf. 'Actually, let me block them for you.'

'Sammy warned me this might happen. I've got a better idea,' said Jess. 'I'll just delete my account.'

Chapter 34

'Bored,' Fia chanted in the living room, banging the lid of the biscuit tin with the flat of her hand. 'Bored, bored, so so bored. This weather is killing me . . . When's the rain *ever* going to stop?'

Having to listen to Fia being bored was even more boring. Her group of friends, none of whom appeared to have proper jobs, had been invited last week to a glitzy press launch in Singapore and were still out there. Fia, having recently fallen out with the owner of the PR company organising the launch, hadn't been invited. Lou said, 'You could help me with the vegetables for tonight's casserole, if you like. There's a pile of leeks and onions on the kitchen table that need chopping up.'

Fia looked as aghast as if she'd asked for help disposing of dead bodies. 'Urgh, no thanks. Gross.' Flinging herself across the navy velvet sofa, she wailed, 'This place is the pits.'

Lou couldn't blame her, not really. For the last six days the rain had been relentless, and the countryside had never looked more sodden. It was depressing, and not the best introduction to Foxwell. Or, as Fia called it, the arse end of nowhere.

Opening the tin, Fia said, 'There aren't even any decent biscuits left.'

'That's because you've eaten them all.'

'Can you go down to the shop and pick up some more?'

'Nice try,' said Lou. 'Except I'm far too busy. You could always go if you're desperate.'

'It's raining. My hair would go all frizzy.'

'So would mine.'

Fia began scrolling through one of the social media apps on her phone. 'It's so unfair,' she moaned, turning the screen to show Lou a video of palm trees, ultramarine skies and azure ocean. 'Why can't it be like that here?'

'Life's unfair. OK, when I've finished doing the casserole, would you like me to teach you how to make biscuits?'

'I'd rather you made them for me. Kitcheny stuff isn't my thing.' She shot Lou a winning smile. 'But you're so good at it.'

This was the thing about Fia: she was gloriously spoiled and irretrievably self-centred, but it was interspersed with flashes of self-awareness. Amused, Lou went back to polishing the furniture while the rain continued to rattle like shrapnel against the French windows. Edgar was upstairs in bed having an afternoon nap. Della was out with Steve Crane, yet again. And Tom was still in London, working crazy hours with his writing partner in between having important meetings with potential film producers.

'Oh, look at Shiv, slumming it at the Ritz.' Fia was now holding up her phone to show Lou a photo of him meeting VIPs at some black and white event. 'Maybe I could go up and see him . . . except the weather's just as vile in London as it is here.'

Shiv Baines was famous for staying good friends with his many exes. He treated them well, bought them extravagant gifts and retained their loyalty and affection. Lou, rubbing vigorously with beeswax polish at a mug ring on the coffee table, said, 'I wouldn't bother. I was chatting to Sammy earlier and he said Shiv's flying back to LA tonight.'

'Are you kidding?' Fia jackknifed into a sitting position. 'Why didn't you tell me?'

Lou raised her eyebrows. 'Er, because I didn't know you needed to know?'

'But now I do, and *hello, bingo!* More to the point, hello, sunshine . . . and heat . . . and getting a proper tan . . . Oh, heaven.' Fia beamed at her. 'It's the perfect answer. I'll go to LA with Shiv.'

Talk about impulsive. Lou said, 'OK, I don't want to put a damper on things, but it's pretty last-minute. You might not be able to get a ticket on his flight.'

'You're so sweet and funny,' Fia exclaimed. 'Shiv doesn't buy tickets! He charters his own private jet.'

Of course he did. Lou listened as Fia made the call and arranged to hitch a ride back to the west coast. With impressive speed, three cases were crammed with clothes and a taxi booked – with Shiv footing the bill – to whisk her up to London City Airport.

'Ta-daaa.' Fia struck a pose at the foot of the stairs, wearing a violet Lycra jumpsuit, silver cowboy boots and a crystal-encrusted Stetson.

What else?

Feeling like a granny, Lou said, 'Will you be warm enough?'

Eye-roll. 'Of course I will.'

'Have you got your passport?'

'Yes!' Fia paused. 'Actually, no. Hang on.' She clattered upstairs, then raced back down again with the passport held between her teeth while she fastened enormously long earrings into her lobes. Then it was time for another pose and a couple more selfies.

'Give my love to Sammy,' said Lou as they heard the taxi pull up outside.

'I'll definitely do that.' Fia's eyes were sparkling. 'I might give him *my* love too!'

'Don't forget he has a girlfriend.'

'I know, but everyone's taking bets on how long that'll last. Let's be fair, now that things are taking off the way they are, he can do a bit better for himself, especially when he's so scute.'

Oh God, was this true? Belatedly Lou's eyebrows slanted. 'Sorry, he's what?'

'It's my word for Sammy.' Fia looked delighted with herself. 'I invented it the other day and now all my friends are starting to use it. Because he's Sammy and he's sexy, scruffy and cute. I don't know how I never noticed it before . . . Oh, don't look at me like that,' she exclaimed. 'It's not just me, it's everyone. And don't forget, I'm the reason all this is happening. He'd still be a complete nobody if it wasn't for me.'

★

It was five days since Fia had abandoned her in order to fly over to LA for some fun in the sun. Della just wished she could have escaped, too, because here there was no sun and she certainly wasn't having any fun.

When the last mouthful of dinner was finished, Steve dropped his knife and fork onto the plate and announced, '*That* was wonderful. In fact . . .'

Della tensed every muscle in her body in an effort not to react.

'. . . in fact, I'd say it was . . . fan-dabby-dozy!'

Della forced herself to smile and nod. She'd known exactly what he was going to say, because Steve was a huge fan of catchphrases and after every meal he liked to declare that it had been fan-dabby-dozy. To the extent that it was now making her want to rip her ears off.

For a sixty-two-year-old man, he wasn't horrendous-looking. He dressed well. And of course there was the silver Bentley Continental and the five-bedroom detached house where he lived alone since the divorce from his posh horsey wife. On paper he ticked a lot of boxes. In real life, sadly, he was starting to drive her nuts. When he wasn't saying *fan-dabby-dozy*, he was fond of greeting good news by exclaiming *yippee-yi-yay*. And if he'd had a couple of Scotches, he liked to sing 'Always Look on the Bright Side of Life' and accompany it with a jerky little shoulder dance that made him look like an oversized puppet on a string.

There were other annoyances too, like the novelty socks and showing them off to people at the slightest provocation. Plus, he liked to rev the Bentley's engine in an attention-seeking fashion whenever it was stopped at traffic lights.

It also profoundly irritated her when he chucked sweet wrappers out of the car window, because what kind of person *did* that?

Today she'd suggested paying another visit to Colworth Manor, ostensibly because their chef created such excellent food but in fact because the owner, Hector McLean, was the best-looking and most charming older man she'd seen in months.

Sadly, despite Della waylaying him on her way back from the ladies' and flirting outrageously during her last visit to his hotel, Hector had made yet another point of reminding her how happy he was with his wife.

Honestly, some men. No sense of adventure.

And – oh, for crying out loud – now Steve had just done it *again*.

'Stop the car,' Della blurted out as they headed back in the direction of Foxwell.

He braked and pulled over to the side of the road. 'What's wrong?'

'That sweet wrapper you just threw out of the window.' She pointed behind her. 'Nobody likes a litter lout.'

He frowned. 'Are you serious?'

'Of course I'm serious. Trust me, it's not a good look.' She might have her share of faults, but littering wasn't one of them. 'You need to go and pick it up.'

Steve's ruddy face reddened still further. 'I just spent a fortune on lunch. You can't speak to me like that.'

'I think you'll find I can.' Lunch had involved enough white wine to make her reckless.

His eyes narrowed. 'You think I don't know what you've been doing? You can't take me for a mug.'

'On the contrary,' said Della, 'I can do whatever I like.'

'In that case, so can I. Out you get.'

Which, when it was a matter of pride and staking her claim to the moral high ground, left her with no choice other than to do just that.

As he drove off, he called out, 'At least I don't go around thinking I'm famous when nobody even knows who I am any more.'

Della shouted back, 'At least I don't say fan-dabby-fucking-dozy!'

OK, maybe getting out of the car had been a mistake. As the Bentley disappeared into the distance, Della realised her tactical error. She was in the middle of nowhere, still several miles from Foxwell. What was more, her bladder was belatedly reminding her just how much wine she'd put away.

And . . . oh *great*, no signal on her phone.

Honestly, this summed up everything that was wrong with the countryside. No phone signal, no department stores, no handy passing taxis and no public conveniences other than the small wood on the other side of the dry-stone wall.

After a couple more minutes of wondering what to do, she gave a *pffff* of annoyance and managed to clamber over the high wall. Under cover of the trees in the wood, she managed an undignified al fresco wee.

While she was in the middle of climbing back over, and laddering her tights in the process, a vehicle came trundling down the road. Trapped with one leg on either side of the wall, as if she were riding a horse, Della looked away and tried to make herself invisible.

The vehicle slowed to a halt and a male voice called out, 'Afternoon! Everything OK over there?'

So typical. She glanced over and saw that the man was driving a flatbed truck. Shaking her head, she said coolly, 'I'm fine.'

'Heading into the woods? Or coming back out?'

Della realised how incongruous she must look, in her emerald silk dress and cream faux-fur jacket. She heaved a sigh and said, stiff-lipped, 'Back out.'

'Can I offer you a lift?'

'I've already told you. I'm fine.' As she uttered the words, her left shoe slipped off and landed in a patch of nettles below.

'OK, Cinderella.' The man, who looked to be in his fifties, sounded as if he might be trying not to laugh. 'But I'm afraid it looks as if your coach and horses have already left.' He jumped out of his truck and made his way over. He had dark curly hair, greying at the temples, and was wearing dusty black jeans and a lumberjack shirt. Once he'd retrieved her lost stiletto, he held up his free hand and said, 'Come on, swing your other leg over and jump down. I'll catch you.'

Della couldn't decide whether to be more cross with herself or with Steve for landing her in this predicament. She jumped,

282

stumbled against the man's chest as he grabbed her, then sprang away and very nearly ended up on her back in the overgrown patch of nettles.

'Whoa, Cinderella. Steady on.' He laughed, revealing a flash of gold tooth. 'It's all right, I don't bite.'

Once she was installed in the passenger seat of the truck, he said, 'Back to Foxwell, I'm guessing?'

'Yes. How do you know that?'

'Because I know you recently moved here.' His mouth twitched as they set off. 'And I know who you are. You used to be on TV.'

Oh for heaven's sake, as if Steve's parting shot hadn't been cruel enough. Of all the comments she was intermittently forced to endure, this was the one she most detested, implying as it did that she was a has-been, a failure. She stiffened and said icily, 'I chose to give up my career when I married. My husband died four years ago.'

'I heard. That's sad.' He paused, moving over to the verge as a large tractor approached and passed them. 'So out of interest, how did you come to be stranded out here, miles from anywhere?'

The other thing about the people living out here in the sticks was their nosiness. Della gave him a regal slow blink and said, 'Is it anything to do with you? No, it is not.'

Her rescuer grinned. 'Fair enough. It's just that Steve Crane was boasting about taking you out to lunch today, so I wondered what you'd done with him.'

See? *See?* 'For heaven's sake, don't you people have anything better to gossip about?'

'Clearly not.' Unperturbed, the man said, 'But that's OK, you don't have to tell me.'

He knew Steve. And Della was starting to realise she hadn't

283

behaved particularly well towards him. She said crossly, 'Who *are* you, anyway?'

A dimple appeared in his left cheek. 'Me? Oh, nobody important.'

And now he was mocking her. By way of retaliation, Della gestured around the front of the truck, then at his well-worn clothes and mud-splashed boots. 'I'd already figured that out.'

He smiled to himself and nodded. After that, silence reigned all the way back to Foxwell. When the truck finally drew to a halt at the gates of Walton House, Della opened the passenger door and said, 'Thank you,' making it clear she didn't mean it.

'Don't mention it.' The man gave her a casual salute and another flash of that rakish gold tooth. 'It's been my absolute pleasure.'

Chapter 35

Edgar had only recently discovered the joys of online shopping, having been shown how to do it by Lou. Anything you wanted could be ordered and delivered to your door without the need for human interaction, which he was all in favour of, obviously.

The most recent item, delivered an hour ago, had been a particularly successful one and had also taught him a new word. Having googled 'rubber thing on walking stick', he'd discovered it was called a ferrule and had ordered one last night. The original ferrule had worn through, which meant the wooden end of his stick had been clacking noisily against the flagstones with every step he took. Now, with the new one fitted, he was looking forward to seeing how long it would take Della to notice the new soundproofing.

Pushing open his office door, he made his way along the hallway to the left, following the distant sound of a female voice in the drawing room.

'. . . Honestly, it was a nightmare . . . So now that's Steve out of the picture. And good riddance, too!'

Della was on the phone to one of her friends. Edgar paused. If Steve was out of the picture, this was *excellent* news; the less

285

time she spent seeing other people, the more time she'd have available to be with him. His spirits lifted; maybe they could start travelling a little further afield, head out on proper day trips . . .

'Oh my God, don't even say it!' Della gave a gurgle of laughter in response to a comment her friend had just made. 'Trust me, I'd never be that desperate. Eddie could have all the money in the world and I still couldn't bring myself to do that . . . bleurgh! And I know he can't help it, but he's hardly riveting company to have around. Honestly, you can't imagine. I'm only here because I don't have any other choice. As soon as he's dead and I get my hands on that money, I'm *out* of here.' She listened, then burst out laughing again. 'Maggie! Yes, me and all my lovely millions. I can't *wait*. We'll have to have the biggest party the moment I've bought my fabulous condo in Dubai!'

Here it was, happening all over again. Edgar froze, engulfed by the familiar doom-laden tidal wave of disappointment and shame. In the drawing room, Della had now moved the conversation on to the designer outfits worn by various celebrities at a televised awards ceremony last night. For a few seconds he considered barging into the room and letting her know he'd heard every word. He'd promised to leave her everything on the strict condition that she kept this information to herself, and she'd clearly – casually – broken that promise. Maggie was one of her London friends, a divorcee with a slew of ex-husbands. Who else knew the details of his second will? Because if Lou got to hear about it, it stood to reason she would pack her bags and leave. And much as she'd deserved to be written out of it in the first place, he didn't want her to go. She was a hard worker and an excellent cook, and despite the message he'd seen on her phone, he found himself still enjoying her company. So what if she was secretly waiting for him to die? At least she still spoke to him as if she liked him.

And she wouldn't be getting the house, which served her right. He'd be the one having the last laugh.

Having silently retraced his steps along the corridor, Edgar returned to his office and closed the door behind him. The next moment he heard scratching and opened it to let Captain Oates in. The little dog wagged his tail and gave a single bark, indicating that he needed to be picked up. Scooping him into his arms, Edgar was abruptly overcome with emotion. His head dipped, his eyes filled with tears and a silent sob juddered his ribcage at the realisation that Captain Oates was the sole occupant of this planet who would miss him when he died.

As far as everyone else was concerned, he was entirely irrelevant. Nobody actually cared whether he was dead or alive. In Foxwell, the residents would relay the news to each other, joke about what a miserable sod he'd always been and marvel at how all that money had never managed to cheer him up.

Would any of them even bother to attend his funeral? Probably not.

Captain Oates reached up and licked his wet cheek, and this time Edgar broke down completely. What a blind fool he'd been to believe that Della had ever regarded him as anything other than a meal ticket. He'd known there could never be any kind of romantic attachment between them, but idiotically he'd assumed they were at least friends.

He was, he now knew, a deluded idiot.

Captain Oates snuffled up against his neck and Edgar said, 'I love you. Do you love me?'

The dog's wiry tail wagged like a metronome, and in his head, Edgar told himself this meant yes.

★

287

The following afternoon, boredom propelled Della down into Foxwell. Edgar had driven off two hours ago and she'd offered to go with him, but he'd said he had an urgent appointment and couldn't wait for her to get ready. Honestly, talk about ungrateful. This was the thanks she got for being nice.

But now that she'd walked down the hill, the sun had vanished and dark clouds had rolled overhead. And here came the first raindrops . . . just wonderful, when of course she'd come out with no umbrella.

Within minutes, the rain was pelting down. Surveying her options and not drawn to any of them, she ducked into the antiques shop at the upper end of the high street and briefly fantasised that the gleaming red Jag parked outside would turn out to belong to a handsome millionaire who'd be enthralled by her beauty and only too delighted to give her a lift home.

Instead, the only person in the shop was the girl with the curly red hair who'd been at the party back in December with Sammy Keeler.

Although if she were still his girlfriend, she didn't seem very happy about it. Her face was pale and make-up-free, and she was wearing a shapeless blue cardigan over a dress that did her figure no favours.

'Don't mind me,' Della said brightly. 'Just browsing!'

The girl looked distracted. 'That's fine. If you need any help, give me a shout.'

Della doubted she would; antiques weren't really her thing. Wandering around the store, wishing the rain would stop, she examined a few china ornaments, wrinkled her nose at a particularly ugly painting, ran her hand over the curved back of an amber velvet chaise longue, then paused to look at her reflection in an old, ornately framed mirror. Her lipstick was wearing off, her hair was damp and messy, and there was a smudge of mascara below one eye. Oh God, was this what her life was coming to? Peering more closely, she wiped away the smudge, then rummaged in her bag for a lipstick to make her look less of a wreck, although why she was bothering on a terrible day like this, she couldn't begin to—

Her hand jerked, the lipstick skidded up the side of her cheek and her heart leapt into her throat, because the door at the back of the shop had just opened and in the mirror she could see a smartly dressed man emerging with a blue and pink spotted waterproof coat over one arm.

He was wearing a beautifully cut dark suit, a crimson shirt, a red and gold paisley-patterned tie and highly polished black shoes.

'Right, all sorted.' Flatbed-truck man addressed the girl in the droopy cardigan. 'I'll take over now. You go home.'

The girl blinked. 'Are you sure? I can stay.'

'Sweetheart, of course I'm sure. You need to get some rest.'

Her shoulders sagged. 'OK, thanks.'

'And don't *worry*.' Having crossed the shop, he dropped a kiss on the top of her head and handed her the spotted coat. 'Everything's going to be fine.'

She sighed. 'God, I hope so.'

When the girl had left the shop, the man turned and looked at Della. 'Hi. Interested in anything, or just keeping out of the rain?'

'Keeping out of the rain.' But there *was* something she was extremely interested in.

Well, *someone*.

He touched his index finger to the side of his face and said, 'You've got a bit of lipstick . . .'

Oh fuck. Swinging back round to the mirror, Della hastily scrubbed at the bright pink tick at the side of her mouth. The

289

more she scrubbed, the pinker and smearier it got. Seconds later, he appeared behind her and said, 'Here, one of these should do the trick.'

'Do you carry baby wipes wherever you go?' She couldn't decide whether the fact that the wipes were doing the trick was annoying or a good thing.

'We keep them in the desk drawer. Great for getting sticker-glue off things and marks off upholstery.' He shrugged. 'They're handy to have around.'

'Do you work here?'

'It's my business.' The dimple appeared. 'And that doesn't mean I'm not telling you. It means I own the place.'

Della couldn't help herself. 'You look . . . so different.'

'Do I?' His eyes glittered. 'That could be because I've been out visiting a client.'

'Can we start over?' She produced her most dazzling smile. 'I'm Della. And you are . . .?'

'Harry Bailey.' He paused, studying her face. 'Harry Wentworth-Bailey if you want the full name. But I prefer to keep it simple. I'm Jess's uncle,' he added, gesturing to the desk where the girl had been sitting until a few minutes ago.

Jess, that was her name. And Steve had mentioned a friend called Harry a few times. Oh God, had Steve told him awful things about her? Della swallowed. 'Sorry about before. You caught me on a bad day. And I thought you were just . . . you know . . .'

'Some scruffy guy driving a truck? I was. I'm also a guy who owns some decent clothes and drives a Jag. Does that make a difference to your opinion of me?'

Was this a sly dig? She decided to brazen it out. 'You could have mentioned it.'

'And spoil my fun? Why would I want to do that?'

'You weren't at Eddie's party,' Della countered. 'I wonder why you weren't invited?'

'I was invited. But I had business to attend to in Milan.'

Some people had an answer for everything. Della changed the subject. 'And what's wrong with your niece? Is she ill?'

Harry Bailey's expression changed. 'Seriously? Surely you've heard what's been going on?'

Why was he looking at her like that? 'What? How am I supposed to know? I mean, she wasn't exactly bouncing around, but I've no idea what's wrong with her . . . Oh, unless she's pregnant! Is that what it is? I had the *worst* morning sickness with mine. Poor thing, she should try . . .' Della stopped, because now he was rudely ignoring her, scrolling through his phone. Pointedly she said, '*So* sorry to be boring you.'

'Jess isn't pregnant.' He held the phone up in front of her. 'This is why she's been worried sick and hasn't been able to eat or sleep.'

Della blinked and brought the Instagram photo into focus until she was able to see that it showed her daughter in an orange sundress, laughing uproariously while she sat on Sammy Whatsisname's knee. Fia's tanned arm was curled around his neck, the hem of her dress was rucked up to upper-thigh level and one leg was kicked up in the air like a cancan dancer.

'They're just having a bit of fun,' she said breezily. 'Perfectly harmless.'

'Maybe so. But your daughter clearly isn't worried about hurting Jess's feelings. When someone asked her if she and Sammy were a couple, she didn't even attempt to deny it.'

Della took a steadying breath. 'Maybe they are, then. I don't know. But they're two adults, thousands of miles away. I can't tell my grown-up daughter what to do.'

'You could try telling her what not to do.'

291

'Or maybe your niece could try telling her so-called boyfriend what not to do.' Fia might be spoiled and impulsive and often thoughtless, but Della would always leap to her daughter's defence. 'In fact, she should be grateful – if it wasn't for Fia, that boy would still be a complete *nobody*.'

'You're on her side. I'm on Jess's. And you're right, they're adults,' said Harry. 'There's nothing either of us can do to change anything.' He stopped, then gazed directly into her eyes, and at that moment, the strangest thing happened. Della felt her whole body start to tingle in the certain knowledge that he was about to kiss her.

Which sounded completely crazy, but it was so real, such a vivid moment of clarity, that she knew she was right.

Frozen, she stared back at him. It was as if time had stopped. She watched, hypnotised, as the dimple in his left cheek deepened and the corners of his mouth lifted. All she could do now was wait for the kiss to follow.

'Coo-eee! Phew, talk about nice weather for ducks! Hello, love, just finished work and I'm after something nice for our Mavis. It's her eightieth birthday tomorrow!'

Harry turned. 'Hello, Moira. Of course, what kind of thing were you thinking of? Excuse me,' he added to Della, making his way across the shop and leaving her standing there like a lemon.

A desperate quivering lemon at that. Now what was she supposed to do? Stay or go? Look completely desperate and needy, or assert her independence and leave?

Except there was no way in the world she could walk out now. Flustered, she began examining a portrait of a hag-like woman in a bonnet.

It took a while, but eventually Moira, who apparently worked in the local supermarket, finished chattering and prevaricating and went away with a chunky amber pendant for her aunt.

The moment she was out of the door, Harry flipped the sign over to *Closed* and Della's stomach flipped too, in anticipation of what was about to happen next.

'You stayed.' He came halfway towards her, and when he smiled, she caught a fleeting glimpse of that gold tooth of his. 'I wondered if you would.'

Attempting flippancy, she said, 'Why wouldn't I? It's still raining.'

'True.' He nodded. 'Are you ready?'

Zinggg went the adrenalin around her body. She licked her lips. 'Absolutely.'

'Come on then.' Turning and heading back towards the door, he said, 'Let's go.'

'Go where?'

He pulled his car keys from his jacket pocket. 'Back to Walton House. That's what you're after, isn't it? Another lift home. So you can get out of the rain.'

The zinging abruptly stopped, like a dying firework. The buzz of excitement evaporated into thin air. Mentally recovering from the answer she hadn't been expecting, Della said stiffly, 'Yes. Thank you. But you don't have to, not if you're busy. I can walk.'

'Hey, it's no trouble.' Harry opened the shop door and pointed his key fob at the crimson Jag to release the locks. 'Always happy to help a damsel in distress.'

They drove up the hill in silence. Della plaited her fingers together in her lap, furious with herself for having got it so wrong. The windscreen wipers went *swoosh-swoosh* and the rain continued to pelt down sideways, sliding across the road as they approached the left turn that led to Walton House.

'You missed it,' said Della as he sped past the stone-pillared entrance.

293

'I'll turn round.' Harry drove on, then braked and pulled into a muddy lay-by. But instead of executing a swift three-point turn, he pulled on the handbrake and shifted sideways to look at her. 'I want to kiss you.'

Oh thank God. At last . . .

Overcome with emotion, she sent up a prayer of gratitude that she hadn't been imagining it after all. She whispered, 'I want to kiss you, too.'

'But I wouldn't want to step on anyone's toes.'

'There aren't any toes to step on.' The words came tumbling out. And best of all, it was true, there really weren't.

'What about Steve?'

'He's out of the picture. He was never *in* the picture.' She shook her head. 'Look, I'm new here. I wanted to make friends and get to know people, and Steve offered to take me out to dinner. But there wasn't any . . . you know, attraction.'

'He must have been disappointed.'

'I could never be romantically involved with a man who wears novelty socks and says yippee-yi-yay.'

'Me neither.' Harry half smiled as he moved towards her. This time he didn't stop. Murmuring, 'Come here,' he drew her against him and their mouths met.

Gosh, he was good.

Oh wow, *really* good. Della was in heaven; this was what she'd been missing, proper chemistry with an attractive man, at long last. Plus he wore good clothes and drove a great car.

Things were looking up in Foxwell. And she deserved it, she truly did.

'Right,' said Harry when the kiss ended. 'Time to get you home. Again.'

'Oh, but . . . I don't have to go back now.'

'Maybe you don't. But I do.' The car had steamed up and he

switched on the heater to clear the windscreen. 'I sent Jess home, remember? Someone needs to take care of the shop.'

Not what she'd wanted to hear, but fair enough. Della said helplessly, 'I don't even know where you live.'

'On the outskirts of the town.'

'What time do you finish? Can we meet up later?'

Harry expertly reversed the Jag and pulled out, ready to head back down the road. 'I'm busy this evening. Maybe another time.'

When they reached the entrance to Walton House, he drove in between the stone pillars and drew up outside the front door. 'There you go. See you around.'

After what had just happened between them? Della bristled. 'Are you joking?'

'I don't know, am I?' He raised an amused eyebrow. 'What's the difference between what I've just done and the pain your daughter is causing my niece?'

Della stared at him. 'Oh my God,' she said slowly. 'How *dare* you?'

Harry shrugged. 'What was it you called it? Perfectly harmless. Just a bit of fun.'

Chapter 36

Sometimes when Talli caught a glimpse of herself and Remy reflected in a shop window or tagged in photos online, she was knocked sideways all over again by how great they looked together.

Like now, at this house-warming party in Wiltshire. There was a huge silver-framed mirror hanging above the fireplace, and each time she cast a casual glance in its direction, it was impossible not to admire what she saw. They were both tall and physically beautiful, and that wasn't being boastful, it just went without saying. They were also intelligent, kind and thoughtful people, each successful in their chosen field.

The house belonged to Will and Gemma Porter and had been drastically extended and redesigned by Remy. The end result was ultra-modern, with glass-fronted balconies overlooking land-scaped gardens and a small lake. Inside, the ground floor was largely open-plan but divided into sections, with a spiral staircase at one end of the house and a lift at the other because Will Porter was a wheelchair user.

The place was finally finished, the family had moved in a fortnight ago and today's party was being held to celebrate this with friends, relations and the people who'd helped to make it happen. Having worked with them from the outset, Remy had become close to the couple.

'OK, brace yourself,' Gemma said as through the floor-to-ceiling windows they saw a people-carrier pull up on the driveway. 'We've had our hour of peace. Here comes the chaos.'

The grandparents had arrived with the Porter offspring in tow, two small sons and a daughter. Talli watched the expression on Remy's face change as the kids burst into the house and instantly made a beeline for him.

Why, though? Why would they zone in on him when there had to be another hundred or so guests at this party to choose from? She stepped back in the nick of time as the taller of the boys came rushing up to Remy – eurgh, there was dried mud on his hands – and began a complicated greeting involving hand grips and fist bumps. Then it was the other boy's turn. Finally the small girl, clutching a bag of sweets, demanded he pick her up so she could plant a sticky-looking kiss on each side of his face. So gross, just the thought of it made her shudder. Also, did the grandparents not even *care* about her teeth?

Talli smiled nicely and tried to catch their eye to say hello, but Remy was the one they adored. The other evening she'd arranged a trip to the theatre in Cheltenham, only to be told by Remy that he wouldn't be able to make that date because he'd promised to take the Porter boys to a football training event.

Watching them together now, both boys chattering away simultaneously as they clamoured for Remy's attention, Talli knew she couldn't put it off much longer. They'd been together for six months. The time had come to take the risk and come clean. Hopefully all would be well and she'd get the reaction she longed to hear. But she also knew that the prospect of actually having to admit the truth gave her palpitations every time she thought about it.

It was so unfair, though; she loved Remy so much. And God knows, it took long enough to find someone you wanted to spend the rest of your life with, let alone—

'Whoops,' Gemma said gaily as her daughter seized a Ribena carton and squeezed it too hard, sending a spray of purple juice over Talli's caramel suede skirt. 'Oh dear, say sorry!'

'It's fine, doesn't matter at all.' It did matter, of course it mattered, but Talli was good at hiding how she really felt. Over the years, both personally and professionally, she'd had plenty of practice.

But it was definitely time to have The Conversation with Remy.

She would do it tomorrow.

Talli planned their Sunday morning with military precision. It was all going to be perfect. They would sleep in, on crisp fresh linen, with fresh flowers in a vase on the bedside table and the fridge downstairs full of his favourite food. She would make a proper cooked breakfast and bring it upstairs for them to enjoy together in bed. Music would be playing in the background and they would read bits out of the Sunday papers to each other. Then they'd have wonderful sex, and after that, she'd tell him. Or actually, maybe tell him first and have the wonderful sex afterwards, once the subject had been broached and dismissed.

She was ninety-five per cent sure he loved her enough not to allow it to change his mind about her.

★

Something was up. Remy had already sensed it, but now he could definitely tell. Talli had insisted he stay in bed while she disappeared into the kitchen and spent forty frantic minutes cooking a full English breakfast for the two of them, then – finally – placing the tray on the bed with a proud flourish. And it had been great, although he was also aware that it was the precursor to sex, which was something he was growing less enthusiastic about, what with his emotions being in the tangle they currently were.

'Isn't this bliss?' She stretched lazily, her bare foot coming to rest against his ankle. 'Sunday morning, no work, just doing exactly what we want to do.' She broke into a smile. 'And there's no one else here to spoil it. Just us. What could be more perfect?'

Should he tell her how he felt? Would it be cruel to do it now, after she'd made such an effort with breakfast? But no, there was definitely something else waiting to be said first. Remy could tell she was nervous by the way her fingers were pleating the edge of the duvet. All of a sudden, out of nowhere, he was filled with ice-cold dread; what if she'd been fibbing about having her period last week?

What if she were about to tell him she was pregnant? *Oh God* . . .

'You're waiting to say something.' He reached for the frantically pleating fingers. 'Tell me what it is.'

Talli drew a breath. 'OK, but it's nothing bad, I promise. I love you. You love me. It's just something you need to know . . .'

She's having an affair. That would be good news.

She has an STD. Not good news.

'. . . and I hope it won't change anything. Because I really want us to carry on being together.' She squeezed his hand. 'Being as happy as we are.'

The suspense was killing him. 'Well, I'm rubbish at mind-reading,' he mentally braced himself, 'so go ahead.'

Another, deeper breath, then Talli gazed into his eyes and said,

'It's about the future. I love our life and I want it to stay like this for ever. I don't want children. I've never wanted them. They're noisy and messy and I've never understood why other people choose to have them. I mean, *why* would you, when you never know what you're going to get? What if you end up landed with kids you don't even like?' She shook her head in disbelief. 'That's what really baffles me. It's like buying a raffle ticket and winning a case of out-of-date dog food, or somebody else's false teeth. I just don't get it. I have no urge to procreate. And I hope that's OK with you, because I know you like other people's kids, but that doesn't mean we have to have our own, does it? I love you and you love me, and that's what matters. As long as we have each other, we don't need kids to make our lives complete.'

Remy saw her chest rise and fall as she took a breath then exhaled with relief. So that was it. She had delivered her pitch; now she was waiting for him to tell her everything was fine and of course he'd be happy to go along with it. She looked confident, but he suspected this was all part of the plan.

'We've been together for six months,' he said slowly, 'and you've never mentioned this before.'

'I know.'

'Why not?'

She shrugged. 'Because when are you supposed to say it? The first time you meet someone, are you meant to blurt it out? That would be bizarre. You wait until you know it could be relevant. Which is now. Which is why I'm telling you. And hoping you feel the same way.'

'I don't feel the same way. You know that.' Remy remembered a conversation they'd had a month or so after their first date. He'd talked about wanting children, and she'd nodded and asked questions, sounding interested and as if she was agreeing with

300

him – without, he now realised, actually agreeing that it was what she wanted too.

'You thought if you told me earlier,' he said now, 'I'd cut my losses and bail out of the relationship.'

He saw the guilty flicker of her lashes.

'Maybe,' she admitted. 'OK, yes. It's happened to me before and I didn't want it to happen again. I don't want to lose you. Because we're perfect. And it shouldn't put you off me, because what if I *did* want children and we tried our best to have them but it didn't happen?' Her eyes widened. 'What would you do then? Dump me, because I couldn't give you what you wanted?'

She was waiting for him to reply to what was essentially a rhetorical question. Remy shook his head. 'No.'

'No, of course you wouldn't! Because that's not the kind of person you are. We'd get through it and build a different kind of life together, and it would still be a great life, and we'd still be happy, don't you see? But I'm being honest with you now, because I'm not the kind of person who'd trick you into marrying me, letting you believe we were going to have kids. I could have done that, but I wouldn't dream of it. Remy, I want to be with you for ever. And I promise you, not having kids will only make our relationship *better* . . .'

She'd honed her speech, laid out her arguments and was being as persuasive as possible. She was beautiful, intelligent and wildly ambitious, and Remy felt nothing but relief. It was as if he'd been handed a giant get-out-of-jail-free card.

'I'm sorry. Of course you're allowed not to want children. But I'm allowed to want them. And I really do.' For the last couple of weeks, the grains of sand had continued to fall through the glass timer, and he'd known it was wrong to keep the relationship going. Finally he had a valid reason to end it.

'OK, don't decide anything now.' Talli's hands were up, stopping him from saying what she knew he was about to say. 'I've landed this on you and it's been a massive shock. You need time to think about it, and—'

'I don't need time. It's a game-changer for me. And I'm not going to change my mind. Sorry,' he added, even though he wasn't.

'Wow.' Talli sat back, tension visible now in her jaw. 'So that's your priority. You aren't bothered about finding your soulmate. All you really want is an oven to put your buns in.'

There it was, the sharp edge to her voice, the disparaging tone. He'd caught glimpses of it before, but she tended to keep it well hidden. But now she wasn't happy, and this was her way of lashing out.

'I'd rather hold out for a soulmate who wants the same as me.' Right on cue, a face appeared in his mind and he determinedly ignored it, because now wasn't the time to be thinking about Lou.

'You'll never find anyone else like me. If you walk away now, you'll regret it,' said Talli. 'I know you will.'

'Maybe.' He already knew he wouldn't. 'But I'm not going to change my mind.'

'So that's it, you're actually serious?' She spread her arms, fingers splayed in disbelief. 'We're done? It's all over?'

Remy shrugged, then nodded. 'May as well make a clean break.'

'Do you even *care*?'

He needed to be straight with her; it would be painful for Talli to hear, but it was the best way. After a pause, he said, 'Of course I care. But maybe, in all honesty . . . not quite enough. Not enough to get past the no-children thing.'

'I can't believe this is happening. I'm starting to think you can't wait to get out of here.'

'It's not that. I just think it's good that we've sorted out something that needed to be sorted out.' Remy couldn't help himself; he was picturing Lou now. Not that he had a clue how she felt about him; for all he knew, that attraction could be completely one-sided. But whether it was or not, he knew he had to end this relationship.

Talli said suddenly, 'Is there someone else?'

His heart rate sped up. 'What?'

'It's like you're already seeing someone. Oh my God, *are* you?'

Ending relationships had always been one of Remy's least favourite things, and during his years at uni there'd sometimes been a degree of overlapping going on. It wasn't the first time he'd been asked this question. Thankfully on this occasion he could be honest.

'I'm not seeing anyone else.' Well, not in the sense she meant.

'Not secretly got your eye on Lou, then?' Talli's tone was ironic rather than genuinely accusing. 'Who knows, maybe that's the plan. Stick it out until the old guy pops his clogs and she inherits everything, then you can move in with her in that great big house on the hill. Not a bad idea!'

What? Remy's eyes narrowed. Nobody knew about the will in which Edgar had left his entire estate to Lou. 'How did you hear about that? Did Lou tell you?' *Surely not.*

'I could pretend she did, but that wouldn't be true. Let's just say I always like to know what's going on in the life of whoever I happen to be involved with.'

It was the way her gaze flickered to his phone on the bedside table that made him realise she'd been reading his messages all along. With nothing to hide, he'd never been one for keeping the contents obsessively to himself. If Talli had seen him using his passcode, she could have gone through everything. And clearly had.

Which explained why she'd happened to casually mention the day after he'd ordered her favourite scent online that she was a bit bored with that one and her new favourite was something else.

Luckily he'd been able to change the order, and Talli had been delighted with the replacement.

'You've been reading my emails.' He and Lou had exchanged several messages around the time of the meeting with the solicitor about the will.

'It's always good to stay ahead of the game.' Talli shrugged. 'Show me a woman who doesn't do it. Anyway, just as well there isn't anything going on between you two.'

'Meaning?'

'Just that Lou's the obliging type. If she finds out you're keen to have kids, take extra care with the contraception. I'm sure she'd be only too happy to be your oven.' Sounding amused, Talli added, 'Show her a bit of attention and she'll get herself knocked up in weeks.'

Chapter 37

'Thank goodness.' Edgar exhaled with relief when Lou, laden with carrier bags, arrived back from the supermarket. He showed her the tin. 'Look at this. Completely empty.'

'Well, it wasn't me. But never mind, panic over. Because . . . ta-daaa!' With a flourish she produced two packets of his favourite shortbread biscuits. 'But don't eat too many, because I managed to get hold of those lamb cutlets you like, so I'm doing them with port and redcurrant sauce for dinner.'

He did like lamb cutlets, especially with that sauce. Frowning, he said, 'And boulangère potatoes?'

'Of course.' She was busily unpacking the bags.

'Did you get everything on the list?'

'Nearly. The only thing they didn't have was nits.'

Edgar frowned irritably. 'What's that supposed to mean?'

Lou produced her phone and showed him. 'That text you sent me. I did ask if they had any, but apparently it's the wrong time of year for them.'

He leaned closer to the screen and saw what had happened. 'I meant nuts. Not nits.'

'I know you did. I'm just teasing. And guess what?' She

rummaged in the next bag and produced two packets of his favourite spiced cashews. 'I got these for you; thought you might prefer them to nits.'

He shook his head, pedantic enough to be annoyed by his own error. 'I should have checked before pressing send. I don't like making mistakes.'

'Ha, that's nothing. Not so long ago, I was messaging a friend and meant to put *I hope he does*. Except I hit the wrong key and put *I hope he dies*. Can you *imagine*?'

Edgar's ears were buzzing. To hide the reaction on his face, he turned away and clicked his fingers at Captain Oates in his basket. Without looking at Lou, he said in a gruff voice, 'And were you secretly hoping he'd die?'

'Oh my God, *no*! Of course I wasn't! I was hoping he'd have a great time.' She laughed. 'How could you even think I'd say that about anyone?'

'Come here, lad.' Bending down to pick up the dog, he risked a glance at her. Lou had no idea he'd seen the message. She'd told him about her typo because it had been a typo, nothing more. And now her cheeks were pink because she was hiding the fact that he'd been the person she'd hoped would have a great time. And that had been on New Year's Eve, when he'd later made the decision to drive up to London and spend the evening with Della . . .

Edgar briefly closed his eyes. He could count on the fingers of one hand the number of times he'd felt guilty, but he was feeling it now.

Oh God, oh God, he'd made the biggest mistake of his life.

★

'Someone on Twitter told me I looked like a cross between a squashed tomato and a warthog,' said Sammy. 'I tweeted back that they were my two favourite things.'

Jess nodded and smiled at him on her phone, because he was doing his best to cheer her up and she wasn't going to let him see her cry. Two days ago she'd been papped for the first time in her life while leaving work, and a stream of unflattering photos of her bundled up against the cold with a pink nose and messy windswept hair had run in a major-circulation newspaper online, comparing her with the other girls currently vying for Sammy's attention.

There was Frini Papadopoulos in a silver mini dress, and there was Fia Lloyd wearing the tiniest crimson thong bikini known to man, both of them exuding beauty and glamour and sex appeal by the bucketload. Who could even begin to compete with such visions of loveliness? Certainly not me, thought Jess. And certainly not the readers of the online article who'd commented in their hundreds, marvelling that Sammy Keeler could ever have had such a lumpy, unattractive girlfriend.

'Hey, are you OK?' He was gazing at her now with concern. 'Whatever you do, don't read the comments online. They're just pathetic trolls.'

'I know.' She sniffed back incipient tears and said hastily, 'Sorry, I think I'm getting a cold.'

'I wish you could come out. I miss you so much.'

'I miss you too, but Harry needs me here.' This wasn't true; she just couldn't imagine anything more humiliating than flying out to LA so people could take yet more dreadful photos of her.

'If anyone says anything, just ignore them.' Sammy reached out to touch the screen, stroking her face from five thousand miles away. 'I love you.'

'Love you too.'

'Are you sure you're all right?'

'Of course I'm sure! I'm *fine*.' This time Jess managed a real smile, because it was what he needed to see.

'None of these girls out here are a patch on you.'

'I know. They're all really ugly. I feel sorry for them.' As she said it, she heard a voice calling Sammy's name.

'I have to go. The interviewer's ready to start.'

'What's this one for?' Well, she knew what they were all for. To promote him and his music.

'It's with Cass Klein for MTV. Do I look OK?' He ran his fingers through his hair and adjusted his black waistcoat.

'You look fantastic. Love you.'

'Love you more.' He blew her a kiss. 'See you.'

The call ended and Jess googled Cass Klein. She was tall, dark and stunning, which came as no surprise seeing as she worked for MTV. Then, because she was a masochist, she looked up Cass's Instagram account, where a clip was playing on a loop of Cass announcing that today she was meeting the divine sex god that was Sammy Keeler, so Frini Papadopoulos had better watch out because she was going to be in full-on seduction mode.

It was relentless. Of course Cass wasn't being serious, but wouldn't any man's head be turned after a while by all this attention?

Don't cry. Don't cry. Jess put her phone away and resolved not to look at it for the next few hours. Sammy had spent his whole life in the shadow of his better-looking, more athletic and more lusted-after big brother. Now it was his turn to step into the spotlight and be paid the kind of attention he could only ever have imagined. It was a dream come true, both professionally and personally. Who could blame him for wanting to make the very most of it?

*

Cass Klein hadn't been backwards in coming forward. When she hugged him once the interview was over, she deliberately pressed her boobs against Sammy's chest.

308

'Er . . . thanks.' Sammy hastily took a step back. 'It was great chatting to you.'

Her lashes fluttered. 'I just love your accent. You're adorable! And I'm free this evening. Wanna meet up?'

All his life he'd seen Remy being approached and propositioned by girls keen to get to know him better. And to think he'd envied him. Feeling his face heat up, Sammy wished it wouldn't *do* that. 'Er . . .'

'He can't.' Fia spoke up from her squashy chair on the other side of the green room. 'He's busy tonight. With me.'

Cass winked at Sammy and lowered her voice. 'Oh well, worth a try. Are you really getting it on with her? Isn't she one of Shiv's exes?'

'She is, but we aren't getting it on. I have a girlfriend back home and I'd never cheat on her.'

Her smile catlike, Cass murmured, 'I know, I saw the photos. And that's a very cute thing to say, because it just makes everyone like you more.'

'I'm not—'

'But you do realise it's never going to last. Far better to dump her now, cut the cord for both your sakes. Then you can get on with really enjoying yourself.'

Sammy stared, then slowly shook his head. 'That's a disgusting thing to say. How dare you?'

The publicity girl sitting across the room leapt to her feet. 'He didn't mean that.'

Sammy's eyes blazed. 'Oh yes I did.'

Later, in the limo heading along Rodeo Drive on their way back to the hotel, Fia touched his arm and said, 'If you fancy some company tonight, shall I come to your room?'

Since arriving in LA on Shiv Baines's private jet – along with Shiv and his newest girlfriend, plus a couple of other exes who

309

all seemed to get along like a house on fire – Fia had become his self-appointed constant companion. 'Why, do you want to play card games?' he asked.

She gave him a mischievous look. 'I was thinking of more interesting games than that.'

At first he'd pretended not to notice the innuendo-laden hints. Now he was totally over them. 'You were never interested in me before.'

'That's because you weren't anyone then. But now you're someone.' Fia grinned unashamedly. 'It makes you a lot more attractive.'

'Is that why you went out with Shiv?'

'Of course.' She shrugged. 'And aren't you glad I did? Because if I hadn't, you wouldn't be here now, that's for sure.'

'Does Shiv know you were only with him because of who he was?'

'Oh babe, he might be ugly, but he isn't stupid. Of course he knows that,' said Fia. 'It's the way the world works, especially out here. Anyway, you still haven't answered my question. Up for a bit of fun tonight? I'll get you in the mood.'

'Thanks, but no thanks.' He couldn't be angry or offended. 'I think you should save your energy for someone you actually like.'

'I like you. I do!'

'But not in that way,' said Sammy.

Fia considered this, then nodded. 'True.' The next moment, her head whipped round and she let out a shriek of excitement. 'Oh my God, that's Harry Styles looking in the window of Vera Wang. Stop the car, I *have* to meet him!'

'The thing is,' said Sammy as she made a lunge for the door handle and practically threw herself head first out of the limo, 'does he want to meet you?'

Chapter 38

It was the first week in March and snow had been falling over-
night in Foxwell, turning the town into a belated Christmas
card. It was all looking beautiful, but Edgar was more concerned
with keeping the Bentley on the road. He probably shouldn't
be driving, but the appointment had been made and he wasn't
going to miss it. Nor did he want Jerry Johnson coming up to
the house, not with Della there. Last week he'd been in his
office, on the phone to his bank, and from the way she'd casually asked about the call afterwards, he knew she'd been
eavesdropping through the closed door.

Yesterday he'd invited her to go out to lunch with him in
Cheltenham, and she'd said no without even bothering to come
up with an excuse – until last night, when she'd struck up a
conversation and apologised nicely for having been grumpy
earlier, then twenty minutes later had asked for yet another loan
to tide her over.

Enough was enough.

Every time he thought about Della now, Edgar remembered
the remarks she'd made about him on the phone to her friend.
Trust me, I'd never be that desperate . . .

He would never be able to erase those words from his mind, nor the sound of her complicit laughter as she'd mocked him. The famous Lucas charm she'd directed at him back in December had worn increasingly thin over time. It was like having a long-stay visitor who wished they didn't have to still be here. All the fun and friendship he'd hoped would continue had died a death.

A delivery van came up the hill and Edgar, heading down, braked to avoid it. Probably yet another parcel for Della, who couldn't seem to get through the day without buying something.

When the van had passed safely, he renewed his cautious journey into the town. He'd been an old fool, but now he was going to make amends for his stupid mistake. The snow was coming down more heavily now, fat flakes tumbling like feathers out of a colourless sky. He'd left Captain Oates back at the house; the meeting wouldn't take longer than an hour. Passing the antiques centre on the right, he saw Harry Bailey and Jess struggling together to slide a walnut armoire out of the back of his truck and into the shop. Further down the road, the woman who worked in the supermarket was heading in to begin her shift; for years he hadn't been aware of her name, but now thanks to Lou he knew she was Moira, married to a mechanic called . . . well, Alan or Dave, something like that, and a grandmother six times over. She was still sometimes annoyingly chatty, but he'd found himself warming towards her when she'd sent him a Christmas card, and a separate one for Captain Oates. Maybe some people weren't as awful as he'd always imagined. Even Belinda from the newsagent's seemed nicer now, having tucked a packet of dog treats in with the card she'd addressed to them both.

Unless she'd only done it because she was after his money too.

The traffic lights ahead were on green when Edgar reached the bottom of the hill, but as he approached them, they changed to red. He slowed to a halt and looked out of the side window at the group of teenagers building a snowman on the triangle of grass outside Val's Café. Not just teenagers either; the two men who ran the pub were joining in. And now the woman who had the cake stall at the market was crossing the road in front of the car, smiling and waving at him as if they were actual friends. After a couple of seconds, during which he double-checked she wasn't waving at someone behind him, Edgar lifted his gloved hand from the steering wheel and kind of bobbed his head in acknowledgement. It must be the snow, cheering up the inhabitants of the town and making them greet people they barely . . . barely . . . what . . .

Jesus, what was happening? A sensation he'd never experienced before was flowing through his brain. Edgar tried to shout for help, and only realised he could no longer speak when a stran-gled groan escaped his throat. His right hand slid from the steering wheel, landing with a thud in his lap, and he felt the strange sensation inside his skull building. A grey mist descended over his field of vision and his body no longer seemed to belong to him. He tried again to call for help, but no intelli-gible sound came out, and now a blackness was rolling from the back of his head to the front, clearing everything in its path like an avalanche . . .

★

Remy was making his way back from Val's Café, having picked up a Cornish pasty and a chicken pie for lunch, when he saw Edgar's Bentley stopped at the traffic lights. The lights were on green and a car waiting behind it was impatiently tooting its horn.

One of the teenage boys who'd been helping to build the

313

snowman sauntered over to the Bentley. Peering in through the side window, he called back with a laugh, 'The old guy's dozed off at the wheel. God, ancient people shouldn't be allowed on the road. Hey,' he tapped on the glass, 'time to wake up!'

Remy began to run; if he knew one thing about Edgar Allsopp, it was that he wasn't the type to fall asleep in his car. Pulling open the driver's door, he saw that Edgar's eyes were almost but not completely closed, there was a grey cast to his skin and his breathing was stertorous.

Beeeeep went the horn of the car behind. *Beeeeeeep.*

'Tell him to shut up,' Remy instructed the wide-eyed teenager. Taking out his phone, he pressed 999. 'Ambulance, please. To Foxwell high street. Right away.'

*

Lou had been dispatched by Edgar to the pet superstore in Cheltenham to stock up on Captain Oates's favourite food. When she took the call from Remy in the middle of the treats aisle and heard what had happened, her heart plummeted. Oh no . . .

By the time she reached the hospital, Remy was waiting for her in the snow outside the entrance to A&E.

His dark eyes were serious. 'You can't see him at the moment. He's being assessed.'

'But at least he's still alive.' Her voice came out sounding wobbly. 'Oh God, I can't believe it. He was fine this morning.' A random memory returned. 'He even offered to turn up the heating if I wasn't warm enough.'

'And he drove down into town without any trouble. They're going to be sending him for a scan. He was still unconscious when they brought him in. Are you OK?'

She was shivering, and not just as a result of racing over from the car park as the snow continued to fall. The last time they'd been here, she'd had the gash in her arm stitched up and they'd passed the time laughing and joking. Back then, she'd loved every minute waiting with him on these hard plastic chairs, being mistaken for husband and wife.

But this was different. This was serious, a matter of life and death.

'Here, you need to warm up.' She'd left her coat in the boot of the car. Remy took off his own jacket and made her put it on.

'Th-thanks.' It smelled of leather and him. 'What happened to the Bentley?'

'I drove it up to the house. Rico followed me and gave me a lift back down. I rang the doorbell a few times while I was there, but no one answered.'

'And I tried to call Della, but she isn't picking up her phone. Maybe she was in the bath, or having a lie-in.' Della obviously needed to know what had happened too.

When the doctor came out to speak to them, he was blunt and to the point.

'Mr Allsopp is very unwell. It looks like a stroke. The prognosis is poor, I'm afraid. But we're moving him to a ward and will keep monitoring him to see what's going on. You're his live-in carer, I believe?'

Lou nodded. 'I am.'

'Well, if there are relatives who need to be informed, I'd recommend they get here as soon as possible. It's likely he might not last too long.'

She swallowed. 'There aren't any relatives. But he has a friend . . . She lives at the same address.'

'Give her a call,' said the doctor.

When Lou did eventually get through, Della said, 'Oh no, poor Eddie, that's awful.'

'You can get a taxi down here. Call me when you arrive and I'll meet you at the main entrance.'

After a moment, Della said, 'Oh dear, I'm sorry, I don't think I can.'

What?

'Edgar's very sick,' Lou reminded her. 'He's in a coma.'

'I know, it's just . . . I hate hospitals, I really do. I find them so . . . you know, upsetting. And I have this thing . . . PTSD . . . from the time my darling husband died . . . I just can't do it right now. Maybe I'll be able to drop by some time tomorrow, if I think I can manage it then. That's the best I can offer, I'm afraid.' Sounding curious rather than distraught, Della went on, 'Are they expecting him to die?'

Die. Lou closed her eyes. 'I think so.'

'OK. I'll phone Tom. Thanks for letting us know.'

Did that mean Tom might come back from London? But it was too late to ask; Della had already ended the call.

Lou put her phone away and said, 'She's not coming. Doesn't like hospitals.'

'OK.'

'Thanks for being here, but you can go now. I'll stay.'

Remy shook his head. 'I'll keep you company.'

'You don't have to, honestly.' His kindness brought a lump to her throat. 'No need to let Talli down.'

'It's fine, I'm not seeing Talli tonight.' He rested his hand on her arm. 'I'm staying, so don't argue. I'm not leaving you here on your own.'

Lou felt a rush of adrenalin at the physical contact, then an even bigger rush of shame because it couldn't have come at a more inappropriate time.

★

316

It was the strangest sensation Edgar had ever known. Something extraordinary had happened and he had no idea how or why, but he was certainly intrigued.

He was in a hospital room, he knew that much. He was lying in a bed with various tubes and wires and beeping machines attached to him, and his eyes were closed, but that didn't appear to be a problem because he could still see himself, as well as everything else that was going on. If he had to guess, he was a microscopic dot of energy hovering in the medicinal air. It was completely fascinating, especially since he'd always roundly pooh-poohed the idea that anything of this fashion could be anything but a ridiculous fantasy.

Yet here he was. And he wasn't even dead. He knew this because he could see the machine monitoring his heartbeat, oxygen levels and blood pressure. He could hear everything, too. Incredible. A doctor was perched on a stool over by the window, scribbling in a folder. A nurse was at his bedside, securing a loose lead to the back of his hand with tape. Glancing up, she said, 'So are you going to Jan's party tomorrow night, then?'

The perching doctor stopped writing. 'Definitely, if I can get away in time. Sounds like it's going to be a good do.'

The nurse nodded vigorously, her eyes shining. 'It does. I can't wait.'

If Edgar had been his normal tetchy self, lying in the bed, he might have opened his eyes at this point and told the pair of them in no uncertain terms to stop flirting and get on with the job of looking after him.

But he wasn't his normal self in his actual body, and from up here it somehow no longer seemed to matter. Since he was clearly unwell, there were more important things to be bothered about.

A glance out of the window informed him that the snow was

still falling slowly but steadily in fat clumps. The next moment the door opened and another nurse appeared, stepping aside to allow two more people into the room.

It was Lou, together with the older of the Keeler brothers. She looked at the nurse and said, 'Are you sure it's OK for both of us to be in here?'

'No problem, love. You said he doesn't have any relatives? Then it's fine, nice for him not to be on his own. You can stay as long as you like.' The nurse lowered her voice. 'As I said, this could be . . . you know . . .'

It was pretty obvious what she wasn't saying; Edgar absorbed the news and realised he was neither sad nor surprised. He wouldn't be around for much longer. This was where it was going to end.

But in the meantime, he was here, *up here*, able to see and hear everything that was going on. And to feel remorse . . .

Oh yes, he might not be sad about his imminent demise, but the guilt was out in force. Lou was looking drawn and sad, her eyes filling as Remy brought chairs over to the bedside and sat her down in the one closest to the head of the bed.

'Oh Edgar. Hello. We're here.' She reached for his aged hand and closed it between both of hers, her thumb gently stroking his arthritic knuckles. 'It's OK, we're here, and I'm not going anywhere. The nurses are being so kind,' she went on. 'They're going to take really good care of you. And don't you worry, you'll be up and about again in no time.'

No time. As in, never. But he still wasn't panicking. Everyone had to die at some stage, and his time was on the brink of running out.

It wasn't until Remy Keeler passed a handkerchief to Lou and she wiped her eyes that Edgar finally realised she was crying.

Then it struck him with a jolt that she was actually trying hard *not* to cry, which somehow meant even more. She was putting on a brave face for his benefit.

'Edgar, can you open your eyes? Try to do that . . . or squeeze my hand if you can hear me. Like this.' She was making a real effort to keep her voice steady. He saw her squeeze his hand, and saw his own hand fail to respond.

'Never mind,' she said. 'Don't worry, just get some rest. And you're not to worry about Captain Oates either. He's fine, absolutely fine. As soon as you're feeling better, we're going to bring him over here so you can see him through the window.'

She chattered on for a while longer, telling him the Bentley was safe at home, and that hopefully Della would be over to see him tomorrow. Then she fell silent and he saw the tears sliding down her cheeks once more. After a few minutes, in an undertone, she whispered to Remy, 'He might still get better, though, mightn't he? Miracles do happen. Even if he can't get around as much as before, we could still get him home. I can look after him.'

Edgar felt terrible. She didn't know. She had no idea.

It wasn't until much later that evening, when Lou excused herself, promising to be back in two minutes, that Edgar discovered he wasn't confined to this room. When she left, he was able to follow her out into the corridor – like a microscopic fruit fly – and saw one of the nurses warn her about the deepening snow outside.

'It's OK, I'm not going anywhere,' Lou told the nurse. 'I'm staying with him.'

But Edgar no longer needed to worry about getting caught in the snow. Leaving her behind, he set off down the long white corridor, then flew out through the main doors of the hospital. Foxwell was several miles away, but no sooner had he pictured it in his mind than it appeared in the far distance. Swooping in closer, he saw the lights on in the snow-covered buildings, a bunch of revellers leaving the Bear Inn, two people kissing on The Triangle outside Val's Café while the snow fell all around them, and an old man wobbling along on his bicycle as a golden Labrador trotted on his lead alongside him.

Leaving the town behind, he swooshed to the right and flew up the hill, past a family of foxes bouncing around as they played together at the bottom of his garden.

Was he imagining all of this? Was it really happening, or was he hallucinating in his hospital bed? He had no idea, but it was certainly different. And now here he was, home. The lights were on all over the house, the Bentley was safely parked outside on the driveway and one of the smaller kitchen windows was a couple of inches ajar, indicating that someone – presumably Della – had been burning toast again.

In flew Edgar, zipping around the ground floor until he reached the drawing room. And there was Della, stretched out lengthwise on the sofa, wearing an embroidered silk kimono and – no surprise there – clutching her phone.

'. . . Oh Saz, can you believe it? And there was me, worried I'd be stuck here for years. But now this has happened, it's looking like I won't have to be. Lou called from the hospital and said it was about as serious as it could get. Apparently the doctors are pretty sure he's on his way out.' Leaning over and reaching for her glass of wine, she spilled some on the walnut coffee table and half wiped it off with her fingers, which would definitely leave a mark. 'Oh, hang on, text coming through . . .' She peered at the screen. 'It's from Lou again. Having another go at trying to get me to the hospital.' She paused to listen, then laughed at something Saz said. 'I know, but I've already told her I don't like hospitals. I explained about my PTSD. And the thing is, if he's in such a deep coma, he wouldn't even know I was there anyway, would he, so what's the point?'

320

Edgar watched her, taking in every last detail of her beautiful face. He'd made a big enough mistake getting her to move down here, but what was done was done. He'd loved her once, despite always knowing she hadn't loved him in return. Really, he'd been the fool, the one at fault. There was no one to blame but himself.

'. . . Yes, I've called Tom to let him know. He's coming down first thing tomorrow . . . Saz, stop it, you can't say that about my son. Ooh, which reminds me, did you hear about Anton shacking up with Lois Atherton's daughter? Can you *imagine?*'

Edgar had heard enough; he left Della to her frivolous conversation with her friend, which he knew would carry on for hours, because they always did. Heading out into the wood-panelled hall and ascending the staircase, he entered his own room and found Captain Oates curled up on the bed. The little dog's eyes were closed, his tail was curled around his hind legs and he was peacefully asleep.

Edgar was suffused with sadness. Captain Oates was his only love. It was heartbreaking to think he might never see him, hold him, speak to him again. How he wished they could have shared more happy weeks, months and even years together. If only he'd known, decades ago, how much joy and meaning a dog could bring into your life. He'd missed out on so much, he knew that now.

Would he still be able to do this, pay incognito visits, once he was gone? He had no idea, obviously, but sensed that the answer was no. Which meant he was here to say goodbye, without being able to speak.

He tried to convey his thoughts to Captain Oates.

I love you.

I love you.

More than you'll ever know.

I wish I didn't have to leave, but I do.

Captain Oates didn't open his eyes. He remained fast asleep, but his tail wagged, just once, which Edgar chose to take as a sign that he understood and loved him too.

The animal rescue place would be happy to know that. And the rest. Maybe he should fly over there and pay them a visit too . . .

But no, there was no need. He felt as if he wanted to head back to the hospital now, to be reunited with his physical body.

As Edgar was leaving the bedroom, Captain Oates woke up, lifted his head and gave a tiny snuffly bark, before closing his eyes once more and going back to sleep.

Goodbye, my beautiful boy. Goodbye.

Over Christmas, and much against Edgar's better judgement, Lou had forced him to sit with her and watch *The Snowman* on TV, because it was a favourite of hers and she couldn't believe he'd never seen it. Pure schmaltz, of course, about the love between a small boy and his snowman, and when it had ended, Edgar had complained that it had been thirty minutes of his life he'd never get back, but in actual fact it had had some emotional moments. Then again, the boy should have known his new friend would melt away; in the end, they always did.

Now, as he made his way back to the hospital, flying through the cold night air with snow falling silently all around him, he was struck by the similarity to that film. Was all of this going to stop when he died? He imagined so, because if he was here for all eternity, wouldn't the sky be filled with other people in the same situation, zipping around in all directions and keeping an eye on what was going on with everyone they'd ever known?

Back in no time, he found Remy Keeler in the corridor outside his room. Keeler was on the phone, saying, 'Lou's devastated and feeling guilty because she wasn't there when it happened. She's convinced herself it was the stress of driving in the snow that caused the stroke.'

Edgar zoomed in closer until he was able to see that Keeler was speaking to his brother in America. On the screen, the scruffy younger brother said, 'It's crazy, he's always been such a miserable old sod. But if he dies, she's going to be distraught.'

Another wave of sadness and regret washed over Edgar. What had he done?

'I know. OK, I'll keep you updated,' said Remy. 'Better get back in there now. I don't like leaving her on her own.'

'Give her my love.'

'I will.'

Edgar followed Remy into the room and they both saw Lou hurriedly wipe her eyes with a balled-up tissue. Edgar thought of all the kind things she'd done for him since their first encounter that day in the supermarket car park when he'd thought she was a mugger. Then, by way of contrast, he recalled Della's grief-free phone conversation this evening with her friend Saz.

The other thing he noticed was the expression on Remy Keeler's face as he rested a comforting hand on Lou's shoulder and gazed down at her while she pushed the screwed-up tissue into her pocket and busied herself straightening one of the lengths of plastic tubing that had got kinked on the bed.

Well, well, this was interesting. He'd known they were good friends. He also knew that Remy had a girlfriend whose name was Talli and who worked as a dentist in Cheltenham. But from the way he was now looking at Lou, he certainly appeared to be wishing they could be more than just good friends.

Edgar experienced another surge of sorrow mixed with shame at his terrible lack of judgement. There was nothing he could do about it now, unless a miraculous recovery was on the cards, enabling him to make amends for the error. But it seemed pretty obvious that his time here on earth was coming to an end. If he'd been granted another hour or two before losing consciousness at the wheel of his car, he would have been able to attend his meeting with Jerry Johnson, admit what he'd done and then explain how a new will needed to be drawn up. Yes, another one.

Except it was too late now. That couldn't happen.

The hours ticked by on the clock on the wall. Edgar watched as Lou held his hand, stroked his fingers and continued to talk to him until exhaustion finally took over. Her eyelids drooped and began to close, her head tilted to one side and she ended up leaning against Remy, the left side of her face resting against his chest.

Remy looked as if he didn't mind one bit.

At one stage a nurse came into the room to check the readings on the monitors and said to him, 'Are you sure you're OK there?'

Remy smiled and nodded. 'Quite sure.'

'If you want to take her home, we'd give you a call as soon as anything changes.'

You mean until I kick the bucket, thought Edgar.

Remy indicated Lou's right hand, still entwined with Edgar's on the bed. 'Thanks, but she wants to stay.'

And once the bucket had been kicked, Lou would discover his duplicity. Then she'd really regret having stayed with him. Edgar concentrated hard on his hand on the bed, wondering if he could have enough influence over it to give Lou's fingers an apologetic squeeze. She would never know how sorry he was to have done what he had.

Nor would he ever know what would happen in the future, how Lou's life might turn out and whether she would find the kind of happiness she truly deserved.

Chapter 39

The hours passed slowly. By seven the following morning, Edgar's breathing had slowed significantly. Remy woke Lou from her fitful dozing, stretched his aching limbs and collected cups of hot coffee from the just opened on-site café.

Together they waited as the end drew near.

A motherly nurse mouthed at him, *It won't be long now*, and he nodded.

Lou said, 'It's all right, Edgar, we're here with you.' Then she turned to Remy with hope in her eyes. 'I think he just squeezed my hand. I felt it.'

But the next inhalation of breath took longer to arrive. The one after that took longer still. Then they waited . . . and waited . . . but the one after that didn't happen.

'He's gone.' Lou's voice was tiny, barely audible.

'He knew you were here with him,' said the nurse.

'I hope so. I'm sure I felt him squeeze my hand.'

They left the hospital an hour later and made their way to the car park. Thankfully the snow had stopped falling and the tarmac had been lavishly salted.

Remy cleared Lou's car of snow first, then his own. He saw her frown as she checked her phone yet again.

'Della still isn't answering. I hope she's OK.'

Remy thought Della was probably still fast asleep. He said, 'Look, I'll follow you back, make sure you get home safely. If you want me to be there when you tell her, I can stay.'

Luckily the roads had been gritted and the journey to Foxwell was uneventful.

When they'd parked both cars on the driveway to the side of Walton House, Lou climbed out of the Mini and came towards him. 'Poor Captain Oates too, I've been thinking about him all the way home. I feel so sorry for him. He won't understand where Edgar's gone.'

'But he has you,' Remy told her.

Fresh tears welled in her eyes and she looked so exhausted he held out his arms. Sinking into them, she said, 'I didn't think I'd be this sad. I just feel so . . . guilty.'

Neither of them had mentioned the will, but he knew this was what she meant. Lou had grown increasingly fond of grumpy Edgar over time, but she would never have come to live and work here in the first place if he hadn't made her that initial crazy offer, the one that had made her realise just how desperate he'd been for her company. Throughout the night, while she'd been sleeping on his shoulder, Remy had also thought about how much he loved her. Because he did love her, there was no escaping that fact now. The problem was, he also knew how impossible it would be to admit it, to Lou or to anyone else, now that Edgar was dead.

Because Lou was set to inherit a property worth millions, in addition to however much Edgar had left in the bank. And how would that look? *Oh, fantastic, you're suddenly loaded, and did I happen to mention I've fallen madly in love with you?*

Entirely believable.

326

He would be judged by everyone they knew.

Worse still, he would be judged by Lou.

But in the meantime, she was here in his arms and he didn't want to let her go. He could feel the warmth of her body against his, smell the faint apricot scent of her shampoo in her hair, and the—

'Whoa, what's going on? Interrupting something, am I?'

The front door had been pulled open and there, framed in the doorway, stood Tom Lloyd. Remy felt Lou's breathing quicken in response to his unexpected appearance.

'What are you doing back here?' Her cheeks were pink.

'It's where I live, isn't it?' He grinned from the doorstep and spread his hands, for all the world as if he were the owner of the house. 'Mum told me about Edgar being in the hospital and the situation looking critical. She thought I should get myself back down here. The car dropped me ten minutes ago.' He waited expectantly. 'Well?'

'Well what?' Remy couldn't help himself; he was repulsed by the eager look in the other man's eyes. But he was also taken aback by the realisation that Tom Lloyd clearly knew about the will. Which meant Lou must have told him.

'Is he dead? Or still hanging on by a thread?'

Remy heard the breath catch in Lou's throat before she said, 'Um . . . where's your mum?'

'In bed with a hangover, I'm guessing, judging by the empty bottle in the drawing room.'

'No I'm not.' Appearing beside him, shivering in her flimsy silk dressing gown, Della looked at Lou. 'How is he?'

'Let's go inside,' said Lou.

'Has he died?' Della persisted.

'I'm so sorry. Yes, he's gone.' As she said it, Remy saw a lone tear roll down Lou's cold cheek. The next thing he saw was the secretly triumphant look exchanged between Della and Tom. What the hell was going on here?

'Ah, that's sad,' said Della. 'Still, at least he had a good innings.'

A muscle twitched in Remy's jaw. He'd always hated that expression.

'Anyway,' Tom addressed him with a glint of victory in his eye, 'no need for you to stay. We'll take it from here.'

There was definitely something going on. Remy replied evenly, 'I'll just come in for a few minutes. There's something I need to discuss with Lou.' What he needed to say was that he didn't trust Tom further than he could throw him and she shouldn't either. Then again, would she even believe him? God, what a situation.

'You look exhausted,' Tom told Lou. 'I am, too. Come on, let me take you up to bed.' And he actually winked. *Ugh*, he was repulsive.

But Lou was already shaking her head as they made their way into the house. 'I'm not tired. I want to see Captain Oates.' The next moment they heard a bark coming from Edgar's office, and Lou hurried down the hallway to find him.

'Oh, I'm sorry sweetie, it's only me.' From the expectant look on the little dog's face, he'd clearly hoped she had Edgar with her. 'He's gone, I'm afraid. He loved you so much.'

Cautiously, because he'd only recently begun allowing her to hold him, Lou picked him up and gave him a brief but heartfelt cuddle. Then she turned to look around the office. 'What's been going on in here?'

There was an almost empty champagne glass on the desk, along with a pair of nail scissors and a vegetable knife. Untidy piles of paperwork were scattered over the fold-out shelf, along with several manila folders.

Remy frowned. 'Are those not usually there?'

328

'No. Edgar's always kept this room really tidy. I don't know what's happened.'

As far as Remy was concerned, it was pretty obvious. He called out to Della, who was clattering plates in the kitchen, 'Lou's wondering why these folders have been pulled out. There are years of bank statements and letters from Edgar's financial advisers all over the desk.'

Della appeared from the kitchen, followed by Tom, who drawled, 'Not actually any of your business.'

'Nor yours,' Remy replied pleasantly.

'Maybe that's where you're wrong.'

Della said, 'Darling, don't—'

'Oh, come on, the guy's dead now. It's going to be common knowledge soon enough.' Amused, Tom added, 'Mum was looking for a copy of the will.'

God, he was loathsome. Remy couldn't believe Lou had fallen for his oily charms. He raised an eyebrow. 'Because . . .?'

Della, at her son's side, lifted her head. 'Because when darling Eddie made his will, he left everything to me.'

Remy heard Lou's astonished intake of breath. What the hell? What had Edgar done? More importantly, *when* had he done it?

'Who else would he want to inherit this place?' Seeing their expressions, Della said defiantly, 'Eddie fell in love with me all those years ago, and he never stopped loving me.'

'So he made the will back then, when he was still living in London?' Remy had to ask the question.

'No.' She exchanged a smug look with her son. 'He did it this year, at the beginning of January.'

Remy shook his head. *Edgar Allsopp, you devious, duplicitous double-crosser.*

But when he turned to look at Lou, he saw that she was doing her best to keep a straight face.

'What's so funny?' said Tom.

Despite her efforts, the laughter spluttered out. She shook her head. 'He left everything to me too.'

'Are you serious?' Tom's expression changed to one of horror. 'What the fuck? *When?*'

'Oh, don't worry, it was back in September. The most recent will is the only one that counts.' Wiping her eyes and now shaking with laughter, Lou said, 'So that means it all goes to you.'

★

Poor Captain Oates. In the absence of his beloved master, he'd taken to following Lou around the house like a lost soul. He was already missing Edgar terribly, she could tell. When she tried to comfort him, she knew she was second best, very much a poor substitute. He'd taken to searching for his master in every room. As she looked at him now, lying sadly on his kitchen dog bed, he gave a pleading little double whine that almost sounded like *Ed-gar*.

It tore at her heart.

'OK, come with me.' She led the way out of the kitchen and he pattered along at her heels.

Hanging on the hook behind the door of the office was the blue and grey fleece Edgar had always kept there to wear when he was chilly or taking Captain Oates out into the garden. It was a few weeks since he'd last allowed Lou to put it into the washing machine, which meant it would hopefully smell of him. If she used it to line the dog bed, maybe it would bring Captain Oates some comfort.

Lou held it out for the dog to sniff. When he tentatively wagged his tail, she checked the pockets to make sure there was no chocolate in there, because Edgar had been partial to

330

Maltesers. But no, there were only his sheepskin-lined suede gloves. Pulling them out, she wondered if they might help Captain Oates too. If it still seemed impossible for her to take in the news that Edgar was dead, goodness knows how hard it must be for a dog to understand that his owner was gone for good.

It wasn't until she balled the gloves up in one hand that Lou realised there was something inside one of them. A pencil, maybe? One of those short ones you got in betting shops? But when she pulled it out, she saw that it was a small old-fashioned key, the kind that might fit into a lock in a piece of antique furniture. Her eyes travelled to Edgar's burr walnut desk and the narrow drawer that Tom had attempted without success to open yesterday.

Chapter 40

'Is Briony here? Is anyone else here?' Lou blurted out when Remy answered the door to her an hour later.

He shook his head. 'No, Briony's out on a site visit. I'm here on my own. What's happened, is there a problem?' The sight of her always made his heart thump faster, but this time it was going into overdrive. What was it? What was she doing here with her eyes brighter than he'd ever seen them before? Please don't say she was about to tell him Tom had just asked her to marry him . . .

But Lou said breathlessly, 'I've done a bad thing.'

'Oh my God . . .'

She broke into a grin at his look of alarm. 'It's OK, I haven't murdered them.'

'Right. Well, probably for the best.' Remy ushered her through to the office. *On the other hand, shame.*

Lou hastily unwound the pink spotted wool scarf from around her neck, then pulled a leather-bound notebook out of her shoulder bag. 'Sorry to barge in like this. Are you busy?'

Never too busy for you. 'More interested in finding out about the bad thing.'

'OK, I found a key. I wasn't snooping,' she added defensively. 'It was tucked inside one of Edgar's gloves. It's the key to the drawer in his desk, the one Della was trying to break into last night. So I unlocked it and found this.' She waved the notebook at him. 'And it explains everything.'

'You've read his diary? *That's* the bad thing?' Remy marvelled at her innocence.

Vigorously Lou shook her head. 'I didn't tell them I'd found it! I heard Tom coming to find me, so I hid it inside my jumper and smuggled it upstairs.'

'Then you brought it down here.'

'I read it first, up in my room. It's sad, but brilliant.'

Her eyes were shining. She was brimming with happiness. Remy said, 'You mean you're getting everything after all?'

'No! Come on, sit down, you have to read it for yourself. They've already arranged for their London solicitors to come down here tomorrow. I have to attend the meeting so they can discuss what happens to me.'

'Do they know you're here now?'

'No, I just said I needed to pick up some milk. They weren't even listening.' Lou's smile was wry. 'Too busy opening another bottle of Edgar's champagne.'

★

It wasn't an actual diary, but Edgar had nevertheless been recording his thoughts for the last couple of years at least. The first eighteen months Remy skimmed through, the entries chiefly comprising complaints about politics, politicians, weather forecasters and various inhabitants of Foxwell who'd had the temerity to cross his path.

Then in September came Edgar's first encounter with Lou. He detailed his decision to make her the offer she wouldn't be able to turn down. Once the deal had been made and she'd moved in, the tone of the entries lightened.

'He liked you more than he let on,' Remy murmured, and when he looked up at her, sitting across the table from him, he saw that she was nodding and wiping her eyes.

'I know. He was nicer about me on paper than he ever was to my face.'

The next section related to Lou dragging Edgar along to Ivy Lodge Animal Sanctuary and was even more moving, detailing as it did the moment he'd fallen in love with Captain Oates.

After that came Lou's insistence that he should make contact with his old friend Della Lucas. Remy nodded to himself, realising from the next few entries that Edgar was learning to be happy, albeit in the two-steps-forward, one-step-back manner of a toddler figuring out how to walk.

Then he turned the page and came to 30 December. Edgar had written:

I've been such a fool. Lou's played a good game and pretended to like me. But today I saw a message on her phone where she'd been speaking to a friend about me. It said: 'I hope he dies'. Of course she does, that's what she's been waiting for all this time. Took me back to being eight, when Elizabeth was killed and I heard my mother sobbing in my father's arms, wanting to know why it couldn't have been me who'd died instead of my sister.

Same old feeling of rejection. It's never going to go away, is it? I know that now. But Lou fooled me. I thought she was different. What a gullible idiot I am. Should have known better.

Remy paused and glanced over at Lou, who exhaled.

'It was a typo. I'd written: "I hope he does". But I didn't notice the mistake. And I had no idea he'd even seen it, but the other day he messaged me and there was a typo, and I jokingly told him about mine. So at least he knew I hadn't meant it. Which I'm so glad about now.' She blinked hard. 'Because I just couldn't bear it if he'd died thinking I had. Anyway,' she indicated the notebook, 'keep going.'

The next entry was on New Year's Day. Edgar was home from spending New Year's Eve in London with Della. He had offered her a home with him, but she had turned him down. So he'd promised to leave her everything if she changed her mind. Which, of course, she had.

And he hadn't felt guilty either. Because it served Lou right.

Remy looked at her. 'Pretty expensive typo.'

'Don't stop,' said Lou. 'It gets better.'

He skimmed through the next entries, in which Edgar gradually came to realise that the happier life he'd hoped for with Della as his friend and companion wasn't going to materialise after all. Then came the overheard phone conversation with her friend Maggie, during the course of which he'd learned how Della really felt about him. Yet again, someone he cared about was just waiting for him to die.

Remy paused. The handwriting here had grown scratchier, as if manifesting the amount of hurt Edgar was experiencing. You could almost feel his pain. It was impossible not to feel sorry for him.

The handwriting in the next entry was calmer. Edgar had written:

Made an appointment to see Jerry Johnson. Told him about the second will. He thinks I'm an old fool, I can tell. But we drafted a third. This is the last one. At least this time I know I won't regret it.

Two days later, he had added:

Final will signed and witnessed. Original stored with Johnson, the executor.

Remy's gaze met Lou's. 'He doesn't say who the beneficiary is. Is it back to you?'

Lou lifted a be-patient index finger. 'Copies of all three wills were in the desk drawer along with the notebook.' With a brief smile, she drew them out of her bag, then laid them out like oversized playing cards on the table. 'Do you want to see them now? Or wait until the meeting tomorrow?'

Her eyes were still dancing; she could barely contain herself.

It was all Remy could do to tear his gaze from her. He tapped the envelope nearest to him and said, 'If it's all the same to you, I think I'd rather see them now.'

★

The meeting took place the following afternoon around the long, highly polished mahogany table in the high-ceilinged dining room of Walton House. Lou took comfort in the knowledge that Edgar would be having the best time if he were watching, enjoying every moment of the drama. This was why he'd done it, after all.

Most of the others around the table, not so much.

The first two wills were invalid, superseded by the third. And in the final Last Will and Testament of Edgar John Allsopp, the beneficiary of very nearly the entire estate was now the Ivy Lodge Animal Sanctuary.

Della's face was chalk white by the time Jerry Johnson finished explaining the situation.

Tom's, on the other hand, was unattractively puce with fury. 'This is fucking ridiculous! It can't be happening,' he roared, slamming his hand down in disbelief. 'He *promised* everything to us. He can't just change his mind without saying anything!'

'I'm afraid he can.' The representative from Kempner and Drew, the firm of solicitors who had drawn up the second will, had driven down from their offices in Holborn.

'As Mr Allsopp's executor,' said Jerry Johnson in his most official solicitor's voice, 'I can assure you that everything is completely in order.'

'But *why*?' Della was distraught. 'He *knew* how badly I needed the money! Why would he do this to me? I loved him,' she went on tearfully. 'And he loved me. We'd only just found each other again, and now this . . .'

'Under the circumstances,' Jerry announced, 'I thought it might be helpful to provide copies of some of the relevant statements made by Mr Allsopp in his own hand, which may go some way to explain his decisions.' He handed photocopied pages to Lou, Della, Tom, and Mary, the manageress of Ivy Lodge.

'Anyone could've written this,' Tom snarled when he'd read the highlighted passages.

'Of course they could, but these aren't legal documents. Unlike the will Mr Allsopp signed on the twenty-eighth of February.' Jerry gave him a brief professional smile.

'This is bullshit. We can contest it.' Tom turned to the London solicitor. 'We'll do that.'

'You're free to contest the will,' the man agreed. 'But I should warn you that it's a costly business. Particularly if your claim is unsuccessful.'

'But that's not fair, because it means we can't afford to do it.'

Della let out a wail of despair. 'How could he be so *spiteful*? He's done this on purpose . . . it's the only way he could get his own back! So what happens to us now?'

'It states in the will that you will receive the sum of seven thousand pounds. You also have two months before you need to leave Walton House.'

'I know what it *states*,' Della's voice rose, 'but where are we supposed to *go*?'

'I'm afraid I really can't help you there.' Rising to his feet, the man from Kempner and Drew slid the paperwork into his briefcase. 'So if there are no further questions, I'll be off.' He nodded politely at Tom and Della. 'You'll receive our invoice for today's meeting in due course.'

'Your invoice for doing fuck all?' said Tom. 'Don't hold your breath.'

When Tom and Della had left the room, respectively raging and devastated, Jerry said drily, 'Wills can heighten the emotions.' He looked across the table at Lou. 'You OK?'

She nodded. 'I'm fine. Apart from Edgar being gone.' It hadn't even been thirty-six hours. So much had happened since then, not least the well-overdue realisation that Tom was a truly repulsive person. Yet another example of her shockingly bad judgement when it came to men.

Jerry's nod was sympathetic. 'I'm sorry I couldn't tell you about the later will, but that's client confidentiality for you.'

'Honestly?' Lou sat back and pushed the fingers of both hands through her hair. 'This might sound mad, but I'm glad it's happened this way. It always felt wrong, knowing I was only here because of the will and Edgar's promise. I never stopped feeling guilty about it. Maybe if I'd worked here for ten years, I might have felt cheated, but it's only been six months. It's actually a weight off my mind, knowing people won't be judging me. And I've enjoyed working here so much more than I ever expected.'

'I didn't know whether or not to tell you this,' said Jerry, 'but now I shall. When he had the stroke, Edgar was on his way to my office. From what he'd said to me on the phone, I gathered he was planning to change the will again.'

Across the table, Mary from the animal sanctuary was starting to look a bit panicky. Lou smiled at her and said, 'Well, I'm glad he didn't.'

Edgar had left her ten thousand pounds and Captain Oates. Who could ask for more? It was perfect.

Chapter 41

The atmosphere in Walton House had been strained, to say the least. Since the disclosure of the third will, Lou suspected Tom and Della were blaming her for Edgar's change of heart. Tom had disappeared up to London for several days, returning late last night. When Lou encountered him in the kitchen, the cloying smell of his aftershave instantly made her feel sick.

'What?' He sounded irritated. 'Why are you looking at me like that?'

'You're wearing a different aftershave.'

'A friend bought it for me. It's her favourite. You have a problem with that?'

Lou swallowed down the wave of nausea; his loss of interest in her had been almost instantaneous. She'd been handy to have around, nothing more than that. Thankfully, the lack of genuine feelings was reciprocated. He might be good-looking, and charming when he chose to be, but she was acutely aware that she'd only ever used him as a way of diverting her attention from Remy.

And that had been a distraction attempt that hadn't worked.

'I told you weeks ago, that's the aftershave Brett used to wear. I can't stand it.'

Tom shrugged, unconcerned. 'Not my problem. Zoe gave it to me and she likes it. I do too.'

Zoe was the girl, she'd belatedly learned from Della, whom he'd been casually involved with for the last couple of months. Lou watched now as he kicked one of Captain Oates's favourite squeaky toys out of the way before opening the fridge. Taking out a carton of orange juice, he glugged half of it down his throat without bothering to find a tumbler. *Good luck, Zoe.*

'I'm going into Cheltenham,' she said evenly, 'to take Edgar's clothes to the funeral home. Do you want to see what I've chosen for him to wear?'

Tom wiped his mouth with the back of his hand and gave a bitter laugh. 'I couldn't give a toss what the old bastard wears. Stick him in a clown outfit for all I care.'

Yet another example, as if it were necessary, of how monumentally disastrous she was at meeting men and thinking they might actually be nice people.

From his basket, where he was nestled next to Edgar's old sheepskin-lined gloves, Captain Oates bared his teeth at Tom and growled deep in his throat.

'Bloody animal.' Tom shook his head at the dog. 'About time you were put down. Then you could be buried with Edgar.'

The last snow of winter might have fallen only a week ago, but a warm front had since swept in, bringing spring to Cheltenham. The sun was shining, the sky a cloudless duck-egg blue, and cherry blossom bloomed on the trees lining the streets of the upmarket district of Montpellier.

Lou had chosen Edgar's smart dark blue suit for him to wear

in his coffin. White shirt, green and turquoise tie, navy socks and, of course, his favourite highly polished leather shoes. She dropped them off with the undertakers he'd specified in his will and confirmed that all the arrangements were in place for next week's funeral.

In no hurry to head home, she stopped at a café on Suffolk Road and sat at one of the outside tables with coffee and a doughnut. Taking out her phone, she started the familiar task of looking for another job, because the way things were going, the sooner she was out of Walton House the better. Much as she loved the inhabitants of Foxwell, it was going to be easier to move away and start afresh, put the past six months behind her and—

'Hey, hello, fancy meeting you here!'

And there in front of her was Talli, looking delighted to see her. Hastily Lou swallowed a mouthful of doughnut. 'Oh, hi!'

Talli's eyes were bright and enquiring. 'Are you here to see me? Did Remy send you?'

'Remy? No . . .' Bemused, Lou said, 'I just dropped some things off at the funeral home, then thought I'd stop for a—'

'The funeral home? Oh, I'm sorry. Who died?'

Well, this was taking a speedy turn for the surreal. Lou frowned. 'Didn't Remy tell you? Edgar had a stroke. He died a week ago, in hospital.' How could Remy have not even mentioned it to her? What was going on?

'You're kidding. Wow! So that means . . . Sorry, I had no idea. You must be . . . Oh, thanks, yes please, I'd love a cappuccino.' Talli beamed at the hovering waitress while pulling out a chair and plonking herself down opposite Lou.

'Why did you think Remy had sent me?'

'My surgery's just around the corner. I come here most days to grab some lunch.' She paused and eyed Lou with curiosity. 'You don't know, do you?'

342

'I don't know what?'

'We broke up.'

'*What?*'

'I mean, I presume you've seen him recently.'

'Of course I've seen him. He stayed with me at the hospital until Edgar died.'

A flicker of a smile crossed Talli's face. 'I'll bet he did.'

Lou shook her head, utterly baffled. 'He didn't tell me . . . I had no idea.'

'Well, congratulations anyway.'

'For what?'

The waitress arrived with the cappuccino and Talli took a sip before sitting back in her chair. 'You've inherited the house, haven't you? Along with everything else. I'd call that cause for celebration.'

'You knew about that?' Had Remy told her?

'I found out, quite by accident.' Talli gave a tiny shrug. 'But I mean, good for you. Who could blame you for taking the job if that was the reward?'

Lou was still reeling from the news about Remy. She said, 'Edgar changed his will. Left everything to Della instead.'

'*What?* Oh, you're kidding! My God . . .' Talli's scandalised laugh contained a mixture of shock and delight.

'Then he changed it again and left it all to the animal sanctuary where we found Captain Oates.'

This time Talli let out an incredulous shriek that caused a nearby pigeon to fly off in a panic. 'So you don't get anything? Nothing at *all?*'

'He left me ten thousand pounds. And Captain Oates.'

'Is that all? And don't they cancel each other out?' Talli wasn't a dog person, and she and Captain Oates had never seen eye to eye.

'Honestly, it's fine. Mind you, Tom and Della aren't so happy. And that's an understatement. Tom's turned out to be a prize

343

dick, but there you go, you'd probably already worked that out for yourself. It's just par for the course with me.'

'Oh, I'm sorry.'

'Like I said, I'm used to it.' Lou shrugged. 'Don't worry about me. But I'm still puzzled as to why Remy didn't tell us you two had broken up.'

Talli took a sip of coffee, then smiled. 'Oh, I have a pretty good idea. You see, we had a difference of opinion, but I told him that after a while, after he'd had time to really think about it, he'd change his mind. So that'll be why he kept quiet about it. He's probably already realised he can't do better than me but doesn't want to cave in too soon. Take it from me, though, give it another week or two and we'll be back together.' She nodded confidently. 'And this time it'll be for good.'

'I'm sure you will.' Well, why wouldn't that happen? They were the perfect couple, after all. Lou dabbed her finger in the dusting of caster sugar on her plate; she'd always known this, from the word go.

'So how about you?' Talli's tone was sympathetic. 'What are your plans? Do you think you'll stay in the area?'

'I'll probably move away. Make a fresh start somewhere else.' Holding up her phone to show Talli the employment site, she said, 'Might go for something completely different, you never know. There's a position here for a receptionist in a new hotel in Cornwall. It's on the south coast, in Lanrock.'

'Good for you,' Talli said warmly. 'That sounds wonderful.' Reaching across the table, she gave Lou's hand a reassuring squeeze. 'It could be just the change you need.'

Neither Della nor Tom Lloyd attended Edgar's funeral. The pair of them had disappeared up to London two days ago, leaving Lou in charge of everything.

344

But it went off well enough. Lou had Jess and Jess's mum with her, and several of the staff and volunteers from the Ivy Lodge Animal Sanctuary felt obliged to attend the church service, along with as many of the inhabitants of Foxwell as she'd been able to persuade to turn up on a bright but breezy Tuesday afternoon in late March.

Remy had been there too, in the row behind her. She'd been intensely aware of his presence throughout the service, but it was neither the time nor the place for that kind of emotion. He'd been snowed under with work, he'd explained, but there'd been no mention of Talli, and she knew that if he had wanted her – or anyone else – to know they were on a break, then he would have told her himself, which meant he clearly didn't.

Following the service and the burial, the mourners retired to the Bear Inn for drinks and awkward reminiscences of Edgar, because no one wanted to speak ill of the dead, but what else was there to say? After just one drink, Remy took Lou aside.

'Sorry, I have to leave. I need to catch a flight to Dallas this evening. Remember the guy who cancelled my meeting with him back in September?'

The night he'd unexpectedly arrived home in the early hours and found her fast asleep in his bed. Lou flushed at the memory. 'The one with the wife and the mistress.'

'That's it.' He nodded. 'He brought another architect onto the project, some local guy, but now it's all going horribly wrong on site, so he's begged me to fly over there, sort out the mess and get the schedule back on track. It's going to take a couple of weeks from the sound of things. I just wanted to let you know. Are you going to be OK here?'

Did he think she was entirely helpless? Lou willed herself to stop thinking about New Year's Eve, when they'd watched the fireworks together at midnight and she'd thought for a magical

345

moment that he'd been about to kiss her. Equally, she refused to think about her thigh touching his as they'd sat side by side in Edgar's hospital room before she'd eventually fallen asleep with her head on his chest. She especially didn't want to think about their first dinner at Al Fresco, when she'd drunk more than she was used to and had flirted shamelessly, convinced that Remy was equally attracted to her, right up to the moment Talli had burst into the restaurant in a blaze of beauty and casual glamour . . .

'Of course I'll be OK. Why wouldn't I be? There's plenty to keep me busy. And I can handle Della and Tom.'

At that moment, the look he gave her made her want to throw her arms around him. But they were surrounded by people, and in her heightened emotional state she didn't trust herself – and it would probably be embarrassing anyway. God knows, Remy didn't need another desperate woman clinging to him like a barnacle in the pub.

She stepped away, and he said in a low voice, 'Well, you look after yourself.'

Lou just hoped Talli knew and appreciated how lucky she was. Clearing her throat so she wouldn't sound froggy, and straightening her shoulders, she smiled up at him. 'Don't worry. I will.'

Chapter 42

When it came down to it, Della had found she couldn't bring herself to visit Edgar's grave without bringing along some flowers.

Only tulips, though. From the supermarket. Well, what could he expect? They were all she could afford.

The funeral had taken place a week ago. Most of the other floral tributes were starting to fade, although there were fresh yellow roses from Lou, who had been paying daily visits because – as she'd put it – she didn't want Edgar to feel lonely.

'Well, here you are,' Della told him now, bending to lay the white tulips on the crumbled topsoil. 'But don't think for one minute that this means I've forgiven you, because I haven't. You've wrecked my life and I still can't believe you did it. You must be laughing at all of us. But mainly me.'

Yet another wave of self-pity swept over her. She hated herself for being so weak, but how could she not feel this way? Her son had promptly moved in with that on-off girlfriend of his in Notting Hill. Fia, still in LA, was having a high old time socialising with the smart set, because that was just the kind of person she was. To Della's chagrin, however, she'd discovered that it was quite a different matter when you were sixty-one

347

and a no-longer-famous actress. Bags and wrinkles were making increasing inroads into her face and neck, but she couldn't afford to have anything done about them.

Even more gallingly, her so-called friends were dropping her at a rate of knots. A fortnight ago, she'd invited herself up to Kensington to stay with Saz, who had *several* spare rooms in that huge wedding cake of a Regency town house of hers. But the moment she'd put forward the idea that Saz might enjoy having a housemate for a few weeks, her erstwhile best friend's attitude had changed dramatically. Saz had even reminded Della that she still hadn't paid back the money she'd loaned her last year.

Tears welled up in Della's eyes; it had all been incredibly awkward, and Saz had evidently spread the word to the rest of their friends, because all of a sudden each time she tried to make contact, they were too busy to speak to her. She was poor, and now that no huge fortune was about to fall magically into her lap, they'd banded together to cast her out of their circle.

What was more frustrating was the fact that she hadn't even liked some of them anyway.

But the fact remained that she now found herself in a major hole with no way of clambering out of it.

'Bit like you,' Della told Edgar, wishing he could hear her and see how devastatingly cruel he'd been. She wanted to call him a bastard but couldn't quite bring herself to say the word out loud here in an actual churchyard.

Up until now she'd been alone, but just then Della heard a car draw up and park on the driveway behind the church. Peering through the yew trees, she caught a flash of colour, then saw who was climbing out of the red Jaguar.

Is this you, God, having a laugh? Talk about kicking someone when they're down.

348

And she hadn't even *said* bastard out loud. Although now she might have to make an exception, because here came another one.

For weeks she'd made every effort not to bump into Harry Bailey, rarely venturing down into the town at all. But when it was unavoidable, she always hurried past his antiques shop on the other side of the road. So of course he had to turn up today, carrying a nicely wrapped bunch of pink peonies.

But he hadn't seen her yet. Having already crouched down beside Eddie's grave, which wouldn't be graced with a stone for some months, until the earth had settled, Della realised she needed more cover. Hastily she scuttled on her hands and knees to the left, ducking behind a neighbouring headstone. Phew, safe. A minute or so later, daring to peek around the side of the stone, she watched as Harry filled a metal urn with water from a nearby standpipe, then unwrapped and arranged the peonies with care so the pops of bright pink were surrounded by their pointy green leaves.

He stood there for some time, gazing down in silence at the flowers on the well-tended grave. Intrigued, Della waited for him to leave so she could head over and see whose name and details were engraved on the white marble headstone.

Except when he did leave, instead of making his way back to the red Jag, he strode over to where Della was.

As she cringed and attempted to make herself invisible, his head appeared over the gravestone behind which she was lurking. 'Hello there. Why were you spying on me?'

Was this her rock bottom? With some difficulty, she unfolded her knees, which audibly creaked as she hauled herself upright. 'I wasn't spying. I was hiding.'

'Ah.' He nodded. 'Why?'

Wasn't shame and misery enough of a reason? 'Oh come on, don't play the innocent. You know why.'

He half smiled. 'Fair enough. I must say, though, I'm surprised to see you here. You missed the funeral, and I gather that wasn't by accident.'

'Maybe I came today to let Eddie know what I think of him and his trickery.' Della brushed dry earth from her knees and said bitterly, 'He reeled me in, made me think my problems were over. Then he did this to me.'

'I heard about that.'

'And it's just not *fair*.' Of course he'd heard. News about the various wills had spread like wildfire through the town, chiefly thanks to Tom disappearing down to the Bear Inn within an hour of the solicitors leaving Walton House. Knocking back shot after shot of Bushmills, he'd told the story to anyone who'd listen. Which had unsurprisingly turned out to be everyone who was there that night.

'It's OK for Lou, she doesn't even seem *bothered*,' Della exclaimed. 'She's like, oh well, never mind, I'll just find another place to live and get myself a new job. But what am *I* supposed to do?'

Harry inclined his head. 'If that's a serious question, I've heard there's a vacancy at the supermarket for a cashier.'

'Oh shut up, leave me alone, don't make fun of me.' To her fury, she felt her eyes fill with hot tears.

'I wasn't actually making fun of you. You'd be more than capable of—'

'No I *wouldn't*!'

'Why not?'

'OK, you want to hear the truth? Even though you already know it?' The tears were sliding down her cheeks, dripping onto her neck. 'Because I'm spoiled and selfish and I can't help it. I'm just not the kind of person who can cope with rotten things happening to her. I'm getting really quite old now.' She could feel her bottom lip wobbling. 'And all I want is an easy life, but

350

it's like I'm being *punished* . . .' Running out of words at last, she broke down completely, scrabbling in her bag for tissues and not even caring what she must look like.

'Hey, come on. I'm sorry. Come and sit down.' Harry guided her over to the wooden bench a short distance away.

By the time Della's bout of noisy sobbing was over, she felt wrung out and even more of a failure.

'There,' said Harry. 'Has that helped?'

'Not really. Because this isn't fairyland.' She didn't even care that her nose must be red. 'Nothing's changed, has it?'

'Look, I'm sorry.'

'For what?'

'Kissing you the other week in the car. I shouldn't have done that.' He paused, looking sideways at her and shielding his eyes from the sun slanting through the trees. 'So you see, you aren't the only one around here who makes mistakes.'

'You were paying me back for something my daughter did.'

'I know. Because you were defending her. It was wrong. I try my best to be a good person, but sometimes I fail. It's called being human. Anyway, I am very sorry.'

His gaze had wandered to the white marble headstone with the peonies. For a few moments he was miles away. Della said, 'Who's that over there?'

'Hmm? Oh, it's Hannah. She was my first love.'

'And you still bring her flowers? That's romantic.'

Harry nodded. 'She was also my third love.'

'You can't say that and not explain what it means.' She watched his face in profile as he sat forward on the bench and looked down at his loosely clasped hands.

'We got together in our twenties for around a year. Then we broke up and I moved away. When I came home seven years later, Hannah was engaged to someone else.'

'Rotten timing.'

'I guess. I'd had a three-year relationship myself, in Tuscany. But that had ended a while before I came back. The moment I saw Hannah again, I knew she was all I wanted.'

'What happened?'

'I told her how I felt and begged her to break off the engagement. But she wouldn't.' He paused as a pair of sparrows flew down, hopping along the path in search of crumbs left by previous occupants of the bench.

'So she married her fiancé anyway.'

Harry nodded. 'We had a three-week affair, not long before the wedding.'

Della's eyebrows shot up; she hadn't been expecting *that*.

'I know.' His smile was fleeting. 'Shocking stuff. I think it was my consolation prize. She loved me, but the other guy was the steady one, the kind she wanted to marry.'

'And?'

'She married him. And they were very happy together. She had three children and was completely faithful to her husband.' Harry brushed away a hovering bee. 'Then one day she rounded a bend too fast on her motorbike, lost control and went head-first into a wall. And that was it; she was killed instantly. All that life, gone.'

'Oh God, so awful.' Della shook her head. 'I'm sorry.'

'But do you understand why I'm telling you this? I slept with Hannah just before she got married. I did a bad thing. We both did. Because we were human. It was wrong and we knew that, but we went ahead and did it.'

She swallowed, taking this in. 'And do her family still live here?'

'No, they moved up to Scotland a couple of years after the accident.' Harry cast a sidelong glance in her direction. 'Before he left, her husband asked me if I'd keep an eye on her grave, make sure it was tidy. And I promised I would.'

'He asked you? Did he know about you and Hannah?'

'Oh yes, he'd always known. She told him years ago, but he'd figured it out for himself way before that anyway. He was a good guy. Well, he still is. We keep in touch.'

'Thanks,' said Della. 'For telling me.'

'That I'm not perfect?' Harry looked over at the church, which had stood there for centuries and presumably witnessed countless love stories, dramas and tragedies over the years. 'No problem. My pleasure. When it comes to being perfect, none of us is.'

Chapter 43

'Thanks, but no thanks,' said Sammy.

Shiv might have frowned, if the Botox hadn't made it as unlikely as levitation. Instead he fixed Sammy with his shark-like stare. 'What do you mean?'

'It means no, I'm not having veneers. I like my teeth just the way they are.'

'Well you shouldn't. They're not white enough and they're not straight enough.'

'And I don't want teeth that look like—' Sammy stopped himself in the nick of time from saying *yours*. Instead he said, 'Something out of a cartoon.'

'You're booked in with the best dental surgeon in LA.'

'Not doing it.'

'Do you want to be a star or not?' A trace of exasperation was creeping in now; Shiv Baines wasn't accustomed to dissent.

'I can be a star with my own teeth.'

'They'll put people off.'

'I could get them whitened.' This was his attempt at meeting Shiv halfway.

'They'd still be crooked.'

'I don't care if they are. Anyway, people seem to like me so far.'

'Some do, others don't. Your approval rating among the fourteen-to-nineteen age group is troubling. Young kids don't like their idols scruffy.'

Sammy almost burst out laughing. Yesterday one of the make-up artists had done her best to persuade him to let her pluck and tint his eyebrows. There'd also been pressure to get his fair lashes dyed black. Thankfully Shiv's watch was now beeping to let him know he had some other poor employee waiting outside to see him. Straightening his spine and noticing a splash of coffee on the front of his white T-shirt, Sammy said, 'Sorry, but I'm still not having it done.'

His tone distinctly cool, Shiv replied dismissively, 'Take a look on social media. Try googling it. See how the kids over here in LA feel about British teeth.'

★

Jess might have grown accustomed to putting on a brave face in public, but inside she was feeling increasingly caught in quicksand, attempting to stay on the surface while the online trolls made determined efforts to drag her down. She'd deleted her own social media accounts, but some comments still managed to reach her by other means and catch her off guard.

It was all very well for people to say she should just ignore them, but when you'd spent a lifetime with very little confidence in your appearance, this was easier said than done. She *knew* she wasn't beautiful, she *knew* she didn't deserve to be Sammy's girlfriend and she *absolutely* knew it was impossible for their relationship to survive.

Maybe if they'd been a couple for longer, they could have battled through. But they hadn't. And the length of time Sammy had been in LA had stealthily increased, week by week. It had been almost three months now. Last week he'd asked her yet again to fly over and join him, but how could she do that to him when her presence would be nothing less than a major embarrassment? The management company's publicity people, Jess knew, were still pushing the agenda that Sammy and Frini Papadopoulos were involved in a steamy romance. And since she only had Sammy's word for it, how did she know it wasn't true?

In all honesty, she reminded herself, he was probably longing for an excuse to be rid of her.

Yesterday she'd been waiting at the counter in Val's Café and had heard a family of tourists at a nearby table talking about the fact that Sammy Keeler lived here. Blithely oblivious to her presence, they'd discussed him at length and marvelled that he hadn't yet dumped his frumpy girlfriend.

Which was always nice to hear.

Last night she'd lain awake and realised what she had to do. It would break her heart, but Sammy would never know that. It was necessary.

And it was for the best.

★

'What?' For a split second he thought it had to be a joke. 'You don't mean it.'

'Sammy, I'm sorry. I really do.'

It was eleven in the morning here in LA, seven in the evening back in the UK, and Sammy had called Jess during a break between recording sessions. Having headed outside, he'd thrown himself onto one of the shaded poolside recliners and settled down for his chat with her. He had to be back in the studio in ten minutes.

And now this.

He jackknifed into a sitting position, seeing the look of shock on his own face, pale and freckled, in the corner of the screen.

By way of contrast, Jess had applied far more make-up than usual, her hair was freshly washed and corkscrewing over her shoulders, and she was wearing an emerald-green velvet dress with a low V that showed off her embonpoint.

Embonpoint had always been one of his favourite words. Up until now.

His mouth dry, he said, 'But . . . why?'

'Oh come on, we both know why. This isn't working out, is it? It's never going to work. It's impossible.'

'That's not fair, though . . . I'm not going to be out here for ever.'

'Maybe not, but most of the time you'll be somewhere else, and how can we even call ourselves a couple when we don't see each other for months on end?'

Horrified, he said, 'Jess—'

'Please don't,' she interrupted, 'because I'm not going to change my mind. Sammy, I'm happy all this has happened to you, but there's no way we can carry on, it just doesn't make any sense.'

'But I *love* you.'

For a couple of seconds, she met his gaze and didn't reply. His stomach tightening, Sammy gabbled, 'Please, we can get through this, I'll do anything.'

'Except you can't,' she retaliated. 'You can't stop people from laughing at me, pitying me, criticising the way I look and the way I dress and the fact that I haven't had fillers.'

'Oh Jess, I've told you, don't read the stuff written online.'

'It's not always online, though, is it? That's the thing. Sometimes they say it to my face.'

In anguish, Sammy said, 'What can I do? Just tell me and I'll do it. Anything at all.'

He saw her pause and take a breath. 'OK, this isn't helping. I was trying to let you down gently. I thought you'd be relieved.'

His voice rose. 'Excuse me? Do I *sound* relieved?'

'Look, I'm sorry, and I didn't want to tell you like this, but there's another reason too. I've met someone else.'

'*What?*'

'His name's Rob, he lives in Gloucester.' Sammy saw her chest rise and fall as she took another, deeper breath. 'He's not interested in music, so he doesn't know who you are. We met at a furniture auction a couple of weeks ago, and he's taken me out a few times. In fact, he's on his way over here to pick me up now. He's nice, Sammy. A good person. You'd like him.'

'But—'

'No.' She held up a hand to stop him. 'Don't say anything else. We both know this is for the best. It was always going to happen sooner or later. You're going to be a superstar and I could never live that kind of life, it's just not me. OK, I can hear Rob's car outside, so I'm going to go now. Don't try and call me, because I won't pick up. You have a brilliant time, OK? And I promise every time I have a bacon and banana sandwich, I'll think of you.' A tear slid down her cheek and she gave a funny little half-wave before ending the video call, leaving Sammy stunned.

With four minutes left before he had to be back in the studio, he tried to return the call and discovered she'd already blocked his number.

He texted Lou: *Jess has just finished with me.*

Her reply arrived thirty seconds later: *Oh I'm sorry. Are you OK?*

A lump rose in Sammy's throat. *No. Have you met the new guy?*

Lou:

Rob? I haven't. But hopefully soon.

Sammy typed: *What's his surname?* He wanted to look him up online to see what he looked like.

358

Lou:

Jess didn't say. She thinks this is for the best, though.

Fuck, typed Sammy.

Lou:

Hey, it's come as a shock. But you'll be fine.

He heard footsteps. Then one of the sound engineers appeared on the terrace. 'There you are.'

Was his heart actually in danger of tearing in two, or did it just feel that way?

The sound engineer made an impatient make-a-move gesture. 'Come on, everyone's waiting for you. Get yourself inside.'

★

There, done. Feeling wrung out with the effort of keeping herself together, Jess changed out of the green velvet dress and into pyjamas and a dressing gown. She took off all the make-up she'd so carefully applied in order to hide her swollen eyelids and blotchy tear-stained skin. Finally she brushed her teeth, then tied back her hair and climbed into bed; it might only be early evening, but maybe at last she'd be able to catch up on some sleep.

Poor old non-existent Rob from Gloucester looked like he was going to be stood up tonight.

Her phone buzzed with a text from Lou:

Lou:

Sammy messaged me. Wanted to know about Rob. He's pretty upset.

Jess:

He'll get over it. What did you tell him?

Lou:

Just what you told me to say.

Jess:

Thanks. Night. Xx

She switched off her phone and closed her eyes. No more tears; she'd done the right thing. It was better for both of them, like amputating a gangrenous toe in order to save the leg.

And she was the toe.

Oh well. Sammy would recover soon enough.

★

Sammy was still catching his breath on the sidewalk outside Shiv's mansion when the electric gates opened and the crazily stretched black limo emerged. He tapped on the window and waited for it to slide down, revealing Shiv in a black tuxedo on his way to an awards show.

'Oh no, not the teeth again,' said Shiv.

'Not the teeth. But I need to see you.'

'You know where I'm going. Can't it wait?'

'Afraid not. It's urgent.'

Shiv murmured something to the chauffeur, who climbed out of the car to open the rear door for Sammy. The air con inside was blissfully cool and the air itself smelled expensive.

'You're sweating.' Shiv grimaced.

'I know. I ran all the way.'

'From the hotel? On foot? Are you crazy?'

'Never more sane. Look, I—'

'You got ten minutes, kid. I'm not going to be late for the awards, so we'll have to talk on the way.'

'My girlfriend's finished with me.'

'She has? That's great news. I was going to tell you to do that.'

Of course he was. There was no point trying to explain to Shiv why this was a terrible thing to say; his brain simply wouldn't compute. He might have signed musicians who'd written extraordinary love songs and brought them to the attention of the world, but all he cared about was money and success.

'The thing is, I don't happen to think it's great news. And I came here tonight to tell you I can't do this any more.' Sammy took a deep breath. 'This isn't the kind of life for me. I want out of the contract.'

Chapter 44

Shiv removed his dark glasses and gave Sammy the shark-eyed stare for which he was famous. 'Is this a joke?'

'No, I mean it. And I'm not going to change my mind.'

'You have any idea how much I could sue you for if you do that?'

'Well, no, but it's probably quite a lot.'

'Quite a lot,' Shiv echoed in amused disbelief, rasping a hand over his designer-stubbled chin.

'Which is why I'm offering you a deal,' Sammy went on. 'I love writing songs. I used to enjoy singing them too, but that was back when no one knew who I was. Being famous isn't for me. I don't like it, I don't need it and I don't want it. I don't care about the online idiots having a go at me either, but I do care when they do it to someone I love. So . . . I want to go home. Actually, that's not true. I *am* going home,' he continued before Shiv had a chance to object, 'but I'd like to carry on working for you, writing songs for your other acts, if you'd be interested in that.'

A long silence ensued.

'You seriously want to give up all this?' Shiv spoke at last. He gestured around them, then through the tinted windows at the massive queue of limos stacked up along the road as they approached the awards ceremony. There were presumably tuxedoed men and fabulously glamorous women in designer clothes inside each one. And who knew, some of them might even enjoy starving themselves for months on end, then dressing up and getting photographed on the red carpet.

'It's what I want more than anything. This isn't my world.' Sammy shook his head with feeling. 'My world is back in Foxwell, where Jess is.' He pressed a hand to his damp and crumpled shirt front. 'I love her more than you could ever understand, and I've lost her. Because she can't cope with all this, and us not being able to see each other. And I can't say I blame her, because it's been shit. I missed her so much, but I thought we could get through it. Except it turns out we couldn't.' The words stumbled out with difficulty, his voice cracking with emotion. 'Because now we're not together any more and she's found someone else. And it's all my fault.'

There was more silence after that, for several seconds. Until . . . *boinkkk*, the limo, which had been crawling along in the queue of traffic, bounced off the rear bumper of the even more stretched limo in front.

Exasperated, Shiv said, 'You need to look where you're going,' to the chauffeur.

'Sorry.' She turned to apologise, and Sammy saw that her cheeks beneath her Ray-Bans were wet with tears. 'I couldn't see where I was going.'

Once it had been ascertained by both chauffeurs that no damage had been caused, they resumed their slow journey. The venue was only a couple of hundred yards ahead of them and it would have been so much quicker on foot, but that wasn't how things were done out here. Only crazy people walked.

'If this ex-girlfriend of yours has found someone else,' said Shiv, 'what's the point of you going back?'

'Because I have to. I can't stay here. Jess is everything to me.'

'Everything to me.' Shiv held up a forefinger and nodded. 'That's a good song title.'

'I love her,' said Sammy. 'I love her, I love her. And if she doesn't want me, I'll wait for as long as it takes.'

'As long as it takes. Another good one. You should be writing these down.'

'I'm leaving tonight,' Sammy went on. 'I can't wait. I need to see her. Maybe she'll change her mind and realise she wants me back.'

'Hey,' Shiv raised his voice to address the chauffeur, 'was that a sniff? You know I can't stand people sniffing. Are you crying again? Goddammit, woman, get a grip.'

'Sorry, Mr Baines. It's just that this is so romantic . . . She's so *lucky*. I mean, imagine having a boyfriend who'd give up everything to have you back.'

'Hmph. Got a screw loose, if you ask me. What if he flies all that way and she tells him to take a hike? Because that could happen. Maybe the new guy's better in bed and—'

'You're all heart,' said Sammy, reaching for the door handle. 'Right, I'm heading off. The quicker I get my stuff packed up, the sooner I can reach the airport. Thanks for everything,' he added. 'I mean it. You've been amazing to work with.'

Shiv waved a dismissive hand. 'Don't say that.'

'I'm serious. I told my girlfriend you're a far nicer person than everyone thinks.'

'Jesus, will you stop? The last thing I want is people thinking I'm nice!' Hastily replacing his look of horror with one of steely determination, Shiv said, 'Besides, you can't just bail out like this. You *owe* me, big-time.'

'I know I do. I'll sign "Angel in the Snow" over to you, and five other tracks of your choice, how about that? They're all yours.'

Shiv didn't hesitate for a moment. 'Deal. You're a mug, by the way.'

'He's *not* a mug,' the chauffeur blurted out. 'He's doing something every woman would want to have happen to her.' Easing the limo to a halt, she turned and smiled at Sammy. 'Good luck.'

'Have a shower, for crying out loud, and change into some clean clothes,' Shiv ordered, fully back in character now as Sammy opened the door. 'You're a sweaty mess.'

Sammy grinned. 'I know. Sorry about that.'

'Got enough money on you to pay for the flight?'

'Just about.'

'Travelling goat class?' Shiv gave an exaggerated shudder. 'Rather you than me.'

'I'd travel in the hold if it was the only way I could get there.'

'Off you go, then.' Drily he added, 'Serves you right if she doesn't want you back.'

Thirty minutes later, while Sammy was flinging his belongings into a case back at the hotel, his phone went *ting* with a message from Shiv's PA and a plane ticket attached. She'd added a note that said: *Shiv called and told me what's happening. He still thinks you're mad but asked me to book you into club class. Good for you, babe – hope it goes well! Xxx*

★

Jess was wondering how much longer Alf Martin planned to linger in the shop, because she was looking forward to closing up. But he was still chatting away about nothing in particular, leaving her to think he was passing the time until the pub opened at 5.30.

Alf was a friend of Harry's, a fellow antiques dealer who'd called by to drop off a box of items Harry had won at auction yesterday. 'Nice piece,' he said now, nodding at the Victorian rocking horse in the window. 'So how are things with you, love?'

'Me? I'm fine.' It felt like knives every time, but she was getting better at putting on a good front.

'Mad, isn't it, to think I used to slip young Sammy a few quid to collect and deliver stuff for me in that clapped-out old van of his. And look at him now!'

'I know.' Jess made a show of checking and closing the drawers of her desk, dropping the hint that it was time he made a move.

'Good lad, he was. Can't say I was ever keen on that music of his, but horses for courses. You must miss him, I reckon.'

'Well, you know . . .' She ostentatiously checked her watch again. *Oh Alf, why can't you just take the hint and go?*

'Whole new life he's making for himself now, isn't he? Hobnobbing with all them famous people, bit different from this place, eh? Don't suppose we'll see him back here any time soon, not now he's got all those girls in bikinis chasing after him. Talk about living the life of Riley.'

'To be honest,' said a voice from the open doorway, 'sometimes the life of Riley isn't all it's cracked up to be.'

Jess had been concentrating on rummaging through her bag for her keys. Her head snapped up so fast she almost gave herself whiplash. What? How . . .? *Oh my God . . .*

'Look at that, talk of the devil!' Alf guffawed with laughter. 'How are you, lad? Just talking about you, we were! Remember when you used to pick stuff up for me in your van? We had some fun, didn't we? Hey, remember the time we went to collect that marble statue from the salvage yard outside Oxford and you reversed into a gatepost? And there was an old woman in a purple hat who threatened to hit you with her umbrella? Ha, right laugh that was!'

'I do remember.' Sammy nodded. 'Look, sorry, Alf, but I'm here to see Jess, if that's OK with you. It's kind of . . . important?'

'Oh, right . . .'

'I came past the Bear just now.' His tone was encouraging. 'Looks like they're just opening up.'

Alf brightened. 'They are? Oh well, in that case, I'll see you around. Unless you fancy joining me for a few pints?' Belatedly remembering Jess was there, he looked at her and added, 'You could come along too, if you want.'

'Thanks,' said Sammy, 'but not today. Maybe another time.'

He accompanied Alf to the exit, then shifted the wrought-iron doorstop out of the way and firmly closed the door.

Watching him, Jess said breathlessly, 'I don't know what's happening. How . . . how are you here?'

'I came back. I had to see you. We need to talk.'

'But . . . but . . .' There were so many questions she didn't know which one to ask first.

'I know, and I'm sorry.' He held up his hands. 'I know you've met someone else now and—'

'What? Oh yes!' God, she'd make a hopeless double agent.

'The guy from Gloucester,' said Sammy. 'What's his name?'

Good question. What *was* his name? Rod? Rich? Ron? Rob? Her brain had turned to candy floss and she couldn't for the life of her remember.

'I've forgotten.' She pulled a face. 'Mainly because I made him up.'

'You're kidding. Are you *serious*?' Sammy's eyebrows rocketed. 'You mean I've flown five thousand miles trying to picture this guy and having endless imaginary conversations with him . . . and he doesn't even exist?'

367

She could feel her legs beginning to tremble. 'I just thought it would make things easier. So you wouldn't have to feel guilty . . . and you'd know you didn't need to worry about me.'

'I was more worried about *me*. So you aren't seeing anyone?' His eyes widened. 'Oh, thank God.'

'But it doesn't change anything,' Jess protested, agonisingly torn, because he was here and she loved him, but the situation was still hopeless. 'You have this whole different life and I can't compete with it . . . You're a new person and I'm still the same old me. I can't be a part of that world. I just don't *fit*.'

'Neither do I. Oh, come here. I can't bear it, I love you.'

He was moving closer, and Jess knew the right thing would be to step back and maintain control. But how could she, when every fibre of her being was fizzing, bristling like iron filings on a magnet with the need to make physical contact, to be back in his arms.

'Sammy, I love you too, but it's never going to work.'

'It will, because I'm not going to be singing any more.'

And then he was holding her tightly and she was clinging to him, her face buried in his neck, breathing in the scent of his skin. Half laughing, she said, 'That's crazy. Singing's what you *do*. You signed a contract with Shiv.'

'I told him. He called me an idiot. But writing the songs is the part I love most. I only ever sang them so other people could hear them. And Shiv understands that, so now we're putting together a new contract. He has plenty of other singers, not so many songwriters. I won't need to be in LA. Or in front of the cameras. Or in a dentist's chair getting my teeth fixed. Because all I want is to be here, with you . . . Mmffffffffhhh . . .!'

But Jess had no intention of stopping; she was kissing him, wrapping her arms around his neck and feeling as if she might explode with joy. Here, alone with Sammy in this dusty shop surrounded by antiques, a kind of miracle had happened that she'd never thought possible.

Finally breaking away, she said breathlessly, 'Won't you miss it? All the glitz and glamour? All the attention and being famous and having a big fuss made of you wherever you go?'

'I promise you I won't miss it. Trust me, it's really not all that.' Sammy spoke with feeling as his fingers entwined with hers. 'From now on, I'm staying here. Out of the limelight. Less Elton John, more Bernie Taupin.'

'Who's Bernie Taupin?' said Jess.

He grinned. 'Exactly. In future I'm just going to be doing my own thing and enjoying life. With my amazing girlfriend.' He drew her against him once more. 'If my amazing girlfriend will have me back, that is.'

The agony and anxiety of the last couple of months had melted away. Her legs were no longer trembling. Jess stroked his wayward hair back from his freckled forehead and wondered if it was possible to be happier than this. 'You know what?' she said. 'I think she just might.'

Chapter 45

Each time he returned from a business trip or holiday abroad, Remy had always looked forward to this part of coming home. Reaching the brow of the hill, with the familiar curve of the road to the right, hinting at what was coming next, then suddenly seeing the valley open up in front of him, with Foxwell nestling in the basin far below and the river glittering silver as it snaked its way across the valley.

Now, on a day like this in late April, the view was even more spectacular. The sun blazed down, wispy cotton-wool clouds hung high in a duck-egg-blue sky and a thousand shades of spring green filled the previously bare branches of the trees and fields beyond. Beneath the woodland to his left, a cobalt haze of bluebells covered the ground, and the hedgerows were studded with swathes of buttercups, celandines and primroses.

As he made his way on down the hill, Remy noted that the town was busier than usual, with cars parked up on both sides of the road. Then, rounding the final bend, he saw the crowds lining the river. Of course, today was the last Saturday of the month. It was Duck Day.

Well, that was how it was known by everyone who lived here.

Forty-odd years ago, the tradition had begun that there would be an annual spring fair held in Foxwell, with music, dancing, special events and competitions, the pinnacle of which was the duck race. Having started out small, it had swiftly grown in size and become ultra-competitive, with people decorating and naming their own plastic ducks and the local bookie taking bets. The numbered ducks were released into the river at the point where it entered the town. Then, jostling and bobbing and with a stream of owners yelling encouragement as they followed their progress on each side of the riverbank, the ducks raced to be the first out from under the stone bridge at the finish line. The winners were plucked out of the water and shown off around town for the rest of the day, while the five hundred or so losers were captured in a net strung across the river, then stored in Dave and Sandy Harding's garage until next year's Duck Day came around.

Remy tapped his fingers on the steering wheel. He'd forgotten all about it because he'd been too busy thinking about Lou, wondering how she was and how soon he might see her again. During the last couple of weeks he'd had trouble thinking of anything *but* Lou. But he'd stuck to his own rule and deliberately not contacted her. As far as anyone else knew, even Sammy, he and Talli were still together.

He might already know how he felt about Lou, but she'd been through so much more than he had. It was only fair to give her the space and time to process the tumultuous events of the past few weeks.

He just hoped to God she hadn't got back together in the meantime with that slimy toad Tom Lloyd.

Home at last. Remy parked in the private space in front of Riverside Cottage and climbed out of the car. He should probably carry his cases into the house and unpack . . . except he couldn't, because now he was here, he was far too impatient. Somewhere among the crowd was Lou, he could sense it, and the longing to see her again was overwhelming. Locking the car and clutching his keys, he crossed the road and joined the throng of people cheering on their ducks. Turning from left to right, he searched but couldn't find her. Maybe she was waiting on the stone bridge at the other end, where the ducks would reach the finish line and—

'Lou, Lou! *Back here.*'

Remy's head whipped to the left as he recognised his brother's voice, eventually locating him on the far side of the bank. Looking scruffier and more cheerful than ever, Sammy was standing next to Jess, both of them gesticulating wildly.

Remy moved closer, squeezing between Dave Harding and Moira from the supermarket. And that was when he saw her, not among the gathered crowds after all, but actually *in* the shallow river, wading across in a short pink and green flowered dress and khaki Hunter wellies in order to free Sammy's duck from where it had got caught up in a tangle of weeds.

His heart turned over at the sight of her, because she was just so natural, always so completely herself. As she reached out with the hooked end of one of Edgar's old walking sticks, she stumbled and almost lost her balance. Shrieking with laughter as the crowd went *ooh*, she recovered and just managed to reach the duck, dislodging it from the weeds and sending it on its way. Everyone cheered and she did a cheerful curtsey, and Remy realised he wasn't the only one who loved her. In the seven months since moving to Foxwell, she'd become an integral part of the place.

The next second, she spotted him and her gaze locked with his. For a magical moment Remy saw her face light up with surprise and what he really hoped was delight. Her mouth moved and he thought she might be saying *You're back*. In

372

response, he broke into a huge grin and nodded, and Lou looked as if she was about to wade over towards him, except now Bob and Rico, on the other side of the water, were yelling at her to turn back and rescue *their* duck, trapped in the rushes.

And being Lou, of course there was no way she could ignore them. Into reverse she went, heading away from Remy, taking care not to slip on the moss-covered stones covering the riverbed. Her streaky blonde hair gleamed bright in the sunlight, swinging around her shoulders as she stretched forward once more, using the walking stick to dislodge the second duck and send it on its way. Her success was greeted with more cheers and applause from the assembled onlookers, and now Rico was reaching down, offering to haul her up onto dry land.

His mouth dry, Remy willed her not to take his hand, because that would feel like a bad sign; he so badly wanted to be the one to rescue her. The next moment, thank God, he saw her shaking her head and saying something to Rico before turning to make her way back through the diamond-clear water, carving a path between the last of the bobbing ducks.

And now here she was, in front of him at last, saying, 'I didn't know you were back.'

His heart took a picture; gazing down at her shining eyes and unstoppable smile, Remy knew this was one of those moments, a memory he would never forget. 'Just got here. I didn't even realise it was Duck Day. Hi.' OK, that hadn't come out in the right order. It sounded ridiculous. He reached down and offered her his hand to help her out, forgetting he still had his car keys in it. Oh fuck.

Plop went the keys into the water, because of course they did. In the space of a few seconds, he'd evidently lost the ability to concentrate and turned into the kind of person to whom stupid things happened.

373

'No worries, I'll get them.' Without hesitation, Lou crouched down and thrust her bare arm into the water, rummaging on the riverbed and using the walking stick to keep her balance. It took almost a minute of feeling around among the stones before she cried, 'Found them!' and emerged triumphant.

'Thanks.' The key fob would be waterlogged, but nothing was going to bother him now. This time when Remy reached down, she clasped his warm, dry hand with her cold, wet one and allowed him to lift her out.

Although it had to be said, she'd brought a fair amount of the river with her. The front of her flowery dress was now drenched, and crouching down to reach the keys meant her wellies had filled almost to the brim with water.

'That was a bit wetter than I was expecting to get.' Laughing, she pushed damp strands of hair away from her face, then did a little jump on the grass so the water fountained out of her boots. 'Thanks for hauling me out. And how are you? Good flight back?'

'Er . . . great.' Remy, who was never at a loss for words, had lost them now. He hadn't felt like this – hadn't *been* like this – ever before in his life. Giving himself a mental kick, he said, 'Good to *be* back.'

The crowds around them had begun to disperse now as people followed the ducks to the finish line. From the other side of the river, Sammy called across, 'We'll catch up with you later, in the pub.' Pointing at Remy, he added with a grin, 'It's your round.'

Remy watched as Sammy and Jess, arms looped around each other's hips, headed for the bridge. 'He looks happy.'

'He's *so* happy. They both are.'

'How about you?' He held his breath.

'I'm happy too.' Lou hesitated, then said, 'Pretty ashamed of

374

myself for ever thinking Tom Lloyd was a half-decent person.' She shrugged. 'But there you go, we live and learn. And he's gone now, for good.'

'Glad to hear it.' Remy couldn't wait any longer; he had to tell her. 'Talli and I broke up.'

'I know,' said Lou.

That wasn't what he'd expected to hear. 'You do? How?'

'Bumped into her in Cheltenham. She told me.'

'Did she say anything else?'

'Not really. She was waiting for you to change your mind.' She searched his face. 'Does this mean you haven't?'

'I definitely haven't. And it's not going to happen. We had different plans for the future.' Having forced himself not to contact Lou while he was away, there was now so much he needed to know. 'How about you? Are you looking for another job yet?'

She nodded. 'I've applied for quite a few. There's a hotel in Cornwall looking for a receptionist, sounds like good fun. It has a giant stained-glass octopus chandelier in the entrance hall that people—'

'Hang on, *Cornwall*? And if they offer you the job, will you take it?' The jolt in his chest was real; was she seriously thinking of moving that far away? For some reason it hadn't occurred to him that she would.

'They have offered it to me.'

Another jolt. *Please*, no. 'And?'

In the distance, by the stone bridge, a great cheer went up as the first duck sailed over the finish line. Lou smiled briefly, then shivered all over and said, 'Sorry, that river's freezing and I can't feel my feet. I'm going to need to get home and change.'

Remy put out an arm and supported her so she could pull off her wellies and tip the water out of each one in turn. There were goosebumps all over her arms, he belatedly realised, her teeth had begun to chatter uncontrollably and her bare feet were pale blue.

'My place is nearer. We have to get you warmed up and out of that . . . I mean, into something dry.' Even as the words were tumbling awkwardly out of his mouth, he was cringing. If that didn't sound like the world's most amateurish chat-up line, he didn't know what did.

Chapter 46

The shower was blissful, scalding hot water sluicing over her body, bringing sensation back into her numb fingers and toes.

She was here, Lou marvelled, right next to the bedroom where it had all started, the night Remy had come home unexpectedly and found her fast asleep in his bed.

Seeing him again today had sent her body into a state of adrenalin-fuelled chaos. One minute she'd been busy doing the job she'd volunteered for, unhooking the plastic ducks that got caught up in the weeds. The next minute he'd been there, deeply tanned from the Texan sunshine, his ink-dark eyes on hers and an unreadable expression on his face.

Well, that wasn't exactly true; she'd had an inkling as to what that expression might be signalling, but what if she was wrong? Maybe she was only willing herself to believe it because she so desperately wanted his feelings to match her own.

She switched off the shower, stepped out and dried herself, then reached for the oversized navy towelling dressing gown Remy had given her. Her pulse quickened as she heard him moving around in his bedroom on the other side of the wall, opening and closing drawers.

He wasn't remotely interested in getting back together with Talli, that much was clear. Which meant there had to be another reason for him having kept the news of their break-up to himself for weeks.

Lou blinked. Possibly because she was so entirely unimportant, he simply hadn't felt it necessary to mention it.

But as she wiped the steam from the bathroom mirror and regarded her reflection, deep down she knew from those magical seconds when he'd looked at her from the riverbank, then from the way he'd been briefly at a loss for words after hauling her out of the water, that she *wasn't* unimportant. When his hand had closed around hers, she'd felt the zap of electricity and known she hadn't been imagining the fact that he'd felt it too.

Was it a coincidence that she'd had The Dream again last night, the one where Brett was back, yelling abuse at her, listing all her faults and telling her she was a useless wife? It happened regularly and she always woke up afterwards feeling drained and miserable. But in last night's dream, for the very first time, she had stood up to Brett and shouted back at him, and the look of horror on his face had been a picture. He'd started to cry and back away, but his hands were so tiny he couldn't manage to open the front door, so she'd had to do it for him . . . then he'd stumbled out of the house, still sobbing, and Lou had never felt so *powerful* . . .

She'd woken up with a start after that, the dream as clear and perfectly preserved as a crystal in her mind. More noticeable, though, had been the sensation of lightness and relief, as if a monster had been vanquished. And after that, she'd felt giddy with joy, confident that this was the last she'd see of the recurring dream. It had almost seemed like fate that it should happen on Duck Day, one of Foxwell's most celebrated days of the year.

And she hadn't even known then that this was the day Remy would reappear.

In the mirror, now clear of steam, her eyes were bright.

Well? Was this fate or wasn't it?

Only one way to find out.

She combed her fingers through her damp hair and changed into the clothes Remy had found for her. The pale grey V-neck sweater was deliciously soft and the white board shorts way too big, but as he'd explained, she could pull the drawstring tight and they wouldn't fall down.

Shame.

'Better now?' said Remy when she rejoined him in the kitchen.

'Much better, thanks.'

He was leaning against the worktop. 'You were going to tell me about the hotel job in Cornwall.'

Had he been waiting to ask her about it all this time? Lou settled herself against the worktop opposite. 'I had a video interview with the owner, Dom Burton. He gave me a guided tour of the place, then showed me the octopus chandelier in the entrance hall. He's quite a character.'

'The Burton Hotel Group.' Remy frowned slightly. 'I've heard of him. Bit of a ladies' man.'

'Oh, he's definitely a charmer.'

After a pause, Remy said, 'You wouldn't want to trust someone like that.'

Lou gave him an innocent look. 'Wouldn't I? He was nice. Fun to work for, I bet.'

'To begin with. Then he'd start flirting with you, and you'd end up getting involved with your charming boss, then it'd all go wrong and you'd end up miserable, having to look for a new job.'

'Is that what would happen?' She couldn't help teasing him;

379

he sounded so *serious*. 'Is it the kind of scenario that sounds vaguely familiar to you?'

Remy exhaled slowly. 'It does. And yes, maybe I am speaking from experience. From back when I was younger.'

'Dom's older than you.'

'Exactly. Some people grow out of it, others don't. I know a woman who had a thing with Dom Burton a while back. He broke her heart. Complete player.'

'I know. I could tell.' Mischievously Lou added, 'I'm getting better at recognising them.'

'When did he offer you the job?' Remy's gaze was unwavering.

'A couple of days ago.'

'And? Are you going to take it?'

'Well, I *was* . . .' As she said it, drawing the word out slowly, Lou saw that he was shaking his head, just fractionally, from side to side. And that was when she knew for sure. 'But then Jess's mum told me there's a position coming up at Ivy Lodge, because one of the women in the office is retiring. They need someone to take care of all the admin, promotion and publicity. And there'd be some helping-out with the animals, too, whenever it's needed.'

'That sounds fantastic.' The minimal head-shake had turned into a vigorous nod. 'Perfect for you.'

'It isn't by the seaside, though. Not like the hotel.'

'But it has animals. So many animals.'

'It wouldn't have a stained-glass chandelier in the shape of a giant octopus.'

'Edgar would love it if you went to work at Ivy Lodge. And I bet Captain Oates would, too.'

This was a clear case of emotional blackmail. Lou said, 'Cornwall's beautiful.'

'It's beautiful here.' Remy gestured at the window. After a moment he said, 'Don't go to Cornwall.'

She held her breath. 'Why not?'

Silence. Followed by more silence.

At last he said, 'Obviously it's your choice. But I don't want you to go.'

'Because you think Dom Burton's a player?'

'No. Well, that doesn't help.' He gazed in desperation up at the ceiling, then exhaled audibly. 'Jesus, this is impossible, why can't I say it? I've never been like this before.'

Oh, how badly she needed to hear the words. 'Like what?'

'It's you,' said Remy. 'What are you doing to me? I want to tell you, but I can't . . . I've made a complete mess of this. I knew you needed time, but then I left it too long . . . and if you were anyone else I'd be able to handle it, no problem at all, but there's so much at stake. I feel scared, and God knows, *that's* a first . . .'

Lou didn't hesitate for another second; when she made up her mind to do something, she did it. And she did it now, crossing the kitchen, closing the short distance between them, then taking his face in her hands and kissing him with an explosion of pent-up emotion that . . . well, if she'd been wearing any, it would definitely have knocked her socks off.

Some kisses are slow and sweetly romantic, some are tentative and shy. This wasn't either of those; it was nothing like that – it was fierce and enthusiastic, joyful and ecstatic, packed with urgency and relief and the overwhelming sense that this, *this* was all that mattered in the world.

Best of all, she knew it was the same for Remy. The endless doubts and fears that everything she'd felt was one-sided had been swept away. Opening her eyes for a split second, she saw that his were closed; all that was visible was the dark sweep of his lashes. But she knew at long last that this was everything they'd both longed for. His arms were around her, one hand was at the nape of her neck, and she could feel the insistent thud-thud-thud of his heart against her chest.

'Well,' said Remy when they eventually drew apart. 'I wasn't expecting that.'

His smile was infectious. Lou said, 'If you hated it, we could always pretend it never happened.' OK, if he took her up on that offer, she would definitely have to leave Foxwell for ever.

But she already knew he wouldn't.

'Don't even joke about it.' His hands were on her arms now, as if he couldn't bear to let her go. 'You have no idea how long I've been waiting for this to happen.'

'You only broke up with Talli a few weeks ago.'

'Before that. Way before that.' He grimaced briefly. 'But you were besotted with Tom.'

This close up, she could see the tiny flecks of gold in his dark eyes. 'I wasn't besotted. I was doing my level best to distract myself from you.'

'The whole time I was in Texas, you were all I could think about.' He traced the curve of her cheek with his thumb. 'You made it pretty difficult to concentrate on overseeing the construction of a hundred-million-dollar shopping mall.'

Lou digested this. 'OK, well you made it pretty difficult to concentrate on clearing out Edgar's wardrobe and taking his clothes down to the charity shop.'

He gave her arm a reassuring squeeze. 'Was it awful?'

'No, it was OK. Bit weird the next day, though, seeing Bez Shackleton heading into the Bear wearing one of Edgar's favourite tweed jackets.'

Remy smiled. 'You need to finish the story, by the way. Are you going to work for Dom Burton?'

'No. I turned him down. I'm going to work for Ivy Lodge. And in my spare time I'm going to study remotely for my

ACCA, so that once I'm qualified, I can do the accounts for the sanctuary.'

He shook his head. 'You are amazing.'

'I'm not.' Lou shrugged. 'I'm just ordinary.' But getting better about putting the bad parts of her life behind her.

He kissed her again. 'Anything but that. Shall I tell you one of the best moments of my life? It was when you came down to show me the three wills you'd found. And you knew you weren't getting the house after all, but you just didn't care. That was incredible. You were actually glad it wasn't going to be yours.'

'I didn't deserve it. And I don't need it. Far better that it goes to Ivy Lodge.' Lou fell silent for a few seconds, lost in thought, then said, 'You know, the best and worst moments in my life have never had anything to do with money. OK, worst.' She counted on her fingers. 'My mum dying. The night I first realised Brett was a terrible husband and my marriage was a disaster. And . . . the night he died, when I actually thought it was my fault and the police were going to arrest me for it.'

Remy nodded. 'Go on.'

'And my best moments?' She had another think. 'Not long before she died, Mum really fancied a bowl of cornflakes one evening, but Dad had gone to the shops and she was feeling too weak to get out of bed. So I made her a tray with a bowl of cornflakes and a jug of milk and carried it upstairs. Then I sat on her bed while she ate it, and she said it was the best meal she'd ever had in her life. And it made me so happy and proud, because I knew she really meant it.' As long as she lived, Lou knew she would never forget that evening; it was perfectly preserved in her memory, along with every detail of her mum's smile. 'OK, second, seeing Sammy and Jess together after he ditched Shiv and came home last week. That was pretty wonderful. He made the right decision. Love beats money every time.' Although with Sammy still writing songs for Shiv, he was hardly going to be struggling in future.

'And the third?' Remy slanted his eyebrows. 'I can tell there's a third.'

'Hard to choose. Maybe Sammy's thirteenth birthday party, when I won the tree-climbing competition and you came second. That was definitely a special moment.'

'I couldn't believe you'd beaten me.' He was looking at her intently. 'Or . . .?'

Lou smiled as his hands slid around her waist once more. 'OK, you and me painting the spare bedroom together up at the house, when I told you I was thinking of taking that accountancy course and you said I should definitely give it a go. Or maybe New Year's Eve, watching the fireworks at midnight. Actually, I've decided,' she murmured. 'It happened about ten minutes ago, right here. When I knew I was going to kiss you.'

'Now there's a coincidence.' Remy drew her against him. 'I think that's my favourite moment, too. Maybe we should try it again, make sure it wasn't a fluke.'

It wasn't. His warm mouth on hers was just as magical as before. Breathing in the scent of his skin, committing it to memory, Lou pressed herself closer, wondering if—

Ddddrrrrrrrr. They both jumped as his phone burst into life.

'It's Sammy.' Remy sighed. 'They're probably wondering why I haven't met up with them at the pub.'

He pressed answer and Lou heard Sammy say, 'Hey, where *are* you?'

'Sorry, busy unpacking. I'll see you later.'

'Are you kidding? We haven't seen you for weeks! We've got some serious catching-up to do.' Sounding stern, Sammy said, 'Get yourself over here, asap!'

Grinning, Remy surveyed Lou and stroked the nape of her neck, making her quiver with lust. He said into the phone, 'The thing is, I'm absolutely shattered. Jet lag's got to me. I really need to catch up on some sleep.'

'OK, tell you what, we'll come to you. Drink up, Jess, knock it back, we're going over to the cottage.'

'Really, please don't,' said Remy, his tone insistent. Then they both heard Jess and Sammy start to laugh.

'And why might that be?' Sammy sounded smug. 'I wonder if it could possibly have anything to do with the fact that you have someone in there with you?'

Joining in, Jess said innocently, 'And you'd rather not be interrupted? Could that be it?'

Sammy went on, 'I know you probably think we're psychic, but actually we heard you'd been seen disappearing into the house with Lou. And the two of you seem to have been in there together for quite a while now.'

'This town,' Remy marvelled. 'Honestly. So who told you?'

'Oh, it was just casually mentioned. By Dave and Sandy Harding.'

'And then by Moira,' Jess added.

'I think it was Jerry Johnson after Moira,' said Sammy.

'Then my mum,' said Jess.

'Then Bob and Rico.'

'Val mentioned it, too.'

'And you don't want to know what Steve Crane had to say when—'

'OK, OK, I get it.' Remy shook his head. 'This is what happens when you live in a place where everybody knows everything.'

'And sometimes they already know it before you do.' Sammy was sounding pleased with himself. 'So, you and Lou . . . is it good to see her again?'

Remy locked eyes with Lou. 'Yes, it's good to see her again.'

'And are you sure you don't want us to come and see you both for a nice long chat?'

'Quite sure, thanks. You two feel free to stay where you are and have another drink. A few drinks,' Remy hastily corrected himself. 'As many as you want. It's Duck Day, everyone's celebrating.'

'Including you two,' Sammy said cheerfully. 'No worries, we'll leave you in peace for the next couple of hours – hopefully you'll have finished all that *unpacking* by then.'

'At last,' Remy said. Switching his phone off, he slid his arms back around Lou's waist. 'Little brothers, they think they're so hilarious.'

'Never mind. He's gone now.'

'Probably telling the rest of the pub.'

Lou's stomach was squirming with lust. 'I don't care.'

'Me neither. And if he doesn't tell them, they'll know within hours anyway.' Lightly Remy traced a finger over the Cupid's bow of her mouth. He bent and kissed her again, then took her by the hand and led her out of the kitchen. 'Come on then, I think we've waited long enough for this, don't you? Time to take you upstairs now.' His dark eyes glinted as he ran his hand down the curve of her spine. 'You can help me unpack.'

Chapter 47

Twenty-six months later

Lou stepped back to admire her handiwork. She patted the black marble headstone and said, 'There you go, Edgar. Looking good. Very smart.'

It was a hot day in early June. Birds were singing in the trees, and bees and butterflies darted around the churchyard, investigating the flowers on offer. Lou had spent the last twenty minutes tidying up the grave, pulling out tiny weeds, deadheading the yellow roses that were now in full bloom and refilling the stone urn with a fresh bunch of orange agapanthus.

She joined Captain Oates on the wooden bench that bore Edgar's name on a brass plaque, and waited. After a few seconds, the little dog wriggled over and clambered onto her leg before settling in her lap.

Lou stroked his head and looked over at the tidy grave. 'Can you believe this, Edgar? It still feels like a miracle every time he does it.'

There were still plenty of people Captain Oates refused to so much as look at. But gradually, over the months following his beloved master's death, he had learned that it was possible to relax and trust *some* people at least some of the time. His default reaction to strangers was no longer a furious glare and a show of teeth. Initially Lou had been the only one allowed to hold him, but he'd since learned that permitting a degree of physical contact wasn't always a bad thing – and while men in bobble hats were still fair game, some others maybe weren't so bad after all.

'So tomorrow we're going to be cutting the ribbon at the opening of the new wing at Ivy Lodge,' Lou told Edgar. 'I mean, officially Captain Oates is the guest of honour, but I'll probably need to give him a hand with the scissors.'

If some people found it mad that she still came to talk to him like this, she didn't give two hoots. Sometimes it really did feel as if he was listening to her – and was probably intensely irritated by his inability to reply. Although she liked to think she could guess what his thoughts would be, to the extent that she could almost hear him voicing them in her head. 'You should be proud,' she went on. 'I'm glad you did what you did. Everyone at Ivy Lodge is so grateful to you, and I love working there so much.' Proudly she added, 'I especially love helping with the accounts.'

A wasp came in to land on the arm of the bench and Captain Oates snarled at it.

'Oh shush, no need for that.' Lou waved the wasp away. 'Right, what else? Oh, it looks like the new owners are moving into the house at last! Val says she saw removal lorries turning into the driveway this morning, so that'll be fun.' Following probate being granted, it had taken over a year for the will to be sorted out and the estate to be finally administered. Walton House was placed on the open market and sold three weeks later, although to the frustration of everyone in Foxwell, the identity of the buyer hadn't been revealed. Rumours had flown around the town, ranging from a porn baron with a gold-plated helicopter to a sheikh with five wives. But the sale had gone through last autumn, and apart from an immediate massive refurb, the place had remained unoccupied ever since.

'OK, sorry, what else?' Aware that she'd been daydreaming and Edgar was probably telling her to get on with it, Lou said, 'Sammy and Jess are thinking of getting another dog to keep Bomber company. From Ivy Lodge again, obviously. And Della's still working in Val's Café.' This snippet of news was almost more extraordinary than the improvement in Captain Oates's behaviour. When the time had come for her to move out of Walton House, everyone had expected Della to hightail it back to London. Instead, to their astonishment, she had chosen to stay in Foxwell, moving into a tiny flat in one of the properties owned by Jess's uncle, Harry Bailey. Since then, a few of the locals had speculated that there could be some kind of below-the-radar romantic situation going on between the two of them, but with both parties steadfastly refusing to admit it, this was another mystery as yet unsolved.

Lou chose not to tell Edgar about the rumours, in case he really was listening. She didn't want to hurt his feelings. Instead, she chatted on about this and that for a while longer . . . Yes, Sammy was still highly in demand as a songwriter while continuing to relish no longer being in the public eye. Talli, on the other hand, was currently an object of great interest to the tabloids as a result of her affair with a just-divorced Member of Parliament. And while Tom was now ensconced in north Wales, having moved in with the daughter of a professional boxer and continued to write screenplays that never got made into films, Fia had turned herself into a TikTok queen and was living the high life in the Hollywood Hills. Oh, and despite Heather's MS

389

symptoms continuing to progress, she was still in excellent spirits and with the help of husband Tony was now writing a popular blog.

Lou gently ruffled Captain Oates's ears. If Edgar was listening, he'd definitely have no idea what TikTok was. Or a blog.

But someone else was approaching now and her heart lifted, because were any of the people Edgar had known as truly happy as she was? Upon his return to Foxwell two years ago, Sammy had bought a modern house on the outskirts of the town for himself and Jess. Lou and Captain Oates had moved into Riverside Cottage shortly afterwards, and life had been exceeding expectations ever since. She'd broken her run of bad luck and found her perfect man at last. Remy was everything she could have wished for: the best company, the best partner. He was kind, he was funny and he made her laugh every day. Every time she saw him, her stomach still gave a secret flip of joy, because he was all hers and who could ask for more? Plus, he was amazing in bed, which was making trying to get pregnant no hardship at all . . .

She lifted her face to his as he reached the bench. Remy bent to give her a lingering kiss, then straightened up and said, 'Captain Oates, is that a tail-wag? Are you actually pleased to see me?'

'He secretly loves you. He's just playing it cool. How did it go?' said Lou, because he was back from a meeting with a potential client in Elliscombe.

'Really well.' Sitting down beside her, he reached for her hand, and *zinggg* went the tiny current of electricity that also still happened each time they touched. 'They want me to design an extension for their hotel. It's an amazing place. But something even more interesting happened on the way back here.' His mouth twitched. 'You'll never guess who I just saw on the driveway of Walton House, standing there as if he owned the place.'

'Ooh, Val said she saw the removal trucks heading in there this morning.' Intrigued, Lou said, 'Is it a royal?'

'Even better than that.' Remy gave her fingers a squeeze and broke into a grin. 'It's Shiv Baines.'

Keep in touch with the world of

Jill Mansell

For up-to-date news from Jill,
exclusive content and competitions,
sign up to her newsletter!

Visit www.jillmansell.co.uk to sign up.

You can also find Jill on social media . . .

Like her on Facebook:
facebook.com/OfficialJillMansell

Follow her on Twitter:
@JillMansell

REVIEW